THE DOWNHILL RACERS

JACK—the strong one. When somebody else's girl got pregnant, they turned to him to marry her.

ANNE—the tormented one. Her body ached for love, but she couldn't give herself to any man.

CHRIS—the ruthless one. No matter how many lives he had to destroy, he had to be a winner.

GEORGIANA—the simple one. No one gave her credit for brains, but she always got what she wanted.

OAKLEY HALL'S BOLD NOVEL THAT CRACKS
OPEN THE SKI SCENE TODAY!

THE DOWNHILL RACERS

by Oakley Hall

A NATIONAL GENERAL COMPANY

THE DOWNHILL RACERS

*A Bantam Book / published by arrangement with
the Viking Press, Inc.*

PRINTING HISTORY
*Viking edition published January 1963
Bantam edition published December 1963
2nd printing .... December 1969
3rd printing*

*Bantam Books are published by Bantam Books, Inc., a National
General company. Its trade-mark, consisting of the words "Bantam
Books" and the portrayal of a bantam, is registered in the United
States Patent Office and in other countries. Marca Registrada.
Bantam Books, Inc., 666 Fifth Avenue, New York, N.Y. 10019.*

PRINTED IN THE UNITED STATES OF AMERICA

Acknowledgments

I would like to acknowledge my great debt to Tom Corcoran, the American who has placed highest in men's Olympic skiing. His generous assistance in checking draft after draft of manuscript helped me make the work as free of technical error as it could be within its own demands, and his sense perceptions and eye for detail were invaluable. I am grateful as well to Peter Klaussen, twice National Veterans champion, for the conversations we had during the early stages of this novel, on competition in general and ski racing in particular. My thanks go also to friends who helped in many different ways, especially: John Buchman, manager of Squaw Valley Lodge; Henrik Bull, long-time racer; Gordon Butterfield, Western Representative of the Head Ski Company and former competitor; Roberta Corcoran, Class A Racer; Don Hamilton, Squaw Valley Lodge Tennis Professional; Jo Marillac, Squaw Valley Ski School Director; Gardiner Pier, M.D.; and Penny Converse Pier, ski photographer.

I have no debts, however, in the way of plot and character. These were my own inventions, and similarities to real people and actual occurrences are coincidental.

OAKLEY HALL

Contents

THE CIRCUIT | I

1

When I remember that FIS year, the beginning, I think first about the night Leary and I stopped in Geneva on our way to Chamonix. I was still in the Army and hadn't made the FIS team, though I was on the Garmisch ski patrol and was able to make most of the races on the European circuit. But Leary had done the best of the American men in the World Championships of the *Fédération Internationale de Ski,* and people were beginning to talk about him as a coming champion.

Georgiana Brown and Anne Patterson had gone down to Chamonix on the train with Mrs. May and the rest of the American girls. Leary and Brown and Anne and I weren't a foursome yet. I still didn't know Anne very well. Most of the top girls had men racers who acted as private coaches—to keep their equipment in shape, advise them on waxes, help them train on the courses, and after a race tell them the mistakes they'd made. Leary did this for Brown, and early in the season Anne had had something of that relationship with Ernst Hochner, a big country boy from Lech. He spoke no English except a phrase he'd picked up somewhere—"Let's go, bay-bee!" —and Anne wasn't the kind to learn any more German than she needed to draw her racing number; so when they were together he would silently hold her hand, and it was embarrassing to see a kind of pulse beat in his eyes when he looked at her. He hit a tree and broke himself all up before the FIS, and the last I heard was that he would probably never ski again.

It was almost dark when Leary and I came into Geneva, and we stopped at a clean little hotel on the left bank of the lake. The manager was offended because we wouldn't take his word that our skis were safe on the VW's ski rack, and he and his pimply-faced son trailed along behind us, arguing and trying to keep us from banging up the woodwork as we carried them to our room.

We were getting ready to go out to eat when we heard music, very faint at first, operatic tunes played on what sounded like a broken-down organ. I went to look out the window, and there in the dusk was a short man in a beret, playing an enormous accordion.

Silhouettes showed in the lighted windows across the street, but he stopped beneath our window, looking up and smiling and nodding as Leary came to sit on the sill. After a while I dropped a silver franc.

"Merci, messieurs!" the man called, and he played for us a long time while I stood shivering behind Leary. It was dark when he wandered on down the street, and after leaving us he didn't play any more.

I can still hear the man in the beret playing that accordion. I don't know anything about music except how to pick out a few folk songs on the guitar, but his music moved me more than any other ever has. It had in it all the mood of the European racing circuit that year.

I know I thought that the accordion player was someone who would understand what we had to do, because he was used to being outside lighted windows, in the cold and dark, but with something he could do well to warm him. Downhill racing is a lonely competition. No one understands what it is like except the racers, and people who are not racers say stupid things that are irritating, that make you feel contemptuous and aloof and even more lonely. Always, in the downhill, there is a chilly, gray, shivering mood, and yet there is the inner warmth of pride that you can do this well, the knowledge that it is a brave thing to do, and over all, of course, that great, tight constriction of wanting so much to win. In downhill, giant slalom, and slalom, you are very much by yourself and on your own. You race the clock and your own estimate of your capacities and limitations, and it is only when you are down and waiting at the bottom for the times, that others are in it with you.

And I guess that like Brown on the No. 3 lift at Aspen, Leary was thinking some of the same things I was. When we had closed the window he sat down with his hands locked on top of his head and scowled at me. "Was he any good?" he asked.

"I thought he was damn good."

Leary had heavy eyebrows that lumped together when he scowled, and when he was thinking he would nod and shake his head and shrug, as though arguing with himself. He said, "Well, do you suppose he decided once he was going to be the best accordion player in the world?"

I shrugged. "I don't know. But I thought he was damn good."

"What if you'd sworn you were going to be the greatest accordion player in the world, and you ended up playing out in the street like that?"

"He sounded pretty happy to me."

He pointed a finger, like a clever prosecuting attorney. "Well, tell me this, Jack. How would you feel if you *were* the greatest, but nobody gave a damn about accordion playing? So nobody knew you were the best. What about that?"

I grinned. "What're you bitching about? You're in the first seed now."

He flushed. Half-jokingly he said, "Hell, you're just jealous."

"Sure I am." Jealousy has adrenalin in it like a race start, but since there isn't anything violent to be done it just turns sickly. But I still grinned at him.

"You are, aren't you?" he said, sounding surprised. "Hell, I thought you weren't. I thought you were built different some way."

"No, just the same," I said.

He stared at me as though there was a lot more he wanted to know, but in the end he changed the subject, and we went out to eat dinner. It was too bad we couldn't have talked about it. He was eaten up to know if I wanted to be the best downhill man in the world as much as he did. It was something he wouldn't have minded admitting, because he was very frank. But I had always felt I must try to hide such feelings. That was one of the ways we were different.

There is rarely, any given year, one best racer, except when someone like Jean-Gabriel Michonneau or Anton Koeller comes along. There are fifteen world-class racers in the first seeding group, and usually no one of them is clearly better than the rest. It ought to be enough to be in that top fifteen. Leary was in it that year, and I made it the next.

There were other times with music in them that year. On the train from one start to another, with all the racers together, we would sing and there would be horseplay and close companionship. But the companionship didn't extend to training or racing. Then the French and Austrians would shut themselves up inside their teams; you couldn't count on a Frenchman to give you the time of day, and if an Austrian gave you the time you could count on its being wrong. The moods during a season are like the moods of the different events in a combined. Midwinter, when the important races are held, there is the chill, urgent do or die of the downhill, but spring is like the slalom, with sun and bright flags, and the races are more fun than crucial and dangerous—although the danger is always there.

Just before going home, in the middle of March, we went up on the Hornli out of Arosa for a picnic, Leary and I and Brown and Anne, Roberto Perez—a Chileño who had attached himself to Leary and me because we were at least from the same hemisphere—Jacques Etienne, who had beaten Leary in the Arlberg-Kandahar, another French fellow, a Swiss from Arosa, and two French girls.

It was a warm day, and a long sweaty hike up to the cornice. From there you could see breathtakingly far down into the valley, and a tiny, perfect village at the

6

timberline, pearl-colored in the sun, to which we planned to ski after we had eaten. The sun was so bright it dazzled the eyes even through dark glasses, and peaks rose all around, shining white and pure and with dark designs of stone set in the snow.

We sat on the rocks a little way from the cornice, with our skis stuck in the snow like a fence. Jacques Etienne's girl, whose name was Madeline, stripped to a bikini; she had very brown, silky skin and dark tufts of hair in her armpits. We all sunned ourselves, talking and joking in bastard French and English, drinking wine from *botas* and eating bread and cheese and salami. We sang American songs and French songs, and Roberto sang in Spanish in a harsh, top-of-the-throat voice. Brown and Leary had their arms around each other, and Brown had such a shining, dewy, freckled look of happiness that it seemed rude to look at her. When she was happy she could look happier than anyone in the world, and when she was unhappy, sadder.

We all sang and clapped a beat while Anne and Jacques tried to dance in their ski boots, and I danced with Madeline, who smelled nicely of sweat and sun. Leary and Brown began to horse around with the wineskins. She squirted him and ran squealing over rocks while he chased her. When he caught her he sat on her, pinning her arms and squirting wine down her throat, saying, "You've got to stop all this drinking, Brownie." When she closed her mouth he squirted wine over her face. "Your face is getting red from drinking all that red wine, Brownie," he said. "You can't giggle and drink at the same time, Brownie." Finally he let her wrestle him down and pour wine down his throat.

But all the time there was the cornice, twenty feet away, and soon we would ski down it—the men would, that is; the girls would hike around below it before they started. Off the cornice it was sheer down, and we would have to turn where it was still very steep, above a rock reef. You couldn't see from the top how far you would fall, if you fell in that turn. So all during the singing and dancing and wine-drinking and horseplay, there was that ahead, and it was that we had come for—off the cornice and down to the pearl-colored village.

The girls had begun to climb down over the rocks, carrying their skis, when Leary called to Brown, "Why don't you come with us, Brownie? It doesn't look so bad."

She turned back as the Swiss went off, poising on the edge of the cornice with his ski tips in space, then tipping slowly forward and suddenly gone, with the gray hump of his rucksack and the tails of his skis disappearing after him. The cornice hung so steeply that we couldn't see him until he'd made the bad turn and traversed far over to the right. Jacques Etienne went next, and then Leary, who didn't even glance back to see if Brown was coming. After a long time Leary reappeared, a third tiny inverted T beside the other two. The other Frenchman went, then Roberto, with a shrill *"Ay-yi-yi!"* The freckles on Brown's face looked like bee stings as she straightened up from putting on her skis. She'd had a bad season since her great downhill run in the FIS.

"Listen," I said. "Do you really want to go down there?"

She pouted and said, "Sure." Stolidly she pushed herself over to the edge and leaned on her poles, studying where she had to go. There was nothing more for me to say; on the circuit Leary told her what to do, and she did it. Finally she pushed off, and I moved up in time to see her come out of the turn and traverse across to join the men. Then I went.

Down the cornice I was falling rather than skiing. I leaned far forward, kept my weight on the downhill ski, and rode out the turn, snow spraying out in a floating, soundless sheet beneath me. With my heart banging like a slow mallet, I slanted over to the right.

When the other girls had joined us we ran down a long, miles-long, beautiful slope, and I wove figure eights with Anne. Anne made lovely round-bottomed, close-kneed, grave turns that were like the repeated chorus of a song; we danced down the mountain toward the timberline, trying to shape perfect links to our chain, laughing as we curved in toward each other, passing and parting, but always swinging back together again. Those few hours, on top, and coming down the Hornli, were worth years. I would not trade the memory of them for money or peace or anything.

There was always on the circuit that edge of danger, like the cornice waiting. I was often afraid, although almost always the fear came after the danger, the close call, was past. It never occurred to me that any of us were frightened all the time, as I found out later Brown was. There were accidents, spiral fractures were frequent, usually someone you knew was in a cast, but I never considered that I—or any of us—could be really hurt. Racers were badly broken up, crippled, even killed, but somehow it was never close, always it was just far enough removed to be unlikely. There was one time, though, that I was frightened for all of us.

We were just back from Europe and I was on terminal leave from the Army. We were a solidly set foursome now, and I was no longer feeling the junior member because I had not been on the FIS team. At Stowe we had everything our way, Leary winning both giant slalom and slalom, Anne the women's slalom, and Brown made a wild, scrambling run to win the GS. And I took second behind Leary in the combined.

After the presentation banquet we left Stowe in Leary's station wagon, heading for New York, where we would stop over a night so Anne could see her mother; then we were going west for the spring races. It was a cold, black night, and the headlights made only a small hole in the darkness. I was driving, and Anne sat close to me with her cropped hair tickling my cheek. From time to time she scraped frost from the windshield with a plastic scraper. Leary and Brown were making out in the back seat. On the roof rack the skis hummed and sang, and whenever there was a bump the cardboard box of trophies would jingle musically.

I wasn't going very fast because I knew there were icy patches in the road; it wouldn't have mattered anyway. The headlights slanted up over a rise, slanted down the other side, and Anne made a muffled sound and stiffened against me. The highway ahead was a shining sheet of ice, and there were headlights crisscrossing the road from the cars that had skidded off. A drain or a waterpipe had broken, and the flooded road had frozen. People standing along the road and among the cars scattered as our headlights came down on them.

There was a gasp from the back seat. Then there was no sound. My hands ached as I leaned forward against the wheel. I eased my foot on the accelerator. Time seemed to sag. I was very conscious of Anne and Brown and Leary, and they were very precious. In that sudden slowing of time the box of trophies clinked, and slowly came the queasy feeling of the rear end slipping out. I turned the wheel, but it didn't do any good. The rear end whipped around like the last man in a game of crack-the-whip, and the station wagon spun down the highway, fast around one time, more slowly the next, past the cars that had run off the road and headlights glaring through the windshield and the windows. Anne sat up very straight beside me, calm and pale in profile, one hand on the dashboard, while faces outside stared in at us horrified and open-mouthed, and people ran out of the way in slow motion. Our own headlights swung out over black ice, swung back toward the people and the cars again, and all at once the tires screeched on bare pavement. I held hard to the wheel as the car swayed, but we were off the ice and back on the highway and heading in the right direction. I let the car drift to a stop.

"Nice going, Jack," Leary said in a casual voice.

The car came to a halt and I opened my door. "You drive, will you?" I said. When I got out my knees buckled. Anne and I got into the back, Leary and Brown into the front. Leary started on again.

Anne leaned on me. She put her arms around me, her mouth came against mine. We kissed hard and warm and short-of-breath. She put her lips to my ear and whispered, "You took care of us, didn't you? I knew you wouldn't let anything happen."

I tried to kiss her mouth again, but now she kept it away, whispering, "Did you think about dying, Jack?"

"Not till afterward."

"I thought about it then, but I wasn't afraid. Because you wouldn't let anything happen to us, would you?"

I shook my head. "No."

Her breath was very warm in my ear. She whispered excitedly, "But do you know? It wouldn't be so terrible and lonely if someone you loved died with you." She laughed. "Would you mind dying with me, Jack?"

And I thought then, as her mouth came back and we kissed and kissed, that I wouldn't mind.

And when I try to recall that FIS year when it all started, I remember being in Aspen for a spring race, and the Aspen No. 3 lift, and the snowcloud.

Someway we had gotten mixed up, and Brown and I were riding together while Leary and Anne were in a chair ahead of us. There is a place on that No. 3 lift where, because of the changing angles of the ascending cable, it looks as though the chairs ahead are rising straight up. The cloud was hanging right at that point.

Anne had the hood of her blue parka raised, and Leary was tilting his skis up and down as he always did riding in a chair, to keep his legs limber. They began to rise into the cloud, and as they did my heart swelled and ached, and beside me Brown made a sound as though she had started to speak but had lost her breath.

Anne and Leary rose and faded into the cloud until there was only the seesaw motion of Leary's Kaestles showing alternately the shiny plastic tops and the yellow Kofix bottoms. Then even the skis were swallowed up.

Our chair thumped over sheaves and we began to rise into the cloud too, where everything was gray-white and chill, and blown bits of snow burned our cheeks. Brown was leaning forward, peering ahead through amber glasses. Her freckled face was strained into an exaggerated expression of anxiety, and I could feel the same strain on my own face.

11

But at last we came out of the cloud and the lift leveled off below the Sundeck. Brown and I slid off the ramp in the sudden bright sun, to join Anne and Leary who were waiting for us by the ranked skis on the wooden racks. Quickly we got back into proper order, Brown with Leary and I with Anne, before we started a fun run down Copper Bowl.

It was an intense, almost terrible moment, watching Anne and Leary disappear into the cloud, and I knew that Brown felt something of what I felt. It is strange that afterward we never mentioned it to each other.

2

In the spring starts that year I was second behind Leary twice and beat him once, and I won the Silver Belt at Sugar Bowl, but only because he fell. So there was not much satisfaction in it, except that Sugar Bowl was home for me, and my father and my own people saw me win.

Then all at once there were no more races, there was no more snow, the season was over, and it was summer. We all went down to the Memorial Day giant slalom at Mammoth because we didn't want to split up yet, but when that was over it was the very end, and I went home to Norden, on Donner Summit, and Brown went home to Reno. Leary drove back to Colorado Springs, where his mother lived, and Anne flew to New York to work during the summer as a model.

My father had a job at Soda Springs clearing ski trails, and he put me on a chain saw for a while, and running the backhoe digging ditches. I saw Georgiana Brown at the Fourth-of-July slalom at Squaw Valley and made a date to take her to a show. She had a summer job at one of the Lake Tahoe resorts, with plenty of free time to water ski. She had heard from Leary that he was going east to stay with his father on Martha's Vineyard and that he was thinking about taking some summer college courses. I had had a letter with the same news, but it was difficult to find things to talk about with Brown, in the summer, so I let her tell me about it all over again.

Long after I had despaired of ever hearing from Anne, there was a letter in a small, round script on blue stationery:

Dearest Jack,

What is a chain saw and *what* is a backhoe? You do such strange and romantic things! Is there room for me to ride around with you on your backhoe?

Went with a group of eagers to ski headwall at Tuckerman's Ravine. Too much climbing and perspiring for not enough skiing. It is *steep!* I really don't enjoy heart-in-mouth skiing as do some—I guess that's why I'm a slalom girl not downhillereeno like Brownie. How is Brownie?

First of month we are all going on cruise on Andy Burman's boat, Bermuda and the isles—Mother's arranging as there will be eligible males aboard. She doesn't understand that I am a Famous Girl Athlete and not interested in men!

At the bottom of the letter she wrote: "Did I say how much I miss you?" I knew it was a kindness, like letting Ernst Hochner hold her hand, but it was the part of the letter I read over and over, and it was what I lived on until I heard from her again, this time an impersonal postcard from Bermuda. Strange and romantic, she had called my summer of working with chain saws and backhoes; to me it was her summer that was strange and romantic —hiking up to Tuckerman's with Dartmouth boys, and beautiful girls in bright dresses dancing on the decks of white yachts with eligible Ivy League men. My own summer was hot, heavy, exhausting work for laborer's wages, and, when I was not too tired in the evenings, walking up the mountain and running down to try to keep my legs in shape—and waiting for snow.

Summer was not so bad. You knew about summer and were prepared for it. But when summer was over there seemed no reason why winter shouldn't begin, and fall was endless. It went on day by slow day, with forest-fire danger rising until a rainstorm broke the heat, with frost beginning to show in the early mornings, with another storm laying a little white on the peaks, with the annual Warren Miller ski movie coming to Reno. Then Indian summer settled in, with its clear, warm days, and hopelessly I tapped the barometer and listened to the old-timers talk about the long-range weather forecast, about the woolly-bear caterpillars and the yellow jackets and the pine cones and all the other prophetic signs of winter. Some of the racers had arranged for an informal training camp at Loveland, over Christmas, but it didn't look as though there would be much skiing before then. As always, the anticipation was almost unendurable.

There was not much contracting work in the fall, and my father and I went hunting together. We both got bucks, and talked about going hunting in Nevada, but never did. In the evenings we watched TV, read, or played cribbage. Often he would try to get me to talk about racing. He didn't understand that I couldn't talk about it yet the way he loved to talk about his ski-jumping days. He was through with jumping except for the memories and a collection of mellow, often-told stories; he knew where he stood. But I was in the midst of racing; for me it was still raw and undigested and I did not know how I was going to place in the great examination that competition was for me. So I wouldn't talk about it, and I think he considered me very modest.

He had been raised in a part of Michigan where there were a lot of Scandinavian ski-jumpers and had been a competitor himself, though never top-flight. Then he had worked as a foreman, helping to prepare the jumping hill for the Winter Olympics at Lake Placid, and as an official during the Games. It was the biggest thing in his life. He had met a lot of important people, people he valued knowing more than anyone he had met since, and with whom he still kept in touch. He had headed me toward ski-jumping right from the start, but by my time Alpine events were more in style than the Nordic, so it wasn't long before I gave up jumping for downhill and slalom like the other boys. He was easygoing, and never objected. If there was an argument he would hold forth that the

Alpine events were sissy compared with jumping and cross-country, but he meant it good-humoredly.

Leary and I often discussed our fathers. Leary's father was infuriated by anyone who didn't work—people who were on unemployment, for instance. Mr. Leary had worked hard all his life and made a lot of money, and he didn't enjoy anything but working and making money. In a way my father was just the opposite, though he had worked hard too. He enjoyed almost everything. He had been a ski patrolman for a good many years, he had helped run the junior races at Sugar Bowl, he loved hunting and gambling in Reno and drinking beer and playing poker with his friends, and he had loved playing hearts with my mother and two other couples while my mother was alive. I knew he liked women and still made out pretty well with them, and he would get into a fine barroom fight about once a year. He liked anything to do with earth-moving, and he enjoyed running the rotary plow and dealing with all the winter and snow problems. The second-best time of his life, next to the Lake Placid Winter Games, was when the *City of San Francisco* got stuck on Donner Summit in the big snow, and he helped organize the crew that rescued the passengers from the train.

But more and more now he was apt to speak of himself as a failure. Maybe as you get older you always think you should have done better things in your life. The worst of it was that I found he was jealous of me in silly little ways. I had gone to the University of Nevada for only a year, but sometimes he would make bitter-edged jokes about his "college-boy son." And he would call people I'd met in the east or in Europe my "rich, eastern buddies." He would say it contemptuously and then pretend he had been joking. It was ironic because he was so proud of his Lake Placid friends, who were, most of them, rich easterners. And it was ironic because one of his favorite sayings was that it wasn't what you knew, it was who you knew: and because of Mr. Gayley.

Mr. Gayley was a San Francisco lawyer who had a chalet at Sugar Bowl and played poker with my father.

His daughter Dodo and I had raced together as juniors, and my father had always been pleased when Mr. Gayley would take Dodo and me to races at Squaw, or Yosemite, or Mammoth, and once to Sun Valley. This had worked into Mr. Gayley's paying my expenses to races when he and Dodo weren't going, and now into an arrangement whereby I was supposed to write or phone him whenever I needed money—although almost always he would seem to know when I was low and send me a hundred dollars without my having to ask.

Once I had been afraid my father would be jealous of Mr. Gayley's helping me, but instead he seemed to feel he had proved something by having a wealthy friend who took an interest in me. And I knew he hoped I would marry Dodo someday. I could see his reasoning. Friends were the most valuable possession you could have, Mr. Gayley was his friend and had done a lot for me, and Dodo obviously liked me. It must have seemed very logical and neat to him. But he never pushed it.

The more I heard about other racers' fathers, the more pleased I was with mine. Mostly he seemed to be happy with me if I did well in a race, sorry with me if I didn't. He was never what is called a "skiing father." I have always remembered a junior race at the Reno Ski Bowl when I was Class III and Georgiana Brown was IV or V. She had taken a flush of gates wrong in the slalom, and her father met her at the finish, gave her a rough push in front of everyone, and called her "a damned little idiot" and other things. When she did well she got a new pair of skis or ski lessons with the latest hotdog instructor; when she did badly she got hell.

On a Saturday toward the end of October, Mr. Gayley phoned my father to say they were up for the weekend and that he had a dead tree on his place that had better be felled before winter. I took the Homelite over in the jeep to drop it for him. He sat on the porch in his plaid shirt and new Levis and watched me fell the pine, and limb it, and cut up the trunk. Once Dodo came out on the deck in a short-sleeved Stanford sweatshirt, to wave at me.

When I'd shut down the saw I went up on the porch to tell Mr. Gayley I'd have the wood split and stacked for him by next weekend.

"No hurry about that, no hurry, Jack," he said. "But you be sure to send me a bill when you've finished the work." He was a thin, bald man with muddy-looking eyes.

"It's my treat, Mr. Gayley," I said.

"Now don't be silly, Jack."

I wasn't going to bill him and he knew it. He asked if I'd like a beer and brought out two Burgies. We drank out of the bottles.

"Well, it shouldn't be long now till snow, Jack."

"I had a letter from Chris Leary saying they were already skiing in Colorado."

"Are they really? I suppose he's training already. I remember you telling me Chris Leary worked harder than anyone else you knew. But you're looking fit, Jack."

"I've worked pretty hard this summer. I've saved some money too." When you try too hard not to say a wrong thing, something is sure to pop out.

"Now don't you worry about that," he said hurriedly. "I'm standing by to take up any slack that develops. And you're not to be embarrassed to shout for help when you need any. This is tryout year, Jack—don't you let anything get in your way."

If you earned a place on the FIS or the Olympic team your bills were taken care of, but in the selection years everyone was on his own and had to scramble.

"You're not worried about making the Olympic team?" Mr. Gayley said, frowning anxiously, shaking his head at me.

"I ought to make it all right. Unless I bust something."

"Well, you're not to skimp on anything this year," he said. "I mean that. I'd like to see you the first American boy to get a medal in an Olympic skiing event. I'd really like to see that, Jack." He took a long pull on his beer.

His face looked unhealthily dark. "Shame you weren't chosen for the FIS last year," he said. "You should at least have been an alternate."

"Well, I got the Army out of the way. And I skied in all the races they did, except the FIS." I went on to tell him about the training camp at Loveland, over Christmas, and immediately thought it must sound as though I wanted him to pay my bills there. Just then cool jazz mewed and muttered as Dodo slid open the glass door of the living room and came out to join us. Her legs were long and thin in her Levis, her arms showed thin where the sleeves of the sweatshirt had been hacked off. She had her black hair cut short, and the back of her neck was blue, like an unshaven chin. She carried a glass of beer.

"Well, hello, stranger."

"Hi, Dodo."

"You certainly need a haircut, Jack Roche."

"You don't," I said and laughed.

She made a face and ran red-nailed fingers through her hair. "Isn't it terrible?"

"It's fine!"

She glanced at her father; she had a way of almost always saying something unpleasant when she spoke to him, or running him down when she talked about him. "Is Daddy exhorting you to win, win, win?"

Mr. Gayley flushed. "Jack doesn't need any exhorting. I don't think anyone can argue the fact that he's number two in the country now."

Leary was unarguably number one, but I had been admired by Mr. Gayley for many years now and I knew that he meant two as above three, not as below one. We had another beer, and then Mrs. Gayley drove up in the Cadillac with bags of groceries to be carried inside. I was asked to dinner, and I went home to shower and change my clothes. After dinner Dodo and I drove to a Reno movie in the Cadillac, and when we came back necked in the car parked under the pines in front of the chalet.

It wasn't as easy between us as it had been once, because Dodo was trying to make me understand that although I might be the number two racer in the country, she was a senior at Stanford and very popular socially. Also she was much more sophisticated then she'd been the last time we'd had a date, and it was clear that I should be going a lot further than I was. Finally I sat up and said, "Listen, Dodo, your Dad's been awfully nice to me."

She retreated to the far side of the seat, pulling herself together. "Yes, I guess he has, hasn't he?"

"Well, he has."

"So I suppose you feel like a gigolo," she said.

I didn't know what to say to that, so there was a bad silence.

After a while she said, "Oh, I know. Anyway, you're in love with that Anne Patterson."

"Who told you that?"

"Never mind who told me. Well—Bruce Carrington told me."

"Listen, Dodo, I don't know how this got started. I just said your Dad's been awfully nice to me. I don't want—"

"Don't," Dodo broke in. "Don't say some damn stupid thing. I swear I'll scream if you say some crummy stupid thing!" She thrust her door open. "Oh, the great number two," she said. "The *so* famous Jack Roche. You damn preoccupied—boor!"

She jumped out and slammed the door, while I got out the other side of the Cadillac. She hurried up the steps of the chalet, under the yellow Bug-Away porchlight, and inside. I couldn't have stopped her if I'd wanted to.

I got in the jeep and drove home, wishing it would hurry up and snow.

3

It was snowing when the plane from Chicago came sliding down into the Denver airport. The plane took a long time in the outrun before it turned and, blowing and scattering snow, cruised back down the runway. There was another wait for the baggage truck and the tractor with the ramp, but finally people began to come off. Anne was one of the last. She had a blue scarf tied over her hair and carried a blue flight bag. She came down the ramp with a man in a gray overcoat and a black hat, and she smiled at him as he stopped to let her precede him through the gate in the cyclone fence.

When she saw me she cried, "Jack!" She threw her arms around me, and the flight bag smacked me on the back. I kissed her cheek while she hugged me hard. She was laughing. The man in the black hat passed, tipped at his hat with his forefinger, nodded, smiled. Anne paid no attention to him. "You came down to get me!"

"Sure I came down. I haven't seen you for seven months. How was it at Stowe?"

She shook her head in an exaggerated way. "Oh, terrible!" She was pale and had dark, slanting smudges under her eyes, but she was the most beautiful girl I had ever known. In the time since I had seen her last I had almost stopped believing she was real. But she was real, and round; her blond hair curled out around the edges of the scarf.

"You look fine, Anne," I said.

"That's just because I'm happy. Actually I'm haggard." She licked at a snowflake that had fallen on her lip. "Mmmmmm—powder." We walked along toward the terminal, arm in arm, and I carried her flight bag. Our hips brushed because we walked so close together. A Christmas carol was playing on the loudspeaker system, and with the music and Anne's hand tight on my arm and the snow falling I was so happy I could hardly get my breath.

"You look so damn fine, Anne," I said.

"*You* look fine," she said. She turned up the collar of her coat and squinted at the sky. "Lovely," she said. "How are you skiing, Jack?"

"Good. How are *you* skiing?"

"Fine, considering Stowe was solid ice. With rocks. Oh, Jack, it's so good to see you, it's like coming home. How are Chris and Brownie?"

"They're here," I said.

Inside the lobby was an enormous Christmas tree with lights, and the caroling was louder. Leary and Brown hurried toward us, and Anne ran to embrace them. The four of us stood in the middle of the lobby all talking at once, and the people who passed smiled at us and often turned back to smile again. Leary had a scab on his forehead where he'd had a fall, Brown had a blue bow and two little Christmas balls holding her ponytail, and Anne wore a fleece-lined greatcoat with snowflakes melting on the shoulders.

"What a wonderful Christmas Eve!" she said. "I was feeling so lonely and bereft on the plane. How long does it take to drive to Loveland?"

"We're not going back to Loveland tonight," Leary said. "Going to whoop it up a little."

"We're going to have our Christmas party here," I said.

"Just the four of us," Brown said. "There's a racers' party at Loveland, but we decided to come down and get you and just the four of us have a party. We've got a tree and some ornaments and a goose for dinner tomorrow. We're going to have Christmas together, just us."

"We've been down here since noon, packing Christmas trees and geese around and trying to keep Jack from looking at his watch every five minutes," Leary said.

Anne kept smiling, her fingers digging into my arm. "Oh, I'm so *glad* to be here!"

"Well, Merry Christmas Eve, Anne," I said.

"Oh, isn't it great?" Brown said. "It's so *great!* It's just the way Christmas ought to be, just the people you *love,* just—" She stopped in a fluster. Her eyes were bright, round, and brown as pennies.

"Come on, let's stop blocking traffic," Leary said,

swinging her around by the elbow. Then he swung her around again so we could all lock arms and move across the lobby together, blocking traffic all the way.

Brown said to Anne, "Wait till you see this goose we've got. It's so fat. We've got these really great motel rooms with a kitchenette and a really good oven. You and I're going to do this goose tomorrow."

"I don't know how to do a goose," Anne said.

"Oh, it's easy!"

By the shops Anne halted and said we had to let her have a little time to do her Christmas shopping. She gave me her ticket so I could pick up her luggage. When she was through we went outside, Anne laden with purchases, Leary with her suitcase and bootbag, and I with her skis in their canvas-and-leather carrier. We walked close together through the parking lot to the station wagon. "Oh, Little Town of Bethlehem" boomed from the loudspeaker system. Snow drifted down and melted on the asphalt.

"It's been snowing most of the week up there," Leary told Anne. "But there're so many people they've got the powder skied out before it even hits the ground. How's Stowe?"

"Boiler plate," Anne said.

"Oh, I hate ice," Brown said.

We loaded Anne's luggage into the back of the wagon and strapped the ski bag on the big roof rack with the other skis. Leary and Brown got into the front seat, Anne and I into the back. I waited almost in a panic until she moved over against me. As I kissed her, out of the corners of my eyes I saw Brown smiling back at us.

"Yeah, it's good you're back, all right, Anne," Leary said as he started the car. "Jack's been in terrible shape."

"We've even played three-handed rummy," Brown said. "What a dumb game!"

"There'll be no more three-handed rummy," Anne said, leaning against me.

Leary drove slowly on the slippery streets through the Denver traffic. Our motel was on the edge of town. It was a fine place. We had two big rooms, each with a bath, and the girls' room had a kitchenette. Leary and I unloaded suitcases, shopping bags, and groceries, while Anne and Brown went inside.

"Packhorses again," Leary grumbled.

Inside, Anne and Brown were decorating the tree, which we had set up earlier, with ornaments and foil from the five-and-ten. I opened one of the bottles of champagne, and we all made toasts to one another, to skiing, to the selection races this year and the Olympics next year. When we had killed the bottle Anne went to take a bath. She reappeared in slacks and a white sweater, no longer looking tired. She sat on my lap and we talked about the summer while Brown and Leary went to clean up.

At dinnertime there was a wrangle over whether to go out or stay in the motel and eat snacks. The three of us voted Anne down, we turned off most of the lights, opened a bottle of champagne, and ate cheese and crackers. But I had promised Anne I would take her somewhere to dance, and we left Brown and Leary, who didn't want to come, and drove to a roadhouse where we danced to a jukebox until Anne had had enough. About eleven we went back to the motel and sat in the car and made out. After a while the kissing became only an ache, empty and insufficient, so that at the same time I was tired of kissing but would never have enough of kissing Anne. It was very late when we went in, Anne into the room where Brown was, I into the other with Leary. We were always very strict in motels and did not fool around.

In the morning Brown knocked on the wall between our rooms and called, "You get up now, we're making breakfast!"

When we were shaving in the bathroom I said to Leary, "You've got lipstick all over your face, buddy." He grunted and scowled at himself ferociously while he scrubbed at his face with a wet washcloth.

Presents were heaped under the tree in the girls' room,

some in colored Christmas wrappings, some in tissue or store bags or boxes. There was a fine smell of bacon frying and coffee perking. Brown was fussing over the stove, where she had Canadian bacon in one pan and scrambled eggs in another.

After brushing her silver-gold curls in front of the mirror, Anne came and watched Brown put slices of bread in the broiler. "Where did you learn to do all these things?" she said, and Brown laughed and said, "Oh, it's just nothing!" The goose lay on the counter, shiny and fat in its plastic jacket.

We ate Brown's breakfast off blue plastic plates and complimented her until she became pink and flustered. After breakfast we began to open presents. The first package Leary handed out was for Brown, a tan-and-white-striped store bag fastened with Scotch tape. Brown took from it a gray boiled-wool jacket with silver buttons. *"Oh!"* she said and hid her face in it.

"Don't go all to pieces!" Leary said, squatting before the tree. "It's that one we saw in Aspen last spring you were so hot for. Remember?"

Brown swung away from us and put on the jacket. With her hands in her pockets she confronted herself in the mirror, turning right and left but keeping her face averted from us. Leary scowled at her.

"Christy, open that package with the blue paper," she said.

Leary tore the blue wrapping off another boiled-wool jacket. Only the buttons were of a different design. "Mother and daughter outfits," Leary said as he rose to put his jacket on. "Which twin is the toniest?"

"Well, you liked it too!" Brown said. "Oh, don't you like it, Christy?"

"It's terrific!" he said, and Brown threw her arms around him and buried her face in his chest. He smoothed a hand over her brown hair. They looked nice in their matching jackets.

Anne went to pour herself another cup of black coffee; she had a very hard time waking up in the morning. When she came back I gave her the Ullr I had had made for her charm bracelet.

Ullr is the Norse god of skiing, and Ullr medallions are for snowbunnies, like fur-lined parkas and reindeer boots. Anne was very sophisticated in many ways, but in other and surprising ways she wasn't at all, and I knew her charm bracelet was very precious to her. This was a gold, fierce-faced, and wild-haired Ullr mounted on a silver medal. I prayed she would like it.

"Oh, Jack!" she said.

"What a *great* Ullr!" Brown said. She and Leary, arms around each other, bent to look at it.

"Oh, Jack," Anne whispered and closed the medal into her fist.

"Have you still got your charm bracelet?"

She nodded. Spots of color were burning in her cheeks again. She went to get the bracelet. It had on it a St. Christopher, a St. Bernard, a tiny pair of dice, and a silver clover-leaf, and I fastened the Ullr on with them. Anne slipped it onto her wrist and gave me a queer, shy smile. "Thank you," she whispered.

"That's a piece of gold I panned myself once," I said. "I had this man in Reno make it up."

"It's beautiful."

"The guy that made it is part Paiute. He promised me he'd build some medicine into it."

The bracelet tinkled as Anne turned it on her arm. I heard Brown whisper, "Find something for Jack, Chris."

Leary handed me a small brown-paper package fastened with Christmas seals. In it was a soft-cover book of folk songs, inscribed, "Time you learned some new songs, buddy. Chris."

Anne had bought lined leather driving gloves for Leary and me. When we thanked her she shook her head and said angrily, "All of you have wonderful presents to give, and all I have is airport junk."

"Well, we didn't give you much time."

"I had plenty of time. I had all fall in New York. I was too busy buying clothes for myself."

"Oh, cut it out, Anne," Brown said.

"They're terrific gloves!" I protested. I felt unhappy because Anne did, but they really weren't very good gloves. Brown had knit racers' toques, black for Leary and blue for me, very fine ones. I had a Swiss army knife for Leary and a teak and silver ponytail clasp for Brown. Anne had a bottle of cologne for Brown.

Leary went to turn on the radio. There was organ music, a man with a fruity voice talking about Christmas through the ages, a Coors beer commercial, finally carols. We sat among the Christmas wrappings and had another cup of coffee, Anne turning her bracelet on her wrist and regarding the leather stationery and stamp kit Brown had given her and the matching appointment book from Leary. There had been a standing joke last year about Anne's borrowing paper, envelopes, and stamps.

"Don't be sour-dog, Anne, please!" Brown said.

Anne made a face at her as "White Christmas" began on the radio. "I just take and take and don't give anything worth-while back," Anne said. She wouldn't look at me. She said loudly, "It's miserable when you find out you don't like yourself."

"Well, *we* all like you," Brown said. "We *love* you."

Anne turned her face away.

"Oh, please be happy!" Brown said.

Anne said in a severe voice, "You don't have to worry. You can cook."

"Cook and knit," Leary said. "She doesn't *have* to be a racer."

"Oh, the *goose!*" Brown cried. She hurried to the kitchenette, and Anne went into the bathroom. Leary was sitting cross-legged on the floor, folding the attachments out from his knife one by one.

"This is a terrific knife," he said quietly. "Thanks a lot. You kind of went all out, didn't you?"

Brown called from the stove, "It's the best Christmas I've ever had. Thanks for the really keen ponytail thing, Jack." She said in a lowered voice, "Anne'll be all right."

"Sure," I said.

When Anne came out of the bathroom she had put

on fresh lipstick. She said in a brisk voice, "It's so simple when you're a little girl. The best Christmases were when you got the best things. I remember when I got a pony. I didn't really want a pony, but it was wonderful getting one." She stopped and said reflectively, "Figgy gave me my first pair of Kneissls that Christmas too, I think." Figgy was one of her stepfathers. He had been a ski instructor at Stowe.

Brown said, "We always have big family Christmases with all the aunts and uncles and Grandma and Grandpa, and everybody quarrels about politics. Sometimes everybody would quarrel so I'd think I was going to get sick. Oh, I'm not even going to talk about it. Chris, you come light the oven for me, will you?"

Shaking the match out, he said, "Let me tell you about this terrific Christmas *I* had. It was before my mother and father got a divorce. Mother'd given me this football, and Mike and I went out in the front yard to play some catch. He missed an easy pass and the ball rolled out in the street and this florist's truck mashed it. Mike told Mother I'd thrown it over his head on purpose, and I called him a liar. I guess I hit him, I forget. So I spent the rest of the day in bed. That was really a terrific Christmas."

When he finished there was an awkward silence, as there always was when Leary told a bitter story about his brother. Then Brown laughed in a strained way. "Oh, how terrible!"

Anne said, "Well, everybody ought to be happy. The people who like to get things and the people who like to give things. Oh, I'm fine," she said as Brown looked at her worriedly.

"It's not that you like to *give* presents so much," Brown said. "It's that you feel grateful for—oh, I don't know how to say it!" She waved her hands in front of her face in confusion.

"Maybe we can do this again next year," I said.

"Oh, let's do!" Brown said. "Let's make a pact! We'll all be on the Olympic training squad and we'll all have Christmas together."

"If anybody's interested," Leary said, "what I'd like for a present next year, only about a year from February —is to stand up in the middle there and get that Olympic downhill gold medal." He cleared his throat. "Well, and the slalom and GS too."

I was embarrassed for him, and I knew Brown and Anne were too. "How about a silver?" I said to ease the moment.

"Oh, I'd be happy with a bronze," Brown said.

"I want the gold because that's first," Leary said. All at once, looking from face to face, he reddened. "Dreams of glory!" he said and pounded his chest. He got up to turn off the radio, which had run into a snarl of commercials. "Well, anyway, I can do more one-legged deep-knee bends than anybody in the world," he said. "Left-legged, that is." He had a trick right knee that bothered him sometimes. "Go for the title, Jack?"

"Any time," I said.

"Loser chore-boys for Brownie."

We faced off and started, Leary counting. I'd never even come close to beating him at this, but now it seemed very important. We grinned at each other as we went down and up together, panting, and waving our arms for balance. My leg began to feel as though the tendons would tear loose.

Anne went out to the kitchen to put her coffee cup in the sink. When she came back she said, "I'm going to see if this Ullr works." Turning it on her wrist, she squinted at Leary and muttered to herself. He began to laugh. He lost his balance at thirty-five and fell, dragging me down with him and yelling that he'd been hexed. We ended up in a heap on the floor, laughing.

"I'm the ex-champ so young!" Leary panted.

Afterward we tried to get Brown and Anne into a contest, but they wouldn't do it. "I'm not feeling competitive," Anne said.

"Let's sing or something," Brown said.

I got the guitar out of its case and played the few songs I knew and the few more I could fake, and we all sang. I tried to work some of the songs in the folk-song

28

book into the key of E. From time to time I saw Anne hold up her wrist to look at the Ullr, and I was happy that she liked it.

Leary chore-boyed for Brown while she got dinner. Outside it was drizzling. At Loveland there would be fine dry powder coming down. We talked about where all the racers were, about equipment and the training races; about who looked hot this year—Harry Butler had improved tremendously, and so had Lorraine Hedquist, though she couldn't touch Brown, who was skiing very well. And I was skiing very well. I had been beating even Leary in the practice slaloms. All at once, reluctantly, like pulling aside a curtain you didn't really want to see behind yet, I began to wonder how far I could go, how good I might become. But I could make myself stop it. You had to have that kind of will—as the night before the downhill you had to be able to button up your mind and stop scaring yourself with the close calls you had had in training runs; as before the slalom you had to keep yourself from going over and over the sequence of the gates, forget about it, and go to sleep.

The day passed slowly in that way pleasant days pass, with nothing to worry about except that it was passing and could never come again.

In the middle of the afternoon we ate the goose and praised Brown to blushes again. Anne was her best gay self, and Leary was in fine spirits and kept us laughing. Anne and I did the dishes, and in the late afternoon we all went downtown to a movie. We had waffles at a pancake palace before returning to the motel. That night we went to bed early so we could get an early start back to Loveland in the morning.

4

In January we went east. We stayed in New York four days, Brown out on Long Island with Mrs. May,

Anne with her mother, and Leary and I in a midtown hotel, though I spent a lot of time with Anne.

Anne's mother was three or four inches shorter than Anne and wore her blond hair long and carefully combed while Anne wore hers whacked off and carefully uncombed. Other than that they looked almost exactly alike.

Anne's mother was married to Roger Bernand, who imported ski stuff, had a shop in New York and a mail-order business. He was her fourth husband. Anne had told me once that usually women who married as many times as her mother made a good thing out of it financially; her mother had not. Anne's father, whom Anne never saw, lived in Buffalo and was a terrible lush. The first stepfather had died and left Anne a little trust fund and the mother a lot of money, which she had blown during her marriage to the Austrian ski instructor Figgy. She had been married to Roger Bernand for five years now. He did quite well, Anne said, but he was Swiss, and tight.

Their house was very narrow and three stories high, dark and shabbily furnished except for a big, skylighted studio room at the top and back, where there were bright modern paintings and Danish furniture. One afternoon I sat with Mrs. Bernand on the couch in the studio while a photographer took pictures of Anne in ski clothes for Bernand's catalogue.

Bernand, a dark man with a hook nose and receding hair, was supervising. He lit a little brown cigar the size of a cigarette and sat down with us while Anne changed her outfit behind a screen. The photographer was putting film into his camera.

"Isn't she a lovely girl, Roger?" Mrs. Bernand said. "She poses very well. She was so awkward when she was a youngster. But she has grown into a perfectly lovely girl."

"Yes," Bernand said, exhaling a cloud of blue smoke.

Mrs. Bernand turned her wide, dark blue, slightly slanted eyes toward me. "Don't you think she's a lovely girl, Jack?"

"Yes, she is."

She continued to regard me, a troubled expression on her face. "Now, let me see," she said. "I know you've told me you're from—Norden? Is that near San Francisco, Jack?"

"It's on Donner Summit, near Sugar Bowl. It's not far from Squaw Valley."

"The National Championships will be at Squaw Valley this year, I believe?" Bernand said.

"That's right."

"Do your parents live in Norden year round?" Mrs. Bernand asked.

"My father does. My mother's dead."

She frowned, apparently trying to recall the conversation on this subject we'd had only two days before. "He's a contractor," I reminded her. Talking to her was exhausting because she never paid attention.

Bernand rose as Anne came out from behind the screen. She had on rose-colored Bogners and a matching, loosely knit sweater. "With boards, huh?" the photographer said as Bernand took a pair of Heads over to Anne. Blowing puffs of smoke, he arranged her with the skis on one shoulder, her face turned toward the camera over the other, her feet in shiny Molitors set apart. She had beautiful legs in the Bogners; I thought how tired she must be of lacing and unlacing boots every time she changed pants. They were taking no pictures of her smiling because she had chipped a corner off a front tooth in a fall at Loveland.

"If you'll parn the expression," the photographer said, "we ought to get the cah a little more around this way."

"It's about worked off for the day," Anne said, "if you'll parn the expression." She winked at me. The photographer snorted.

"Such a trim little behind, darling," Mrs. Bernand said.

"We'll just have you in the striped pants and then wind up," Bernand said around his cigar. The photographer made the chirruping sound that meant he was going to shoot. "Now only with the poles," Bernand said, and

Anne was relieved of the skis and given a pair of black poles to lean on.

When she had clumped behind the screen to change again, Mrs. Bernand rose to pour herself another martini from the silver jug, Bernand sat down and looked at his watch, the photographer patted a yawn.

"I really must insist that you get that tooth capped, darling," Mrs. Bernand called. "*So* disfiguring. You look so solemn with your mouth closed always, and so raffish when you do smile. Darling, you must let me make an appointment with Dr. Block."

"No time," Anne said. "Must mush on to Franconia tomorrow." She draped the pink sweater over the screen on top of the other clothes there.

"Early tomorrow," I said.

"What a grind, eh, the circuit?" Bernand said. "But so much fun when one is young."

"Oh, but anything's fun *then,* Roger," Mrs. Bernand said, and he grinned and nodded.

Then he said to me, "I have talked to my good friend Walter Nello who writes articles for the sports magazines. He is very interested in doing an article on you four comrades, how you will race together for us in the Olympics. Racing. Playing. All those things. Many pictures. He says for certain later in the winter he will do it."

"That sounds simply fabulous," Mrs. Bernand said. "But we must be very careful not to hurt Mrs. May's feelings again this year by not consulting her. So touchy. How are you and Elizabeth May getting along, darling?"

"I don't have to get along with her this year," Anne said. "I'm not on any team. As a matter of fact she *spoke* to me the last time I saw her."

"Raddled old Lesbian bitch," Mrs. Bernand said mildly. "It really is too bad that things are done so haphazardly in this country and Elizabeth May can simply shoulder her way into charge of our poor girls. But on her side of it she does spend a great deal of money paying for transportation and coaching and things like that. I really didn't approve of the way you went around Europe so independently last year, my darling. But I would hate to see you cowed by her like poor Georgiana Brown."

"I don't think it's like that," I said.

"She's staying out there because May asked her to," Anne said, behind the screen. "Brownie's just sorry for her. I guess she's grateful too. It's pitiful really. May wishes she had a daughter just like Brownie."

"Well, I do disapprove of older people feeding on the young," Mrs. Bernand said and tipped her martini glass to her lips.

Anne came out in blue-and-black-striped pants and a big-patterned sweater. She pulled over a folding chair, sat down tiredly, and put her unlaced boot in my lap. I laced it for her, she dropped her foot with a thump to the floor and raised the other. Mrs. Bernand watched us with a troubled expression. When they had finished taking pictures Anne sat down again and I unlaced her boots. Bernand left with the photographer.

"Charles McCammon has phoned several times, dear," Mrs. Bernand said. "He's very anxious that you get in touch with him while you're here."

"Maybe I'll call him tonight," Anne said. "No, I won't either."

"Surely it would be the gracious thing to—"

"I don't want to get married, and I'm so tired of arguing with him about it. He loves to argue. I guess it's a good thing for a lawyer to get lots of practice arguing."

"But surely if you made him understand that you couldn't possibly marry until after the Olympics, my darling—" Mrs. Bernand drew a long breath. "You didn't tell me he'd asked you to marry him, dear."

Anne sat wiggling her toes in gray socks in my lap. I was wishing I were somewhere else, but she smiled at me, showing the chipped tooth, and it was all right. "Didn't I?" she said to her mother. "I guess I didn't because I know I can do so much better than that."

"Anne, darling," her mother said in a strange, soft voice; she sounded as though she were trying to comfort Anne for some hurt.

33

"It was that day we went for a drive up to Connecticut," Anne said. "He wanted to show me the house he was going to buy for us. It was a split level with a big sunny playroom for children." She began to laugh. "I reminded him that earlier he'd been talking about a house in Stowe," she went on. "He said of course we'd have a cabin at Stowe, we'd drive up and look at listings the next weekend. But this was the house where we would live. I said how would it be if I lived at Stowe and he came up to visit me weekends."

"Oh, Anne," her mother said.

"I said but what I really wanted was a chalet in Klosters and a nice little apartment in Paris, and he could send me money every month and come over and visit me on his vacations."

"Oh, *Anne!*"

"I didn't really say that," Anne said. She rose and went behind the screen, stripping off the sweater. Mrs. Bernand brushed at a strand of hair and glanced at the martini jug. I asked if I could get her another, but she said she thought she'd better not. She wore a plain black, expensive-looking dress and a thin gold chain around her neck, which she touched with a forefinger from time to time.

Finally she asked politely, "I think you said your father was a contractor, Jack? Does that mean he contracts to build buildings?"

"He does earth-moving and things like that."

"Oh, I see."

Behind the screen Anne laughed. Mrs. Bernand's face turned pink, puzzled, worried, and disapproving all at once.

Anne reappeared in her green quilted robe, barefoot. "Mother, I'm going to lie down in my room for a while. Is it all right if Jack goes down and makes some sandwiches?"

"Yes—yes, of course," Mrs. Bernand said. "There are lots of things in the refrigerator, I think, Jack. There must still be some of that good Danish beer." As we left the studio she stood looking after us, holding her empty glass in one hand and the wrist of the hand that held the glass in the other.

When I brought the sandwiches on a plate and the two bottles of Tuborg with glasses inverted over their necks, Anne was lying on her bed, filing her fingernails. The shades were drawn and a lamp with a scalloped shade was turned on. There was a fashion magazine on the bedside table. I put the plate on the magazine, sat down on the edge of the bed, poured beer into a glass and handed it to her. The beer left a mustache of foam on her upper lip, which she licked away with the pink tip of her tongue.

"I suppose I could be a model," she said. "I suppose I could stand it."

"You'd be good at it."

"I'd probably get fat if I wasn't skiing."

"Your mother isn't fat."

She leaned forward to put down her glass, holding her robe closed with her left hand. "Yes, she is," she said, pointed a finger to her temple to show where, and laughed.

"She doesn't like me very much, I guess."

"You worry her. I'll tell her it's nothing before I leave —I don't really like to worry her. I'll tell her we're only friendlies. Fellow athletes." She looked at me candidly and said, "It's true, isn't it?"

"Sure."

"Of course I'd tell her that even if it wasn't true." She reached for a sandwich.

"I don't know if I want you to get that tooth capped or not," I said. "I read somewhere that it's the flaw that makes for true beauty."

Her eyes widened and moistened. "That's nice, Jack," she said. She took a bite of the sandwich and, her cheek bulging, gave me the long, candid examination again. "Points for that," she said. Then she said seriously, "Do you suppose I've been good for you, Jack?"

I grinned and nodded. Good for me like a chocolate éclair, I thought, that was cool, sweet, and delicious, and left you with cavities in your teeth. But she had been good for me. Skiing in Europe, and on the circuit now at home, was not exactly a new world for me, but it was certainly new country, and at first I had felt called upon, for protection, to try out the various poses of shyness and aloofness, and for a while to pretend I was hard-boiled, a rough-cut mountain man like my father. It was Anne who had helped me out of my poses, and now I was at ease in almost any company and considered myself clever at covering up when I was not. Questions like Anne's mother's, as to where I was from and what my father did, no longer threw me into defensive rages.

I took a long drink of beer, and Anne said, "I think I have been. So that's something anyway."

"Sure you've been good for me. No mother to teach me, what would I know about life if it wasn't for you?"

"Do you suppose I could make a career of teaching young boys about life?"

"This young boy is two years older than you are, old girl."

She chewed another bite of sandwich reflectively. "Well," she said, "I'm not going to marry Charley Mc-Cammon before the Olympics, or after them, or ever. If I couldn't do any better than that I'd—especially now that I have the one flaw of true beauty."

"You never told me about him," I said. "She wants you to marry him, huh?"

She nodded. She put her hand out for her glass, and I handed it to her. "She thinks she's an authority on picking men. She's done so wonderfully at it herself. Charley's thirty-four. He's so badly coordinated he can't even—I don't know what he can't even. Anything. Dance; he can't even dance."

"Does he ski?"

"He thinks he does. He skis like a ski patrolman coming off the mountain with a toboggan with a body in it. The first thing he'd do would be to figure out some way I couldn't ski because I'm good at it and he's not."

" 'Most beautiful natural skier this country's ever seen,' " I said. It was what one of the ski magazines had said of her last year. "Have you met anybody yet you'd want to marry?"

"There was a boy I met in Bermuda when we were

there. He was half French and half English and he had
a lovely accent. He was a Scuba diver, looking for
archaeological things down there. His name was Raoul.
He came of very wealthy people, I think."

"You never can tell," I said, trying to make a joke of
it.

"No, you usually can," Anne said seriously. "I've got
an awfully good eye."

We sat in silence for a while and I was so unhappy it
began to seem ridiculous and in the end I almost managed
to laugh at myself.

Anne said, "I guess I'd better take a nap now. Do
you think we ought to go out on the town tonight?"

"Can't afford it," I said.

"I'll get some money from Roger." She finished her
beer, gave me the empty glass, and leaned back on the
pillow with her eyes closed. "I ought to get what he'd
have to pay a regular model," she said. "Just so I don't
ruin my amateur standing. But who'd know?"

"Well, we have to get off early in the morning," I said.
I didn't want to go out on the town.

"I suppose I should stay in and have a good, long chat
with Mother." Sighing, she said, "And I suppose the
thing to do is have Charley over for cocktails. I'll call
Brownie and ask her to come in and spend the night
here so we can get an early start. That way I couldn't
possibly go out with Charley tonight."

"Remember you have to stay in training." I leaned over
and kissed her and rose. "See you in the morning. We'd
better plan on leaving about seven."

"Oh, my God!" Anne said in a tragic voice. She was
reaching for the fashion magazine as I went out.

5

Whenever I was low, all the worries would start
circling like Indians riding and shooting around a wagon
train. I would worry about money, about going back to

college, about what I was going to do when the racing season—the great season of many seasons that inevitably had to end some spring—finally ended. I worried very much about letting down people like my father and Mr. Gayley, who had faith in me, who were in a way betting on me. And I worried about keeping my balance over Anne.

When I was low it would come on me that I had no chance of ever beating Chris Leary, that the best I could hope to do was trail along in second place behind him. And out of that, if my mood was bad enough, it would all begin to seem a fake: the courage, the "downhill guts," only a swallowing of dose after dose of meaningless medicine, and all the finely trained summoning of muscle and instant reaction and pure dogged will not only not heroic, or even admirable, but foolish; and the splendor of mountains and rocks and evergreens and the snow covering, so beautiful that you ached with it and your eyes watered sometimes—yet all you knew to do to the beauty of that clean snow was frantically to make tracks all over it, like scribbling your name on someone else's painting. And then I would feel guilty to be so wrapped up not only in racing but in skiing itself, which was somehow like kissing Anne Patterson, unsatisfying and insatiable. Yet there were so many memorable days skiing, when it was the most important thing in the world, filled with joy and certitude—the actuality worthy of the anticipation, which I have found to be true of very few things.

It was half snowing and half raining as I walked down Fifth Avenue toward the hotel. Snow isn't exciting in a city, it's only trouble and mess. Tires sizzled as cars passed, and doormen stood in the street and blew whistles at taxis. Buses ground by stinking of exhaust fumes. An old convertible skidded and smacked a Cadillac with a sound like a load of sheet metal being dumped, and I stood and watched the argument and a cop in a black slicker and cap cover trying to sort out the traffic. Suddenly, with the horns tooting, I was so lonely and homesick I felt as if I were falling down a well.

I'd thought Leary had gone to meet his brother, but

he was sitting cross-legged on the bed in the hotel room, in his shorts, looking at a new ski magazine.

"Here's another one of those articles about downhill racing being too dangerous," he said as soon as I came in. "Too many racers getting hurt and a couple of guys killed last year. How there ought to be more control gates and only natural bumps. Why don't they leave it alone? Anybody can back out of a race if the course looks too tough." He grinned. "Of course they haven't been around to consult me yet."

He had very small ears set close to his head, and his features were delicate and aristocratic, like those of some spoiled prince in an old painting. The edges of his eyelids were always reddened, as though he never had enough sleep. He was talking in the too-fast way he had when he was nervous or excited. "Did you stick it to Anne that we have to get rolling early tomorrow?"

"I told her seven."

"I just talked to Brownie. She's coming in to stay with Anne tonight. Christ, I get sorry for her with that damned old bat May riding her. And her father too. She can't take that kind of pressure."

It was strange to hear him say that. He himself rode Brown pretty roughly about her racing. I started to ask about his brother, but he hopped off the bed and paced across the room and back, saying, "Everybody but me walks to and fro. I walk fro and to."

"You're walking forth and back," I said.

He began to walk backward, grinning. "Right!" He did some one-legged deep-knee bends. "Yeah, and down and up."

When he stopped, panting, I said, "I thought you were going to meet your brother."

"I called up and told him I couldn't make it."

"I thought it was supposed to be important."

"Well, I thought I'd better get the wagon checked before we started up to Franconia. They have to have it all day." He did some more knee bends. "What the hell's the point anyway?" he went on. "He was just going to give me a bad time. You know, last year was supposed to be *it*. I was supposed to go back to school this year, settle down."

"What's your brother got to do with it?"

"He's Jesus Christ, that's all. My father's got it worked out that he can't talk to me, so he gets Mike to do it. Jack, tell me this, will you? How come people just can't stand it, you can do something better than anybody else?"

"I don't know," I said. It seemed strange that while there was no question about his downhill courage, he couldn't face his brother. And it was strange to think his father could not talk to him. My father and I had no trouble that way. We had always spent a lot of time together and done many different things together. Around Norden I was "Charley Roche's boy" more than I was Jack Roche.

"Just so damn jealous," Leary said. "You know what I notice? The ill will. People wishing so hard you'd fall on your face. You can smell it on them. The bigger you get, the more you can smell it."

I sat down in the chair, kicked off my after-ski boots, and crossed my feet up on the bed. He was looking at me almost resentfully, as though I had criticized him for not having gone to see his brother.

"You know what he said?" he asked. "Said I was going to play around so long and never finish college, I wasn't going to be fit for anything except running a gas station. I told him that was fine with me."

I'd never met his brother Mike. They were from somewhere near Boston originally, but their mother and father had been divorced when Chris was ten, and he and Mike and the mother had moved to Colorado Springs. Both Chris and Mike had returned to the east to prep, but Leary had flunked out and gone back to Colorado to high school, and had become a hotter and hotter racer on the junior circuit. Mike had been graduated from Yale and was now at the Harvard Business School, while Leary had quit Denver University after a semester. Mike had done everything right, Leary said, and he had done everything wrong—except to become the best downhill man in the country, which was neither right nor wrong, it was only out of line.

I remembered the stories Chris had told me about fights with Mike—Mike provoking Chris into chasing him and Chris never able to catch him, and crying and cursing in frustration until Mike turned and beat him up; Mike making trouble and managing to fasten the blame on Chris. Skiing was the only way he'd ever beaten Mike, and as soon as he'd beaten him Mike had quit racing. The stories had made me glad I had no brother, older or younger.

"You don't know how lucky you are," Leary said. "Your dad isn't riding you all the time to win like Brown's, or to go screw around in college like mine. It's really tough when somebody's always after you with a needle."

"I guess so."

"I can take it better than Brownie though. I just don't give a damn any more. You know, next year's the Olympics. You'd think the Olympics would mean something. And five tryout races this year. Mike acts like he's never heard of the North Americans or the Stowe Internationals or the Harriman or the Roch or the Nationals. He'll just go screw me with Dad. He always does."

"Maybe you ought to talk to your father."

He came back and sat cross-legged on the bed again, scraping his fingers through his cropped black hair. "I can't take it!" he said. "He and Edith just sit there and look at me like I'm a bug, and he chews up his cigar and talks about the mill. He thinks getting a goddam degree's the only thing that counts in the world. Christ, everybody's got a degree. What the hell's so great about a crummy B.S.? I guess it's just that he had it all worked out. Mike was going to go to Harvard and be the business end, and I was supposed to get a B.S. and be research. You know why? Because I got an A in a science course in high school once.

"I can't stand it," he went on. "I just say all these stupid things. I get it all rehearsed, what I'm going to say, but it comes out wrong or else I'm afraid to say it. It's great for Mike, you know. He's going to the B School, the mill's going to be his meat. He and Dad sit around eating cigars and talking about how they're going to move down to Arkansas and all that cheap nigger labor. But it's not my meat. I don't love it. I don't even think about it. I'm a downhill racer, and I guess nobody in the family is ever going to understand about it. And I just don't give a damn any more." He closed his mouth tightly and glared at me, hunching his body over his black-haired legs. There was a long pale scar dotted with suture marks on his left shin, where he'd sliced his leg open with a ski edge. He said through clenched lips, "Goddam them. I'm number one in the country and it doesn't mean a thing to any of them."

Uncomfortably I said, "Well, it's a sport a lot of people don't know anything about."

"Yeah, sport. That's it. They think we're playing. That's what Mike thinks, I know. Having fun. It's really fun coming down some icy goddam mountain at sixty miles an hour in flat light. I've done a lot of thinking," he said, looking down. "You know, there's so little men *have* to do in the world—in life. The only really important thing is the human race going on. Women have the babies; a man's job making babies is damn small. Well, once he went out and shot deer or planted corn, things like that. But that's all easy now. So he has all this time, he sits around and thinks up things to do. You know—wars. Or he paints, he's an artist. Or he invents ways to kill deer faster or plant his corn easier, so he has more time. What he does mostly though, he makes money. That's the best thing he's thought of to do yet, that really passes the time. And if he makes a lot of it he can think he's terrific.

"What I'm trying to say is, men don't have anything *really* to do, so they invent things and pretend they have to do them so they can think they are great and important. But it's all phony. Except for one thing that isn't. That's —oh, you know—doing something nobody else can do as well; making a mark; footprints in the sands of time and all that crap. Only it isn't crap.

"So I'm close to making a mark," he went on. "I mean a

real mark, so I'm something really important and nobody can take it away. And they want me to give it up, or anyway do it half-assed, for something that's really phony where I'll never be anything or make any kind of mark at all. And I think it's goddam cruel."

He looked up at me anxiously, and I realized this must be the speech he had rehearsed. He was trying it out on me.

I said, "Well, you can't ever explain anything to anybody that's not a racer."

Leary nodded.

"I guess what they'd say—earning a living for a wife and kids—isn't so phony."

"Well, I don't have any wife and kids," he said. "And I'm not going to have."

We sat there. I was thinking that when it got too tough for Brown or Anne, they could get married and have babies and so be neatly out of it. But there was no easy way out for Leary or me. When you had subscribed all of yourself to succeeding at something, there was no concealing the fact that you had failed, if you failed.

To change the subject I said, "Brownie's father's pretty bad. I used to see him around at the junior races. There're a lot of fathers like that."

He seemed relieved to talk about something else too. "Jesus, he's on her all the time. He used to go with her to all the races, and now he writes her letters and she has to call him up every time. You know, before I started going with her last year she'd hardly ever been out with *any*body. I guess he told her if she was going to be a racer she didn't have time for men, period. She broke loose a little last year, in Europe, but it's still bad. I guess he's very big in Reno, in real estate, and he's a partner in some car agency, but you'd think all he had to worry about is whether she's going to make the Olympics or not. He's going to buy her a Porsche if she makes the squad."

"She'll make it."

He wagged his head at me, his eyebrows lumping together. "I don't know. I don't know whether she's trying to win just to give him a kick or because she's scared *not* to. But you've got to do it because *you* want it. It's got to come from inside you. Doesn't it?"

"I don't know where it comes from," I said.

He gave a fake yawn and got up again. "I'm going to take a shower," he announced. "Then let's go pick up the car and get something to eat, okay?"

"Okay," I said.

He went into the bathroom, and I heard the beat of the shower. I was feeling depressed again, and I sat slumped in my chair, wondering what it was and where it came from, the secret and essential ingredient you had to have to be better than merely very good, to be the best. I was a better athlete than Leary, and a better skier, but I could never beat him in downhill unless he had a fall, and could beat him only with luck in slalom. He didn't even enjoy skiing as Brown and Anne and I did. But he was a real competitor, and so he was a better racer.

Anne didn't seem to have the essential ingredient. She was what's called a "natural skier," and she had had a lot of early training from her stepfather—Figgy had been an international-class racer. She could win in slalom, at least, almost whenever she wanted. But the will or desire was never strong—she didn't care enough.

Brown was stronger and a better athlete, but she had nerve trouble. In one start she would take silly and dangerous chances and, with luck, make a spectacular run; then she was apt to fall unaccountably apart in the next race. She was very young still, though, and should learn to pace herself better.

Leary had said you couldn't do it to please your father or because you were afraid of him or for any reason that was not out of your own self, yet it seemed to me in a way he was competing as he had once tried to catch Mike, whom he was never able to catch, and as though he must impress his father, who was never impressed. But he was number one in the country; whatever the ingredient was, he must have it. Maybe it was simply the love of winning. Leary loved to win so much there didn't seem to be anything else in the world for him.

I decided not to think about it any more. It seemed to

me that by trying to discover what urgency possessed him, that did not possess me, I was only psyching myself out of ever being able to beat him. I tried to think, instead, of driving north to Franconia tomorrow, the four of us together again; and the day after that, when we would be skiing on the hard, icy snowpack of New England, with the weather clear and cold and the Chief-of-Course setting the downhill, the blue gates drawing the course excitingly down the mountain in a new trial and examination, the blue flags shivering in the wind.

6

It was snowing again as we climbed the slalom course on Cannon, and gusts of wind came down the mountain and blew the snow in startled flurries. The hill was a maze of red, blue, and yellow flagged poles, and the ascending line of racers twisted slowly up alongside the course. We individually memorized the combinations of gates as we climbed, deciding where to go high or low, where to go for speed, where to check. The trickiest part of the course was near the bottom, where there was a sidehill hairpin leading into a three-gate flush and an offset H. Then there was a jog through two closed gates and the short schuss to the finish.

Skis on my shoulder, poles in my left hand, setting my boots in across the fall line to grip here where the hill was steep, I stopped when Karl Neuer, ahead of me, paused to study a combination. Snowflakes floated down and melted on my face and lay like tiny lace doilies on the sleeve of my parka and the gloved hand gripping the tips of my skis. Karl Neuer and Franz Beck were two Austrians who were teaching at Stowe and racing in the eastern starts.

Neuer muttered in German and plodded on. He had won the giant slalom but had fallen yesterday in the downhill and had no chance for the combined. Leary had won the downhill, Franz Beck had been a close second, and I an even closer third, but anyone in the first ten except Neuer still could win the combined by winning big in the slalom. In the first seed for the North Americans were Leary and me, the Austrians, a hot young Canadian named Markle, Benny McInerny and Joe Hammond from last year's FIS team, Tom Boyd, who had been in the last Olympics as well as the FIS, Jackie Samuelson, who had also been in the last Olympics, and Harry Butler, who was new on the circuit but had made a good record last year.

Weekend skiers stopped along the course to watch us as we climbed, and from time to time the snow lightened and T-bars were visible against the lacy snow-covering of the trees. I kept yawning. Everyone has his own way of reacting to a race, and though in slalom there is none of the fear of speed that is present in the downhill, there is tension enough. Leary was always very nervous until just before starting time, but I would go around yawning all morning, drowsy, unable to concentrate; people would seem a blur, everything too complicated to cope with— until my number was called at the top. Then the adrenalin would flow as though a faucet had been turned on, and I would have to fight my nerves like trying to push a cat into a paper bag.

At the top of the course, racers and officials were crowded around the starting gate, and racers were tying on their numbers, filing edges, warming up, or merely waiting. The bright colors of sweaters and racing parkas, pants and toques, were muted and watered-looking in the white-on-gray day and the falling snow. Leary was pacing up and down to keep his legs limber. My own legs felt dull and weak.

Only the first fifteen or twenty gates were visible, their colored blobs of flags hanging limp. Below that, the course whitened into obscurity. The gatekeepers were taking up their positions, and sideslippers packed the new snow that had fallen. Someone was testing the phone connection in a mechanical voice. From time to time a racer, to relieve the tension and warm up, would take off down alongside the course and crank off four or five tight turns, while the rest of us watched appraisingly. I closed my eyes and, moving a finger like a metronome, recited the order of the gates to myself.

Near me, Tom Boyd and Jackie Samuelson were talking together in a relaxed fashion. They were both wearing their Olympic sweaters. Racers who'd made an Olympic squad always seemed to wear some piece of Olympic gear, as though to remind the rest of us that they'd made the Winter Games—what had we done? On the other side of me Bill Birks was unmusically singing:

"Downhill racers sing this song, doo-dah, doo-dah,
Downhill course is goddam long, oh, doo-dah-day!"

No one ever sang at a downhill start; there you waited and suffered silently. The slalom mood was more relaxed. But there was a sudden swifter beat to my heart as the starter yelled, "Clear the course!" The gatekeepers took up the cry, echoing it down the hill. A gust of wind fluttered the flags. Leary came over to stand with me and we watched the first forerunner start down. He made smooth, stylish turns, not trying for speed. When the second forerunner went down, the snow had let up a little and we could see more of the course.

The first racer, Joe Hammond, burst out of the slot with a flurry of poles. He had been a downhill wonder once, but he had never come back after a broken leg. Karl Neuer ran second; he skated, rowed with his poles, banged past the flagged gates, and worked for every fraction of a second.

"Three in the slot, four on deck, five in the hole."

I was five. My stomach rose six inches and hung there queasily. There were sharp, aching flutters in my legs. I moved up above the starting gate and waited there, flexing my knees. The loudspeaker at the bottom boomed Joe Hammond's time, distant and hollow, quarreling with its echo—59.6.

The starter counted down for McInerny, who leaned out of the slot: five . . . four . . . three . . . two . . . one . . . *Go!"* McInerny started down, and Franz Beck,

47

in his white earband, threaded his way into the gate. "Four in the slot, five on deck."

The Canadian boy, Markle, face lost behind his goggles, spat out his chewing gum and came up behind me, Leary behind him. Neuer's time was 53.8. There was cheering down below. "Good grief," somebody said. Suddenly the T-bars and the weekend skiers were clearer, and the trees beyond them stood in puddles of blue shadow. The sun had broken through.

When the starter began his count-down on Beck I had a moment of panic as the succession of the gates went blank in my mind's eye. I closed my eyes and gritted my teeth and summoned them back. "Go!" the starter said, and I slid into the slot Beck had vacated. He had started faster than Neuer, too fast, I thought. Coming out of the fourth gate he had to check, throwing out a sheet of snow. He took the fifth gate off balance, one of his skis jerked up, but he recovered. The starter touched my shoulder and said, "Roche?"

"Ho."

"Get set."

I pulled my goggles down over my eyes, leaned out and set my poles. He began to count.

"Time for number three, McInerny, North Conway —fifty-seven and four-tenths seconds."

I flexed my knees to the rhythm of the starter's counting.

"Go!"

I drove myself out with my poles, breathed explosively, "Hanh!" so I would not forget and hold my breath, and went down fast through the first series of gates, which presented no problems, taking the last of them so close the small of my back brushed the upper bamboo. There was a scrape of steel edges on ice as I cut hard around. My downhill ski slipped, then held, and I drove with my poles; drive! and drive! and a step up with the uphill ski and weight it and bring up the other, and drive! again. High through the next gate and skate once—*too fast! too fast!* I ran the tails of my skis out in a snowplow for an instant, smacked them together and cranked around but still too fast. Just in time my edges bit and came around but off balance now—*no!* I got my balance back as though the protest had done it, and now two open gates; shoulder in past the bamboo, around hard again; drive! drive! drive! with poles stabbing and the burn of snowflakes on my chin. Twist the right shoulder through this gate, and around and left shoulder through the next; out of the corners of my eyes now the banner at the bottom fluttering FINISH and the blink of the holes cut to let the wind through; I cursed out loud as my skis almost went out from under me driving through the next, closed, gate, but my ankles strained to cut the edges in, and driving with my poles again I dropped into the offset hairpin. Now the final flush: elbows in and narrow, I steered the tips of my skis two inches to the right, a little to the left, shaving bamboo gates, and into the H. *Careful here!* The tails of my skis cracked a gate but I kept my balance, and there was the consciousness that from the number of close calls I'd had I must be making fast time. I ducked through the H, jogged once more, tucked, and schussed down to the finish, where the big banner hung limply now, as though holding its breath. At the last instant I came erect and flung my poles out ahead of me to break the beam of the electric timer, swept into the outrun, and jarred to a stop.

There was applause from the people standing around the roped-off outrun. Panting, I pushed the goggles up on my forehead and moved slowly over to where Neuer, Beck, and McInerny stood by the timing shelter.

"You looked fast so far, Jack," McInerny said. "Good run." Beck made a saluting gesture, and Neuer put out a gloved hand to shake mine.

"Very good run, Jock."

"Thanks. Yours too." Hearing my name, I turned and waved at Anne, Brown, and Alice Beard. Markle was on course now.

My stomach fluttered as the loudspeaker came to life. "Time for number five, Roche, Norden, California —fifty-three and five-tenths." There was a cheer. Karl

Neuer banged a fist on his thigh. I grinned toward Anne and Brown, who were clapping.

Markle shot out of the hairpin into the last flush. He hooked a tip on a pole, tottered, almost recovered, got off balance again in the H. He was falling for the last twenty-five yards, but he didn't hit the snow until just before the finish and plowed across in a tangle of arms and legs, skis and poles, to laughter and applause. But he had made a good run. A ski patrolman went over to help him up.

Then Leary was on the course, the speeding dark blur of his body seeming to leap from gate to gate. "He's going to be fast or can-up," McInerny said in his know-it-all way. Neuer muttered, "Too fast comes," and Beck spoke to him in German. The loudspeaker announced Markle's time: 54.8.

I heard Brown cry, as though Leary could hear her, "Slow down, Chris!"

He didn't slow down. His movements had a jerky, half-completed look; but there was something heartbreakingly sure about him. He checked so hard before a flush he was lost in a spray of snow, and I thought he had fallen. But he hadn't fallen.

Brown cried out again, "Go, Christy!"

"He is very excellent, your friend," Neuer said to me solemnly. "But sometimes foolish."

I nodded and watched Leary sweep out of the offset hairpin. He started through the flush down the fall line, twisting his shoulders like an awkward but enthusiastic dancer, each shift of weight giving him just enough deflection of line, shouldering past the bamboo poles so that they vibrated behind him. He slammed across the finish and deep into the outrun before he stopped.

There was cheering and clapping and whistling, and now I didn't look toward Anne and Brown. McInerny didn't have to inform us that this was the fastest run, but he did anyway. Leary poled over to us, grinning arrogantly, eyes alight, panting.

I cleared my throat and said, "Great run."

"Great run, Christy," McInerny said. "Best time so

far." Neuer held out a hand to shake Leary's. Beck and Leary shook hands. Leary leaned on his poles and grinned up at the loudspeaker. You arrogant bastard! I thought. It seemed a long time before the announcement came. "Time for number seven, Leary, Colorado Springs: fifty-two and eight-tenths."

The cheering broke out again, and McInerny slapped Leary on the back. "Oh, hell," Leary said, grinning. "I thought I could bust fifty-two." He moved over toward Brown and Anne, stopping to shake hands with people along the way. Karl Neuer was watching him sourly, and I realized that I must be wearing the same expression. Above us the finish banner cracked and bellied in another gust of wind. I turned to look up the hill; the racer on course had missed a gate and was climbing frantically back up to it.

It seemed to me then that it was hopeless. That had been the best slalom run I had ever made. Leary had put out just a little more, borne down on the accelerator a little harder, and made mine not only a second, but second-rate. I had beaten him in slalom in training races, and I had beaten him in the Gibson at North Conway. But this was the North Americans, the first tryout race, and he won the important races. What I wanted more, much more, than to beat him in slalom or giant slalom, was to beat him in a downhill, but now that seemed even more hopeless.

His time on that run was the best of the day. On the second run Beck and Tom Boyd beat him, but his total time was good enough to win the slalom, and with his first in the downhill, and fourth in the GS, he won the combined going away. I surprised myself by backing into third place in the combined behind Beck, and it was fine to take a third in the first selection race, better than I had dreamed of doing last year. But there was no joy in it for me, as there would have been no joy for me, either, in a second.

THE SWING WEST | II

1

We came over the pass on packed snow and slowly down the switchbacks behind a mud-splattered semi with its stack smoking and brakelights blinking off and on. I was driving the station wagon and I cut around the semi on an inside curve. The driver raised a hand to us, and Anne waved back. Pines were dropping their loads of snow in sudden showers, and black spots of asphalt began to show in the road. The tire chains would clink and clatter for a moment before they ran silently again. Leary and Brown were asleep in the back seat, and Anne and I did not talk so as not to waken them.

They woke when we ran out of the snow and I had to take off the chains. Yawning, Brown said, "Can we have a comfort stop, please?" I stopped at a gas-station-grocery-PO at the foot of the grade, and Brown and Anne went to the john while Leary fished in the glove compartment for the credit card, and I got out my shaver. Taking turns at the wheel, we had driven straight through from Stowe to the Rockies, and we were all tired.

When I came out of the men's room Anne was wandering back toward the car with her blue toilet kit, Leary was signing the gas ticket, and Brown was coming out of the store carrying a grocery bag. When we started on again, with Leary driving, she took a wedge of cheese and a box of soda crackers from the bag. Cutting slices of cheese with Leary's knife, she made sandwiches of the crackers and handed them around. Brown was always in charge of the commissary.

"Home again," Leary said as he swung the station wagon out to pass again the truck I had passed on the grade.

"Home for you westerners," Anne said.

"This is only home for Chris," Brown said. "Home for Jack and me is the Sierra."

"Well, we'd goddam well better do better at home than we did at Stowe," Leary said.

The Stowe Internationals had been a disaster for him and for Brown. The downhill course had been boiler plate. Leary had clobbered twice, Markering-out the second time. Brown had also fallen in the downhill and twisted her knee, and had made two miserable slalom runs; it was a sad comedown after her win in the North Americans. Anne, who was on her home ground at Stowe, had won the women's combined. I had skied over-cautiously in the downhill, but so many racers had canned-up on the ice that I had sneaked into fourth place in the combined, best of any of the American men. Now we had a breathing spell with some starts that didn't matter much, and no more downhill until Sun Valley. Then came the three big western races, the Harriman Cup, Roch Cup, and National Championships, with the selection committee watching us again.

"We'll clean up at Arapahoe just because it doesn't matter," I said.

"They all matter," Leary said. He had been very nervous and quick to anger since Stowe.

"Well, Anne did just wonderfully," Brown said. "At least we can all be glad Anne did so well."

"We easterners have had a lot more experience on ice than you westerners," Anne said, pouting her lips at the mirror from her toilet kit as she put on lipstick.

"You be glad for Anne," Leary said with a glance at Brown. "That's about all you've got to be glad about. You looked like a Class C racer in the slalom, Brownie."

She didn't reply, busying herself making more cheese and cracker sandwiches. As she turned to hold one out to me, I saw that there was a swollen pink look around her eyes. "Jack?" she said.

"Thanks."

"Are we going to drive through to Arapahoe tonight?" Anne asked in a change-the-subject voice.

"We ought to get in about ten, I think," Leary said.

"I'm tired," Brown said suddenly. "Let's stop at dinner-time and sleep in a motel."

"Oh, hell, let's go on in!" Leary said.

"I want to stop," Brown said. "Let's vote on it. I vote to stop."

"Against!" Leary said angrily. He'd been picking on Brown all the way, as though it were her fault he had clobbered at Stowe.

"Let's stop," I said.

Anne gave me a raised-eyebrow look. When there were ties in the voting we had a system of making poker hands out of license numbers to decide the issue.

"Goddam it!" Leary said. "If we stop tonight, that's just that many runs we miss in the morning. It's already Wednesday."

"Oh, let's stop if we find a decent place," Anne said easily. "We're all tired and crabby. I'll promise not to make any fuss about getting up early."

"Good," Brown said.

"I sure don't understand you," Leary said, glancing at her again. "You're the one that makes all the trouble about wanting to stop, and you're the one that ought to be up there training hardest."

"I should have flown out with Mrs. May and the other girls," Brown said. "Then I'd have been at Arapahoe yesterday."

"Well, why didn't you?"

"Because you wanted me to come in the car!" she cried at him.

"Don't get hysterical."

"I've got a *right* to get hysterical!"

Leary started, "Now, listen, Brownie—" But she cried, "Oh, lay off me! Will you please lay off?"

There was a long silence. The back of Leary's neck was red. I met Anne's eyes for a moment, then I looked out the window at the snowbanks along the highway.

Brown began to pass around cheese and crackers again. "Well, you don't know what it's like," she said to no one in particular. "Why can't I have a bad race sometimes like everybody else? Mrs. May is really terrible sometimes. And Daddy—" She stopped. She had to phone her father after every race, and I was sure he had not congratulated her on her showing at Stowe. In an apologetic voice she said to Leary, "Well, you don't have to get on me too."

"I just don't see why you have to get so goddam hysterical about everything," Leary said.

With a pursed mouth Brown handed a cheese and cracker sandwich to Anne.

"Well, I don't," Leary went on. "You were really a mess at Stowe. Crying and—"

"I fell really badly!" Brown said. "I don't know why I didn't get really hurt. Anybody—"

"You were a wreck before the downhill. You had yourself psyched out about the ice before you started. Why the hell wouldn't you take the line I told you to?"

"Well, I *was* scared," Brown said calmly enough. "I get awfully scared sometimes before the downhill."

A women's downhill start was an even grimmer scene than a men's, and when he could, Leary stood by with Brown to try to calm her down; but Anne didn't want me there at all.

"I suppose you never get scared," Brown said.

"No," Leary said. "If you train right there's nothing to be scared about."

She stared at him with her mouth half open.

"Why don't you quit it?" I said to Leary.

But he said doggedly, "I don't know anybody else that gets into that kind of a fit before a downhill."

"Let's talk about something else," Anne said.

"I'm a coward," Brown said in a shaking voice. "That's all. I can't help it."

"Oh, Christ," Leary said.

"You're such a brave downhill racer," Brown said.

"You're so great. You were really great at Stowe. Why don't you worry about your own runs?" Her voice began to shrill. "Everybody keeps worrying about *me*. Why does everybody have to make such a stink about how I did? I hate racing, I *hate* downhill. Why can't everybody just leave me alone? Everybody's on me and on me—"

"Brownie," Anne said, and Brown stopped and leaned against the door.

Leary's neck was red again and there was an aggrieved and put-upon set to his jaw.

We all had the sense to keep quiet for a time, and then at dark we began looking for our kind of motel. We finally found one with green, peaked roofs on the cabins that advertised steam heat and winter rates, and we got one cabin with kitchenette and one without. Brown and Anne went to shop for dinner while Leary and I took showers.

"What's the matter between you and Brown?" I said.

Toweling himself, he gave me a surprised look. "What do you mean, what's the matter?"

"You've been bitching at each other all the way."

He got a black turtleneck shirt out of his suitcase and dove into it. As his head came out he said, "Nothing's the matter. She just goes all to pieces if you criticize her; you heard her."

"It's goddam unpleasant for Anne and me."

He gazed at me blankly for a moment. Then he scowled and said, "Tough."

I started to get mad, but I realized that the way I had put it to him he couldn't very well have said much else. To ease the strain I said, "Well, maybe it's just her time of the month."

But that didn't please him either. He glared, then turned away from me to finish dressing.

After we had eaten we lounged on the twin beds, drinking wine by the light of a candle stuck in a saucer on the table. I played the guitar and we sang, and it was almost good again after a bad day. I thought about all the times I'd been lonely, because times like this were so much the opposite of lonely—not merely not-

lonely, for that was only the middle of the scale. I
didn't know the word for the other end, which was what
we had, but now I was very worried that something
was going to destroy it.

I was starting to pick out "On Top of Old Smoky"
when I saw Leary lean around and kiss Brown hard
on the mouth. Their faces hung together, shadowed in
the candlelight, Brown's rounded, Leary's hard and lean;
something about them seemed very intense. But Brown
pulled away and said in a breaking voice, "No, leave
me alone. Leave me alone!"

Leary drew back. I looked away. Anne and I
started singing, but they didn't join in, and after a time
we stopped. The silence then was like ripples spreading
from a rock thrown into a pond. Leary watched Brown
with an ugly expression as she poured the last of the
wine into her glass.

Anne sighed. "Let's go for a little ride, Jack."

I put down the guitar and started to rise, but Brown
said, "No."

"You don't need to go," Leary said stiffly. He stood
up and raised his glass. "How about a toast? No more
bad races."

"Hear, hear!" I said. We all drank but Brown, who
sat with her face averted in the shadows. "Here's to
us!" I said. But it didn't work; the heaviness, a kind
of sadness, remained. I was sorry for Leary, who had
tried to make amends and had failed.

Anne said in a flat voice, "We'd better get to bed
early if we're going to get up early."

Anne and I said good night; Brown and Leary said
nothing. Leary and I went outside in the freezing air
and across to our cabin. He kicked off his after-ski
boots furiously. In bed he turned his back on me, and
when I had switched off the light and got into the other
bed I could hear his breathing.

"What's the matter, Chris?"

"We should have driven on through, for God's sake."

"I guess you're right."

"We'd be there by now, goddam it. Well, I'm sick of it."

"Sick of what?"

He was silent for a time. "For one thing I'm goddam sick of sitting around in motels drinking wine and pretending it's so cute being in a motel together and being such good little boys and girls. It's so goddam cute. And all this all-for-one and one-for-all three musketeers crap."

I grinned painfully in the darkness. I didn't want him to be sick of that. I asked, "What's wrong with Brownie, Chris?"

"I'm really disappointed in her," he said in a fake voice. "I used to think she had the stuff. But she's not going to make it. She's no competitor."

"Oh, for God's sake—"

"You sure can't say I haven't tried to help her," he broke in. "I've tried like hell to work her out of this goddam thing with her father—and everything else. I went over every inch of every course with her last year. And I'd go up there and hold her hand at the starts. You'd think she'd show some appreciation, Christ sake!"

"You've been riding her too much."

"I ought to've known you'd take her side. Goddam it, you don't know anything about it." After a pause he said, "You didn't see that famous run she made in the FIS. She can't ski that well. She was lucky she didn't kill herself. She'd talked to her father on the phone and he got her jazzed up and she went all out and looked like she was going to kill herself trying to win it. It was the same thing at Stowe. Only that time she wasn't so lucky. She's so scared of getting hurt now it's pitiful. She keeps talking about Janice Haney—in a wheelchair for life and all that."

"That scares me too."

"It scares everybody, but nobody else goes around talking about it all the time. It's all part of this damn thing with her father. It's his fault too. You remember how everybody used to say she had more downhill guts than any of the other girls—she's just used them all up."

"But what're you going to do?" I said. "If she's in trouble, you—"

"I've been trying to tell you! I can't even say anything to her. She just gets hysterical. I don't want to talk about it any more, okay?"

"Okay," I said. I was feeling a little sick from too much sweet wine. The bedclothes rustled as Leary turned over. I'd forgotten to set the alarm and I had to get up to turn on the light to find the clock. Leary pulled the pillow over his head.

When I had turned off the light again I lay staring into the darkness, wondering what we could do for Brown.

After a long time, Leary said, "What do you suppose it's like when it's over?"

"What's over? You and Brown?"

"Oh, Christ!" he said. "No—you know, what happens to champions? When it's over."

"You're going to run a gas station," I said.

He grunted as though he'd tried to laugh. "Okay. What about you?"

"I'd like to get in on the ground floor at some new ski resort."

"Instructor, you mean? That's crap, Jack."

"I'd rather work on the mountain. Snow safety or lifts and tows, something like that. I wouldn't mind being an instructor though. I don't think it'd be so bad."

"I think that's real gigolo crap."

"Okay, think what you want to think."

"Don't get mad."

"Then don't keep telling me what I'm probably going to have to do when I quit racing is crap. You can go big-deal it in some damn mill of your Dad's. Great for you."

"You think that's great? That's really crap."

"Well, don't get mad."

He laughed a little. Then he said in an overcasual voice, "I sure don't want it to be over. That's going to be rough. But just so you did *some*thing. You know."

"Sure," I said. I was thinking about Brown again. He had said he was sick of the three musketeers crap, and he had seemed to be saying that he and Brown were through. If they were through, the four of us were through, and that was something I didn't want to be over. I had known it would have to break up sometime, but I wasn't ready yet. "Maybe she'll be all right," I said. I turned toward him, but I couldn't see him in the darkness.

"I sure hope so," Leary said.

2

To make it simple, you can say that downhill is speed, slalom is turns, and giant slalom turns at speed. At Arapahoe there were slalom and giant slalom only, but the GS was a long one, almost a downhill course. It should have been Leary's meat, but he skied more cautiously than usual, and Tom Boyd beat him and Harry Butler almost did. Then he got into trouble on his second slalom run and I beat him in the slalom. He never tried to pretend he was a good loser; after the slalom he wouldn't talk to me.

Brown had another bad weekend. She had very slow time in the GS, and in the first slalom run was even worse than the Class C racer Leary had called her, coming down the course all jerky turns and locked knees. She looked as though she knew she was going to fall and wanted to make sure that, when she did, it would be uphill and sitting down, so she wouldn't get hurt.

I watched the second slalom run from halfway up the course. Brown did only a little better this time. I watched Leary talking to her at the bottom. She was listlessly picking at the knots tying on her racing number. Leary in his black sweater and toque, his body slanting toward her, leaned forward on his skis, while Brown stood with her face turned down and her red-brown ponytail flowing out of a hole cut in the back of her cap. She would turn her goggled face up to him and nod, flex her knees and nod again, look down and slide her skis back and forth in the snow. It was an overcast, below-zero day, and the colored poles and flags and the girls twisting down the course didn't even look gay through yellow lenses. Times floated up from the loudspeaker at the finish. The spectators who had lined the lower part of the course were leaving now that all the top-seeded girls had come down. I couldn't see Anne at the bottom, so I waited where I was.

As the last of the girls ran the course, Brown came side-stepping back up the hill. She paused to get her breath and smiled wanly at me.

"Going to take another run when they're finished?"

She nodded. Tear streaks showed on her cheeks. She cried when she had done badly and often cried too when she had won; it was as though tears were necessary to release the tensions she had built up for a race. She said, "I don't know what's wrong with me. I'm just tttttt-*terr*ible!"

"Maybe you've got your skis on upside down."

She managed a bark of a laugh and started on up the hill, sidestepping, reaching up with her uphill pole, her pants tightening over her neat round behind at every step. The gatekeepers and officials were coming down now, and the line through the gates was a well-worn rut. I stood watching Brown climb to the top. Leary had disappeared. Brown waited at the start until everyone was off the course. I waved at her when it was clear, and she started down, very fast.

She struck a tip in the rut halfway down and fell.

She sat up, but she didn't get up any further. "Jack!" she called in a strained voice. I started up toward her as fast as I could go.

As soon as I reached her I knew she had a break. She was sitting on her left leg, which was caught under her and turned down, with the ski sunk in the snow up to her boot. The binding hadn't released.

She stared at me with round eyes. Her face was waxily

64

pale. "What a stupid way to break your ankle," she whispered. "Oh, goddam it!"

"Maybe not," I said, panting.

"The damn release didn't let go," Brown whispered. "Oh, goddam it, Jack. It's broken."

I took off my skis, crossed them in the snow to signal the ski patrol, and bent over to free her boot. She whimpered and cursed as I lifted her by the armpits and laid her back in the snow with her legs straightened. I took off my parka and put it over her.

"I don't like it here," she said in a fuzzy voice. "It's so damn cold. It's never cold like this at home."

"There ought to be a ski patrolman along in a minute."

"Why does everything happen to me, Jack?"

"Maybe it's only twisted," I said, but she shook her head. "Listen, Brownie, if it's broken the worst that can happen is you'll be out a year. But probably a lot less. I—"

"A year!" she cried. "That shoots next season too!"

"Brownie—"

"A *year!*" But all at once her face was at odds with her frantic voice. The relief in her face was so naked I had to look away from her. I'd seen that before in racers who had broken a leg—relief that it had finally happened and wasn't worse, and the relief of the terrific pressure suddenly gone. "A year," Brown said. "Why, that's—" She stopped.

A big ski patrolman in his rust-colored parka was coming toward us with a toboggan. "Somebody here need a lift down the hill?" he called cheerfully. He had a scoutmaster's face and voice. He took an interminable time splinting Brown's ankle and was fussy about my helping wrap her in the blankets from the toboggan. But he was very strong and sure snowplowing on down the hill with her to the aid station. I sat with her while she waited to see the X-ray. Once I went outside, found Harry Butler, and asked him to go tell Leary that Brown was hurt.

The doctor was with Brown when I went back inside. She had a navy blue blanket wrapped around her and was gazing with a set jaw at the black and pale smudges on the slide the doctor held. He was young and red-headed, with a plaster-smeared apron on. "It's broken all right," Brown said.

"You'll be in a walking cast before you know it," the doctor said.

Still staring at the plate, Brown said, "Do I have to go to the hospital?"

"I can cast it here. I'll put a short cast on, and you can go home and have your own doctor look at it."

"I don't want to go home," Brown said, sounding like a spoiled child. Then she nodded. "Yes, I guess so. Okay."

Mrs. May came in. She was sunburned, wrinkled, and lean, and she wore a red jacket, a corduroy skirt, and after-ski boots with gum soles an inch thick. Behind her in the doorway were Alice and Lorraine and Joanne Grimes, and behind them I saw Anne with her eyebrows raised questioningly. I made a sign at her as of breaking something between my hands.

"Georgiana!" Mrs. May said in her harsh voice. "What the devil have you done?" Brown made a rusty sound and hid her face. Mrs. May said, "You haven't got a spiral, you silly little thing?"

"It's my ankle," Brown said, and Mrs. May glared at the doctor and the X-ray he held. She said to him, through her teeth, "She would have been the best female racer this country ever produced by next season. What a tragic, simply appalling thing! I can't bear it!" She shouldered me aside to lean over and embrace Brown, and all at once there was gentleness in the harsh voice. "Oh, you poor thing. Poor child."

I moved toward the door. Leary was standing with Anne. He looked irritated.

Mrs. May said, "Well, you must be got home, I suppose. I'll telephone your father."

"Oh, don't call him," Brown said. "Please don't call him. I'll call him."

"Don't be silly. Now don't get upset yourself—why, haven't they given you anything, dear?" She looked savagely at the doctor.

"Mrs. May, he'll just come," Brown whispered. "I don't want to make him come all the way out here just because I—I'll just go home." She broke down, and Mrs. May tried to comfort her. I squeezed out past the girls looking in the door to join Anne and Leary.

"Let's go have a beer," Leary said, and we left.

Lorraine came with us. The rathskeller was full of racers talking about the race, and about the next start, at Winter Park, and about Sun Valley and Aspen, Stowe and Squaw Valley, the FIS last year and the Winter Games next. Now that Brown was out, the women's competition was going to be between Anne, Lorraine, and Alice Beard.

McInerny had cornered Anne, and I was stuck with Lorraine, who was trying very hard to pretend that Brown's broken ankle wasn't the most wonderful thing that had happened this year. I listened to her telling how much better she was doing and how much better she was going to do and eavesdropped on Leary being the World's Greatest Authority on Downhill to Bill Birks, and all of a sudden I was sick of racers and their talk. I excused myself and went over to sit by myself.

After a while Anne joined me. "You look depressed," she said.

I nodded.

"So am I."

"Well, you shouldn't be. You were great in the slalom. How'd you come out in the combined?"

"Second," she said, wrinkling her nose. She sat looking over at the others for a time. "I don't like anybody," she announced.

"That's the way I was feeling. Except you."

A long dimple cut her cheek. She smiled at me, showing the chipped tooth. "And I you." Then she said, "Christy's a cold toad, isn't he?"

"I don't know whether he really is or just thinks he's supposed to be."

Her charm bracelet tinkled inside the sleeve of her parka as she picked up her beer. Hearing it, she pushed back her cuff and fingered the Ullr. "He's been good luck," she said. "Do you know I haven't made a bad slalom run this season?" She knocked wood. "But Brownie needed him today. Poor Brownie. What will she do, just go home?"

"Just go home, I guess."

"That will drive her out of her mind." She sighed. "I almost felt sorry for Mrs. M. just now."

I nodded.

"I think how she must have been wishing it was Patterson who got hurt instead of Brown. I almost wish I had."

"Getting tired of the circuit?"

Nodding, she said, "Do you know? The trouble with me is that I just can't seem to get myself worked up about it." She made a spread-fingered gesture with her hand as though to mask her face. "About anything." She said quickly, "I don't know if I could be the best female racer this country's ever produced or not, but I could be damned good. But I don't really care enough. Isn't it too bad?"

Before I could answer, Leary sauntered over to us. "Jo says May's got Brown in a room upstairs here. I guess we ought to go see her."

"Why don't *you* go see her?" Anne said.

"She'll want to see all of us."

"If there's anything I can't bear it's sloppy sentiment," Anne said.

Leary said sulkily, "There'll be other people there anyway. I wouldn't be seeing her alone. Let's all go."

So we all went upstairs. Alice let us in. Mrs. May wasn't there. "She's pretty dopey," Alice whispered.

Brown was lying in the center of a double bed with her ponytail like a pet on the pillow beside her head. The cast on her left foot lumped big under the covers.

She smiled at us in an unfocused way as we stood around the bed. Anne and I waited for Leary to say something.

"Well, Christ sake, Brownie," he said.

"I'm all dopey," Brown said. "He gave me something to make it not hurt."

"Looks like you've got a good big cast there," I said. She nodded and grinned with pale lips. She closed her eyes. "Well, I've got to go home, I guess."

"Mrs. May's been trying to phone her folks," Alice said.

Leary cleared his throat. "He'll come get you, huh?"

"She can't get hold of him," Brown said. "They're down in San Francisco, I think. No, I'm just going to fly home, I guess. Flying's best. You know—quickest and all."

"Sure," I said.

Leary stood there with his hands in his pockets, looking as though he wished he was anywhere else but here. I felt like kicking him.

"How long would it take to drive?" Anne asked.

"Couple of days," I said. I saw what she was thinking. "Well, maybe a day and a half if we went straight through, taking turns driving."

"Let's do that," Anne said.

"Oh, that would be wonderful!" Brown said. "Oh, I'd love that!" Her voice broke. "It was just—it's just that it's so kind of sudden to just drop out of—everything. I mean, just go home on the plane and that's—you know—the *end* of it. I mean, I'd love it if we could drive—" Abruptly she broke off, looking at Leary.

He said loudly, "Well, we can't though." He said to me, "We can't do that, Jack. We wouldn't get back to Winter Park till Thursday or Friday, and we'd be bushed. You can't not do any training for a race, Christ sake!"

"We ought to be able to get back by Wednesday night if we really push it."

"We're supposed to be in training! You can't drive like

that and not get any sleep or exercise or anything; your legs would be shot. I mean, I'd like to take Brownie home, but I just don't see how we can do it."

"Well, to hell with the Winter Park race then," I said.

"I vote to take Brownie home," Anne said.

"Goddam it," Leary said, "we can't do it. I'm not going to do it."

Alice looked embarrassed, Anne hard-mouthed. Brown lay there with her face very small and tan on the pillow. She said, "Oh, I vote against it. It really is silly."

"Sure it's silly," Leary said.

Anne said, "Jack and I need a rest from the circuit. Lend us the wagon and we'll take Brownie home and meet you in Sun Valley."

"You can get a ride with Boyd and McInerny, Chris," I said, but all at once it seemed to me that Anne and I were conspiring to make him look bad, and that the whole idea was, as he and Brown had said, silly. But then I thought of driving back from Reno alone with Anne.

Leary shrugged. "Sure, take it. I don't give a damn." He started for the door, and I saw Brown's face crumple.

"Hey!" she cried. He stopped and turned. "Hey, sign my cast, will you, Christy?" She worked her leg free of the covers and exposed the white rough cast. Leary stood looking down at it until someone produced a pen. He bent to write his name on Brown's cast, then he left.

Anne and I stayed a little longer, making plans to leave as soon as the banquet was over, and pretending not to notice that Brown was crying.

3

It was a foolish trip. Through western Colorado and over Soldier Summit it was icy, mile on mile of treacherous driving where your hands ached on the wheel and a knot spread between your shoulders. We came into Salt Lake City in a blizzard and had to lay over for a day, and there was ice again crossing the salt flats to Wendover. There was not much to say, and the singing was thin without Leary's loud, tuneless voice. We had made a bed for Brown in the back of the wagon, but she was uncomfortable and sometimes irritable. She would fall into depressions that pervaded the car, or else she tried too hard to be cheerful, which was worse. It was a bad trip.

We stopped in front of Brown's house, in Reno, at two o'clock in the morning.

It was a two-storied brick house with bare trees in front of it. As soon as we got out of the car a dog came rushing up, barking and almost knocking Brown off her crutches, while she cried, "Monte! Oh, good old Monte!" as though the dog were her only friend in the world. The porchlight came on, and Mr. and Mrs. Brown and Brown's sister Caroline, who was fifteen and fat, in blue flannel pajamas, appeared on the porch. There was a great deal of milling, embracing, and introducing while Caroline held Monte, a small, hangdog, hysterical collie. In the living room Anne promptly curled up on the couch and went to sleep, and I found myself at the table in the kitchen with Brown and her mother and father.

Mr. Brown, whom I hadn't seen for four or five years, was gray-haired now. He was a big man with a triangular face and heavy lines, like parentheses, at the corners of his mouth. He wore a purple silk robe. He'd made himself a drink, and he sat in the corner of the breakfast nook with his arms folded on his chest, looking grim and anxious, while Mrs. Brown questioned Brown about her ankle. The sister had gone back to bed, and the dog was under the table at Brown's feet. Mrs. Brown was making coffee.

"We'll get Ned Wright to look at the leg tomorrow," Mr. Brown said as his wife poured coffee. "Oh, I mean today, don't I?"

Brown laughed in an exaggerated way. With her family she had a set of mannerisms different from those

71

I was used to, which made her seem phony and not so likable.

"I talked to him Sunday," Mr. Brown said. "He says a broken ankle's nowhere near as serious as a spiral. You can get back on the boards much sooner. Of course he can't tell a thing until he gets some pictures."

Brown stared at him with her lips sucked in tightly. He reached over to pat her hand. "Maybe you'll make the Olympics yet, kiddo."

"Oh, there's no chance of getting selected for the team now, Daddy," Brown said in a low voice. She bent down to scratch the dog and whispered, "Good old Monte."

"Such a shame," Mrs. Brown said as she filled her own cup with coffee. "Mrs. May was so nice on the phone, Georgie. Wonderful praise for you. She said you'd been working so hard and skiing so well."

"Oh, I didn't ski well at Arapahoe. Just terribly."

"You didn't do very well at Stowe either," Mr. Brown said. He took up his glass and drank.

"I don't know what's been wrong," Brown said.

"Did you fall on your first or second run, honey?"

"Oh, it was after. Chris told me what I'd been doing wrong, and I went back up to come down the course again. You know, try to get it back again. And, just—zip, I caught a tip!" She made gestures. "Just all tied up someway," she said with a laugh, while Mr. Brown stared at her from under his eyebrows, his chin tucked down into the lapels of his purple robe.

"You don't know why?" he asked.

"George—" Mrs. Brown started, but stopped as he turned to glare at her. She rose and went to put the percolator back on the stove.

"No," Brown whispered and left her pale lips shaped in the O after she had said the word.

"You'd had plenty of rest?"

"Oh, yes."

"I understood it that Elizabeth May said you hadn't been getting enough rest, you and Chris Leary and Jack and Anne Patterson out on a party every night or driving all over the landscape."

"That's not true," I said, and Mr. Brown's eyes swung toward me. They were a little bloodshot, and they did not quite meet mine.

"George," Mrs. Brown said, "Mrs. May said the only possible explanation she might have was that Georgie—"

He said in a heavy voice, "So it was simply a matter of not enough rest, wasn't it, honey?"

"I guess so," Brown whispered.

"So there you are. That's why you couldn't ski well. Why did you say you didn't know what was wrong?"

"I don't know."

"Oh, be fair, George!" Mrs. Brown said. "Mrs. May said Georgie had been working so hard."

He ignored her. He said to Brown, "Of course it's your career, not mine."

She didn't say anything.

"Isn't it?"

She nodded. I heard the cast thump as she moved her leg. I saw her trying to smile.

Mr. Brown drained his glass. "So you won't make the selections. So you won't be in the Olympics this time. Doesn't it seem just a little too bad, honey? You were simply out of training. It sounds pretty stupid to me."

"I guess it was pretty stupid, Daddy."

"So now you're out. And Elizabeth May said you could have been the best woman skier this country's ever had. But I guess she was wrong. You don't have the sense to be the best woman skier this country's ever had."

My jaws ached as I watched Brown nodding. Tears ran down her cheeks. She brushed at her chin where they had collected.

Mr. Brown turned to me and smiled as though everything were fine. "You've been doing well, Jack. Your father must be proud of you. Is he still up on the summit there?"

"Yes," I said.

"I don't think I've seen him since you and Georgie were juniors together."

"I guess not," I said.

"Chris Leary's been having some bad luck lately, but he is certainly the class among the American men. Wouldn't you say so?"

I nodded.

"The only international caliber skier we've got. Though you beat him for the Silver Belt last year, didn't you?"

I nodded and looked straight at him; it was important that he wouldn't meet my eyes. "I've taken him in slalom and GS a few times," I said. "I haven't ever won a downhill from him unless he's had a fall."

"That's funny, since you're bigger and heavier than he is. It seems you might be beating him in downhill because of your weight."

I felt my face burning. "That weight business is over-rated," I said. "But I haven't got the guts, I guess. He takes a faster downhill line than anybody else in the country."

"Yes, I've heard that," Mr. Brown said. He looked pleased with himself. "Well, that's downhill racing, isn't it?"

Mrs. Brown said quickly, "All the local people will be pulling for you in the Nationals, Jack. You're the local boy even here in Reno."

I managed to grin at her. Brown was sitting with her shoulders slumped and her face turned down.

"You ought to go to bed, Brownie," I said, but she shook her head.

"Have you two heard about the wonderful new resort that's going in over on Lake Tahoe?" Mrs. Brown asked. "Millions of dollars. A man named Patten's behind it."

"Going to have two doublechairs and some Pomas," Mr. Brown said. "Of course the money will be made out of the subdivision. I've got a few bucks in it. I wrote you about it, honey."

"It sounds wonderful," Brown said in a dull voice.

Her father put his hand on hers again and squeezed it. "Ankle hurt, honey?" he asked gently.

"It does a little, Daddy."

"Well, you're to see Ned Wright today. He's the best bone man I know of. I told you I talked to him already, and it may not be as bad as it looks."

"I've got the X-ray in my bag," Brown said.

"Remember that time you hurt your leg in Yosemite, honey?"

Brown smiled a little.

"I was so damned mad," Mr. Brown said indulgently. "I was trying to get you out of the hotel to look over the course—remember how bad you used to be about looking over the course? And all you were interested in was trying on your fastcaps to see which one matched your sweater or was the most becoming or some damned thing. I remember I kept trying to tell you you had to grab every advantage you could, but all you wanted to grab was the most becoming hat." He shook his head and laughed. "I suppose that's something women are born with." More soberly he said, "But you fell and hurt your leg when you took that gate wrong, honey. Remember how you did? All because you wouldn't get out there and memorize that course."

"I remember," Brown said.

I was ashamed of her because she wouldn't stand up to him, and I hated him for making me ashamed of her. But if he had made her into a coward there was credit due her for some of those downhills she had run in her fear. He had tried to make me out a coward too. I sat there, exhausted, looking at him and hating him.

Mrs. Brown said, "That's the way girls are, George. I'm sure Georgie wasn't any different from the rest of us at twelve or thirteen."

Mr. Brown rattled the ice in his glass as though trying to make up his mind whether to have another drink or not. "Well," he said, "what's fretting about hats and colors going together and all that if it isn't concerning yourself with attracting men."

"Oh, George!" Mrs. Brown said, laughing.

"Oh, yes it is! Even at twelve or thirteen. Isn't it, honey?"

"I guess it is, Daddy," Brown said. She sounded exhausted too.

"You bet it is. And if you're going to have a racing career there just isn't time for any of that. That's all there is to it. So it's all part of the same thing, that time and this one. There's just no place for that. You see that, don't you, honey?"

His face was flushed, his smile loose-lipped. All at once I couldn't look at him any more. Brown was nodding silently, her freckles showing dark on her sallow face.

"I think you children ought to get some sleep," Mrs. Brown said. "You look worn out, Georgie. Now let's not sit here and talk any longer."

"I'm awfully tired," Brown said. With her cast thumping, she slid out of the kitchen nook. I rose and handed her her crutches.

"Thanks, Jack," she said.

4

In the morning Anne and I left Brown's house early so we could get some skiing in at Squaw Valley before I went to see my father.

It was pleasant to feel like a celebrity at Squaw, where I was even more famous than Anne. We took the lift up KT-22, rising over the skiers coming down the Poma Hill, and over the swale with our skis riding high above the two great firs there, and steeply up the steilhang to the top. We hiked around to the start of the women's downhill course, and I led Anne down it, taking it slowly with short turns in the fall line. We came low around the Poma Hill, ran through the moguls there, and up the ramp to the chair again. In the chair, with the bar down and our skis on the footrest, we gazed up at the lines of ascending and descending chairs.

"They like you here," Anne said.

"It's just local-boy-makes-good stuff."

"Well, it's nice to be skiing with a local boy who's made good."

"I guess you could ski with anyone you wanted to," I said. In profile to me she gazed up the mountain, smiling, a dimple cutting her cheek. "So beautiful," I said. "And the slalom queen. You could have any man you wanted."

"Oh, no," Anne said.

"What do you mean, oh, no?"

"Because I want Santa Claus."

The chair began to climb more steeply. I looked down into the tops of the firs and thought of the cable snapping, Anne screaming and clutching me for help. Somehow, holding her, I would jump for those firs and, like Tarzan, bear her safely down.

"People would say you married him for his toy bag," I said.

"And they'd be right," Anne said. The lift leveled off over naked, mossy juts of rock. "Let's get this bar up," she said, and I lifted the bar and we swung our skis free of the footrest.

This time I led her over to the saddle and down, swooping down, through the pines standing on their blue shadows like Christmas tree bases. There was still a little powder in among the trees, and running through it with your skis invisible and silent was like sliding down through vales of air.

We went cross-country for a way, then down a gully that formed a sun trap. We took off our skis and parkas and lay down on a flat rock with the sun in our faces. I put my head in Anne's lap, and she squeezed a handful of snow so water dripped into my dry mouth.

I kept my eyes closed against the sun. I said, "Maybe there isn't any Santa Claus."

"That's mean," she said in a soft voice. "Mean to say that, Jack."

"But maybe there isn't."

"There'll be a reasonably accurate facsimile."

"Wealthy," I said.

"Oh, rich," Anne said. "Very rich. Someone who will love me and think I'm beautiful and cherish me, and who is very rich. Let's not talk about this, Jack."

"All right. Can I have another drink?"

The icy drops fell and tickled in my throat again.

Anne said in the soft voice, "Who do you want, Jack? Next to me."

"I'm going to be a monk."

"No, really."

"Oh, well, Brownie, I guess." I said it in a feeble effort to make her jealous.

"Really?" She sounded surprised.

"Why not? She's cute and round instead of beautiful like you, but she's the greatest female—" I stopped. I was tired of that joke.

Anne didn't say anything. I opened my eyes to see the blurred shape of her face against the sun. "Okay, that's enough about me," I said. "Who for you?"

"I told you. Santa Claus."

"No, really!"

"Nobody," Anne said.

"What about that Raoul you told me about?"

The shape of her face bent closer. She kissed me on the mouth. "We have to stop this," she said. "We're just making each other unhappy." She pushed to make me sit up, then jumped off the rock. Watching her put her skis on, I knew there had never been any hope for me.

"Let's just fun ski today," Anne said. "Do you remember what fun it used to be just to ski? Not racing or practicing or training or learning a course—just skiing?"

"I'll try to remember," I said and got off the rock to join her.

We ran on down to the bottom and then took the Squaw No. 1 lift to Tower 26, and the tram to the top to ski the headwall. Then we rode Squaw No. 2 to the top of Siberia. Halfway down the first face, a man in a red earband waved and called to me. He came over and stop-christied, a boy named Fred Wales with whom I'd skied in high school.

"Hi, Jack."

"Hi, Fred. How's everything?"

"Good enough. I've been reading about you in the ski magazines and the papers, man."

"What're you doing now, Fred?"

He made a face. "I'm working in the ski shop here, kind of ski-bumming."

"Racing?"

"Not much. I make a few starts, Class B. I don't have too much time for it."

He looked up past me. I turned to see Anne coming down the face past the slow skiers and the fallen skiers and the sitzmarks, cutting long curving lines through the steep-faced humps of moguls as though they didn't exist, her knees deeply bent, her poles working crisply, the whole curved springing shape of her body shifting beautifully in her turns. She flourished a pole at me as she passed and went on down the bowl at speed, but so gracefully she looked like a movie of herself in slow motion.

"Jesus Christ, who's that?" Fred Wales demanded.

"Anne Patterson."

"Jesus," he said. He watched her until she stopped. Then he turned back to me. "Saw in the paper that Georgie Brown broke up. Too bad." He poked holes in the snow with the tips of his poles and said in an embarrassed voice, for we had once been good friends, "Hey, man, you've been going great. I remember back in Class III I could push you pretty good. Now it makes me feel great to see you pushing Chris Leary so hard."

I grinned and foolishly bounced on my skis. "Thanks," I said. Anne was waiting at the bottom of the bowl, gazing up at the people floating above her on the lift.

"You going to take him in the Nationals, Jack?"

"I'll be trying." I wasn't as sick of saying that as I was going to get.

"Be pulling for you, man. What're you doing out here now?"

"Seeing my Dad. We're taking off for Sun Valley to-night."

"You and Patterson?" He made a big thing of it with his eyes and mouth.

I said, "No, nothing like that."

"Oh—well, be seeing you next month, man. Great luck and stuff."

I said so long and felt a little unhappy with myself as I skied down to join Anne.

"Let's go down and eat," I said. "Then I'd better go see my father. Do you want to stay here and ski while I go?"

"I'd like to meet him," Anne said. "Is he nice?"

"Sure he's nice," I said.

5

Just west of the summit there was a sign on the highway that said CHARLEY ROCHE CONSTRUCTION. We turned off on an oiled road to a Y, the left branch of which led up to the house, the right down into the corporation yard, where there were piles of old iron and oildrums and junk, and the equipment was parked in sheds with galvanized iron roofs.

The corporation yard was visible as we drove up to the house, and I saw Anne gazing down into it. The yard looked better than usual, with snow covering the barrels and scrap in woven shapes, and piled like ice cream on the cabs of the dump truck and the cranky old rotary snowplow. There were plowed tracks around in the snow where the jeep blade had maneuvered. The jeep pickup, with its doughnut tires, stood in front of the house.

Anne said, "What's that funny-looking scoop on the back of the little tractor for?"

"That's a backhoe. You dig ditches with it."

"Oh, that's a backhoe!"

I stopped behind the jeep, and we got out. From the

porch you could see across to Mount Disney and Mount Lincoln, where tiny skiers were moving against the snow. The peaks were bright in the sun and stained with the shadows of the trees, the sky above them dark blue.

My father came out the door in a rush and gave me a bear hug, saying, "Hey, Jackie! Hey, sonny!" He was my height, but he weighed two-thirty; he was all muscle under a layer of fat, the strongest man I'd ever known. He had a square red face, pale blue eyes, and not much hair left. I introduced him to Anne, and he said, "I've heard a lot about you from Jackie here, Miss Patterson. Now you two come inside." The knotty pine living room was overheated, as always. Rock and roll from KHOE thumped like a loose tire chain on the radio. The fireplace was full of newspapers and cigarette butts and milk cartons, the mantel above it crowded with trophies.

"Now you kids sit down," my father said. "Have you had your lunch yet?" I said we had, he asked if we'd have a beer, and bustled out into the kitchen while I helped Anne off with her parka. Then I went outside to the station wagon and brought in the carton of hardware I'd won on the circuit so far. I set the trophies out on the table and, looking at the array of them, I was pleased until I remembered how many were seconds and thirds behind Leary. But there were three slalom firsts, the Gibson Cup, and the medium-sized gold-plated skier on his wooden stand from Arapahoe. Usually the formula was: the bigger the race, the smaller the trophy.

Anne was watching me curiously. "Proof I haven't been just ski-bumming around," I said. I sat down with her, wishing I felt more at ease. A truck went by on Highway 40, tearing the air with its roar and tire whine. I could hear my father fussing in the kitchen; he was very awkward when dealing with things that didn't matter. Anne glanced around the room with appraising eyes, and I tried not to be ashamed of it.

When my father returned with the beer and glasses he said, "Well, look at the loot!" He picked up the cups, bowls, and medals one by one, examining the inscriptions.

81

He knew which ones mattered. When he came to the North American second, he said, "Chrissie took first, huh?"

"That's right," I said.

"You kind of got past him at North Conway and Stowe though. Had a fall in the down-mountain at Stowe, didn't he?"

I nodded and poured beer into my glass.

He looked sideways at Anne. Then he winked at me and said, "Well, you are running in class now, aren't you, sonny?"

I was supposed to take it that he was referring to the trophies so he could make a big thing out of explaining that he meant Anne. I only grinned, and he looked disappointed. He said to Anne, "Well, you are the finest-looking young lady I've ever seen in company with this fellow, Miss Patterson."

"Why, thank you!" Anne said. She said it just right.

"Hey, you've chipped a tooth there, haven't you? That's too bad."

"She had a fall at Loveland Christmastime and got a crack in the mouth."

"That's a shame."

"Jack likes it this way so I haven't had it fixed," Anne said in her easy voice.

"Well, now—" my father started, but he didn't go on, and I was grateful for that too. He set the Gibson Cup in the center of the table and squinted at it. I wondered why he hadn't asked if I was going to make the Olympic team. He said, "Say, I was sorry to hear Georgie Brown broke her ankle. George Brown's in a state, I expect."

"Yes," I said.

"He is that way." He shook his head. "Well, that leaves you alone at the top of the heap, doesn't it, Miss Patterson?"

"No, indeed," Anne said. She sipped her beer.

My father leaned his chair back on its hind legs. "I know how it is," he said. "Somebody gives you a tough time, you might say in kidding you wish they'd crack up so you could get past them. But you don't really mean it.

I know; I was a pretty fair jumper in my time. Did you know that, Miss Patterson?"

"Jack told me, Mr. Roche."

He nodded. "I've seen it with Jackie," he continued. "I remember when he was a junior and used to trail behind Brucie Carrington in every race. Jackie'd get so mad he'd bust things. Though I don't think he ever wished Brucie had any broken legs. Maybe you did though, sometimes, huh, Jackie?"

"I never did beat him," I said. "He hasn't been racing much since he went to Stanford."

"Well, now it's one-two with Chris Leary," my father said. "Same thing all over again. Well, I've always told Jackie riding the circuit's one thing, but watch out the circuit doesn't get to riding you."

Anne was looking at him with a little frown.

I said, "I guess I'd better get used to running behind Chris. I don't seem to be able to beat him much unless he clobbers."

"Positive thinking," my father said. "Positive thinking, now."

"Jack's a better skier than Chris," Anne said. "And I'm a better skier than Brownie. They're just better at winning downhills."

My father laughed as though he found that a wonderful joke. He let down the front legs of his chair and leaned his elbows on the table. "Well, there's just one piece of advice I've got," he said. "Don't forget to have a good time. You're making friends on the circuit now you'll value all your life. I had something to do with the Lake Placid Games," he said to Anne. Then he went on quickly, "I know there's a lot of hard work and training, but don't forget you're having the time of your life. We're sure looking forward to seeing all of you in the Nationals out here. I guess you are a shoo-in, Miss Patterson. And Jackie might make out on his home ground."

"Positive thinking," I said.

He laughed, but all at once he seemed to run down, and we sat in an awkward silence. I was thinking about the Nationals, and people asking me if I was going to beat Leary, and the people at Squaw Valley who had made me feel like a celebrity. Squaw Valley was just far enough away so that I wasn't merely Charley Roche's boy as I was here.

My father stretched to tuck his shirt front back under his belt. "Whose wheels're those you've got out there? Yours, Miss Patterson?"

"It's Chris's car," I said.

"He didn't come out with you though, huh?"

"There's a race at Winter Park he wanted to make."

"He works pretty hard, doesn't he? Pretty serious about it."

"He doesn't have much fun on the circuit," Anne said.

My father laughed again. "Say, you're terrific! You're from Stowe, are you, Miss Patterson?"

"From New York now," Anne said.

"Do you—you come from a big family back there?"

"No, I'm an only child. Like Jack."

It wasn't what he had meant, but he let it pass. In the overheated room I could feel sweat tickling my sides. There was another silence.

"Are we keeping you from something, Dad?"

"Well, I've got to go up by Jacobs' and pull out a couple of cars got snowed in there. But they can wait awhile. Hey, have you heard about this fellow Patten? He's putting in a resort at Silver Ridge. Right on the lake, so he's got winter sports, and the lake for summer. He's a good man. Big ideas and the backing to make them work."

"Mr. Brown was talking about it," I said.

"I'll be doing some work for him when the snow gets off the ground this spring. Talked to him about you. He's anxious to meet you, Jackie." There was a louder blurt of music from the radio, and he went to turn it down. "Another beer, Miss Patterson? Jackie?"

"No, thanks," I said.

"No, thank you," Anne said.

He came back and sat down again.

"What do you mean, you talked to him about me?" I asked.

"Well, you know—about you getting in at the start over there. I mean, it's going to be a big place." He looked from me to Anne, smiling uncertainly. "Well, I know how the world looks to kids your age—wide open and all yours. But when you get older it gets tighter and tighter, and there's not as much of it yours as you thought, and when you see a hole that just fits it sure looks good. Or a slot for your son. Bill Patten is a good fellow, he's really got a head on him. Got a nice-looking daughter too, Jackie," he said quickly, as though to slide it by unnoticed. "Well, what Bill and I were talking about was his ski school there. He knows he has to have a big name for a draw, but too many times it's all big name and no school. He swears he's going to have the best ski school in the Sierra.

"Jackie, you're a natural for it. Everybody says there's never been a better example of a textbook skier. Now what Bill's thinking about doing, he's thinking about getting André Cuvier for a couple of years, start things up, know-how, big name, and all that. But we were talking about you going in with Andy. You'd need a little money to put up, show faith in the project and all that—there's no strain there. Then you'd work into it after Andy went on his way. You are no mean name yourself, Jackie. If you won the Nationals—" He stopped as though he wished he hadn't mentioned that.

I felt Anne looking at me. My heart was pounding, hard with resentment. "When's he think he's going to get started?" I asked.

"The way they talk they'll be going by next season. Jackie, he's got so much backing—"

I said carefully, "Well, I'm afraid that's a little too soon for me, Dad. Because of the Winter Games next year."

He licked his lips and wagged his head a little. "Well— I mean, it's up to you, of course, Jackie. But you know? It's what we always talked about—you getting in on the ground floor like that. You remember."

"Sure," I said. "But I can do a lot better after I've been in the Olympics."

He wagged his head again, stared into his glass of beer.

I said, "Anyway, what I really want is to be up on the mountain someway. I don't want to be an instructor much."

"Jackie, a person kind of has to do what he can do that's special." He rubbed a hand over his glistening forehead; he looked worried, flustered, ashamed, and unhappy. "Well, I shouldn't have brought it up just now," he said. "But you'll be seeing Bill Patten when you come out for the Nationals. He'll see to that, I know."

"Sure," I said. Anne sat beside me, looking aloof and cool as a magazine advertisement in her big-collared sweater. I said, "Well, I guess we'd better run along so Dad can get those cars pulled out. We've got a long drive to make." I said to my father, "We're heading for Sun Valley."

Nodding, he said, "Sun Valley and then Aspen, huh? Those are tryouts, aren't they, Jackie?"

"That's right," I said. "And the Nationals."

Anne and I rose.

My father got up and kneaded my shoulder. He laid his other hand on Anne's. "Well, positive thinking, you two," he said. "I'll be looking for you out here next month. Good to have met you, Miss Patterson." In a stage whisper he said, "I don't want you to think I'm not proud of this boy here. I just think he's the best, that's all."

I helped Anne on with her parka, and he helped me on with mine. I felt his hand in my pocket. Outside in the sun-warmed air our boots crunched on the windrow the jeep blade had left. I looked at the bills my father had put into my pocket—two twenties.

"Thanks," I said as we shook hands.

"Wish I could afford more. But Gayley was up last week. Now don't you hold off writing him if you need anything. And drop him a line now and then even if you don't. He appreciates that."

Anne sat in the wagon with the hood of her parka thrown back, dark glasses on, and a streak of sunlight bright on her cheek. She smiled a good-by at my father.

"That one looks good enough to eat," he whispered to

me as he walked around with me to the driver's door.

"See you next month," I said.

He wrung my hand one more time before I got into the car; it was as though he were apologizing for something. He slammed the door for me. "Don't forget to have fun!" he called. He stood and waved after us as I drove down the hill to the highway.

"He's a little jealous of you, isn't he?" Anne said after we had driven in silence for a while.

"Well, he's jealous of some funny little things."

"No, I mean he's jealous about your being on the Olympic team. But he doesn't want to be. I think he's nice."

I didn't know what to say. I thought of Leary saying that they were so damned jealous, that you could smell the ill will.

"It's funny about parents," Anne said. "They work so hard so their children will be better than they were, and then they're a little bit jealous when they are."

We started down Donner Summit then, and I began to tell her about the Donner party, to change the subject.

6

When we got back to Brown's house in Reno, late in the afternoon, Brown was lying on the couch in the living room with a pillow under her left knee and a book face down on her stomach. She had on green and white pajamas, no lipstick, and her hair was out of the ponytail and lay thickly around her head on the pillow propped against the arm of the couch. Her sister, watching TV in a chair across the room, paid no attention to Anne and me.

"How was Squaw?" Brown asked cheerfully.

"Fine," I said. "How's your ankle?"

"It's aching away. Hey, turn that down a little, will you, Carrie?"

Her sister turned the volume down imperceptibly.

"What did the new doctor say?" Anne asked.

"Nothing. Just—nothing much. You want anything to drink or eat or anything?" It was strange that she had become a less familiar person already.

"We've got to take off, Brownie," I said.

She nodded. "Well, I'll have a walking cast on pretty soon," she said. "I can come watch you in the Nationals, I guess." Brightening, she said, "Maybe if I can scrounge a ride I'll come to Aspen for the Roch."

"Come bring us luck," Anne said.

"I'll be your Ullr," Brown said. She made motions as of fanning her hair out wildly, like Ullr's. "Listen," she said, "will you call me after the Harriman and tell me how everyone did?"

"Sure," I said.

"We'll all call you," Anne said, meaning Leary too.

Brown's face tightened into a thin smile. "He's so damn —funny," she whispered. "I guess you can't be mad at somebody for acting the way he can't help acting, can you?"

Anne didn't answer.

Brown turned her face toward me. "Do me a favor, Jack?"

"Sure."

"Listen, you know how he is. Don't get mad at him. He needs *some*body. He's kind of mixed up, Jack. You know—about his father and his brother. I know he's awfully unhappy sometimes."

"Sure, Brownie," I said.

"We're going to miss you terribly," Anne said. "We'll probably all come unstuck without you along to hold everything together."

"Don't you dare!" Brown said almost angrily.

"Well, we'll call you after the Harriman," I said. "And maybe we'll see you in Aspen."

Anne bent to kiss Brown.

"Good-by!" Brown said. "Good-by, Jack!" I bent to kiss her too. I had meant to kiss her on the cheek, but she moved her head and my lips brushed her small, chewing-gum-scented mouth.

"We'll see you, Brownie," I said.

We collected Anne's toilet case, my shaving kit, and the other gear we hadn't already stowed in the car, and there was another round of good-bys as we went out. I remembered to take Brown's three pairs of skis off the rack and set them inside the garage.

It was dark before we got out of Reno. Anne's skis and mine hummed and buzzed on the top, different notes for different speeds, different keys for different trips. They always made their presence known on the roof, and it was an exciting and urgent sound, part of the whole exciting, urgent round of the circuit, of racing and moving on and racing again. Now the sound was different because Brown's and Leary's skis were missing.

Anne and I had a late dinner at the Basque restaurant in Winnemucca. She drove as far as Wells, where we turned north on 93 for the jump to Twin Falls. When we filled up with gas I took over the driving. After a coffee stop, in the thick darkness with the headlights fleeing ahead of us over the black tape of the road, over the white spaced line and the dirty windrows of snow, Anne sat very close to me. I put my arm around her, and she leaned heavily against me in the humming silence.

I put my hand inside her sweater and under her shirt where there was no bra, touched her nipple, cupped my hand over her warm breast as though it were very fragile. She stretched, changed her position slightly, sighed. I could feel her looking at me. Gently I stroked her breast and kept my eyes on the road while she stretched, sighed, breathed deeply and more deeply, arched her back, sighed more heavily. Gradually she slipped down until she lay across my lap and I could slide my hands inside the tight band of her stretchpants, her belly sucking in and my hand cupping there while she sighed more deeply and gasped once, and then resumed the slow sighing until the care began to wander on the road, and I slowed, stopped and shut off the engine, and turned toward her.

Her arms locked around my neck, she said, "Jack!" in a flat voice of warning, and she held me against her as though for protection. "No. Please."

"Please," I said.

"No," she said in the flat voice. "No, I can't. No." And something in her voice and in her straining arms made my own ardor pass. She said nothing more and after a while released me and sat up again beside me, but not touching me now. I started the car. The headlights fled before us again, the hum of the wind in the skis rose in pitch.

Anne leaned over against the far door. "If I could only explain it to you," she said.

"Never mind, Anne."

"It goes—up and up. It's because I trust you that it— It goes up—" she said and stopped.

I said, "Then what happens?"

"Then it's just ugly," Anne said. "I'm so sorry."

After a time she tried again. "Then it's just ugly and it's all gone and it's only— I don't know how to describe it. And then I get so afraid. No, not afraid of you. Just afraid, and that makes it worse and worse. Afraid I'll never be any good to anyone. Something got left out. It's so terrible to think you can never be any good to anyone."

I cleared my throat. "Someday there'll be the right guy and it'll be fine." Even though I couldn't see her face, I knew she was looking at me with the expression she had when I'd said something stupid.

She said, "Thanks. But I don't think so."

"Sure there will."

It was so long before she spoke again that I began to think she had gone to sleep. But finally she said, "Somebody is going to get gypped so badly. Because they're not going to get anything for their money. Not just nothing worth having. Just nothing at all."

"You know that's not right, Anne."

"We got started wrong," she said. "It should have been Chris and me. Because there's nothing there either. And you and Brown." Her voice shook for the first time. "But I've loved having you love me."

"There's always going to be someone around in love with you."

"Not for long," Anne said. "But I'm a damned good skier, aren't I?"

"Best natural skier this country's ever seen," I said.

She began to laugh. She sounded hysterical. When she stopped there was nothing more to say, and after a while I knew she was asleep. I cursed her, hating her, but I loved her and ached for her. I cursed half aloud as I drove, repeating the same stupid words over and over and getting a kind of solace out of the repetition.

Beyond Twin Falls morning came, lighter and lighter gray, and then pink, and blue-shadowed as the orange sun came up. Anne woke as we came into Ketchum, with Sun Valley just ahead, rubbing her eyes and leaning forward and gazing out the windshield to try to make out where we were.

"Oh, we're here," she said. "Good morning, Jack."

"Good morning, Anne," I said.

7

After breakfast in Ketchum we went on into Sun Valley and checked in at the Challenger. We were a day early, but we were fixed up with beds in the chalets. I was too tired to sleep, and I lay awake still driving Highway 93, trying not to think about Anne and trying to get myself back into the mood of the circuit, which had been broken. I got to thinking about the downhill course for the Harriman, which year in and year out was the toughest and most dangerous, thinking in particular about the Rock Garden and the moguls and the schuss on Exhibition. I didn't go to sleep until I had managed to blot that out of my mind too.

In the middle of the afternoon I got up, shaved,

showered, and dressed, and wandered around the inn, watching the fat yellow buses with ski racks on their sides bringing the skiers back from Baldy. I went over to the swimming pool where the mist rose excitingly, and skiers with dark faces and pale bodies hurried into and out of the water. I wandered over toward Dollar to watch the beginners' ski classes. I was thinking about Silver Ridge and Mr. Patten, and I was trying to feel what it would be like when it was over, when I was an ex-champion or ex-almost-champion, and had to make a living in some resort like this.

The sun was very low over peaks like haystacks when I finally looked in at the Ram and found Anne with Bill Dye, the Chief-of-Course, and another couple who were in Sun Valley to watch the Harriman—Eddie Black, a veteran racer, and Gracie something, who had bright yellow hair and an eastern accent. The Ram was filling with people coming in after skiing, and there were a lot of ski instructors squiring bunnies from their classes. The combo began to play, Eddie asked Anne to dance, and Bill Dye, Gracie, so I was left alone.

I watched Anne and Eddie Black moving onto the crowded floor. Her bare arms looked very white against her black sheath dress. She never wore the Lanz print dresses the other girls favored, and she looked fine in high heels. It was funny to see the other girls in dresses at the banquets, with the line at their necks where the skiers' tans ended, and tilted forward and unsure of themselves in high heels—girls who were so competent on skis. You were always aware that they were racers dressed up, except for Anne.

I loved to watch her dance. As she and Eddie Black swung apart, her face was remote, secret, faintly smiling. Her smile deepened and dimples cut her cheeks for an instant as she swung back toward him. I loved to see the quick, springing curve of her thigh as she changed direction. Once she smiled at me, revealing the dark flaw of her chipped tooth, managing to convey that she would rather be dancing with me.

When the four of them came back to the booth a

waiter brought another round of beer, and glüwein for Gracie. Bill Dye leaned toward me across the initial-carved table. "Did you hear Jean-Gaby's going to fore-run the downhill?"

"Who?"

"Jean-Gabriel Michonneau."

"I didn't know he was in this country."

Gracie held up her arms and squinted as though she were aiming a gun. "Bang! Shot down and nailed up on the wall."

Anne looked puzzled, Eddie laughed, and Bill Dye made motions toward a nearby booth.

"They're over there," he said, and Gracie clapped a hand to her mouth. He said to me, "He and Helen Moles-worth got married in Megève, and she brought him back here."

"Who's she?" Anne asked.

"Just a couple-three million bucks," Eddie Black said.

"Chock full of money," Gracie said.

"She was married to one of those Aspen people. He died a couple of years ago. She's got a place at Aspen. She likes"—she flushed—"she likes ski instructors quite a lot. Anyway, she's got Jean-Gaby now."

"She's been married five or six times, I think," Bill Dye said. "Each time a step up in Dun and Bradstreet—till Jean-Gaby. Molesworth was in oil, I think. Now I guess she's turned a corner where she can let Jean-Gaby marry *her* for her portfolio."

"Well, it makes me sick," Gracie said. "He was such a terrific racer. Really the greatest."

Jean-Gaby Michonneau had been one of the greatest champions, as Gracie had said. He had retired from rac-ing before the last Olympics, and I had thought he was working for the French government, planning new ski areas.

"You've met Jean-Gaby, haven't you, Jack?" Eddie Black asked. When I said I hadn't he looked pleased to be one up on me. "Hell of a nice guy," he said.

"Liz May got him up from Aspen to give you girls some pointers," Bill Dye told Anne.

"I met him at the FIS last year," Anne said.

"Well, I think it's sickening," Gracie said.

I said to Bill Dye, "How far up is the last gate on Exhibition going to be?"

He laughed. It was always the important question about the Harriman downhill course, since the speed of the schuss down Exhibition depended on where the last control gate was placed. "Oh, I think we'll be easy on you this time," he said.

He began to complain about his troubles as Chief-of-Course, and about the Harriman having to be held early this year because of a conflict with the Nationals at Squaw.

Joe Hammond and Charley Catten stopped by the booth. They were just out from Winter Park, where Leary had won the combined, with Tom Boyd second and Harry Butler third. Alice Beard had won the women's. Leary was riding with Boyd and McInerny, and Joe didn't think they'd arrived yet. "Where's the last gate on Exhibition?" he asked, and everyone laughed.

Anne and I got up to dance, but her mind wasn't on it. "Let's go say hello to Jean-Gaby," she said. She took my hand and we went over to the booth Bill Dye had indicated.

Jean-Gabriel Michonneau rose when he saw her. He had coarse black hair combed straight back, a thin, dark face with a prominent mole on one cheek. "Ah, mademoiselle!" he said with a little bow. Anne introduced me, and I shook a wiry hand; he half bowed again. "We are hearing so much about you this year," he said to me. "And may I present my wife? My dear, this is Miss Anne Patterson and Mr. Jack Roche."

"Hello," Mrs. Michonneau said, smiling at me. She had shoulder-length silver-white hair framing a pale, heart-shaped face in which the only color was a pink mouth and sharp blue eyes. "We saw you dancing," she said. "What a handsome young couple, we said, didn't we, Jean-Gaby?" She had a soft voice that made you feel you must hold your breath in order to hear her better.

"Ah, yes!" Jean-Gaby said. The mole on his cheek

gave his smile a wry twist. I wondered if there were secrets of downhill racing he could reveal, if he chose. "Ah, won't you please sit with us?" he asked politely.

"Thanks; we're with some people," I said, although I knew Anne wanted to stay.

Mrs. Michonneau's pale eyes in her marshmallow-colored face inspected me. "I hope Jean-Gaby and I will see something of you two before the race this weekend."

"Well, we'll be up on Baldy training every day."

"You must see Anne Patterson ski, my dear. She has very much style."

"I can see she has. So few people have real style."

"Thank you," Anne said.

We all said good night, see you tomorrow, as though we were old friends already. I knew people like Helen Michonneau at Sugar Bowl and Squaw Valley, wealthy people who skied a little as an excuse for having après-ski parties, and who liked to hobnob with racers. But they didn't really like us, as almost always race officials who hadn't been racers themselves didn't like us, and they patronized us and talked about things we knew nothing about. We went to their parties when we were invited, as though by royal command, but we all resented them.

Anne and I danced another set, silently. Finally she asked, "Why didn't you want to stay and talk to them?"

"She gives me he creeps."

"Oh, does she?" Anne said. "I think she's fascinating." It was as though we'd had a quarrel. When we went back to our booth everybody was talking about going to the Quonset Hut for pizza. We started out with them, but Anne whispered, "Let's go somewhere by ourselves."

Outside in the darkness, walking on the resinously squeaking snow, we left the others. We drove into Ketchum for a hamburger, then went to a movie and held hands and ate popcorn. But I felt out of touch with Anne. After the movie we went back to the Challenger. Anne was to room with Alice, I, as always, with Leary, who hadn't arrived yet. We said good night as though we were casual dates.

Leary came in sometime during the night. In the morning when I went to breakfast he was still asleep, but when I returned the room was redolent of camphor and wintergreen, and he was sitting on the edge of the bed, kneading liniment into his thighs. He mixed liniments in different combinations, like racing waxes, and tried them out. "How was your trip?" he asked without looking up.

"Okay," I said, watching him rubbing and beating his mixture into his legs. On the circuit your legs took on a character of their own, as a sort of attached but autonomous part of yourself. They had their good days and bad days, and you always thought of them with a capital L. "Congratulations," I said.

"Thanks." He stood up to pull on his longjohns. "I did all right. I almost canned-up on the first slalom run, but I managed to hold it."

"How was the GS?"

"Tough. Harry had a hell of a good run for second. Tom was third." He stood there not quite facing me. "It was good for me," he said in a different voice. "Got my confidence back."

I nodded. I said, "Jean-Gaby Michonneau's here. He's going to forerun the downhill. He's married to some rich bag."

"Yeah?" Leary said. He banged each thigh in turn with the knife of his hand, as though giving them the finishing touch. "You ever see him race?"

"I saw him four or five years ago at Sugar Bowl."

"How was it with Brownie?" he asked abruptly.

"Okay. She was all right. We promised we'd call her after the Harriman."

Frowning, he watched me fish the keys to the station wagon out of my pocket. I dropped them with a jingle on the table between the two beds. I decided not to thank him.

"Anne okay?" he asked.

"She's okay. She's kind of mad at you."

His face reddened. "Well, to hell with *her!*" he said. He looked hard at me. "Well, I guess you think I'm a crud for not going along."

I shrugged.

"I don't like looking like a crud," Leary said. "But I can stand it. I mean I really don't give *too* much of a damn how I look."

I didn't say anything to that either, and he began pacing up and down—or fro and to. It seemed a long time since we had had any laughs together on the circuit.

"Listen," he said. "I like Brownie all right. I like her a lot. But I had to back off. I can't get married, Christ sake!"

"Married?"

"She wants to get married," he said, avoiding my eyes. "Of all the goddam silly ideas. I can't get married. I don't *want* to get married. Jesus, my father'd really love that. You can't go screwing around getting married, you've got to concentrate on racing. Look how we were at Arapahoe. She had me all fussed, and she'd got herself so— That's how she broke her ankle, I know. I had to get her off *that* idea, and get myself back in phase. I could've just as well have got myself really bugged and gone on losing the rest of the season!"

"Okay," I said, but I liked him better when he said he didn't give a damn what anyone thought of him than when he tried to blame Brown for everything. I felt as out of touch with him as I had with Anne last night.

His eyebrows were a fierce bar across his forehead, and his eyelids had the red-edged, sleepless look. He said, "Jack, I'm not in this goddam thing to come in any place but first."

"Neither am I," I said.

"I mean every race, whether it's a tryout or just for fun. I'm going to make that Olympic team. And I'm going to cop something in the Games."

"Okay," I said. He looked relieved; I supposed he had thought I was going to give him a worse time about Brown. But I wasn't his conscience. "So what's different?" I said. "Everybody wants to be another Jean-Gaby or Toni Koeller. All that's different is you don't mind saying it out loud."

He looked at me blankly. He would not talk about it

97

so much if he hadn't been so sure of himself, I thought and I hated that confidence.

"It's just like downhill, Jack," he said. "The whole thing is. You've got to pick your line and then hold it. You've got to be able to hold it."

I nodded.

"That's the way it is," Leary said. Then he said defensively, "You said you were in it to win too."

"I'm in it to win, but I don't know if I want to be a goddam machine. What if you hold your line so hard you get there, you win everything you ever wanted to win, you're *it*, except you find out it's not really you that won everything, it was just some goddam machine?"

Leary shrugged. "Maybe that's the way it's got to be."

"That's all right, huh?"

"If that's the way it has to be." He shrugged again, as though the subject no longer interested him. "Who'd Jean-Gaby get married to?" he asked.

"Helen somebody. Molesworth."

"Christ, I know her! She's got a place in Aspen. Jesus. She used to eat instructors, I heard, boots, skis, and long-thongs. What'd he do that for? I thought he had some great job with the French government."

"Maybe he couldn't hack it."

"Jesus," Leary said. He sounded as though he had a cold in his nose. "What'd he marry *her* for?"

"Maybe he decided he didn't want to run a gas station."

"What the hell're you talking about?"

I got up and went to stand at the window. Sun Valley needed snow. The slopes of Dollar were rutted and moguled and the snow was dirty. In the east you skied on ice on narrow trails, and here the trees were scrubby, the moguls too big, and it was too cold. But home in the Sierra there was always enough snow, often there was deep powder, and seldom ice; the mountains were rugged, friendly and big treed under a deep blue sky and a warm sun. Or so it would seem to me when I was homesick.

"I got some bad news," Leary said.

I looked at my hands, cross-hatched with edge-cuts, callused from my bootlaces. "What's that?" I asked.

"I'm getting the shaft from my father," he said in the stuffed-nose voice. "I'm flying too high, he says. If that doesn't mean he's trying to shoot me down I don't know what it means." I turned toward him; his face looked very tight across the cheeks. "They can't stand it," he said, almost as though he understood and forgave them. "They've just got to cut you down some way. He's mad because I didn't go see Mike that time in New York. He won't even *write* me himself, he's got to dictate it to my stepmother. 'Your father says—'" he mimicked.

"No more allowance?" I asked.

He shrugged elaborately. "He didn't slam the door. If we can agree about certain things— That means I agree to do it his way. Well, I don't mind lying to him."

"I can always write Mr. Gayley for some money," I said. "Anyway, there's not much longer to go this season. We'll get expenses, and we can scrounge skis and sell them. You'll be all right."

Boots clumped and voices muttered down the hall outside our door. Leary pulled on his stretchpants and left them unzipped while he got into his black turtlenecked shirt. Tucking it in, he said, "Let's go over on Baldy and look at the downhill." He zipped up his pants. "I'm not worried about this season," he said in a tight voice, "or next year. I can ride the Olympic squad next year. I was hoping to get down to Portillo this summer though."

I shook my head; that would cost a lot of money.

"It'd be like having another season under your belt," Leary said. "Ski all summer. It's just that much more of a leg-up on everybody else."

"I guess that's right," I said.

"So I'm screwed out of that," Leary said.

8

There was the familiar yet always new excitement of starting out in the morning on another mountain as

Leary and I rode over through Ketchum on the bus with a bunch of other racers. Everyone was loud, shrill, over-friendly. On No. 1 we shivered in the cold with the canvas covers drawn over our legs. No. 2 climbed above Exhibition, and here you shivered too, not so much from cold but from looking down at the gradient and the moguls—steeply set snow mounds carved by skis, with their tops gleaming in the sun and hammocks of shadow at their bases, some of them five or six feet high. In the downhill you made a difficult turn at the top of the Exhibition run, traversed those moguls very fast, too fast, because it was difficult to slow down, three or four times, and then, depending on where the last control gate was, schussed to the bottom at fifty or sixty or seventy miles an hour over a washboard of bumps, and shot into River Run, where it was flatter, where you needed all the speed you had been able to accumulate on Exhibition, where the downhill was won or lost.

At the top of No. 2 Leary and I changed to No. 3 and rode on up to the warming hut at the top. We skied down Ridge Run, which was the first schuss of the downhill, mamboing slowly to warm up, our breath steaming. The cold felt like a glaze on my face. We went on down through the Rock Garden, which was badly torn up, over the road and down between the lift towers, which would be padded for the race, and around the hard fallaway leading onto the top of Exhibition. We stopped there, looking down the moguls. Another skier stood at some distance from us, a lean man all in black, with goggles on and a black cap.

"Who's that?" Leary asked just as the other pushed off.

"I don't know." I watched him gelandesprung off the first mogul, lift again from the second. Then he had his speed, and he went across Exhibition on a steep traverse, bouncing off the tops of the moguls with his knees working like pistons, almost in a blur, and his crouched body flowing smoothly along the line of his descent. He made a fine turn and traversed across the other way. Skiers up and down the slope had stopped to watch him. He finally swung uphill to a halt.

"That's Jean-Gaby," I said.

Leary kick-turned and skated over to where Jean-Gaby had started and without a pause started down the line the Frenchman had taken. He didn't do as well, and I wondered if a letter like the one he had gotten from his father could affect one's skiing. Halfway along the first traverse one ski tilted away from the other, one pole jerked up for balance. But he tucked his legs up and was airborne for twenty feet before he came down, in control again. I started down before he made his turn, but I didn't have to prove anything to Jean-Gaby Michonneau, so I chose a slower line. When I caught up with them they were shaking gloved hands. Leary had met Jean-Gaby during FIS week. I shook hands with him too. With Europeans, you shook hands every time you met.

"That was beautiful recovery," Jean-Gaby said to Leary. "Very nice."

"Thanks," Leary said, leaning on his poles. A frozen bit of mucus showed in one nostril. "You're going to forerun Saturday, I hear."

"Ah, yes," Jean-Gaby said with his crooked smile. "I will make a very careful forerun for you young fellows."

"You didn't look very careful coming down here," I said.

He seemed nakedly gratified. "Ah, thank you. But it is nothing here."

Leary was frowning and banging a hand against his thigh as though he had a cramp. Jean-Gaby said to him, "But you must not let the hands come up, so. You must pardon me if I tell you this. I am now a coach, I have been asked to come here to ski with the girls. To help them a little."

"Hell, no, I don't mind," Leary said, but I saw that he did. Standing erect, he held his poles too high, then too low, then out from his body.

Jean-Gaby smiled and didn't seemed displeased. "You recovered very well," he said. "But once I saw a fellow

101

have his pole through his stomach that way. Of course it would be very rare to fall just so. But sad."

"Sure," Leary said, nodding, doing more calisthenics with his poles.

Jean-Gaby gave signs of the conversation being at an end, and there was an awkward moment as we hesitated over who was going to lead off. But Leary deferred to Jean-Gaby, who led us down to the bottom of Exhibition and in a schuss down River Run. He rode a very fast ski; the distance between him and Leary widened considerably as we ran down over the flats to the downhill finish.

On the lift going back up again we could see Olympic, which was part of women's downhill. The girls were coming down through the moguls there. I waved to Anne, but she didn't see me. Lorraine took an eggbeater fall and the Markered-out of a ski. Her curses were shrill as breaking glass on the frozen air.

At the top of No. 2 Jean-Gaby asked us to have a cup of tea with him. Leary was sullen and silent, staring ahead at the Frenchman who had already been what he was not yet and might never be, and who still rode fast skis, as we trudged up the long flight of stairs to the Roundhouse. Inside there was a fire blazing, and Helen Michonneau came toward us through the skiers warming themselves around it. Her pale hair was caught in a blue earband, she wore blue pants, a slightly darker blue sweater, her boots had blue tongues. Her body had a slumped, boneless look, like a stuffed cloth doll; in the daylight she looked much older than she had last night. She smiled at Jean-Gaby as he strode long-legged toward her, taking off his goggles and cap. Black coarse hair was pasted to his head. He kissed her on the forehead, and she touched a hand to his cheek.

He started to introduce her to Leary, but she said, "Oh, I've met Christy Leary at Aspen. Hello, Chris."

"Hello, Mrs. Molesworth—I mean, Mrs. Michonneau."

She laughed at his mistake. "Hello, Jack Roche," she said in her listen-carefully voice. "I rode up on the lift with your lovely leggy lady."

102

"We saw her going down Olympic just now," I said.

When we had found a table and had sat down with our cups of tea, Helen Michonneau produced a silver flask from her belt pouch, doctored her cup and Jean-Gaby's, offered it to Leary and me, and smiled when we thanked her, no. She rested a hand on the table next to Jean-Gaby's hand, so that they just touched. "Did you have a nice run, darling?"

"Ah, not bad!"

"We were glad to hear he was only forerunning," I said.

Stirring sugar into his tea, Leary said to Jean-Gaby, "You're not going to be racing any more, huh?"

He shook his head, smiling.

I was finding it hard not to stare at his wife's hand. It was an ugly hand, darkly blotched and old, with bulging veins. Now it rested on top of his like a toad. "Jean-Gaby is very precious," she said. "I couldn't bear to have him broken up in a bad fall."

"Perhaps I will race again as a Veteran," he said. "Who knows? Right now I am at that curious place"—he extended his hands—"where I am not so foolish brave as I once was. Nor yet so wise as I would hope to be."

"Well, you don't win downhills with wisdom," Leary blurted.

"But yes!" Jean-Gaby said. "Of course one must also be very good. I am very good still."

"The best in the world, darling," Helen Michonneau murmured. I managed to laugh, and Jean-Gaby laughed, but Leary didn't even try. Just then the girls came stamping into the Roundhouse, Lorraine shaking her hands and blowing on them, Evelyn Squires hurrying over to the fire to sit down and loosen her boots. Mrs. May followed them in, wearing her khaki fur-lined parka and her green Alpiner's hat with resort badges pinned all over it. She had a face like a rusty hatchet. Anne came to join us, and I went to get her a cup of black coffee.

When I came back Helen Michonneau was saying, "I have a very pleasant house in Aspen, and I wish the three of you would come stay with us the week before the Roch Cup races. I will promise faithfully that no interference will be made with your training."

"I will also promise," Jean-Gaby said. "And I must tell you that my wife has a very fine cook."

I wondered how it felt to be married to a rich wife and have everything belong to her: her house, her cook, her car. And be her husband like her other things. Maybe it didn't matter to him; but as I looked again at her dark, ugly hand resting on his, I thought that it probably did.

"We'd love to," Anne said. "Thank you very much." She looked at me.

"That would be great," I said reluctantly.

Helen Michonneau smiled at Leary, who was holding his cup in both hands.

"Fine," he said. "That's very nice of you, Mrs. Michonneau."

"Helen." She smiled. "You are all to call me Helen. Please. Then that's lovely, that's all settled. It's too bad your friend Georgiana Brown had her accident and can't be with us."

"She might be coming to Aspen," I said. "She said she'd come if she got her walking cast on and could get a ride."

Mrs. May came striding toward us. She asked Jean-Gaby if he was ready to take the girls for a run, then sat down to talk to Helen, snubbing Anne. Leary and I excused ourselves and went outside to put our skis on.

When we stopped at the top of Exhibition, Leary said, "Well, that's fine. I don't mind scrounging off her at Aspen, do you?"

"It's fine."

"How can he stand it, Christ sake?"

I shrugged. I thought about my father slipping into the conversation the information that Patten had a daughter. We watched while Jean-Gaby led the eight girls down Exhibition. He came in short turns down the fall line, with Lorraine behind him. Skiing between Jean-Gaby and Anne, Lorraine looked gracelessly thick, like a fireplug on skis. Jean-Gaby waved a pole as he passed us, and so did Anne. The serpentine they formed, with Mrs. May trailing far behind, curved on down Exhibition, looking like an all-girl ski-school class following a handsome instructor.

"He won't ever race again," Leary said.

I felt anger like a headache at his jealousy. "Well, that's a break for us, isn't it?" I said. "One and two instead of two and three."

"What the hell're you talking about?" Leary said. "He's too old. You heard him. Anybody can look good down a little piece of the mountain."

"Uh-huh," I said. I jabbed the tip of my pole into the pack, making little blue holes, like wounds.

"He couldn't last the whole course like that," Leary said.

Maybe nobody could last it, I thought; fast and with grace. Aloud I said, "Come on, let's go. If you stand still too long here they have to chip you loose with an icepick." We skied on down through the moguls.

9

That night at dinner in the cafeteria, Bill Dye announced the training hours for the downhill course. The downhill races were to be held on Saturday, the slaloms Sunday, and the presentation banquet Sunday night. There was no giant slalom in the Harriman.

After dinner there were to be ski movies at the Opera House, including some of the last FIS, but Anne wanted to dance. I wasn't well enough dressed to go into the Duchin Room, and the Ram was crowded, so we wandered over to the Quonset Hut and danced to the combo there. When the combo was out we sat in a booth and nursed beers. Anne had bought a new sweater. It was beige and had a big collar. She liked big collars that made a sort of ruff below her face and hid the skier's tan line.

"Isn't it nice?" she said, smoothing her hand over the wool. "I had them send the bill to Roger. I hope he won't mind. He and Mother are having some trouble."

"That's too bad."

"They're always having trouble, but this time sounds a little more serious. Mother says she's moved out. But maybe he threw her out." I saw she wasn't as casual about it as she was trying to pretend.

"Someday somebody will take you away from all that," I said.

She smiled at me. She looked thoughtfully around the big, barren room, and her hand stroked her sweater again. She said, "Helen wears clothes well."

"Who?"

"Helen Michonneau. I almost wanted to clap when I saw her in that blue outfit."

"She looked like a snow bunny. You look better than that in chopped-off Levis and an old sweatshirt. All she was showing was that she had a lot of money to spend on bunny clothes."

"You don't understand," Anne said. "I think she must have been like me once."

"She's never done anything athletic in her life."

She looked annoyed, as though I were stupidly refusing to see her point. She sipped her beer, sighed. "I suppose only women understand about clothes. I don't know how to explain it. Oh, if I'm very lonely, or everything seems bad, or I'm scared, if I can just buy a new dress or a suit or a sweater or even a pair of shoes— Can you understand that?"

"Did you buy that sweater because you were scared of something?"

She looked down. "Oh, a little," she said. "Oh, not scared exactly."

"Of the downhill?"

"Oh, no. About Mother and Roger. I'm afraid she's been seeing Figgy again."

The combo was coming back in, scraping, and shuffling as they took their places. The piano player trickled his fingers down the keyboard. I said, "Did the sweater help?"

"Don't I seem happy and secure?"

"You always do."

"I think I do when I think I look nice," Anne said.

"Because when you're being paid attention to you're all right. When no one's paying attention to you you're not even there. Have you ever felt like that?"

I shook my head.

"People pay attention to Helen Michonneau," Anne said. "*She* has style. If you have beautiful clothes and wear them well, then everyone looks at you and you're being paid attention to. It's the same with racing—winning anyway—people are watching you do something well and admiring you."

"I guess so," I said. The combo began to play, people came out to dance. Anne's eyes looked very dark and far away.

"There's something else about beautiful clothes," she went on. "It's like— It sounds silly, but it's a kind of inviolate thing. It's only nice material touching you, and people looking at you. Not sexily really. But as though you are a painting. I mean, admiring you that way. Aesthetically—that's what I mean."

"Sometimes you like to be touched," I said.

"Just in a certain way," Anne said calmly. "Just as though we were dancing; like dancing. Only aesthetically. As though I'm being paid attention to and admired." Her voice tightened. "Let's dance, Jack," she said, and her voice tightened another notch. "I love to dance," she said, "and wear beautiful clothes and be admired, and nothing else. Isn't that a wonderful way to be?" Then she got up and we danced, and while we danced the remote and faintly happy expression came over her face, as though she had gone far off to a place that was very pleasant and safe.

"How about one more beer?" I asked. "Then we'd better get to bed."

"Let's wait till the combo comes back and dance one more set."

"All right."

I saw that she had come all the way back.

She frowned at me. "But you don't really want to. You think racers ought to get more rest."

I shook my head, although it was true. "We can stay for another set."

"You're just saying that because you love me," Anne whispered.

"Okay," I said.

"You do love me, don't you?"

"Yes."

"That's better than a new sweater," Anne said. "I love for you to love me." She closed her eyes and held her steepled hands up to touch her lips. She whispered, "I love clothes and dancing and for you to love me."

My face was burning. "Well, I can dance another set with you, but I can't do much about buying you clothes."

"And sports cars," Anne said in a hurting voice. "Have you ever seen a Facel Vega? It's French. It's beautiful. I love beautiful cars too. But do you know? I'm not sure I love racing any more."

"No?"

"But I want to win the Nationals this year, and I want to win in the Winter Games next year. Maybe I want to win as much as Chris does, but in a different way. And I can win if I really want to. Do you know I can?"

"Sure you can. If you want to put out in the downhill no one can touch you. There's no one even close to you, Anne."

"Tusch, Anne," she said. "That's what Ernst used to say, 'Tusch!' I could beat everyone if I really tusched," she said. "It's just that I don't want to get hurt. Ernst got hurt so terribly training for the FIS."

I remembered the way Ernst Hochner had looked at her, and I knew I would look at her that way, too, except for having seen him. I poured the last quarter inch of beer into my glass.

Anne said, "But if I let myself go in the Nationals I can win the downhill and the GS beside the slalom. Then there will be lots of publicity—photographs of me. And if I win in the Olympics—I'd be able to get fabulous modeling jobs. I could make fabulous money. Some of them make incredible amounts of money—a hundred dollars an hour. Then I could wait and see about getting married. Maybe I could make so much money you and I could—" she stopped.

I pushed at my glass and said, "Nobody makes that much money."

She laughed, and I tried to say lightly, "Anyway, it would be history repeating itself. Because I'll probably be a ski instructor by then. Like your mother marrying that Austrian."

Anne stared at me with her eyes dark and blank. "Oh, Figgy," she said. "Oh, you mean Figgy."

"Then if we had a daughter I could teach her to be the greatest female skier this country's ever had. And when she won the Nationals—" I stopped; I had blundered into a place where I was not welcome. Anne was rubbing her forehead as though she had a headache.

"Jack," she said in a tight, urgent voice. "Let's go over to the Ram and dance just one more. Please."

"All right," I said.

Quickly she got to her feet and took up her greatcoat. She fluffed her fingers through her hair, looking at me as though she didn't see me. I helped her on with her coat, we went outside into the face-crinkling cold, she took my arm. We didn't speak as we walked over to the Ram.

The first person we saw when we entered was Jean-Gaby. "Ah, you must come and sit with us, you two," he said. He sounded a little drunk. He took Anne's arm and mine and convoyed us to a table where Helen was sitting with Leary and another couple—a red-headed girl and a dark-faced man with a froglike Texas voice. His name was Dixie Rigg. I didn't get the girl's name.

There was considerable milling around while another of the initial-carved tables was brought up and butted to the first. Anne was placed between me and the Texan. Helen was talking to Leary in her low voice, while he nodded from time to time. Both Jean-Gaby and Dixie Rigg were smoking cigars. As soon as we were all settled the redhead decided she had to go to the ladies' room, so all the men had to stand up again. I wished I were in bed at the inn. Yawns were coming on me, and I saw from the tension in his nostrils that Leary was having the same trouble.

"From near Waco there," I heard Dixie Rigg say to Anne in his gravelly voice. A little later I heard him say, "Yeah, I'm in oil, honey." When the waiter came he took charge of ordering drinks. Leary and I asked for beer, but Anne said she didn't want anything, which offended Dixie Rigg. Finally, laughing, she ordered a beer too.

Jean-Gaby, chewing his long cigar, looked sad. Once Helen patted his hand. She and Leary seemed to be discussing European ski resorts. The music started raggedly, and Dixie Rigg asked Anne to dance before I could. His dark face was round and jolly, and his sunburned dark hair was neatly parted in the middle. He looked thirty-five or forty and he bounced when he danced.

"We ought to be in bed," I said to Leary.

"What time is it?"

"Quarter after ten."

"You must, you know," Jean-Gaby said suddenly. "When Anne comes back I will command that she go. It is too late. Nine-thirty is too late."

Helen's face was startlingly white in the dim light. She wore pearls and a black sweater buttoned at the neck over a low-cut cocktail dress. "I don't think Anne takes her training as seriously as you boys do," she said, smiling at me.

"She doesn't have the competition we have," I said.

She laughed. The red-headed girl came back, saying, "Where'd old Dixie go?"

"He's dancing with Anne," Helen said.

"Oh, yeah?" the girl said. I got up as she sat down again, but no one else bothered. She said to me, "You're a racer?"

"Yes."

"What's your name again?"

"Jack Roche."

She looked at me blankly. "Oh, yeah." She took a big swallow from her glass and stared across the table at Leary, who was talking to Jean-Gaby.

"Of course one must be lucky," Jean-Gaby said, shaking his unlit cigar over the ashtray. "To be a champion one must be very lucky. Are you lucky, my friend?"

"Sure," Leary said. "I guess so. Sure I am."

"That is correct," Jean-Gaby said, nodding. "One must always think so, at least." As she listened, Helen's mouth slackened into a repellent downward curve. Jean-Gaby turned to me. "And are you lucky, Jack?"

"Sure," I said.

"Goody for you," the redhead said.

"Were you lucky?" Leary asked.

Jean-Gaby made a shoulders-mouth-eyebrows shrug. "Ah, I thought so then. But there are many different kinds of luck. It may go deep or stretch very long. Or it may stop very sudden—*bom.*" He made a hatchet motion with his hand. "For a racer," he went on, "for a champion racer I have thought sometimes the very best luck would be he is killed in an auto accident the next day after he has won his last great race." The final words sounded very loud as the music ceased.

Helen said in a harsh voice, "That is so very, very flattering."

With an exaggerated gesture he laid a hand on her shoulder. "Ah, my dear, I must explain this to you. Right after you have won a great race it is very lovely. But soon a sadness comes. One thinks it can never be again. These two will know this feeling."

"Chris might," I said. "I haven't won a great race yet."

Leary tried to look stern, but instead looked pleased.

Just then Anne and Dixie Rigg came back to the table. "Well, you are a sweet-dancing little honey, honey," Dixie was announcing, his hand still on Anne's waist. The redhead was looking up at him.

"We'd better go, Jack," Leary said.

"Time to go, Anne," I said.

Dixie Rigg put up an argument, but Jean-Gaby shook his cigar at him, said he was the girls' coach now, and Anne should have been in bed an hour ago. Finally the three of us made it outside.

"Who the hell's he?" I said to Leary.

"Christ, I don't know. Some old friend of Helen's or her last husband's or something."

Anne didn't say anything, walking between us with her hands in the pockets of her greatcoat. The evening had been, for a while, bittersweet romantic and wonderful; then it had turned bad.

"Ahm in oihl, honeh," I said, and Leary laughed.

"Oh, he's sweet though," Anne said. But then she laughed too, and that helped.

10

The Harriman Cup was midway through the try-out races for the Olympic team, and the selection committee would be watching the results. The next day training began in earnest, and from that night on we were usually in bed by nine, dead-tired, and up early to wax and be on the lift as soon as it opened. The week unwound like tape from a reel which turned slowly at first, but faster and faster as the spinning center was uncovered.

Training for the downhill, you had to find the fastest line that you could hold. You tested your line in sections—working on the Rock Garden, on the airborne route over the road and down between the lift towers, on the fallaway at the top of Exhibition, the traverses over the moguls, and the schuss from the last control gate there—always being careful to overlap the sections so your legs did not get used to resting at certain places. During the training days you worked hard but at the same time tried to husband your strength toward those few minutes on Saturday when all you could muster would be needed.

Inevitably there were falls, as you found out where you had chosen too fast a line, and, because the course was rough and unfinished still and you were running it at speed, inevitably there were toboggan cases. Miles Doyle got a spiral fracture in the Rock Garden, and

Don Preger a compound in the schuss. I took a terrific eggbeater at the top of Exhibition, with Jean-Gaby watching, and broke a ski.

The girls were training on Olympic, but their training hours were not the same as ours, and Jean-Gaby was often on the men's course, watching us critically. I think all of us would have given a lot to know what his criticisms were.

The men racers ate lunch at tables reserved for us in the Roundhouse, and we would talk about the course.

McInerny said, "Well, they finally got mattresses up on those lift towers."

I said, "They've got them tied on so tight there's about as much give as a sock over a baseball bat."

"They're just to protect that damn orange paint," Harry Butler said.

Everyone except Leary laughed, a little nervously— we were all afraid of those two lift towers. During the lunchtime joking and discussion Leary only listened. He never joined in the talk during training, as though he were afraid of giving something away, but he didn't mind bragging after a race. Nobody but me liked him much.

Brushing a hand over his blond crewcut, McInerny said, "I'll never be able to hold that bastard at the top of Exhibition."

"I watched Jean-Gaby run the course yesterday," Charley Catten said. "He took it real high there. You saw him, Benny."

"Okay, he held it high," McInerny said. "Maybe he uses some special kind of fallaway-holding wax."

"Well, I sure waxed wrong today," Harry said. "What are you guys using?"

He was looking at Leary and me. It was not a question you asked, because wax formulas were personal and private. And it was not a question Leary, picking at the herringbone tread of his boot sole, was going to answer. Harry was younger than the rest of us and apt to be brash and tough-talking. It was a pose I had used once. He had a pleasantly skewed nose and dark marks under his eyes that made him resemble a raccoon.

"Eight, white, and five," I said.

He bared his teeth at me. "Not on this snow, buddy, not on this snow. You had a close one down the moguls there, didn't you, Sugar Bowl?"

"Pretty close," I said. "But not *too* close."

"Hi, Tom," McInerny said as Tom Boyd and Joe Hammond sat down with us. They immediately began to talk about past Harrimans: about the famous run in the fog, when so many racers crashed at the bottom of Exhibition, running into one another and into the toboggans and trees, that the spectators who were there to see the crashes were screaming up the course to stop the race; about the time Chandler fell three times on Exhibition, each time getting up and trying to go on, even after he had broken a ski, and crying when a course policeman persuaded him to quit; and they shook their heads over all the racers who had hit those lift towers.

"Listen to the snow come down," I said, and everybody laughed.

"It's a wonder any of you old-timers are still alive," Charley Catten said.

"You can't psych me out on this course," Harry Butler said. "I'll take Exhibition over the Nosedive and the Seven Turns at Stowe any day. One mistake and you're in those damn trees yelling timber. I have nightmares about going off in those damn trees at Stowe."

After lunch, on the lift to the top, Leary said, "That was funny hearing Harry talk about Stowe like that. You have nightmares like that, Jack?" He seesawed his skis.

I hadn't thought about it when Harry was talking, but I thought about it now, and, like a TV picture without sound, in my eyes there was Anne out of control and throwing up her hands just as she hit a tree, terribly. Leary turned to look at me as I said, "Oh, sure, sometimes."

"I don't," he said. "I have this queer dream where I'm going like hell but the wind is stopping me. It's a really frustrating crazy thing. I keep tucking and tucking but it doesn't do any good. It's like there are bumps all over me or my clothes are coming loose. I just keep slowing down."

I swung my skis as he was doing and tried to rid myself of the picture of Anne crashing. "You'd better not have any bumps sticking out on you tomorrow," I said, "because I'm going to go for it."

"Harry's going to get off a really hot run one of these times."

So am I, I said, but not aloud. Up on top we slid down the ramp in a wind that pushed and plucked at our clothes. All around were the peaks of the Sawtooth Mountains, with trees on their north slopes and bare ground showing on the south. There were roads and buildings on the mountains, which looked tame and worn-down compared to the Sierra. I wished I hadn't seen that terrible picture of Anne in my mind's eye. Now there was a required non-stop training run, and that was all I should be thinking about.

The race was at noon on Saturday, and when I got up on top the warming hut was jammed with racers and equipment and skis spread bottoms up between chairs, and there was the guttering-candle smell of melted wax. I found a spot, lit my meta tablets, and mixed my wax. I painted and scraped it thin and smooth. As soon as it had set I took my skis out on the packed snow and leaned them against the building.

Over at the start there was a crowd of racers, spectators, and officials. I recognized Bob Graves, from the selection committee. Racers wore tight, striped pants, racing parkas, and helmets; numbers were beginning to blossom. Now there was little talking among the racers, now faces were bluish white and lips blue. I kept away from the crowd, standing by myself and yawning. I remembered to eat the chocolate bar I had brought along. Harry Butler wandered by without recognizing me. "Luck," I said, and he looked startled and said, "Luck." Leary came over to stand with me, stiff-mouthed, with a bruised-looking face.

"You've got your boots on inside out," I said.

His eyes started down toward his boots; he scowled at me. I yawned back at him. A loudspeaker began squawking instructions. "Good luck, Chris," I said as he moved away. I went over beyond the start to look down the first schuss, where the double poles guided the course down and down.

I tightened my boots, tied on my number, closed all my zippers. I rubbed a little 48 on the bottoms of my skis for a fast start. My nose began to drip and I wiped it on my glove, my glove on my pants; then I took off my gloves to fasten my helmet. All at once I felt very taut, secure and contained in my helmet, tight parka, and pants. Racers were cutting a few turns down the mountain and sidestepping back again.

The first forerunner started down.

The crowd around the starting gate had grown. Now Jean-Gaby was in the slot, crouched and straining like a coiled spring. He resembled a Mohican with his ear-band pushing his hair into a topknot. In the first schuss he looked as though he'd spent most of his life in a tuck. He went very fast out of sight. My number was called.

The loudspeaker blatted and quarreled with itself. One minute, Dan Arganbright; in two minutes, me. Dan moved past me into the slot, stepping with his skis as though he didn't want to touch the freshly waxed bottoms to the snow until it counted. "Good luck," I said.

"Yeah, good luck, thanks," he mumbled. He looked at me, unseeing. "Yeah, good luck to you too, huh?" He went into the slot, pumping his goggles in and out.

The starter was scowling at the phone. "Thirty seconds," he said. "Fifteen . . . ten . . ." His hands made bread on Dan's back. He counted down to one. "Go!"

Dan drove himself out of the slot, skating; then he tucked.

"Number two in the slot. Number three on deck."

I went into the slot, thrusting my gloves through the loops of my poles, checking my helmet, number, zippers, anything that might catch the wind. I pulled my goggles down but held them out from my face to keep them from fogging. The languor and the yawns vanished. I flexed my legs. The starter worked at my back to relax the tight muscles, counting. I fixed my goggles in place, leaned out and set my poles, began to bounce in time to the counting. The "Go!" came. I made a good start.

Encapsuled in speed, hunched down in my tuck, nothing existed but the course rushing toward me. My legs were reacting well, my skis felt fast. And now, at speed, it was as though my body were clicked over onto the automatic pilot of my reactions while my mind turned slowly and separate on ahead, to the rough terrain of the Rock Garden, to the lift over the road and the descent between the towers, to the fallaway leading into Exhibition, where I had fallen in training.

Through the Rock Garden there was a sense of people watching. I lost my balance for an instant, recovered; lost and recovered it again; I was making fast time. Then out of the Rock Garden and the orange towers looming. Now the lift over the road, legs tucking up, and airborne long out over the road and down with hardly a jolt, to sweep safely past the obliquely set, mattress-and-straw-padded towers. Next the fallaway.

My line was high, and I came very fast down toward the ridge; *too fast!* Before I could stop myself I had risen out of my tuck to windcheck and stem. I cursed aloud and forced myself down again, but I had slowed enough to take the fine edge off my line, and my skis held too easily on the turn. Crossing the moguls, I picked up speed again, with slamming, knee-springing shocks as I hit the tops of the bumps.

Now turn and slant across the other way, faster and faster and no way here to check, and turn again, with the staccato, continual jolting on the bumps draining the strength from my legs. But at last the final gate on Exhibition, and down into a tuck again for the long schuss toward the slot at the bottom that from here looked the size of a keyhole, and speed and the tearing strain in the thighs mounting but sound blotted out now in a muffled vacuum of concentration.

I squirted through the hole between the lift terminal

and the trees, where people were watching and the to-boggans waiting, and into River Run and the long flat where all that counted was already done—my wax and my speed down Exhibition. Ahead was the funnel-shaped crowd at the finish. There were more bumps here, but these were only bad because my legs were almost gone. It was a tremendous act of will now to stay down, to keep knees loose and ride flat skis. I caught an edge and, in that terrible slowness of the brink of disaster, felt my balance going. I had to rise out of my tuck to recover, then into it again. I sailed across the finish line and into a stop turn and almost fell. I leaned on my poles, panting, sweating, stomach heaving, too weak to move. There was clapping all around, a padded sound of glove on glove. Finally I pushed myself over toward the timer's shelter.

The loudspeaker announced: "Time for Jack Roche, Norden, California—two: thirty-nine and six-tenths. That is fast time so far." I stood with Dan Arganbright and waited for the rest of the first seed to come down. I was still fast when Catten finished, when McInerny, Hammond, Samuelson, and Boyd had finished.

But Leary came down in 2:39.2, and I was second. I hadn't cried since I was a junior. I shook Leary's hand and said, "Great run," while he grinned and swaggered. Harry Butler had 2:40.8, but no one else was even close.

11

In the women's downhill Anne was a close second behind Lorraine Hedquist. I saw her only on the last schuss, and she came down through the bumps very well, pumping hard across the finish. But when she was down, leaning on her poles as though she had no strength left, her face was gray with exhaustion. Photographers got her to pose for them, and, when the placing was definite, she and Lorraine and Nolly Keyes posed together, and she and Jean-Gaby. I saw Mrs. May watching her with pursed-mouth dislike.

When I finally reached Anne she had her color back, and she looked happy and excited—from, I supposed, all the attention. I congratulated her, and she wrinkled her nose and whispered, "I thought I was running it fast enough to win."

"She's a real downhill racer."

Anne laughed. "I suppose it would be maddening for her to have a girly-girl beat her."

"You certainly are the photographer's honey, girly-girl."

"Wasn't I though?" She touched my arm with her gloved hand. "You almost beat Chris, didn't you?"

"Not quite."

"You don't have to beat him by much in the slalom to win the combined. Then we'd be Harriman Cup winners together, wouldn't that be fine?"

She could beat Lorraine in slalom wearing barrel staves, but the downhill was worth more than the slalom in the combined standings, and it wouldn't be as easy for me to beat Leary as she made out.

"Are you positive-thinking the way your father said to do?" she asked.

"Sure I am," I said.

"That was a goddam good run of yours," Leary said. He was sitting on the edge of his bed in his red long-johns, round-backed. He looked very tired. "That was a goddam good run Harry made too."

I grunted.

"You were damn close," he said. He lay back on the bed and gazed up at the ceiling. "I've lost another two pounds. I'm going to be really down by the end of the season."

Although it was discouraging to have the best downhill run I'd ever made only good enough for a second, I thought how it must be for Leary to have me pushing him closer and closer, only four-tenths off his time, and Harry Butler coming on. Each time now Leary would have to put out more because I might put out more. If I hadn't checked at the top of Exhibition I would have won.

"Jesus," Leary said, "I'm getting so I think, is this all one season?"

I sat down and eased my boots off. "Well, it's not so far from being over. Just the Roch and the one at Alta and the Nationals. Then it's just spring races."

"Two more tryouts," Leary said. "We're in for the Olympic squad, do you know it? You too. Unless something happens."

"Yeah," I said.

"I'd really like to get down to Portillo this summer," he said. "Ski all summer, really work. I'd really have a start on next season."

"Money," I said.

"I've got a hunch Helen Michonneau might put up for it. I'll bet she would." He fell silent, staring up at the ceiling, while I struggled out of my pants and went to take a shower. When I came back he hadn't moved.

"Hey, Jack, do you ever look at yourself in the mirror and say, Oh, you crappy guy!"

"No, I say, Oh, you handsome bastard. And a great athlete too." But he sounded depressed and serious, so I said, "Well, I look at myself and laugh sometimes."

"I get awfully sick of being a crappy guy sometimes," Leary said.

"Cut it out."

"I mean, up on top today you said good luck and all. But I don't say good luck. You know why? Because I don't wish anybody any luck."

"You're a real competitor, Chris," I said uncomfortably. "That's all."

He turned over on his side, facing away from me. There was a hole in the heel of one of his gray socks. "I was just thinking about it," he said. "We had kind of a great time, you and me and Brownie and Anne. And Brownie and I are—you know. And Anne won't talk to me much any more. And there I am up on top hating your guts. Really great."

I didn't know what to say. I pulled on my Levis.

Finally he said, "Then I come down and I'm fast by four-tenths and you come over and say, Hey, congratulations! Or, Good run! Or something. You know what I would've done? I'd have said some crappy jealous thing or made excuses. You don't do that."

"Well, don't think I was happy for you."

He grunted.

"You're kind of low, aren't you?"

"I almost had it," he said. "I was really out of control coming down over the road there. I came so close to clobbering on that lower tower—I don't know how I missed it."

So he had been in trouble too and still had beaten me by four-tenths.

"Hell, I guess I'm just a little shook," he said. He forced a laugh. "It'll pass."

"It better," I said. "I don't have to get much away from you tomorrow, and I like the looks of those slalom courses."

"Yeah?" Leary said. "Well, I may be low but I'm not worried."

It snowed during the night, and Sunday morning the new snow was shining in the sun. The slalom was delayed an hour while we packed out the powder on the courses on Ruud. On the first slalom run I had the best time; and, waiting for the second start, I had a tight, shaky, almost triumphant feeling that I could make it. But in the second run Leary and McInerny beat me; even though I won the slalom and was a close second in the combined, I was sick with disappointment.

Jean-Gaby and Helen were at the finish to congratulate Leary and me and Harry Butler, who was third. They introduced us to people whose names I didn't hear. There were photographers from two skiing magazines and the area newspapers to take pictures, and a man with a gray mustache and a beret, who was from one of the big sports magazines, was bossy and impatient, ordering us to make some runs through gates while he took more shots.

The photographer brought Anne over to pose with Leary and me. "Where's the other one Roge Bernand was talking about?" he demanded. "The first place guy's girl friend, where's she? I want her in here too."

"She broke her ankle last week," Anne said. "She's gone home."

"Oh, Christ," the photographer said.

When the women's slalom started I took him up alongside the course with me and pointed out combinations where there would be trouble, since he wanted to catch a fall. The slalom was all Anne's. She came down the course in her baby-blue stretchpants and white sweater, making liquid turns. Her face as she passed us was not strained like the other girls', but smiling as though she were enjoying herself, almost the expression she wore when she was dancing. She won the first run by eight-tenths, the second by almost two seconds, and she got a great deal of attention. Alice took second place. Lorraine had a bad fall at the combination where I'd stationed the photographer, missed a gate, and was DSQed.

Helen, Jean-Gaby, Dixie Rigg, and some of the other people we'd met appropriated Anne, so I had no chance to congratulate her. I didn't see her till later in the afternoon when Leary and I, after we'd had a swim in the pool, were drinking beer in the Quonset Hut and enjoying the unraveled, rundown feeling of the races being over and nothing to face now but the banquet. She came in alone. She wore a cocktail dress under her greatcoat and she looked fine. I thought she seemed very much at home in Sun Valley.

She leaned over with her hands on the table and said to Leary, "Let's go call Brownie now."

"Well, I thought I'd wait till after the rates go on."

"I promised we'd call her right after the slalom."

"Well, okay," Leary said.

We got some change, found a pay phone, and Anne and I waited outside the open door while Leary, who seemed very nervous, made the call.

"Hey, hello, Brownie?" he said in a high voice that didn't sound like him. "How're you doing? . . . Well, but how're *you* doing first? . . . Oh. . . . Well, I mean—you know. . . . You haven't, huh? . . . Oh, well, I won. . . . Yeah. . . . Well, Jack won the slalom. He got second in the downhill, and I got second in the slalom. . . . Yeah, Anne won big. There's going to be a big write-up and pictures in one of the ski mags, and. . . . Lorraine got DSQed in the slalom. . . ." He listened for a long time, and I saw the back of his neck turning red. "Listen, Brownie," he said. "Listen. . . . Listen, sure it's a damn shame. We'd have won everything between us the way we used to do. . . . Listen, Brownie. . . ."

He listened himself for a long time again. "So maybe we'll see you in Aspen, huh? Well, you'll know before then though? . . . We'll be staying with—well, Jean-Gaby Michonneau's married this Helen Molesworth and we'll be staying at her place."

He glanced back at Anne and me, nodding to the phone. "Sure . . . sure, you will." Abruptly he said, "You want to talk to Anne, Brownie? Here." He backed out of the booth, passing the phone to Anne.

Anne talked to her, and then I did, and heard Brown's tearful voice congratulating me. I said I hoped we'd see her in Aspen. She asked to talk to Leary again, and he squeezed back into the booth to say good-by. When he had hung up, the three of us stood together outside the phone booth. Leary looked very gloomy.

"Well, when shall we take off for Aspen?" I asked. "After dinner or first thing in the morning?"

"I don't care," Leary said.

Anne stood with her hands in her coat pockets, her pink mouth pouting thoughtfully. She said, "Helen and Jean-Gaby are flying back to Aspen with Dixie Rigg. He has a Beechcraft. They've asked me to come with them."

"Oh," I said. "Sure."

"I think I'll go with them," Anne said.

"Sure," I said, nodding.

"I mean, I suppose it isn't *really* respectable for a girl to go on long car trips alone with two men."

"That's right," I said. "With Brownie not along." I felt as though I'd been kicked in the stomach. Anne looked at me sideways out of her wide, dark eyes. "Well, we'll see you at the banquet," I said. "And then at Aspen."

"We'll go early in the morning, I guess," Leary said. "You want us to take your skis?"

"Please," Anne said. She turned full toward me and said, "Jack, don't be all polite and funny with me. I really shouldn't be driving all over the place with you and Chris. I don't care how it looks, but I oughtn't to get Mrs. May any madder at me than she already is."

"Sure," I said. "Anyway, I think it's great, Anne. Have a good trip."

She took my hand and squeezed it hard. Then she swung away and left us. Leary and I stood watching her go.

"You really like her, huh?" Leary said.

I didn't answer.

"I wish Brownie wouldn't cry like that," he said. "I get all unstuck when she cries like that. Then after a while I just get mad."

"Let's go have another beer," I said.

ASPEN | III

1

Coming into Sun Valley, you wonder where the mountains are; coming into Aspen, you wonder where the snow is. From Glenwood you run up along the Crystal River and Roaring Fork, and there is only a little snow showing on the north slopes. There is a little more and a little more as you gain altitude, and white peaks in the distance, but you are surprised when you see people skiing at Buttermilk. Then you cross the bridge into Aspen and you can see Ajax Mountain, and all at once you realize that what looked like bare ground are thickets of aspens with their branches making a smoky brown shadow on the snow.

When Leary and I drove into Aspen on Tuesday afternoon there were clouds coming up behind the mountains like smoke from behind stage flats, and there was the heaviness in the nostrils of snow on the way. Leary drove down past the Hotel Jerome to the center of town. Everyone on the streets was in ski clothing, looking in shop windows, carrying skis, talking on corners, and there was a walking-wounded in a sheepskin jacket humping along on crutches. Cars on the streets bore license plates from many states.

Leary stopped at the ski-club office to see if we had any mail. I had a postcard from my father which didn't say anything about the Harriman but wished me luck in the Roch. They'd had a four-foot storm on the summit. And there was a note from Mr. Gayley, enclosing a check for a hundred dollars. Leary had a packet of mail tied with brown string. He sat behind the wheel, his lips pursed, reading a long typewritten letter. He scowled briefly at a mimeographed form from a brown envelope, then jammed the rest into the glove compartment.

"What's the government want?" I asked.

He shook his head once. "Nothing." He started the engine.

"You know where she lives?"

"I've been there."

We drove past the shacks and restored shacks of Aspen. Helen Michonneau's house was visible a long way down the street, a white gingerbread mansion with a wrought-iron fence around the yard. A green jeep stood in the drive, and Leary pulled the station wagon in nose to nose with it. The first snowflakes were beginning to come down, floating and fragile like bits of tissue paper.

A woman with a German accent and blond hair done up in two coils like earphones met us at the door. There was some calling back and forth between her and Helen's voice before we were admitted. Helen appeared, in a tan loden jacket and a skirt with red braid around the bottom. Her pale hair gleamed in the dim entryway.

"You've come, and you've brought snow with you!" she said. "How thoughtful!"

She took us into the living room, which had wine-red carpeting and red and orange furniture, red-orange walls and a white ceiling. One wall was entirely taken up with framed photographs, hundreds of them, and there was a little black iron fireplace. I'd never seen a room like it, and Helen laughed at my expression. "It really is a nice room," she said in her confidential voice. "It will grow on you, you'll see." I was deciding that she wasn't as bad as some of the other rich bar-skiers, and that she wasn't bad-looking if she didn't let her mouth sag into the fish-mouth, when I realized that the room had been cunningly decorated into a fancy frame for her. In it the marsh-mallow face was only pleasantly pale and her metallic hair was softened.

She asked Leary how our trip had been and acted fascinated and frightened for us when he told about the three-car accident we had just missed being part of. I was wondering where Anne was.

"How was your plane trip?"

"Oh, very festive. Dixie has a very sweet little bar in his Beechie. He's a very fine pilot. He used to pilot Cling Haggin's plane, you know, before he went into the oil business for himself. Poor man—he's had to fly back to Texas to solve some dreadful crisis or other. Now what may I get you two to drink? Alcoholic or otherwise? Beer?"

"I'd like a beer, please," I said.

"I would too," Leary said. "Can I help you, Helen?"

They went out together, and I moved over to examine the photographs on the wall. Helen Michonneau was in each of them, always with a man or men. There were a couple of old-time movie actors, political figures, men in uniform, and many people in ski clothes. Almost all the photographs were inscribed, but it was hard to make out the signatures under the glass that covered them. Helen had been beautiful when she was young. There was a painting of her over the mantel, with color in her skin and life in her hair, eyes bigger and darker, lips parted to say something in the confidential voice. I started as the fire in the fireplace cracked and threw sparks against the screen.

On one of the coffee tables was Roger Bernand's catalogue, and I picked it up and paged through, looking at the photographs of Anne, worrying about her and depressed because I was jealous and because it was silly to be jealous. Everything that had been so good on the circuit was petering out, turning bad; I was feeling tense and lonely. I went to the window and parted the striped drapes to look at the snow falling. It was almost dark and cars went by with headlights on. The street was covered with snow now, and flakes fell softly against the background flush of Aspen.

When Leary and Helen came back I heard her say, "You're not to worry. I'm sure there's something I can do." Leary was carrying a tray on which were beer mugs and a plate of cheese and crackers. Helen had a martini glass. We all sat down. I wondered what Leary wasn't to worry about.

129

"Have you heard if it's going to be a big storm?" I asked.

"Oh, I think Jean-Gaby said it would be six inches or so." She sipped her martini. "And have you done your stint in the Army already, Jack?"

"Finished last year. I'm done unless something happens."

"I'm afraid we are all done if something happens," Helen said.

"Where's Anne?" I asked.

She leaned forward to put down her glass. "Mysteriously seeing her stepfather, who has flown out here. Something concerning her mother. I was not told."

"Oh," I said.

"So many problems," she said. "Racers shouldn't have personal problems. I've heard Jean-Gaby expostulate about that many times. Are you beset with problems too, Jack?"

"Just trying to get down the mountain faster than Chris."

She laughed again. Leary was drinking his beer in nervous sips, picking his mug up and putting it down with unnecessary motions. Someone came in the front door, stamping.

"Oh, there's Jean-Gaby!" Helen said. He came into the room, with snowflakes in his black hair, to shake hands with Leary and me. He bent to kiss Helen, who raised one of her ugly hands to touch his cheek.

He said, "Ah, the beautiful snow! When the snow descends, the soul rises up!" He illustrated.

"That's very poetic, darling!" Helen said.

He bowed to her, asked if anyone's glass was empty, and went out with Leary's mug and Helen's martini glass.

"Such a fine person," Helen whispered, gazing after him. "And trying so hard to find himself. Poor Jean-Gaby."

Embarrassed, Leary and I pretended we hadn't heard. A telephone rang distantly.

The German woman appeared; Mr. Roche was wanted on the telephone. I excused myself and was led to a little room off the entry, where there was a telephone on a desk, and above the desk a smiling photograph of Jean-Gaby and Helen with their arms around each other, holding skis.

It was Anne. "What's the matter?" I asked.

"Everything."

"What?"

"You're going to have to tell Helen I can't be there for dinner. I'll spend the night here too."

"Where? Spend the night where? With your step-father?"

"No. With Brownie. We're at the Palomino. It's a motel."

"Well, she's invited here, isn't she?"

"I don't think she'd better come tonight," Anne said.

"I thought you were seeing Bernand."

"That was earlier. He's gone now. He's divorcing my mother and he wanted me to help."

"Help?"

"He's going to divorce her because of adultery," Anne said in a dry voice. "He's afraid she'll countersue. He wanted me to give evidence against her."

"You wouldn't do that, would you? I don't—"

"No, but he thought I would," Anne broke in. "That I'd give evidence about certain things if he'd promise not to bring out others."

"The son-of-a-bitch!"

"No. He's not, Jack. He's just so furious at Mother."

"Because she—"

"With Figgy," Anne said. "It's because it was Figgy, and he hates Figgy so much."

"Well, I'm sorry," I said. "Can I do anything?"

"You can not be all stiff-necked with me the way you were Sunday night."

"All right. I'm sorry."

"Tell Helen I'm sorry about tonight."

"What about Brownie? Am I supposed not to mention she's here?"

I heard muffled voices speaking at the other end of the line. Then Anne said in my ear, "You can tell Chris she's here. I'm going to spend the night with her, but she's not feeling well and can't come over there. You can fix that."

"All right," I said. "How was your trip?" I hadn't meant to ask that. I wasn't going to say anything about Dixie Rigg.

"It was fine," Anne said.

"Listen, will we see you on the mountain tomorrow, or should we come over there, or what?"

"Come over in the morning," Anne said. "It's the Palomino Motel. Be sure Chris comes too," she said, and as she hung up I realized that she had sounded angry.

2

Jean-Gaby said, "But if the girl is sick perhaps we must do something."

"Anne would've said so if she needed help," I said.

They all looked at me, and I felt caught in a lie. Leary shifted his eyes to gaze at the wall of photographs. "Anne is a perfectly lovely girl," Helen said in a detached voice. The German woman came to say that dinner was ready.

At dinner Leary was very quiet while Jean-Gaby talked about the ways money was raised for the French ski teams. He inquired into Leary's financing, and mine.

Helen said, "So there is always someone to take care of you if you are good enough."

"That's right," I said.

"It's not just the money," Leary said. "They ought to fix it someway so you don't have a whole lot of other things to worry about beside training. It's hard enough to get to sleep just worrying about a race."

Helen's hand patted Leary's while Jean-Gaby waved his fork like a teacher's pointer. "In this country there is a difficulty," he said. "In this country the young men race for only this little while. Then one must go to work, one must begin to make one's place in the world. Skiing is only a game for these few young years. But in Europe it is enough to be a champion skier. Anything a champion. That is a worth-while thing, a fine thing. And when one can no longer race there are many fine employments to choose from in skiing.

"One is asked why there are no great ski champions in this country. It is so simple. It is because it is not enough to be a champion here. If one is to be champion it is this he must work for every moment. There is no time to prepare to be also a doctor or professor or any other thing. There is time for only this."

"That's right," Leary said.

"But what happens if you fall in love?" Helen asked in her soft voice. She smiled. "Here you are existing for this one very strict purpose—but what happens if you fall in love?" She looked from Jean-Gaby to Leary and raised her eyebrows inquiringly at me.

"I guess you can't afford to," I said.

Jean-Gaby said harshly, "One cannot afford it because women take the strength from the legs."

"You are talking about sex, Jean-Gaby. I was speaking of love."

I felt my face prickling. As though he hadn't noticed the reprimand Jean-Gaby said, "But it is very simple, my dear. One is already in love with racing and one does not fall in love twice at once."

She laughed and seemed to forgive him. "Is that true, Jack?" she asked. "That you are so in love with racing you have nothing left for some lovely girl you might meet?"

I didn't like her presuming to think she could tease me about Anne. Jean-Gaby said, "You embarrass these boys, my dear." He didn't say it pleasantly, and the corners of her mouth wrenched down in anger.

"But I'm trying to approach something important, darling," she said. "You have criticized this country because our racers are not cared for properly. Because there is no proper organization. I remember your telling me something of what Chris was saying just now—the intense concentration needed, in training as well as the races themselves. I would like to learn exactly what is needed to protect our racers from distractions—from money problems, from their draft boards, or—"

"It would be a very fine thing if this could be done," Jean-Gaby said. "Were you thinking of yourself, my dear?"

"Yes, I was. I was thinking of the way Elizabeth May helps the girls' teams. She contributes a great deal of her own money to their expenses. And I'm sure she must get a great deal of satisfaction for her money." Then she said in a cold voice, "And haven't you been thinking of *your*self, darling?"

He just looked at her.

"Of course, if I were to do this I wouldn't think of having anyone but you coach the boys. Men, I should say, shouldn't I? As Chris says, they should train summers in South America, and in Europe in the winter. You would be pleased to coach them, wouldn't you, darling?"

"But of course," Jean-Gaby said woodenly.

Leary was scowling and picking at the edge-cuts on his hands. Finally the German woman came with coffee.

When Helen brought up the subject of Brown again, Leary quickly rose, said he was dead-tired, and asked if he could go to bed. Helen went to show him his room, while I sat at the table with Jean-Gaby. We talked about racing; it was all we had in common.

"It is the very great need," he said. "The need to win. It is very important." He clenched a fist and shook it. "Always I had the need to win," he said. "And your friend has it. I think with luck he could be a great champion."

I nodded, with a bellyache of jealousy.

"With luck," Jean-Gaby repeated. "And not if he will only remain in this country. The competition is not enough, it is too easy for him here. He must go to Europe where he will be beaten and beaten, so he must *wish* and *wish* and *wish* more. To make more sharp this need. Here he wins too much."

I nodded again.

He said suddenly, "I do not wish to hurt you, Jack. I like you very much, and I do not much like your friend.

One does not like another who is too much like oneself. But I think he has in him this rare thing to be a champion."

If he meant I did not have the ability, maybe he was right; but if he meant I did not have the need, then he was wrong. I stared at the candleflames. Glowing through the wine in the bottoms of our glasses, they made little bloody spots on the tablecloth.

"Ah, Jack," Jean-Gaby said. "It is you who are the lucky one. For you will be able to live your life. Your friend will not."

"What about you?" I asked. My voice sounded as though I had a sore throat.

"Ah, I try," he said. "But it does not go well." He grinned and shook his head. "Not well."

I was conscious of his eyes studying me. I was feeling many things, none of them pleasant. After a while he said abruptly, "You have a little fear, I have noticed. I can see that. Chris has none. So one is built, so another. I have had this little fear also."

I nodded once more.

"Now I am a physician," Jean-Gaby went on. "I will tell you how to cure this little thing—no, not to cure, only how you must do so it will not hurt you. You will try what I tell you, and if it works for you, then you will tell me I am a good physician."

"Sure," I said and remembered him watching me on the downhill course at Sun Valley.

"With this little fear you must be very careful in the training. I think you must never make the training runs fast. Do you know why? Because the course is never as good in training as it will be for the race. It is always more difficult. So"—he raised a finger at me—"never at full speed. Because never you must frighten yourself with a bad fall in training, or almost a bad fall. Because then in the race, where you have fallen or have been frightened, there is this little thing in you to slow down at that place, when you must not slow down. I have seen you train much too hard; much. I have seen you fall, you have broken a ski, it could have been very bad. I think it

135

is there you have lost the downhill. The physician says
you must try this in training at least one time. Will you?"

"Sure!" I said. I was trembling. "Thanks. Sure, I know
that's where I lost the downhill. I checked at the top of
Exhibition. I—"

"Ah, did you?" Jean-Gaby broke in and looked pleased
with himself.

There was a quick rap of heels as Helen returned. We
rose for her. When we had seated ourselves again Jean-
Gaby said, "Brandy, my dear?"

She ignored him, leaning toward me to whisper, "Why
was he so upset, Jack?"

I licked my lips; I had thought he must have told her
already. "I guess he must have got a notice from his draft
board. Didn't—"

She shook her head impatiently. "That was just a
notice for a physical examination. He is a little worried he
might pass this time. No, I want to know why he was so
frightened when we were talking about Georgiana Brown."

"I don't know," I said. "Was he?"

Jean-Gaby had lit a cigarette and his eyes were slitted
against its smoke.

"Why would he be afraid of her?"

"I don't know," I said. "I don't think—"

"What kind of girl is she?"

"She's a terrific girl!" I said.

She leaned back, sighed. "Yes, I would like some
brandy, darling. Jack?"

"No, thank you."

Jean-Gaby rubbed out his cigarette and poured brandy
into two tiny silver glasses. I felt that they wanted to talk,
but not in front of me, and I wanted to think over what
Jean-Gaby had told me. I asked to be excused and said I
thought I had better get to bed too.

"Good night, Jack," Jean-Gaby said. "You will think
about what the physician has said?"

"I'm thinking about it right now," I said, and he looked
pleased again.

Helen led me up the stairs, which were quiet, with red
carpeting. Little brass triangles in the corners of the stairs

caught the light. But the second floor hallway was dark, and I could just make out the pale cloud of Helen's hair ahead of me.

"Here is your room, Jack." There was the click of a door opening, but still she didn't turn on a light.

I felt that she was standing very close to me, though I couldn't see her. I put my hands in front of myself; all at once I was sweating. But she whispered, "Good night." I sensed that she had moved away, and after a moment saw the shape of her at the head of the stairs.

I blundered inside the room, flipping my hand along the wall for the switch. Sweat trickled like snail tracks inside my shirt. The light came on, a milky glass ball that hung in the center of the room, which was small, with a dormer window and a single bed covered with a blue counterpane. I had started to close the door when Leary's voice whispered, "Jack!"

He came in, in his blue pajama bottoms. He closed the door and leaned back against it. "What the hell did Anne *say?*"

I told him.

"But what the hell's it all about?"

"I don't know." We stared at each other. Then I said, "Listen, what is it about the draft?"

His eyebrows met and humped together as he made a face. His eyes were reddened from the long drive. "Hell, I got a notice I was supposed to go for a physical, and I didn't. I'm kind of in trouble about it."

"For Christ sake!"

"She thinks she can fix it up. She knows a lot of people. I got by on my knee before, but I don't know if I'll make it again. And she knows this doctor that'll give me something so it sounds like I've got a heart murmur or something."

Anger came up in my throat. "Great!" I said.

"Well, why the hell not? I suppose you wouldn't have got out of it if there'd been somebody around to fix you up!"

I wondered if I would have. Perhaps I was only jealous because no one had tried to fix it for me; and because

Jean-Gaby thought Leary could be a great champion and didn't think I could.

"How the hell did Brownie get here?" Leary demanded.

"She probably got a ride with somebody coming out."

"Anne didn't say anything about her father bringing her or anything, did she?"

I realized that he did look scared. "What's the matter, Chris?"

He slumped against the door and blew out a long breath. "Nothing," he said. "Just—Christ, I don't know how you get so screwed up all at once. Listen, Jack, don't get mad at me, huh?"

"Hell, no. Why?"

I thought he was going to tell me what was wrong, but he changed his mind. "Hell, nothing's wrong," he said. "I'm just—I don't know—jumpy."

"Did she make a pass at you?" I asked.

"Who?" He scowled at me, and I jerked my head to indicate Helen. "What? Oh, hell, no. No, it's nothing like that. Say," he said, in a falsely hearty voice, "there's a three-way combined this weekend, remember? Tryout race. We've got to get to training." He made a queer, grasping gesture at his forehead, as though to pull out something that was protruding from it. "We're racing, remember?" he said. "Hell, I'd better let you get to bed."

He didn't move right away, blowing another long breath. Then he said, "Well, see you early," slipped outside and disappeared. The door clicked softly shut behind him.

3

They were in number five. With Leary a step behind me, I went down a roofed walk with my breath steaming in the early cold. I knocked on the door of number five, and Anne's voice called, "Who is it?"

"It's Jack."

She let us in. Her eyes were pleasantly swollen with

sleep. "Hello, darling," she said to me; she didn't speak to Leary. Round-bottomed and narrow-bodied in her long red underwear, she went back to sit on her twin bed, yawning and stretching her arms up. Brown was sitting up in the other bed. A gray suitcase was open like a clamshell.

"Hi, Brownie," Leary said.

"Hi, Chris," Brown said. Her freckles showed prominently; she had lost some of her tan. Leary and I took off our parkas, and I went over to sit on the bed beside Anne. She hugged me to her hard for a moment.

Leary stood looking down at Brown. They seemed to be having a silent conversation.

"Brownie's three months pregnant," Anne said.

"I just missed my third one," Brown said to Leary and drew her knees up to make a tent of the covers.

"You go to a doctor?" Leary said.

She shook her head.

I was trying to count back three months. It must have been at the beginning of the season, but we had been so many different places then—

Leary had turned slightly toward me, red-faced, his black toque in his hands.

"Well, I don't know what to do," Brown said apologetically.

"You didn't tell your father and mother yet, did you?" Leary asked.

"Oh, no," Brown said.

Suddenly I couldn't look at her any more. I felt like hitting someone.

Brown said, "I guess I wasn't really sure till I missed the third one. It should've come four or five days ago. But it didn't. So I was sure. I mean, you can't just go on the whole time thinking you're going to get it *next* month. I mean—well, I knew Nancy Erickson was coming out here so I just came out with her and some others." Her voice ran down.

"Got your walking cast, huh?" Leary said.

"Oh, yes," Brown said. She laughed a little. "It's so

139

kind of funny there are two things at the same time. I mean—isn't it? I mean, I can't ski for a year anyway."

"That's pretty lucky all right," I said.

"Little mother," Anne said humorously, gently, and Brown tried hard to smile at her. Something in my chest ached and moved. Anne said to Leary, "You can buy those things in any drugstore, didn't you know?"

Leary turned redder still.

"And I felt terrible about the Christmas presents *I* gave," Anne said.

"Was that when it was?" I asked.

He nodded.

"It wasn't anybody's fault," Brown said. "We just got carried away; you know how you get carried away."

"No, I don't know how you do," Anne said.

There was a silence, as though we were waiting for something to happen or someone else to arrive. Leary pulled and stretched at his cap. Finally Brown whispered, "I don't know what to do."

"You can't jump off tables with that ankle," Anne said.

"We've been talking about things to do," Brown explained to Leary. "I mean, how to miscarry—or getting an abortion."

"That's murder," Leary said. "You can't do that, that's murder."

"That's silly," Anne said.

"I thought you'd quit being a Catholic, Chris," Brown said.

Leary said, "Well, I guess we'd better—" He stopped, muscles bunching along his jaw. We waited, but he didn't go on.

"What about your folks?" I said to Brown, thinking about her father. Immediately I wished I hadn't brought it up.

Brown made a little O of her lips. "Oh, I was afraid to be there even. I was afraid they'd just look at me and see, some way. Oh, it's so nice to be here with all of you," she said.

I said to Leary, "What're you going to do about it?"

"I don't know what to do. I've got to think."

"Oh, I don't know what to do either," Brown said, as though excusing him.

"I can't even think right now," Leary said. He made the gesture as of pulling out something stuck in his forehead. "Christ!" he said to me. "There's a goddam race this weekend and we've got to go get our passes and stuff." He shook his head as though he was trying to clear it. "You'll be here, huh? I'll see you later, Brownie."

"Sure," Brown said. "Sure, I'll be here, Christy."

"Don't forget to come back," Anne said.

"What the hell do you think you mean?" Leary said in a weak bluster. He grimaced at me just as Brown made a warning face at Anne. "Come on, Jack," he said.

I rose and got back into my parka, while Anne stared at me meaningfully.

"Well, I'll see you later, Brownie. I've got to do some thinking," Leary said, but now he made no move to go on out, and there was another ugly, silent moment.

Brown threw back the covers and got out of bed in her pink and white flannelette pajamas. The rubber heel of her walking cast thumped on the floor. "Look!" she said and did a one-legged deep-knee bend, holding her left leg with the cast stiffly out before her. Coming up, panting, she said, "That's hard!"

She took a hobbling step over toward Leary. She caught hold of his arm, shook it once, and whispered, "Christy, I'm not going to be any trouble. I don't want to be any trouble."

He patted her shoulder. He looked sick. She hobbled back to the bed, moving her left leg with an awkward, sideways motion. Anne watched, her nostrils white in her tan face, sitting slumped on the bed, her breasts showing dull-pointed in her red underwear.

When Leary and I went outside, a truck with a blade on the front was scraping and jolting past in the street, pushing the new snow into a windrow along the curb. Dark-bellied clouds were still passing over, but it had stopped snowing.

"I'll let you off somewhere," Leary said as we got into the station wagon. "I've got to go do something."

"Do what?"

"Well, I've got to think, Christ sake!" He started the engine. Our breath frosted the inside of the windshield.

"All that great talk about being gentlemen and lady athletes in motels," I said. "I'll bet you were sick of it, all right."

"Where do you want off?" he said.

"Up by the Golden Horn, I guess. Where're you going?"

"I want to be by myself for a while." He turned up toward the center of town. He said in the blustering voice, "Don't try to crap me you never got into Anne's pants."

Everything turned pink and mushy in my eyes. For an instant I thought I was going to hit him.

" 'You can buy those things in any drugstore, didn't you know?' " he mimicked furiously.

"Shut up!" I said.

He didn't say anything more, and I closed my eyes and tried to understand what he must be feeling—trouble with his father, trouble with his draft board, and now this trouble. I remembered his telling me about the dream where he was trying to schuss but bumps on him or loose clothing kept catching the wind.

"Let me out here, will you?" I said.

He stopped the station wagon and sat staring straight ahead while I got my boots in their jack out of the back, and my poles and Vector downhills off the top rack. Then he drove away down the street.

4

All the other racers would be on Ajax, so I went up Bell to ski by myself. The new snow was almost knee deep on Back of Bell, and I ran down through the trees, enjoying the softly floating give of my skis in powder, in the lovely quiet. On pack there is always the rattle of your skis and the scrape of edges, but in powder all sound is muffled, and in that special silence you can listen to the pleasured beating of your heart, and everything is spotless and transformed with the snow covering it, and snow is crouched on the limbs of evergreens like friendly white animals with whiskers of pine needles. There is an almost frantic need to ski fast and wring from the powder the enjoyment while it is so intense.

They say that skiing fresh powder snow is like deflowering virgins. It is true that you always choose untracked snow to run through, to leave your tracks in, your mark on. There are places like the headwall at Squaw where you can see the linked vertical S's of your turns all the way from the lodge, and it is as though you have put the signature of your appreciation on nature, made your mark where no mark had existed. I wondered if Leary had some sort of feeling like that now about Brown, or if he only felt that she and nature had trapped him.

After a couple of runs I went up on top to come down Gentleman's Ridge, which was marked closed due to avalanche danger. It was a dirty trick on the ski patrol, who would have to sweep my trail to be sure I had gotten out, but there were no tracks at all here, and I had a lot of poison to ski out of my system. It was good to be away from the other skiers, swooping down the ridge and running flushes of trees like slalom gates, with powder rooster-tailing like spray behind a hydroplane when I made a hard turn.

Once I fell and slid a long way under the snow. I lay there for an instant, looking up at the faint light through the snow covering me. Then I sat up, spluttering, with powder in my mouth and burning down my neck and inside my gloves. Cleaning my glasses and slapping snow off my clothes, I thought about the time my father and I, cross-country skiing, had cut loose an avalanche. I was very young, but I was not frightened because I was with my father and because I knew the mountain crews often cut preventative avalanches with their skis. But afterward the sight always stayed with me —the slow parting behind my father's skis, like thick cloth cut by scissors, the snow starting to roll, and, as it picked up speed, the sudden dark rocks showing in it. When my mother died I went again to where we had started the avalanche. I was twelve then, and I thought I would cut it loose again and this time go down with it, to die in my grief in that wild tumble of snow and rocks. Alone and frightened, I realized that I felt no grief that my mother was dead, that all I felt was the knowledge that I too had to die someday, and I still held that avalanche in reserve, as my private property, until the day when my doctor would tell me I had cancer or that my heart was bad, or whatever it would be for me.

Feeling lonely now, instead of pleasantly alone, I skied down off the ridge and ran very fast through the cut-up powder of Copper Bowl and went over onto Ajax. The girls were on Ruthie's Run, but I didn't see Anne with them. On top I met Bruce Carrington skiing with Bill Birks. This was the first big race Bruce had been to since he had started pre-med.

We shook hands. "You and Chris've been having everything your own way this year," he said. "I thought you needed a little real competition."

I caught myself worrying that he would be able to beat me now, even out of training, as he had always done when we were juniors. I asked him how school was, and he said it was damned dull during ski season. Dodo Gayley was engaged to a fraternity brother of his, he said. I asked if they'd seen Leary.

He shook his head. Bill said, "We just got up. What a lift line!"

Bruce pushed his goggles up on his forehead and looked at me with his hard blue eyes. "When're you going to take one away from him, Jack? You're about due, aren't you?"

"I'm sure due," I said. "Let's make a run, shall we?"

They deferred to me, and I started down Ruthie's.

I skied with Bruce and Bill, and looked for Leary, until noon. Then I went down, left my skis at the ski shop, and walked to the Palomino Motel. When Anne let me in she looked furious. Brown was still in her pajamas, lying face down on the bed with one arm hanging and her fingers plucking at the nap of the blue shag rug beside the bed.

"What's the matter?" I asked Anne.

"Where's your friend?"

"I thought he might've come here."

"He hasn't," Anne said. "He sent Helen instead."

"You don't know that for sure," Brown said in a muffled voice.

"Who did then?"

"Maybe Jack did."

"I didn't," I said, not understanding. "For what? To ask you to come stay at her house?"

"Not exactly," Anne said. She said to Brown, "It had to be Chris."

"Oh, I guess so," Brown said.

"What did she want?" I asked.

"I'd gone to make a phone call, and when I came back Helen was here," Anne said. "I wasn't wanted, so I went on up to the ski club. When I came back again she was gone. With her knitting needle."

"With her what?"

"That's a figure of speech," Anne said. Brown turned over on her back. Her face was red and swollen, her eyes swollen, as though someone had hit her. She raised her left leg and stared at the cast.

"Can you get dehydrated from crying?" she asked in a small voice. "I hate crybabies," she said. "I'm such a miserable crybaby."

"Listen, what happened?" I asked.

"She meant to help," Brown said. "She meant to help Christy anyway."

"She wants Brownie to have an abortion," Anne explained. "She had it all arranged, the doctor and everything. No strain, no charge, no——"

"I guess I seem awfully stupid," Brown said.

145

I sat down in the chair at the little desk. Brown let her cast fall to the bed with a thud. She said, "Maybe she meant to help and she just got mad because I— Oh, I don't know. But I hated her so."

"She got mad?"

"She called me stupid. She called me a scheming little idiot. She was awfully mad." Her voice shook a little. "Is—is Chris sleeping with her, Jack?"

"No," I said. "I don't think so. No."

Anne's face was full of pity. She bared her chipped tooth at me in an angry smile.

Brown said, "Her hands are so ugly. Have you ever seen her hands? They're horrible. He isn't, is he, Jack?" she asked.

"He wouldn't do that."

Anne said, "She must be so used to running people. But she couldn't run our Brownie."

"Maybe it was just stupid and contrary of me," Brown said. "Anne, it was what—it was what we'd kind of decided to do anyway. I don't want Chris to marry me if he doesn't want to. I mean, I know it's the obvious— I guess it's the only thing to do. But she was so horrible about it."

"Well, I'm proud of you," Anne said in a husky voice. "Somebody told me once I could be the best skier in the world if I only had your downhill guts. Was it your downhill guts, Brownie?"

"I don't have any downhill guts!" Brown cried. "It's all a fake! Anyway, you wouldn't have been proud of me. I just got hysterical. You know, I know people walk all over me a lot. But mostly I don't care. I don't know what got my back up so this time. She was just trying to help Chris. Do you think I'm stupid, Jack?"

"No," I said. "I think you're great."

"Great with child," Anne said.

Brown laughed and sobbed at the same time. I thought about Leary hinting to Helen Michonneau about Portillo, asking Helen to get him out of trouble with the draft board, and now to get him out of trouble with Brown. I thought of him saying, "Don't get mad at me, Jack."

"It's probably the only sensible thing to do," Brown said. "It's what Anne and I'd decided I had to do anyway. But I kept thinking: the poor little thing, what'd it ever do to make everybody want to kill it. Oh, Anne, of course I know it's not a poor little thing, it's nothing yet. But I thought: what if they *did* something, you know, *taking* it, so I was all wrecked up inside and I couldn't ever have any babies. My Aunt Irene has something wrong with her so she and Uncle Robbie couldn't ever have babies, and she's a terrible person, with little yappy dogs and— All of a sudden I got so afraid of being like that. And she kept after me and after me. It was like having somebody pushing you—pushing you so you'd be off balance and right away pushing you again. She wouldn't listen to anything I said. I don't even want to think about it any more."

"She's pretty bad," I said.

"I wish you'd stayed here, Anne. It wouldn't have been so bad if you'd stayed here."

"Maybe it would have been worse," Anne said.

There was a silence. Finally Brown said, "You know, if Chris had come and asked me, I would've done it."

"Would you?" Anne said.

"Yes."

"But now you won't."

"No, I won't. You know, maybe I was so mad because he didn't have the guts to come himself. And I won't do it now. I just won't!"

"Then what're we going to do?" Anne asked.

"I don't know," Brown whispered.

5

I finally caught up with Leary on the No. 3 lift. He was on the platform in his black toque and parka, and I pushed up along the line and was glared, muttered, and yelled at for a crasher. But I managed to make the chair with Leary. "Where've you been?" I said, as we swung up off the platform.

"Skiing the mountain," he said. He wouldn't look at me. "There happens to be a goddam important race this weekend."

"The race must go on," I said. "That's the human race."

"That's really funny," Leary said. "Ha! Ha!" He was sitting on the handles of his poles, with the baskets stuck out ahead of him. His hands, in black finger-gloves, were doubled into fists. Our chair climbed up above the soft points of the evergreens.

"See Helen yet?" I asked.

"What do you mean, have I seen Helen yet?"

"Since she went to see Brownie."

He shook his head once.

"Well, Brownie won't do it."

He shrugged, his lips tucking into a thin, down-slanted line.

"So what're you going to do?" I said.

"Goddam it, I'm going to race this weekend!" He began to seesaw his skis. "Goddam it, what am I supposed to do, just be a stupid jerk and marry her? Well, I'm not going to do it!"

"You've got to," I said. I said it in anger, but it sounded phony, and my anger too seemed phony. Maybe I was sorrier for Brown, but I was sorry for him too.

"The hell I have to!" he said through his teeth. Then he said, "Listen, what the hell would my father say if I did? And Mike. They think I'm a playboy already. Well, I don't give a damn what they think. But I care what I think. I mean, if I did that, it'd mean the whole thing really didn't matter so much as I'd made out." He turned to look at me almost pleadingly. "Jack, if I do it, everything comes apart. Can't you see?"

In a way I saw. But I said, "Listen, I don't know how you feel about her or anything. But there're only two more tryout races. She'd be having the baby before next ski season, so if you married her, and you wanted to, you could check out then, couldn't you? But the baby'd have a father and all that. And Brownie'd have a hell of a lot easier time of it."

Leary tipped his Kaestles up and down, shaking his head. "I can see that letter from my stepmother," he said. He gazed up along the line of lift towers. "Yeah, summer's coming," he said. "But I've got to get down to Portillo this summer. I mean, the kid has to be supported someway. And *she* does. That's the hook they catch you with—I can see that letter now. No. I mean, if you stick yourself with trying to do the fair thing, then you're stuck all the way. You've got to be consistent."

I didn't say anything, and he continued, "Sure, I've really got her screwed up. But the only way out is for me to screw myself forever to fix it. So I'm not going to."

"You said the other day you were sick of being a bastard," I said.

"I can stand it," he said in a hard voice. "Listen, Jack, I'm just not going to screw myself out of the only thing—the only thing I've— I'm not going to wreck everything just to make it easier for Brownie." He paused, then said in a different voice, "Do you think I wouldn't take it out on her forever, how she ruined my goddam life? And the baby too?"

That was something Helen had told him. I could almost hear her soft, insistent voice saying it. "That's shit," I said.

"All right," Leary said quickly. "Maybe it is. But I won't do it to myself, Jack."

The lift leveled off for a way, then began to climb steeply. Last year I had been riding with Brown here, and we had watched Leary and Anne disappear into the cloud.

"You know what I can do?" Leary said loudly. "I can shut it right out of my head. I can block it right out. It's Wednesday, and there's a GS and slalom and downhill this weekend to think about. That's what I have to think about, and I can shut Brownie's being pregnant and all that right out. I guess that makes me a real bastard."

"I don't know," I said. "It's just that it's such a hell of a thing for her. You never met her father, did you?"

"I can't even think about it till this weekend's over," he said. "I mean, I'm not going to. Sure it's a hell of a thing for her, and it's my fault. But I'm not even going to think about it." We came up onto the flat top of the mountain, approaching the get-off ramp. Skiers wedelened down the slope, beneath our skis. "Anyway," Leary said. "She had her chance."

We slid off the ramp and stopped. I leaned on my poles, facing him. "What do you mean, she had her chance?"

"Well, I don't know what happened between her and Helen. But Helen had it all fixed up. She knows this doctor that would do it, and she was going to pay for everything."

"This the same doctor that's going to fix you up for your physical? He must really be a great guy."

Leary's face turned dark red.

"If you're going to be consistent, be consistent," I said. "You said it was your fault. You're goddam right it's your fault. Don't try to blame her for anything."

He stared at me, his eyes hidden by his dark glasses and his mouth tucked into the tight line. Finally he said, "Okay."

"Okay," I said.

"But it doesn't change anything. I'm not going to— marry her. You might as well get that straight. I can't do it."

"Okay," I said again.

He looked relieved. "Let's take a run," he said. "Let's go find some powder."

I followed him down.

6

Brown was alone at the motel, sitting in the chair with her cast propped up on the bed. She wore cut-off Levis and a moccasin on her good foot. There was now, as there always had been, an uneasiness when we were alone together. It was hard not to look at her bare legs. I bent over to examine the cover of the paperback she had been reading and asked how it was. And she asked how the skiing was.

"Where's Anne?" I asked. "I didn't see her on the mountain this afternoon."

"Well, I told her she ought to go, but she wouldn't." As though she didn't want to say it, she said, "Well, she went to rent a U-drive and pick somebody up at the airport."

"Dixie Rigg?" I asked.

She nodded. "It's a funny name, isn't it?"

"He's a Texan with oil wells."

"And his own plane. Anne told me." She smoothed her hands over her thick, shining, reddish-brown hair; she wore on her ponytail the clasp I'd given her for Christmas. She smiled uncertainly at me. "Did—did you see Chris up on the mountain?"

"We skied together this afternoon."

"Oh." She nodded. "Good."

I sat down on Anne's bed across from her.

"Where would you like to eat dinner, Brownie?"

"Oh, you don't have to take me out to dinner. I didn't come here to be a big stupid burden on everybody. Aren't you supposed to be eating over at Mrs. Michonneau's?"

"I don't want to eat there. I want to take you out to dinner. Listen, Brownie, don't talk as though nobody would want to take you out to dinner."

"Well, but let me take *you*. Since we are kind of alone. I've got some money."

"I've got plenty of money. Where do you want to go?"

"I don't want to see Mrs. May or Alice or Lorraine or anybody. Can we go to that place in a cellar where we went last spring and ate spaghetti?"

"Sure," I said.

"Jack," Brown said, "let's not talk about Christy, okay?"

"Okay. Or about Anne either."

Her eyes looked sideways at me, half frightened. But she smiled and said, "Well, okay! Should I dress up?"

"Have you got just a sweater and skirt? I can't change without going back to Helen's."

"You look fine," she said, pushing herself up. "Would you take my suitcase into the bathroom, Jack? I'll get changed in there."

"You change here, and *I'll* go in there." I went into the bathroom, closed the door, and laughed at my face in the medicine-cabinet mirror. I had seen Brown change her clothes many times. Traveling on the circuit, none of us had been embarrassed to be seen in our underclothes. I tried to laugh at myself and Brown about it, and I tried not to think about Anne meeting Dixie Rigg at the airport.

Brown called, "Okay, you can come out, Jack."

She was standing before the mirror over the decaled blond bureau, brushing her hair. She had on a quilted skirt, a green stocking on her good leg, and the jacket Leary had given her. She was pleasantly round. She fixed her ponytail and bent closer to the mirror as she put on lipstick.

"Can you feel anything?" I asked.

Her eyes met mine questioningly in the mirror.

"I mean the baby."

"Oh! Oh, no. I guess it's awfully tiny yet. I feel a little thicker here, is all." She made a gesture toward the front of herself. "But I can't tell what I weigh because of the cast."

"Do you get sick in the mornings or anything like that?"

She had finished her mouth, but she still stood facing

the mirror, so that I was talking to her reflection. "Well, I threw up a few times," she said. "But do you know? I worried so much I think I worried myself sick. I'd wake up early in the morning and it would be so bad I'd start to cry. And sometimes I'd get sick."

"Stop worrying," I said, and her eyes looked at me again.

"I'd better write a note for Anne," she said, turning toward the desk to find paper and pen. She fixed the note to the frame of the mirror. "It's so great to be in a walking cast," she said. "You should have seen me clobber on my crutches once, going upstairs at home. Right over backward."

"Do you want me to get a cab?"

"Oh, I'm fine if we take it easy."

We walked downtown, keeping to the back streets so we wouldn't meet any of the other racers. Ajax, where the downhill course was, loomed ghostly pale over Aspen.

It was slow going for Brown down the narrow stairs to the cellar, where a piano was playing beside a tiny dance floor. It wasn't crowded yet. We sat down in a booth in the corner, a fat waitress came and lit two candles stuck in bottles, and we ordered beer. When the waitress had gone I blew out one of the candles.

"That's better," Brown said. "I like it dark too."

"I guess you won't feel neglected if I don't ask you to dance."

She laughed. The waitress came back with glasses and bottles of beer.

"I suppose I'll get tight," Brown said as I poured beer into her glass. "Such a damn big emotional mess of a day. It was really terrible this morning. I'm still all shaky."

"Go ahead and get tight."

"Do you know? I've never really been tight."

"Haven't you?"

"I've always been scared to, I guess." In the hurried, talking-too-much way she had when she was nervous, she rushed on to say, "I wouldn't be afraid to get tight with you, though."

"Thanks," I said.

"Do you know what? This friend of mine and I were talking about you once. Do you know what she said? She said you were the only person she knew who wasn't always pushing and worrying and trying to— I think she said you'd never crash a lift line to get ahead of other people. She said you were the only person she knew who understood other people, and it was because you weren't always thinking about how to crash the lift line. You know, she didn't really mean a lift line, she meant—" She waved a hand.

I poured myself some more beer. Brown hadn't touched her glass yet. "I thought you were going to get tight," I said.

"Oh, that's right." She picked up her glass; but instead of drinking she held it against her cheek as though to cool herself. "Do you know why I've never been tight really?" she said in a strained voice. "I was just afraid somebody'd catch me, and not being twenty-one. I've always been afraid of so many things! I don't think other people are afraid as much as I am."

"What about your downhill guts?" I said.

"I wish people wouldn't keep talking about that. I don't think anybody else gets as scared before a downhill as I do."

I remembered Leary talking about her fit of hysterics before the downhill at Stowe. I'd seen her too, a number of times before a race, her freckled face gray with fright under her white helmet, her mouth twitching. But until Stowe she had been able regularly to beat all the girls who were not frightened or who concealed their fright better. And at Stowe she must at least have suspected she was pregnant. I watched her sip her beer.

"Shall we eat now?" I asked.

"Let's eat now."

I flagged the waitress, and we ordered spaghetti. A man with a string bass had joined the piano player, and there were four couples in ski clothes dancing. "I wish we could dance," Brown said.

154

"When do you get your cast off?"

"Oh, a long time yet," she said vaguely.

We sat in an uncomfortable silence until the waitress brought us oblong plates heaped with spaghetti and sauce, and garlic bread and salad. I ordered a half bottle of red wine. But still it was hard to talk. Everything I would think of to say seemed to have Leary or Anne in it, and I knew that Brown was having the same trouble. When we had finished, the waitress cleared away the dishes and brought coffee. Brown sat intently stirring cream and sugar into her cup.

I said, "Listen, back at the motel I said I wanted to take you out to dinner, and you said I didn't have to. You remember?"

She nodded.

"Well, don't do that. I wouldn't ask you to come out to dinner if I didn't want to."

"Yes, you would," Brown said in a stubborn voice. "You would because you feel sorry for me. I'm not saying you *didn't* want to," she added.

"I don't want you saying things like that though."

"All right," she said. She looked puzzled.

I took a deep, shaky breath and said, "Because I'm going to ask you to marry me and I don't want you saying, 'Oh, you don't have to do that.'"

She didn't move or look at me. There was a creamy curve of candlelight on her cheek, which shook with the trembling of the candle flame. After a time she folded her hands in front of her and said, "That's so funny. I was going to ask *you*."

"We ought to make it pretty soon, I guess."

She nodded quickly. "People are so good at counting months." She still wouldn't look at me. "It's so funny," she said. "I was trying to get up my nerve to ask if you'd marry me just till the baby came. I just didn't have the nerve." She managed to smile. Finally she brushed her eyes past mine. "Yes. I will," she said.

"Okay."

"I was going to say, 'Jack, I'm in this terrible trouble

155

and I don't know what to do. Could you just be married to me till September?' But you can't ask someone to do something like that. Oh, Jack!"

"I was afraid we were going to have to sit around and argue about it," I said. I moved my hand across the table toward her. She looked at it as though she didn't know what it was for. Then she clutched it with her small, hard hand.

"Oh, Jack, thanks."

"Everything's going to come out all right," I said.

"Oh, Jack," Brown said in a blurred voice. She squeezed my hand once more and released it. "Sure, I'll marry you, buddy. Jack, I won't be any trouble. I'll just go home and watch TV till you get through with the circuit. You just come and see me sometimes. You know, for appearances. And then if you'd be there when the baby comes. And then—" She stopped.

I said, "We'd better get busy and decide when we're going to get married and then what we're going to do. Maybe as soon as the races are over this weekend. I'll skip the Alta race and we can go home and get things fixed up out there. We ought to be talking about it."

"Just like regular—people," Brown said. "Getting married, I mean." Her eyes were very bright and round. She leaned forward. "You know what? You're going to win the Roch this weekend. You'll win it, and I'll pretend you won it for me."

"Well, I'll win it for you then," I said. I laughed, but all at once I was sure I was going to win it. It was a breath-quickening feeling, it was solid, it had no shaky edges to it. Trying to think about it coolly, I felt even surer. I had been pushing Leary harder and harder, and sometime I was going to pass him. There had been a barrier I had to break through, and now it was gone. It was gone because Jean-Gaby had made me realize just how much I wanted to win by telling me that I did not want to win enough, and he had handed me the razor with which to shave off those few tenths of a second that won or lost races. And yet that wasn't all. It was as though, by marrying Brown, I was seizing an advantage, pushing myself

156

to the head of the lift line Anne had thought I would not crash, found a secret that, although it cut no tenths-of-seconds off my time, in the end would add them to Leary's, like those bumps and loose clothing that slowed him in the schuss in his dream. But the certainty that I was going to win pushed that unpleasant part back to the edges of my mind.

Brown said, "Well, shouldn't we just elope, Jack? Just go off and get married?"

"Whatever you want. We could go home and have a big wedding if you want."

"Oh, wouldn't that be silly with my ankle? And the bride wore a lovely white cast with rosebuds painted—" Her face sobered. "Oh, no, it wouldn't be fair to let Daddy spend all that money."

I was thinking about her father too. I remembered Leary asking if he had brought her to Aspen. He was frightened of Mr. Brown as in New York he had been frightened of meeting his brother, who was going to give him a bad time. He had no fear, Jean-Gaby had said; but he was afraid of these things, while I was not. I poured the rest of the wine into our two glasses, and we made a silent toast.

"I guess your father's not going to be very pleased," I said.

"He'd be a lot less pleased if I didn't get married," Brown said. It seemed a very good joke, and we both laughed. Then she looked worried. "Daddy's going to be the bad part," she said in a low voice. "He might be pretty—mean. To you, Jack."

"That's all right."

"There's no way they won't know why we got married," Brown said, "I mean *think* they know. I mean, I'll have to go to the doctor and they'll have to know when the baby's due. I can cheat a little, but nowhere near enough. But maybe that just makes it easier."

"You can play it by ear."

"It really is easier if you don't lie," Brown continued earnestly. "I mean—it is, isn't it? It's just that when you get scared you lie. Scared people always lie. Have you noticed that? It's the other way too; liars are scared people. I've been just a terrible liar. And I'm a bad liar so I'm always getting caught. I don't have to be that way with you, do I, Jack?"

"Hell, no!" I said.

Unhappily she whispered, "But what about Anne? What'll Anne say?" Before I could reply she said almost pleadingly, "But it's only till September or so."

"We weren't going to talk about them."

"I'm sorry. Okay."

When I thought about Anne I had a poisoned, shameful feeling that somehow, before I had beaten Leary, I had beaten her. And as the band finished a number, and the rhythmic sound of dancing changed into a confused shuffling of feet on the dance floor, Brown whispered, "Jack, here she comes!"

I turned to see Anne and Dixie Rigg coming across toward us. I wished that Brown hadn't left the note and that they hadn't come; but there they were. Anne's hair shone like blended silver and gold in the candlelight. I rose to shake hands with Dixie Rigg.

"Well now, you two folks," he said as Anne introduced him to Brown. They sat down with us, Anne beside me. Her hand caught mine and squeezed it, between us on the seat, to reassure me. Dixie Rigg wore a brown suit, checked shirt and bow tie, and his black hair was neatly combed into two thick waves so that he resembled a bighorn sheep. "Well, what are we all drinking here?" he demanded as the waitress came over.

She was bringing our bill. He took it from her. "Here, I'll take care of that. We're going to be drinking with these folks now. What are you drinking, honey?" he said to Anne.

"Maybe we'd better have champagne," I said.

He looked at me with his eyebrows hooked over black buttons of eyes. Brown had turned her face down.

"Hadn't we better announce it?" I asked her. She wouldn't raise her head. I said, "Well, Brownie and I are going to get married."

"Well now, you kids!" Dixie Rigg said. "Well, that is

nice! Honey," he said to the waitress, "you bring us the finest bottle of champagne you have got, hear?"

Anne's hand caught mine again. Her fingernails cut into my flesh. Brown looked up at her as she said, "Why, of course! It's perfect!" And then she said something I didn't understand: "Dixie, I made you come for nothing."

"Not for nothing! Don't be silly, honey! This is an occasion I am happy to be in on, I sure am. These nice friends of yours. Why, this is wonderful—you two kids!"

"When did you decide this?" Anne asked.

"Just now," I said.

"What do you think, Anne?" Brown said in a low voice.

"I think it's wonderful. Where's that champagne, Dixie? I want to drink a toast."

"That fat girl is real slow, isn't she? Maybe I ought to help her along." He left the table, saying, "You folks pardon me, I'll try and get some action here."

I leaned back in the booth. Beside me Anne was sitting up very straight, her fingers picking at the top button of her sweater. She was smiling at Brown. She said, "It is the right thing. I never even thought of it."

Brown looked miserable.

"I think it's wonderful," Anne said. "Brownie, I'm so —glad for you." When she turned toward me the candlelight made circles of shadow of her eyes. "I'm a prophetess, did you know? And I see you will be happy ever after." She raised a finger and made a mysterious signature in the air. "So be it," she said.

"Anne," Brown whispered, "it's just till the baby comes. It's just till September—"

Dixie Rigg returned with a silver-capped bottle of champagne in a bucket, followed by the waitress with glasses. He made a big noise twirling the bottle in the ice and being officious and jerk Texas, but it was hard to dislike him. He bounced the cork off the ceiling, poured the champagne, and Anne raised her glass for a toast.

"To the dearest people I know—I've ever known!" Her voice began to shake. "To the very best people I've ever known, long lives and happiness and good—and good—"

She stopped and put her glass to her lips. I heard the click as the edge tapped her teeth.

"That's a fine toast, honey," Dixie Rigg said. "Hear! Hear!" People in nearby booths were craning their necks at us and smiling. "Let's all drink up now," Dixie said. "I've got a little toast here too."

He poured champagne into his own glass—no one else needed any—and said, "Well now, this toast is: Here is *cham*pagne to your friends, and pain to your *sham* friends." He beamed.

"That's very nice, Dixie," Anne said.

He leaned his elbows on the table and fixed his eyes on me. "Well now, Jack, I don't mean to butt in where it's not my business, but what's the plan here? Have you got a plan yet?"

"We were just talking it over when you came in."

"Can I put in for maid of honor?" Anne said.

"Oh, yes," Brown said. "Oh, yes, please." Then she fell silent, and I knew she was thinking of Leary, as I was. Anne pushed her empty glass toward Dixie Rigg.

"I'll ask Chris to be best man," I said.

Brown licked her lips. Dixie refilled Anne's glass. He said, "I have got this little old Beechie sitting down at the airfield, and we would certainly be pleased to offer our services. She is slow but comfortable, and she can take five, six people without a bit of strain. So if there is any place I could take you kids—how'd you like to go to Hawaii to get married? Or Acapulco, that's better yet. I have got a friend in Acapulco, he likes to really spread it around; I'll bet he would do things proud for you two kids. Now let me think where else—you got any ideas, honey?"

"Acapulco sounds wonderful," Anne said. "But it's their wedding, Dixie."

"Why, of course it is. I'm the biggest horner-inner there ever was—I've been told it a thousand times. Don't you two let me bulldoze you into anything. But I sure would like to help, honey," he said to Anne.

The piano and the bass went into action with a heavy

beat and a silver tinkling of notes. Couples began moving out onto the little dance floor.

"Do you mind if I dance with your fiancé?" Anne asked suddenly.

"Oh, no!" Brown said. "No, you—" She stopped. I got up.

"Well, if you're sure you don't mind," Anne said.

We left the booth to dance to the slowly pulsing music. The piano player drank from a bottle of beer while a girl in tight green stretchpants leaned on his piano and talked to him. Anne's fingers touched the hairs at the back of my neck.

"What a silly thing to do," she said softly.

"No, it's not."

"Of course it's not." She was as light a dancer as she was light on her skis. "Did you know I phoned Dixie and asked him to come?"

"Did you?"

She laughed in my ear. "It's so funny. Because Chris went running to Helen. And I went running to call Dixie for the same thing."

"What same thing?"

"To get Brownie fixed. I knew he'd have the connections, the know-how. He keeps talking about know-how. But you had the know-how this time, didn't you?"

We circled past our booth, where the champagne bottle lay tilted in its bucket. Brown, her hand to her cheek, was nodding to something Dixie was saying.

"I never thought you were clever before," Anne said. "But you saw the things all the clever people missed when they panicked and went to call for help from their influential friends."

The beat of the music changed to a faster tempo, but we stayed close together so we could talk. Anne whispered in my ear, "But you love *me*, don't you? You love *me!*"

"Yes."

"Say it, please."

"I love you."

"You can love Brownie a little, just so you love me the most. Always the most. Will you love me always, Jack?" She laughed in a whisper. "It won't cost you anything to say it."

"I guess I will," I said. I didn't know if I would love her always or not, but I loved her now. Her fingers stroked lightly up the hairs at the back of my neck.

"That's such a cheap trick," she whispered. "I'm not usually as cheap as that, am I? Does it give you an erection?"

I didn't answer, and she stopped doing it. She said, "Well, you'll get a divorce in the fall after the baby and everybody's going to think you're a terrible heel. Will you mind?"

"I guess not."

"I'll divorce Dixie after a year or so," she said. "Maybe you and I can get married then. I'll get a big settlement. I won't stay married to you though. I'm going to marry lots of times, and I'll get big settlements every time the way Helen did—not like Mother. And I'll be one of the ten best-dressed women in the country. Wait and see. But in between times we can see each other. Would you like that?"

"Are you going to marry him?" I asked. I felt as though I were smothering.

"I think I might. It's funny how things make you decide. Like you and Brownie."

"Anne, don't do it because of that."

"It was mean of me to say that. Do you know what it is mostly?"

"What?"

"Mother's gone back to Figgy, and there's going to be a terrible mess in court. Because Roger's been playing around too. And I can't help him the way he wants—if I did Mother wouldn't get any money and then probably Figgy would walk out on her. But I can't do that. But then I can't go home. I won't have any place to go."

I looked at the bits of light caught in her hair. "Why not?"

"Figgy's pretty terrible. I'm afraid of him. I really am afraid of him."

"What'd he do to you?" I said thickly.

"Well, when I was a little girl—when Mother was married to him—I had to sleep in the same bed with them. That was what he wanted, and Mother was so crazy about him she'd make me do anything he wanted. And after they'd got a divorce even."

"I'll kill him!" I whispered.

She moved a little away from me. Her eyes examined my face; she looked very grave. All at once she shook her head. "No," she said. "I'm lying. Jack, I'm just the way I am. It's nobody's fault. Please, you're to forget what I said then." She moved close to me again. "But I think I will marry Dixie," she said. "You know, he's what I always said I wanted. Isn't he like Santa Claus in a way? He is funny and Texas, but he's sweet and dear and he loves me. Anyway he says he does. Tell me it's all right."

"No," I said. "He's too old and—"

"Do you know what happened? When I called him up to tell him I wanted to help Brownie I thought the operator might be listening, so I tried to be roundabout telling him what was wrong. Do you know what he thought? He thought *I* was pregnant. Isn't that wonderful!" She trembled against me when she laughed. "And he had business to do, some very important deal, but he flew right out. He said, 'Say, sounds like they've got you between a rock and a hard place, honey,' and he came right away. He was going to fly me to Mexico City where there's a wonderful doctor who does things like this. And he was disappointed he couldn't help *me*."

"We'd better go back to the table," I said.

"They can wait till the set is over. Brownie won't mind. After all, we're saying good-by."

I didn't ask if Dixie Rigg would mind.

"But it's not good-by at all," Anne continued. "I'm going to see you all my life, see you and see you. Jack, I am a prophetess. Anything you do will come out right."

"Everything you do will come out right too, Anne," I said.

"Oh, no," she said. "No, I don't think so. It will all look lovely and shiny, but it will just end up in a mess." Suddenly she said in a sober voice, "I'm hysterical, aren't I? I'm on a talking jag."

We danced in silence for a little longer, and then the set was over. Anne took my arm as we went slowly back to the booth. "Do you know?" she whispered. "I'm sorry for Chris Leary." She smiled at Dixie as he rose, and there was no time to say anything more.

"Why, you two kids didn't do any dancing at all," Dixie said. "You just walked around. I thought you were a real high-flyer, honey. Well, it's pretty thin music here, I guess."

"We were only going through the motions while we talked," Anne said. "I was telling Jack that if he isn't good to Brownie, I'm going to make a wax figure of a big Norden oaf and stick pins in his legs."

"Oh, stop it, Anne," Brown said. "Please don't make a *thing* out of it. You know it's just till——" She made motions with her hands.

"Can't I kid Jack a little?"

"You've been kidding him too much. He doesn't look very happy."

"I'm happy!" I protested.

"Yeah, let's all get happy here!" Dixie Rigg said as he leaned over to pour champagne in our glasses. "Come on now, you racers have to drink up. We have got to whup things up here happywise. We will finish this bottle and then we're going over to the Jerome where the music is not so damn thin and do some real dancing—for a starter. Now drink up here!"

"Jack and Anne have to race this weekend," Brown said. "They have to get to bed, Dixie."

Dixie scowled at her and growled at me. "Fine, full-blooded boy like you isn't going to let himself get sent off to bed the night he has just got himself fixed to get married, is he?" He aimed a finger at Anne. "And that little lady there—I bet you she could party every single night and be even world-beatinger than she already is. Isn't that right, honey?"

"Right!" Anne said.

"And besides," he said to Brown, "we have got to get your wedding plans fixed up, lil cripple girl. We have got to decide on Acapulco or—hey!" He snapped his fingers. "Billy Weaver. He is singing at one of those places on the strip at Vegas. He's a *real* good friend of mine. We could really have a time in Vegas. That appeal to you, honey?"

"I don't know," Brown said. "Oh, I don't know!" Suddenly she covered her face with her hands.

"Dixie," Anne said, "not too boisterous."

He turned painfully red. "Oh, I am sorry," he said. "Please, you must all boot me in the pants if I get too big-mouth. Please do that for me."

Brown said, "It's just that—it's just that I don't want everything to move too fast."

"Honey," Dixie said, "I know just how you feel. You drink up now and everything'll slow down."

We drank up. When the bottle was finished Dixie insisted that we go to the Jerome. Brown and Anne went off to put on lipstick, and I went to the men's room while Dixie paid the bill. Presently he joined me at the urinal. "That's a fine little girl you've got there, young fellow."

"Yes, she is," I said. I zipped my pants. Something was needed, and I said reluctantly, "Anne's a fine girl too."

"She sure is that."

When I was drying my hands on the blower, Harry Butler and Dan Arganbright came into the men's room. "Hello, Roche," Harry said. "Hey, Roche, what's this we hear, you and Patterson're getting hooked? Champagne corks shooting off, all this getting married talk; no snow?"

"Brownie and I," I said loudly.

"*Georgie* Brown?" Danny said.

I introduced them to Dixie Rigg to try to get them off the subject. "How do, sir," Harry said as they shook hands. He said to me, "*Brownie?* What the hell is this, mixed doubles?"

Dixie Rigg stood by with his brown face flat and secret like an Indian in a western movie.

"Brownie and me," I said to Harry. "Now you're getting hold of it. Why aren't you guys home in bed? You call yourselves racers?"

"We ought to be," Danny said.

"Going, going," Harry said. "But I have got this little doll-baby from Omaha. She had never been with a real honest-to-God ski racer—" He stopped and squinted at me. "Married, huh?" he said. "Well, you're all through then, Roche. Maybe I can move up a goddam notch and be the trailer instead of the trailer's trailer. Big deal."

"See you on the mountain," I said.

"Well, congratulations, Jack!" Dan said, but Harry was silent now, purse-mouthed, as though he thought he'd talked too much. Dixie and I went out, and, with nothing to say to each other, waited for Brown and Anne.

Dixie drove us to the Jerome, with Anne beside him, and Brown and me in the back seat. The first people we saw when we entered the lobby were Leary and Helen Michonneau, standing together near the desk.

I was holding the door open for Brown and Anne. Brown stopped, blocking some other people who were trying to come in, and whispered to me, "Oh, Jesus, Jack—"

Behind her someone said, "Pardon us," and she had to move forward out of the way. Anne and the other people came past, and just then Helen saw us. Dixie called out, "Why, hello there, Helen honey!" And Leary turned toward us.

He had on the jacket that matched Brown's. He took a step back and leaned his elbows on the desk behind him. He gazed at a point between Brown and me, his eyebrows a frowning bar across his face, while Dixie went over to embrace Helen.

Anne said brightly, "You had better congratulate the engaged couple, Chris."

"What?" Leary said.

"Brownie and Jack are going to be married. Isn't that terrific?"

"What?" Leary said, like a deaf person. He grinned foolishly.

"What's this?" Helen demanded.

Anne repeated what she had said while Leary continued to grin as though there was a well-meant joke going on but he couldn't quite make out what it was.

"What's *this?*" Helen said, coming up to Anne. Helen was dressed in a creamy white sweater and stretchpants, and her face, framed by a blue earband, was almost pretty. But she had no shape in the pants; there was only the tightly filled configuration of the material itself.

"These two fine kids are going to get married," Dixie told her. "And Annie and me're trying to figure out where they want to go—Acapulco or maybe Las Vegas. Billy Weaver's there. I'll bet you and Jean-Gaby'd love to come along too—wouldn't that be fine? Chrissie too," he said, nodding to Leary, who was staring at me. "Jean-Gaby here?" Dixie asked.

"He's in a race committee meeting," Helen said.

"Say, great, Jack," Leary said in a rusty voice.

Helen put her arms around Brown. "Why, it's wonderful! It's so wonderful! Such a happy surprise!" She turned to embrace me; her cheek, pressed against mine, didn't feel like flesh but like some heavy, expensive material. She kept repeating that it was wonderful. "Isn't that wonderful, Chris?" she said when she released me.

"Say, it's terrific, Jack," he said. He cleared his throat. "Brownie."

"Well now, come on now," Dixie Rigg said. "Let's all come along. I am furnishing the champagne tonight, and there is going to be no skimping production or consumptionwise either. Come on, Helen honey, you and Chrissie come along and we'll leave word for Jean-Gaby to come in and join us."

There was more milling and exhausting waiting while he dickered and pulled his weight with the headwaiter. Finally, with a great disturbance, two tables were placed together for us, we were seated, and champagne in buckets appeared. The bandleader, reading from a card, announced, "This next number is in honor of Miss Georgiana Brown and Mr. Jack Roche, just engaged to be married. Let's give the happy couple a good big hand!"

There was a round of applause. People were gazing

and smiling at our table. The band began to play a jazzy arrangement of "Here Comes the Bride," and a waiter with a ski-bum's tan poured champagne into our glasses. Leary maintained the foolish grin, as though he thought no one could see him behind it. Anne leaned across the table and whispered to Brown, "Can you stand it, Brownie? I can get you out of this if you can't." Brown just shook her head a little. She smiled at Leary, as though that was something she had to get done.

"When'd you decide about this?" Leary asked.

"Just tonight," I said.

"Just a little while ago," Brown said.

Leary wet his lips and nodded.

"It's just till—you know—fall," Brown whispered.

Leary bent forward as though to hear better. Then he said, "Oh," and leaned back. Dixie was lighting a cigar. He patted Anne's shoulder. "Hey, come on, everybody!" he said. "We have a lot of bubbly to get through here. Now, drink up, Helen honey." He sounded coarse and suddenly drunk. I watched him squeeze Anne's arm. "Hey, how you doing, honey?"

I looked away as, smiling brightly, Anne said, "Oh, finely, finely."

"Got to get you that tooth fixed, honey," Dixie Rigg said.

Helen said to Brown, "But you should be married right here, Georgiana." Everyone stopped talking and listened; her voice had that quality. Smiling, massaging her hands together as if they were hurting her, she said to Brown, "Don't you think so, dear? Right after the race Sunday, before the banquet. Here in the hotel. Will you let me give you a love wedding for a gift, Georgiana? It will be my pleasure."

"Oh!" Brown said. "Oh, no. I can't let you do that. We were just going to—you know—elope."

Helen's mouth turned down for a moment, and it was as though gears shifted in her voice. "But I've said it would be my pleasure," she said. Brown kept shaking her head. "But I would love to do it for you!" Helen in-

sisted. "I think it should be a skiing motif, everyone in
ski clothes—"

"Oh, I can't get stretchpants on over my cast," Brown
said. "I can't—"

"You are not to worry about anything, dear," Helen
said, smiling again. "We can sew you into them, can't we?"
She laughed. "You hear so often that girls look sewn
into their Bogners. And the bride's attendants in matching sweaters and Bogners, blue, I think. Don't you think
so, Anne?"

"Why not?" Anne said.

Looking at me with her sharp blue eyes, Helen said,
"I presume Chris is going to be best man, Jack?"

I nodded. Leary laughed once, like a cough.

"I was set on flying these kids to Acapulco or somewhere," Dixie Rigg said in a lugubrious tone. "And you
are taking it all away from me, Helen honey." He had
his hand on Anne again, and I saw Leary watching him
with a stifled expression. I wanted to get out, and get
Brown out, but it was so complicated with her bad leg and
Helen making plans and Dixie drunk that I knew we
couldn't escape gracefully. And it occurred to me that
the kind of wedding Helen was talking about might make
everything easier with Mr. Brown.

"Let me tell you something," Helen said, and it was
strange to see everyone, even Brown, lean forward to
listen like conspirators. "I have this very good friend
who is a staff writer for *Life* magazine—Peter Dudley.
I'm going to call Peter about this wedding of yours,
Georgiana. I think it will fit perfectly into their '*Life* Goes
to a Party' series. I really think it will. And in conjunction
with the Roch Cup races, which they may be covering
anyway—don't you think that might make a memorable
wedding, dear?"

Brown didn't answer.

Helen said, "I really believe the more that is made of
the wedding, the more the marriage will amount to. Fly-
by-night weddings make fly-by-night marriages. When
I've been married, I've always seen to it that *much* was
made over it."

Dixie beat his hand on his leg with laughter.

"That's right! That's right, Helen honey!"

She flushed but, with her eyes fixed on Brown, continued, "There is not a single thing you need worry about, dear, until Sunday afternoon. Then we will make a tremendous fuss over you." She said to me, "Don't you forget to get the license"; to Brown again, "Oh, your parents. Will your parents want to come, dear?"

"I don't know," Brown said. The ski-bum waiter came around to fill our glasses again. "I—just don't know," Brown said.

"Well, you'll call them and let me know right away, won't you?"

Brown nodded, looking down at her folded hands.

"If your father doesn't come, Jean-Gaby can give you away," Helen said. "I think that would be very nice."

With his cigar jutting from the corner of his mouth, Dixie Rigg said, "How'd you like to go to Acapulco on your honeymoon, lil cripple gal?"

"I'd love to! But Jack has to race at Alta next week. And then the Nationals are after that."

"You athletes!" Dixie said in a perishing voice. He said to Anne, "Well, come on, highflyer, let's fly high." They got up to dance. Leary gave me a contorted look of misery and sympathy and anger and turned to watch them, the muscles pulled tight along his jaw.

"How's your sense of humor?" I said to Brown.

She shook her head. "Not too good." She raised her glass and whispered, "Whoopee!" She watched Helen beckon Leary down into Dixie's chair. "Jack," she whispered, "can you stand this kind of wedding? Because it might help."

"I thought about that too."

"It just might."

"Do you want to call him tonight?"

"Tomorrow. I'm too tired tonight. I'm just bushed."

"Do you want to try to get out of here now?"

"Oh, I guess we shouldn't just yet." Frowning at the people on the dance floor, she said, "I wish Anne'd make

170

that jerk behave. I think he's terrible. Would you pour me a little more champagne, Jack?"

I got up to reach the bottle. I poured some for Helen too. The edges of Leary's eyelids looked as though they were bleeding. I permitted myself one glance at Anne and Dixie; he was a terrible dancer. Anne had said that what she'd told me about Figgy wasn't true, and I didn't know what to believe. But I had believed her when she said she had no place to go now. When I thought about Anne there was a strange sensation of moving ponderously toward the edge of something.

When I sat down beside Brown again she was sipping her champagne as though she had made up her mind, at last, to get tight.

"It's going to be fine," she said in a low voice. "It's really going to help. It's just that I get so tired of everybody running me around."

"Well, nature's going to be running you around from now on."

She smiled. She smiled for a long time, as though that idea delighted her. Then she set her jaw determinedly. "Well, I'm not going to phone. I'm going to send a telegram."

"Good," I said.

"I'll send a night letter," Brown said. "I'd just come all unglued on the telephone."

"Do you want me to phone him?"

"No," Brown said. "I'm going to send a night letter."

When the music stopped, Dixie and Anne came back and more champagne was poured. Jean-Gaby appeared. Helen told him the news, and he came over to shake hands with me. He was very formal and distant, and he ignored Brown. "This is very surprising news, my dear fellow. Congratulations."

He said it as though I'd offended him. I thanked him, and he turned away. Still standing, I said loudly to Brown, "Well, I'd better take you home now. I've got to get some sleep."

Dixie Rigg started a noisy argument, but again it was

Jean-Gaby who insisted that Leary and Anne and I must get our rest, and Helen said she was sure Georgiana must be exhausted. Then they all decided to leave, which was not what I had wanted. We made our way out to the lobby.

Leary said suddenly, "—keep your hands off her!" There was a scuffle where Dixie was helping Anne on with her greatcoat, and in a swift shifting movement Dixie and Leary were standing facing each other with Anne behind them, her face white as paper.

"I said keep your hands off her!" Leary said. Dixie said something sibilant and inaudible, and Leary pulled back a fist and shoulder. Helen said, "Chris, stop it!" and Jean-Gaby stepped between them. "Dixie, you're quite drunk," Helen said, and with that it was over and dissolved before anyone else in the lobby had noticed.

"Jack," Brown whispered, gripping my arm. "Please, let's go. I want to go. Right now." She started out the door ahead of me, and I followed with my parka skewing across my back as I thrust my hands into the armholes. Outside it was very cold. "Let's go, let's hurry!" Brown said frantically. "Please, before they come out!"

I took her arm and we started across the street as fast as she could go. We made it out of sight of the hotel entrance before anyone appeared. Brown's breath was steaming. Once she stopped and took a Kleenex from her pocket and blew her nose.

"Oh, poor Christy, he must feel so rotten," she said. We started on again. "But maybe he feels better now. Everything's got all turned around. All at once everything's so unhappy and awful for everyone else. All at once I'm the only lucky one."

We walked along past dark shop windows, slowly, for the sidewalk was broken and uneven here. Two couples came toward us, talking and laughing. When we stopped to let them by, one of the men said in a loud, jokester voice, "Oh-oh! Bad luck to see a casualty. Don't look. Bad luck!"

"Oh, drop dead," Brown said.

"Oh, bitter; bitter, Just—"

"Shut up," I said.

He stepped toward me and I stepped toward him. I wanted to hit him. But one of the girls pulled him back, there was some muttered talk, and then the four of them went on toward the Jerome, no longer laughing. I hoped I had spoiled their evening.

"Jerks," Brown said shakily. We turned the corner. I was trembling. Finally we could see the tree in front of the Palomino Motel, dotted with colored lights like a giant Christmas tree. I thought of the little Christmas tree in the motel room in Denver, and Leary and Brown giving each other the matching jackets, and those two jackets in the lobby of the Jerome, and I thought of Leary telling Dixie Rigg to keep his hands off Anne, and starting to swing on him, but slowly enough so that he could be stopped in time. As Brown had said, maybe he felt better now.

We walked along the covered walkway to number five. Facing the door and fishing in her pocket for the key, Brown said, "I'll be better tomorrow. Will—will you come see me when you come down off the mountain?"

"How about breakfast?"

"Oh, you don't need to—" She stopped herself. But she shook her head. "No, I'm going to sleep in. I don't want any breakfast. Come and see me after the lifts shut down." She unlocked the door, stepped inside, and turned to face me. "Good night, Jack. I don't know what to say except—thanks."

I said, "Good night, Brownie," and she smiled a little. She closed the door, and I started the long cold walk back to Helen's house.

7

As I walked slowly across Aspen there was a feathery frosting falling from the clear sky, like dew turned to snow. I was trying to think what being married to Brown would be like, but no picture came. Instead I

173

saw myself poised at the top of the downhill and then panting at the bottom and waiting for my time to be announced, which was the fastest time. And I saw myself at the banquet at the Red Onion receiving the Roch Cup. By then I would already be married.

Imperceptibly the snow came down. In the lights it gleamed pale and brilliant on the streets, like a dusting of diamonds. Music was thumping in one of the restaurants as I passed. A VW came cautiously toward me, the skis on its back pointing toward the sky, and sad headlights like bloodhound's eyes.

At Helen's the porchlight was on. The green jeep and Leary's station wagon with its ski rack like antlers were in the drive, and the Cadillac stood in front. Dixie's U-drive was not in sight. Lights were still on inside the house.

Leary was alone in the red room, sitting in the high-backed loveseat with his legs stretched out and his stockinged feet crossed on the coffee table. He was looking at a ski magazine.

He glanced up casually and said, "Hi."

I sat down opposite him, my fingers tingling in the warm room. I almost asked where Anne and Dixie were, but instead I said, "Well, I guess I'll go to bed."

"I was just looking at this magazine," Leary said. "You see all this stuff about shorter skis?" Then he made a face and said, "Well, you and Brownie're getting married, huh?"

"Yes."

"So I look like a real bastard."

Something beat in my head like wings. "I'm sure sorry about *that*," I said. But I remembered his telling me how his brother had always contrived to make him look bad, and I said, "I'm not trying to make you look any way, Chris."

"Oh, hell," he said, tossing the magazine onto the coffee table with the Roger Bernand catalogue. "I don't know why I can't just say thanks. It's just so damn hard when you look like a bastard and somebody else's the big hero."

I had practiced what I would say when and if he
thanked me, but now I had forgotten my speech. "Listen,
Chris," I said. "It would have cost you too much, I guess.
It doesn't cost me anything. Forget it."

"What do you mean?" he said. "What do you mean,
would've cost me too much?"

"What you said up on the mountain today."

"Oh." He looked down at his hands. "I don't know
why I'm so goddam belligerent," he said. "Nobody did
anything to me. You're doing this. And Helen tried to
fix up. And Brownie didn't ever do anything except— She
didn't do anything at all, she's been terrific. But there
wasn't ever so much between Brownie and me, Jack.
Except—that. Not like you and Anne."

"Never mind, Chris."

"You think I don't feel like hell? Well, I do." Staring
at his hands still, he said, "The idea is you stay married
till fall, huh? Then you get a divorce or something? Then
what?"

"I don't know."

"Listen, I'd better tell you this. She didn't want to do
it. I mean, she really didn't want to."

"Forget it!"

He wiped the back of his hand across his mouth. "That
was really great about me being best man. You'd think
it'd make her sick to her stomach."

"It's to please me. Anne'll be maid of honor."

"Jesus, it's a bad joke. But you've always been strong
for the four of us."

"Well, that's all over."

He nodded. "Well, it must feel great to do a keen good
thing."

I couldn't tell whether he was being sarcastic or not,
and I felt the beat of anger in my head again. I said,
"I'd rather not think about it in a crappy way like that."

"I didn't mean it like that."

"Well, it feels good then," I said. "Sure it does."

"Well, I felt like hell," Leary said. "I just wanted to
take a crack at somebody, I didn't even care who it
was. I was so sick of that Texas prick with his hands all

175

over Anne, and you with that goddam silly grin trying not to look at them. But you know? He would've taken me apart right there and chewed me up if Helen hadn't stopped it. Jesus," he said in a flat voice.

"Well, thanks for thinking about me," I said.

He nodded, stiff-faced.

"Listen, Chris. Nothing was ever going to happen between Anne and me. Don't worry about that. I'm a poor boy and she has to have a rich boy."

"He must be damn near forty. Is he that loaded?"

"I don't know anything about it. The only thing I know to do is forget it."

He smeared his hands over his face. "Forget it, forget it," he said. "Christ, the way everything changes! About a month ago it seemed like I was on top of everything, and now everything's on top of me."

I got up and said I'd better be going to bed.

"I guess I'll stay here and read awhile," Leary said, reaching for his magazine. I was almost to the stairs when he said, "I know you did it for Brownie, Jack. But thanks."

"It's okay," I said without turning. I went on upstairs, wondering where Anne and Dixie Rigg were.

8

The operator said, "I have a collect call for anyone there, from Jack Roche in Aspen, Colorado. Will you accept the charges?" And my father's voice said, "Sure. Hello, Jackie."

"How are you, Dad?"

"Fine, Jackie. Fine. What's up?"

"I'm getting married," I said.

There was a silence. "You're getting *married?*" he said. "Oh, to Anne Patterson. Say, she is really a beautiful—"

"No, to Georgiana Brown, Dad."

"Georgie?"

"Listen: it's one of those things. I have to."

"Oh," he said. After another pause he said, "Oh," again, differently. Then he said, "That's kind of too bad, isn't it? When's the kid due?"

"September."

"I always thought you had things figured out so you wouldn't get in any of that kind of trouble."

"Well, you know how it is."

He sighed. "I know how it is. Well, Georgie's a fine girl."

"She's a fine girl."

"But I thought you and Anne Patterson—"

"There never was anything there."

"Well, I wish I liked George Brown better."

"Me too."

"He know about this yet?"

"Not yet."

He sighed again. "You'll need some money, I guess."

"I thought you might want to come out for the wedding. It's going to be a big deal. It's Sunday after the downhill. Helen Michonneau's running it. She's married to Jean-Gaby Michonneau. And maybe you'll want to come watch the Roch. I've been positive thinking."

"You have, huh?" he said, as though he didn't understand.

"I think I'm going to win."

"Oh, you do? Say, did Chris Leary get hurt or something?"

I closed my eyes. "No. I'm just going to win, that's all."

"Say, it's great to hear you talk that way, Jackie. I don't know if I can. GS is Friday and the slalom Saturday?"

"That's right."

"I'll try and make it. Where can I get hold of you?"

I gave him Helen's number, and he said he would try to get to Aspen by Friday, but it might be Saturday. "That's fine about you getting married," he said. "And don't you worry about a thing. Half the people I know got married for the same reason. Don't you worry about it."

"Thanks, Dad."

"And say, it's fine to hear you saying you're going to win it this weekend. I've been telling you all along all you had to do was think that way."

"Well, good-by, Dad," I said.

"Good-by, son."

"Hello, Jack," Brown said. She wore her Levi shorts and a pink-and-white-striped shirt. Her freckled face was scrubbed-looking, and her hair shone. She had on dark glasses.

"Didn't Anne come by?"

"She just left. Jean-Gaby's going over the women's downhill with them this morning." She had been writing on a piece of stationery with a *Holiday* magazine for backing.

"You didn't sleep in after all," I said.

She indicated the paper. "I've been trying to write this damn telegram—night letter."

I said, "I think my Dad's going to come out for the wedding."

"That's wonderful. Well, here's what I've said: 'Marrying Jack Roche after race Sunday hope you will be happy for me love Georgie.' But it's silly to send something that short night letter."

"It sounds fine."

"First I said a lot of other things. How Helen was going to do the wedding and maybe there'd be *Life* photographers there and all that. But I took it all out." Slowly she scraped the paper into a wad in her fist. She tossed the wad at the pink metal wastebasket beside the bureau. It bounced off the wall and fell in.

"Good shot."

"Well, you know, he's going to be mad whether I make a point of asking them to come, or if I don't. So I'm not going to. They can come if they want, but I'm not going to ask them. Then they won't come."

"Maybe you'd better ask them. That might be pretty raw, not to."

"No, I'm not going to!" she said in a tight voice. "He'll

just make me cry the whole time. I'm not going to cry at my own wedding, with those photographers there, and ruin everything for everybody."

"Maybe if you asked them but didn't make it sound as though you were too anxious for them to come, then they wouldn't. But at least you'd have asked them."

She grinned at me as she took off her dark glasses. Her eyes looked hot and pink. "Oh, good," she said. "Oh, isn't it terrible how being scared makes a crook out of you? But that's good, that's what I'll do, Jack. Like 'Can you come?' at the end?"

"Maybe 'Can you come on such short notice?'"

"Oh, that's good! I'm so glad you can be crooked too. He won't come."

"Do you know what my father said? I told him we *had* to get married—you know. He said we weren't to worry about it, half the people he knew got married for that reason."

Brown laughed. "That was nice of him. Jack, hadn't you better be going up to train? It's Thursday already."

"I'm going up right away. Helen wants us all to come to dinner tonight and talk about the wedding. She's going to try to get this *Life* guy there too."

Her ponytail bounced as she nodded. "Anne thinks we ought to let Dixie Rigg take us down to Acapulco for our honeymoon. He knows some fabulously rich Mexican who has a kind of palace there."

"It'd be great if it wasn't for the Nationals. I thought I'd skip the race at Alta, but I can't miss the Nationals."

"Oh, I told her we couldn't," Brown said quickly. She picked up her glasses again but didn't put them on. "She came in right after you left last night," she said, as though I'd asked her about Anne.

"Well, I'd better get up the mountain," I said. "Do you want to meet me for lunch?"

"Oh, you don't want to come down, do you?"

"Don't say that."

"I'm sorry." Her face darkened. "Jack, I'm sorry I'm such a mess. I guess I just haven't got used to nature running me around yet. Well, okay. Where shall we meet?"

"Let's have a hamburger at that place at the bottom of No. 1. About one o'clock, so it won't be so crowded."

"You're so damn good, Jack," Brown whispered.

Up on top the sky was the color of dirty lead, and the light was flat. Everyone looked bug-eyed with yellow lenses on. Leary and I ran slowly down the catwalk under the lift, following the course down Zog Park to the top of Ruthie's. The bumps looked tough; but Ruthie's Run was not as steep as Exhibition.

On the catwalk over to Spring Pitch, Harry Butler and Bruce Carrington caught up with us, and we stood in a huddle discussing the course, with Leary, as usual, contributing nothing. Harry skied off into the trees to take a leak.

Bruce wore a high, buff-and-brown Norwegian cap that made him look seven feet tall. Leaning on his poles, he said, "Hear you and Georgie Brown are getting married, Jack."

I nodded. "After the downhill Sunday. Can I get you to be one of my boys?"

"Pleased to be," Bruce said. He studiously didn't look at Leary, who was fidgeting. "Remember that time at Slide Mountain?" he said. "I guess Georgie was about thirteen. They had her forerun the GS? Remember that?"

I nodded.

"She came down there so fast I think only one of the women beat her," Bruce said. "She's a great girl. Congratulations."

"Thanks."

"What're you going to do, Jack? Settle down and stop this ski-bumming?"

"Maybe after the Olympics."

Harry came poling and skating out of the trees in a rush; he didn't want to miss any more talk about the downhill course than he had to. Back with us, he leaned languidly on his poles and looked bored as Bruce said, "Well, I was really surprised to hear it, Jack. I thought you were a dedicated type, non-stop-to-the-top and all that. Georgie too."

I felt uncomfortable until I glanced at Leary's face; then it began to seem funny.

"Love conquers all," Harry said, bouncing up and down on his Kneissls.

"Well, I was thinking about the Junior Nationals here," Bruce said. "You guys remember them."

"You won the combined," Leary said.

"I was supposed to win it," Bruce said. "I was the hotdog that year. But that was the hour of decision for me. Whether I was going to head for D.U. or Colorado and see how far I could go racing, or forget it and go into pre-med, the way I knew I ought to do. Sure, I won the combined, but you and Chris had me scared. And Bobby Chandler. You were all coming on too fast. You were really pushing me, and I knew damn well I wasn't going to be the hotdog long."

"I saw Bobby clobber at Mount Mansfield," Harry said soberly. "Jesus. You could hear the bones break like a twenty-two going off. You saw him, Chris."

"I just saw him when they were taking him down," Leary said.

"Those goddam trees," Harry said.

"Anyway," Bruce said patiently, "I knew you guys were going past me pretty quick or we'd all kill ourselves. It was all just too damned much sweat. I thought I was going to have a nervous breakdown worrying about keeping out in front that year. Talk about a monkey on your back. I just had to face it—I'm not the competitor you guys are. You too, Harry."

"Not me," Harry said. "I'm just a young fellow trying to get along. I don't care whether I win or lose, it's just how I *ski*." He illustrated graceful turns with his poles and upper body while we laughed at him.

Bruce said to me, "You and your damned deep-knee bends. And sitting with your back against the wall. You really psyched me out, you bastard." He slapped me on the arm with his gloved hand. "Who was it said, 'Don't look back, something might be gaining on you'? Every time I looked back you were gaining on me."

I managed to laugh. "Well, I didn't ever catch you," I said. "You quit the circuit on me."

"Nobody has anything to spare for any deep-knee bends on the senior circuit," Leary said. "All you try to do is save your legs, Christ sake." He gave me a confused, accusing look.

Screwing his gloves through the loops of his poles, Bruce said to Leary, "Well, I'm glad it's you he's gaining on now, not me. I guess you won't be sorry to see him married and off the circuit."

Leary laughed loudly, as though it were a terrific joke.

"Yeah, well then you can look back and see *me* gaining," Harry said. He bounced up and down. "Come on, let's go down and look at that next straight shot there."

We ran down to the top of Spring Pitch, where there was a tough turn. The blue flags hung limply between the blue poles. Below us Aspen was laid out like an aerial photograph of a town, drab in the flat light.

9

It was late before Leary and I finished side-slipping the giant slalom course and came off the mountain. There were a number of cars parked in front of Helen's house. Inside Mrs. May was perched on the arm of Brown's chair, and Anne and Helen and Jean-Gaby were in conversation with a graying, crewcut man, who wore corduroy knickers and black-rimmed glasses. I could feel Mrs. May's eyes on me as Leary and I were introduced to the newcomer, who was Peter Dudley from *Life*.

When I moved over toward Brown, Mrs. May caught hold of my arm, hard-fingered, and said she wanted to talk to me. We went into the telephone room and she closed the door. "I hate to be made a fool of!" she said.

I tried to look serious, but it was like being called into the principal's office for something someone else had done. "Georgiana has told me the situation," she announced. She had a way of talking as though her upper lip were stuck to her front teeth. "How would you like to try to chaperone a gaggle of girls while every young rooster—" She stopped. Her eyes had yellowish, red-veined whites. "Well, you outwitted me," she said. "I congratulate you. But of course I overestimated Georgiana," she said, staring straight into my eyes. "We always overestimate those we think are like ourselves, don't we? I should never have permitted her to drive all over the country with you and Chris Leary, and especially not with Anne Patterson." She said Anne's name through her teeth. "I should at least have had the perception to see she was treading dangerous ground and notified her father. I can imagine what kind of an example Anne Patterson furnished. I know that kind all too well. But the Anne Pattersons of the world never get into trouble, do they? It is always some precious little unsophisticated fool like Georgiana. Damn you *men!*"

I didn't know what to say. I didn't know whether she was going to attack me with her fingernails or burst into tears.

"I'm so *mad,*" she said. "I'm so— Well, we will see if the new FIS ruling on professionalism won't shake that poise." She swept a hand in front of her face as though brushing something away. "But let me congratulate *you* on your very good taste," she said. "Once there was a young man who—" She stopped again.

I didn't know what she was talking about, and I was getting a little scared. But she took a step away from me, and when she went on it was not so violently.

"So you are going to marry her," she said. "I suppose that makes you feel very virtuous. Of course it is the end of her career. She would have been a world champion."

"I guess so," I said. She is well out of anything that has to do with you, you old bitch, I added to myself. Brown had always been her favorite, and her favorite goat, but I hadn't realized Mrs. May hated Anne so—as though because Anne was beautiful and she was ugly,

Anne was her natural enemy. She was a terrible old bitch, and insane. I remembered the story that she had slapped Brown after Brown had lost a combined in Europe with a DSQ in the slalom.

Mrs. May said, "May I ask what you intend to do about notifying Georgiana's father? She tells me she has done nothing yet."

"I'm not going to do anything," I said.

"Then I suppose I must," she snapped.

"I don't think it's your responsibility, Mrs. May," I said. "She went home when she broke her ankle, and she came back here on her own. It's up to her to get in touch with him, and I guess she's afraid he'll give her a bad time. And maybe she's had enough to last her awhile."

"Perhaps you think you've given her a good time?" Mrs. May cried. Then the hard, inflamed eyes seemed to soften a little. "I've taken her over to stay with me at the Jerome. Of course she's had bad times. Well, you *are* going to marry her. You deserve some credit for that. You mustn't think I'm altogether furious at *you*. I'm furious at—I'm merely furious. I find it disgusting when men and women persist in acting like animals. But there is some relief when honor is discernible amongst the wreckage." All at once she slapped me brusquely on the shoulder, as though I had passed some kind of test, and we went back into the red room to join the others.

Helen was sitting on a stack of TV cushions, talking to Brown, who nodded back at her with a kind of mechanical fascination. Mrs. May went over to them, and I escaped upstairs to shower and change my clothes.

The talk at dinner was all wedding, mostly among Helen, Anne, and Peter Dudley, for it seemed to be definite that *Life* would have a photographer on hand. Brown was consulted occasionally, Mrs. May once or twice, and I not at all. Leary was sitting next to Jean-Gaby, and they were talking about Portillo. Dixie Rigg, I learned, had flown back to Texas on business.

Helen had arranged for a ski shop to furnish light blue Bogners for five bridesmaids, and she was buying as her own gift five blue sweaters. She knew where she could get men's white sweaters that had been rejected by a ski school, but I was asked if I could find ushers who had black stretchpants. I said I thought I could.

Peter Dudley was very drunk. His eyes kept drooping closed. Then his lips would move as though he were talking to himself, his eyes would open, and he would wave his fork. For a while everyone listened when he did this, but when it turned out to be meaningless we stopped paying attention to him. Finally he said loudly, "Got to do the ski poles bit." He leaned his knife and fork together in a tent shape. "Military dealio," he said. "Bride and groom going along under crossed ski poles and all that standard operating crap." He opened an eye at Brown, nodding. "We'll make something out of that cast though. That'll be good."

Brown smiled weakly, and everyone acted as though the crossed ski poles idea was very fine and original, except Leary, who asked to be excused. The Roch Cup combined was a three-way, and the giant slalom was in the morning.

Soon after Leary had gone, I asked to be excused too. Anne, sitting next to Peter Dudley and nervously turning her charm bracelet on her white wrist, paid no attention to me. I saw Mrs. May glance from her to me. Then everyone seemed to be looking at me as I stood behind Brown's chair. Anne smiled mockingly as I put my hand on Brown's shoulder and Brown laid her hand on mine. Helen smiled too, and Peter Dudley grinned floppily, and even Mrs. May assumed a pleasant expression. Jean-Gaby was frowning. Sunday I was going to find out just how good a physician he was.

"Ah, good night, Jack," he said, and everyone chorused good nights. I went upstairs. No light showed under Leary's door.

He had said that no one had anything to spare for deep-knee bends on the senior circuit, so I did ten one-legged dips off each leg. I flopped into bed too tired to brush my teeth or put on pajamas. For a while I reviewed the GS course, guiding myself down it, but my thoughts were always pushing ahead to training for the downhill, to the downhill itself. Half dozing, like a spectator, I watched myself tucked in a schuss, crouched with my gloves and the grips of my poles almost before my face while the baskets stuck out behind like tailfeathers; down the first slow schuss, faster down Zog Park, where there was a straight shot with a closed gate at the end, faster down Ruthie's, lifting over the road, holding the turn into the catwalk—then I was finished and watching Leary come down the last schuss, very slowly, because a great wind was sweeping up the hill at him. And people began shouting my name, *"Jack! Jack!"* But it wasn't the Roch finish, it was the winner's ceremony after one of the alpine events in the Winter Games with the "Star-Spangled Banner" playing and the movie cameras rolling, and it was I, Jack Roche, standing in the center, with the second- and third-place winners on my right and left, lower than I was, while above the music they called my name—

Suddenly I was awake in the dense black enclosure of the room, for someone had whispered, *"Jack!"* I raised my hand to grasp the hand that had touched my face and felt the bracelet on the bare arm.

"Jack, it's *Brownie*," Anne whispered with a shaky whisper of a laugh.

"Hello, Brownie." I shivered and ran my hand up her bare arm, and felt the pad of muscle caught tense beneath her shoulder, and smoothed my hand down the cool flesh of her side.

Now I could make out the shape of her, bending over the bed. I turned my hand under her body and felt the hard-pointed small shape of her breast. She whispered, "Is there room in there for you and me and my cast?"

"Sure." I turned back the covers and she got in beside me. She had nothing on but the bracelet. Turning quickly over on her face, she whispered a muffled "Oh, you knew I was coming."

"I was too beat to put my pajamas on."

Her breath was warm against my shoulder when she spoke. "We're not going to do anything, so don't keep turning toward me like that. That's right—just stay like that. This is just a preview. I was afraid you might be thinking about backing out of marrying me Sunday and going back to Anne. Do you think I feel nice?"

"Yes," I said. "Nice."

"Really nice? As nice as Anne?"

"As nice as Anne."

"I love you so, Jack," Anne whispered.

I didn't know who was supposed to be talking. "Anne —" I said. My tongue felt like wool in my mouth.

"Shhhhh! Stop that! We are going to have a terrible marriage if you slip up and call me Anne every time you get passionate. Are you still in love with Anne?"

"I guess so."

"Well, you'll get over *that*, won't you?"

"Maybe I will."

She bit my shoulder. It hurt. "No, I won't," I said. I smoothed my hand along her side again, where her arm protected her breasts. Even my hand ached for her. But almost coldly it came to me that someday I was going to hate her.

"That feels nice," she said. "Did you use to do that to Anne?"

"Yes," I said through my mouthful of wool. I opened my eyes on the darkness again. You damned teaser, you dirty teaser.

She whispered, "Jack, I have to know. Did—did you ever sleep with Anne?"

"One night in Aspen."

"Did you go all the way?" she whispered in a parody of Brown's clear, little girl's voice.

I didn't answer, and Anne said, "All right, I'm through playing that game. It's not very much fun."

I said, "Anne—I have to know. What did Figgy do to you?"

I knew I shouldn't have said it as soon as I had spoken. She was silent for a time. Then she said, "Nothing. Let's not talk about that. That's not any fun either." Now there was a heaviness, a dullness, as though an electric current had been turned off. "I came to say good-by,"

Anne said. "Do you suppose we could take a chance on my staying here all night? Of course we wouldn't do anything."

"Sure," I said. But out of the unhappiness the mention of Figgy had caused, or maybe it was because I wanted so badly to beat Leary, suddenly it seemed very important that I get enough sleep before the giant slalom. It was as though half of me wanted her to go, half to stay. Then she turned toward me with her cool body startlingly warm against my leg, and nothing was so important as having her there.

"Preview," she whispered.

"What do you mean, preview?"

"No, don't do that. We'll just get all excited. No, Jack, please don't! Just stay like that. We don't want to get carried away," she said and laughed. She touched me; there was a jingle of the charms on her bracelet. "I want you to stay just like that about me till you come back to me."

"Come back to—"

"After Brownie's had her baby."

"You're going to marry Dixie."

"That was just the way I felt last night. Of course I'm not going to. It was just that I was feeling bereft. Then I thought I wanted to go down to Acapulco and meet his friend. Luis. He's tremendously rich and his wife's just died and he's not very old, and Dixie says he's very handsome and very nice. But I don't want anybody but you really."

"Listen—you said you loved me just now."

"It's just that you've made me jealous, you see. So clever."

"Anne, you know it's just—Brownie's just—"

"Shhh! I want to be sure you'll come back to me, because then you'll see. Then I'll make such good love to you. But you have to come back to me. Then we can make love and I'll love it, I know I will. Jack, you can make me love to, can't you? Like Sleeping Beauty. No, don't move."

"Sure I can," I said.

"Don't you know I can't stand for you to marry Brownie?"

"I won't then."

"But you have to."

"No, I don't."

"Yes, you have to. Because you'd do that and I'm so proud because really you love *me*. No, I don't mean proud, that's outside, and it's something inside. It makes me feel all warm and romantic and lost, but in a good way. And I do love you. It's so wonderful to realize all of a sudden that you love somebody. You have to marry her because I love you for doing it. But afterward you have to come back to me. Do you suppose we could get a job running a ski school together or something?"

"Sure we could."

"Swear you'll come back to me though."

"I swear it."

"If you do I'll be your lovely hotpants girl and I'll sleep with you whenever you want."

"Every night?"

"All right."

"Swear it."

"I swear it on my Ullr."

"Ten times every night."

"You won't be able to ski."

"Five times then."

"Such a man. How many times with Brownie?"

"None."

"Don't be silly. I don't mind. Well, I mind a little, but you can practice with her so you'll be perfect with me. No, don't do that. You have to wait. Do you know what? You're going to be proud of me. I'm going to win everything from now on. I'm going to race like a mad girl. I'm going to win here, and I'm going to win the Nationals, and then I'm going on to be number one girl in the Olympics. Mrs. May won't be able to stand it, but I'm going to. Jack, I don't want to be like Helen. I thought I wanted to be like Helen, but I don't. I want to be a girl athlete and have just you love me. We'll be ski-school directors and never have any money, and get old and brown

189

and leathery together. And we'll have our Olympic medals hung up in a little glass case. You're going to have a gold medal too, aren't you?"

"Sure I am."

"And we'll both win the Roch Cup this weekend."

"Right!"

"Won't that be fine? We'll win everything because we're celibate. Oh, but you won't be for the Nationals. I'm afraid you won't win that."

"You're jealous."

"I'm just a tiny bit jealous."

"We'd better go to sleep. GS tomorrow."

"You can touch me once before we go to sleep," Anne said. She moved a little. "There, that's nice. But that's all until you come back to me."

Later when I wakened the black of the room had grayed. I could make out the shapes of the window and the dresser and the black pool of the mirror. Anne was gone. Apparently she had decided not to take the chance of spending the night. For a frightened moment I thought she might have been only a dream. But she had been real, lying naked and cool beside me, talking and talking.

10

If he liked the course and the snow, Tom Boyd could beat anyone in the country in giant slalom. The Roch GS was his kind of course and he didn't have to tell the rest of us he was going to be hard to beat, but he did anyway—he was good at that kind of thing too.

He started eighth, so I watched him from the bottom. He sailed smoothly down the course as though the gates were placed exactly where he would have chosen to turn even if they hadn't been there. He didn't fight and scramble like most of the rest of us, and he didn't look particularly fast, but he won by a second and a tenth. It was old-timer's day, with Hammond second and McInerny hird. Leary got in trouble and lost his line but still made ourth, while I had a plain bad run for fifth—two and a aalf seconds out. I was glad my father hadn't arrived yet, o see my run, and I was sorry Jean-Gaby had seen it. It was a bad morning, and I blamed myself for thinking back to last night with Anne, and ahead to the downhill, instead of concentrating on the race I was running.

It was Anne's kind of course too, and she won the women's GS, with Alice and Lorraine tied for second. In the afternoon we trained on the downhill, where a couple of gates had been changed, and I ran it faster than I had before, but not at more than two-thirds speed, as the physician had recommended. The last thing we did was help pack out the next day's slalom courses.

At Helen's there was a message that my father had been delayed and wouldn't arrive until Sunday. I went to bed right after dinner and concentrated fiercely on checking and rechecking the combinations of gates in the slalom courses. But a part of my mind roved always ahead to the downhill or reran the GS in self-recrimination. I tried impossibly to compute the FIS points if I picked up seconds in the downhill but missed in the slalom, if I failed to win the downhill but won big in the slalom. I had to win the slalom. I reviewed the slalom gates in an increasing panic that I was getting no rest.

But at least it was better than going over and over again what I felt about Anne, what Anne felt about me, what was going to become of Anne, and of Anne and me. Finally I discovered that it was best to turn my thoughts to the wedding after the downhill Sunday. That was not so complex or so demanding as Anne or the slalom; there I knew what I must do and could do, and there, somehow, I was invulnerable.

There was a good crowd to watch the slalom. On the first run Leary had fast time until I came down and clipped him by four-tenths. No one else was close. Back on top, waiting for the second run, I forced him a chocolate bar. I was thinking that more and more often now a run would be the best I'd ever made. I had a strange, detached sensation of being in a glass box where no one could touch me and even sounds were muffled.

I stood gazing down the second course, which had the same start and finish as the first but was trickier. Jean-Gaby sideslipped to a stop just above me. His eyes were hidden behind dark glasses, his stiff hair was rumpled. He had on an official's armband.

"You made a very fine run, Jack," he said.

"Thanks."

"Now how will you do on this second run?"

I licked the chocolate out of the corners of my lips. "I guess I'll take it easy this time."

I couldn't make out his expression behind his dark glasses. He stared at me steadily, waiting.

"There's no use worrying about Chris," I said. "He'll go all out this time, and if he stands he'll win. He'll win or can-up trying too hard, and I'll take a chance that he won't stand."

Jean-Gaby had hardly spoken to me since the night Brown and I had announced that we were going to get married, and I thought he had lost interest in me. Now he nodded once, severely. "That is correct." He skied off down the hill and took up a position beside the gate-keeper at the top of the tough flush.

Leary didn't fall, but he came too fast into the flush where Jean-Gaby was watching, ran off the course, and finished with bad time. I took no chances on my run, but I suffered through the wait for the rest of the first seed to come down. Harry Butler beat me in the second run, but I won the slalom by enough of a margin to put me out in front on FIS points going into the downhill, with Leary far behind. I could give away time in the downhill and still win the Roch Cup, but I wanted to beat Leary in the downhill this time.

I stood halfway up the women's slalom course and watched Anne win the first run. Then I joined Brown and Helen and Peter Dudley at the bottom. Anne had fast time in the second run too. When she came over to us Brown hugged and kissed her. Brown sounded almost hysterical as she cried, "Oh, you looked *so* great, Anne! You looked so *great!*"

There was color in Anne's cheeks, and the chipped tooth showed when she smiled. She gave me her gloved hand to press, and I felt the shape of the bracelet under the sleeve of her sweater. Her eyes had the excited, faraway look. "You looked fine, Anne," I said. She moved over to Helen, who hugged her. She had an unbeatable lead in the women's combined.

After the race I walked back into town with Brown. She wore her long black parka and a pair of old stretchpants with the left leg pinned together over her cast. We went down into the crowded basement of the Golden Horn. I found a place for her to sit near the fire and, as soon as someone moved, squeezed in beside her. It was hard to talk over the noise of the jukebox and the raised voices and the clatter of boots going up and down the stairs.

"It's so great you won the slalom!" Brown said. The waitress brought our beers. She had a ski-bum's tan. She started away, then did a doubletake and said, "Oh! Congratulations, Jack Roche!"

"Thanks," I said. People near us looked around. Brown's hand caught mine and pressed it. When the waitress had gone I said, "I guess you felt pretty unhappy watching the girls coming down."

Brown shook her head. "No, I didn't. It's like being out of jail." She hunched her shoulders up as though she were cold. "Do you know? I think Anne'll win the downhill too. I don't think I could beat her any more."

"You always did in downhill—if you stood."

She shook her head again. "Everything's changed around. I think you're going to beat Chris tomorrow too. And he always used to beat you. You looked so great today, Jack. You're—I don't know—you've got everything pulled together some way. Everybody was talking about it. Did you see Christy crying?"

"No. Was he?"

"He was crying," Brown said with an ashamed satisfaction in her voice. "I thought—well, I thought he might be kind of going to let you win because—you know. But he was crying. You looked so good on that first run, Jack. You know, when he makes a run that fast it's just luck if he stands. But you looked in control all the way." She took a sip of beer and licked at her upper lip. "And Lorry was crying just now," she said. "Because Anne could walk down the mountain tomorrow and still win the combined. Mrs. May was trying to comfort her. Didn't you see them? It's just like being out of jail," she repeated and took another swallow of beer. "Did you ever cry when you lost, Jack?"

"When I was a junior I did. Or I'd try to hurt myself. I'd kick something to hurt my foot, or I'd hit my fist against something."

"Aren't we funny people?" Brown said. She gazed across the crowded room as though looking for someone she knew. After a long time she said, "I'm not going to race any more."

"Aren't you?"

"Do you know what I'm going to do next year? I'm going to the U. of Nevada and get a credential so I can teach school."

"That's a good thing to do," I said. I thought of Anne asking if she and I could get jobs as ski-school directors together. That part, at least, had been a dream.

"What are you going to do when you get through racing, Jack? Are you going back to college?"

"I'll just get a job. In skiing, some way."

"Instructing?"

"I'd like to be on lifts and tows, or snow safety, or permanent ski patrol. I was on the ski patrol at Garmisch. But I suppose I could make more money instructing if I get to be a big name."

"Oh, you will," Brown said as though it were settled. Then she nodded. "I wouldn't mind instructing either. With kids. I'd like to teach kids and run a junior racing program and all that. I think I could fix it so they had some fun. I never had any fun when I was a junior."

I drank my beer, trying not to think about Leary crying, trying to concentrate on the downhill tomorrow.

Brown touched my hand. She said in a low voice, "Jack, you don't have to marry me—it's all right now. I'm over being scared. It'll be all right."

"Can't back out now."

"Jack, I mean it." She was staring at the people coming down the stairs, and her little chin was set hard. She whispered, "Jack, you said you would when I was so scared I thought I'd die. But now I'm not any more. Jack, I don't like feeling like a—like a—oh, I don't know what I feel like!"

"You don't have to feel any way. What's the matter, Brownie? Did I do something?"

"No. Just that nature is—" She shook her head so hard her ponytail leaped. "You're in love with Anne."

"We weren't going to talk about any of that."

"I'm so chicken," Brown said. "If I wasn't so chicken I'd say, 'Well, I won't marry you, you're in love with another woman.' It's just that I'm so chicken about everything."

"You're making me depressed, and I just won the slalom—I ought to be feeling great."

"I'm sorry," she said. She took her dark glasses from her pocket, put them on, and looked at me. "Okay, I'll cheer you up. Do you know what they're going to do to me? They're going to sew me into a pair of Bogners for the wedding. It's Helen's idea. They're going to rip a pair of Bogners up the inside seam so I can get into them with my cast, and then they're going to sew me into them. Don't you think that's funny?"

"That's pretty funny."

She finished her beer, put the glass down, and folded her hands in her lap.

"Do you want another beer?"

"You'd better get up on the mountain, hadn't you?"

"I guess I'd better."

"I think I'll go back to the hotel and take a nap. Mrs. May's got some sleeping pills, and when I want to take a nap I just take a pill and—zip!" She snapped her fingers.

I helped her up and into her parka. A couple immediately backed into the places we had vacated. As we made our way toward the stairs someone called, "Congratulations, Jack!" It was no one I'd ever seen before. "That was a beautiful run, Jack," a girl with pink lipstick said, and a middle-aged man patted my shoulder as I passed him. "Good luck tomorrow, Roche."

I said, "Thanks," embarrassed at the attention being paid me and the eyes that were turned toward me, and anxious to get Brown up the stairs and out of the Golden Horn—but at the same time I was very pleased.

11

Friday night I had hardly slept. Saturday night I slept as though I had been doped. Sunday morning I felt exhausted, my legs as heavy and useless as damp bread. Enclosed in my glass box again, I yawned through a completely silent early breakfast with Jean-Gaby and Leary. Helen and Anne weren't up yet.

Outside it was gray with a little snow coming down. The light was going to be bad. It was my wedding day, but all I could think about was the light and my legs. After breakfast I spent ten minutes in my room rubbing liniment into my thighs.

Just as we were leaving the house my father phoned to say he was in Aspen and to wish me luck if there wasn't time for me to meet him. I said I'd see him after the race, and I felt an unreasoning annoyance that he hadn't been here yesterday for the slalom and that he should bother me now. You never liked to talk to anybody before the downhill.

Then the day began to move. It shook itself into slowly decreasing circles, of riding the lift, and waxing, and moving on up to the start. Snow came down gently, off and on, out of low-hanging clouds; and because of the snow and the flat light the racers were even more silent than usual, in a mood that was more depressed than grim. On top, Bruce Carrington, his face very pale under his

red and black racing helmet, his skis held upright, reminded me of an illustration in a boys' book I'd once
had—a knight on vigil in a chapel, leaning on his lance.

It was a big race; there were sixty Class A racers from
all over the country. I watched them come slowly up
toward the start in their racing parkas and helmets and
striped pants, their skis on their shoulders. Many of them I
didn't know, but almost all seemed to know me. They
nodded and called me by name as they passed.

From Bill Birks, who had attended last night's Calcutta Pool for the downhill, I learned that I had gone for
twenty-two hundred dollars, Leary for thirty-two hundred;
we were the top two. I watched Leary pace past, his blue
lips pursed as though cinched with a drawstring. He
ignored me. Harry Butler was checking the tape that covered the airholes in his goggles. Boyd and Samuelson, in
their red, white, and blue parkas, were standing together,
pretending to be chatting casually.

Everyone began to tie on his racing number as though
on a signal. It was ten minutes to starting time. I relaced
my boots tightly. I laid my Vectors out on the snow,
fitted my boots into the Marker toepieces, clamped the
turntables closed. I ran a few turns, worrying about my
legs, which felt dead. I sidestepped back up and ran
down again, and they began to come to life. In the starting
gate the telephone crackled and muttered. Yawning, I
watched the snowflakes dotting the black tops of my skis.
Down the mountain only the first few control gates were
visible.

The first forerunner left a foot-wide, inch-deep groove
down the exact center of the course and faded into the
falling snow.

The second forerunner leaned out of the gate with
Harry behind him. Boyd was running second, I third,
Leary sixth. All at once I stopped yawning; my mind
began to reach out for the feeling of certainty I'd had, very
slowly and carefully; it was like looking in your wallet for
a check you were afraid you had lost. But it was still
there. The second forerunner started. There was an in-
tolerable time while we waited for him to get down.

"Number one next. Number two on deck. Number three get ready." An official beckoned to me. Harry slid into the slot.

"Ten seconds," the starter said.

Pulling his goggles down, Boyd moved up behind Harry. The starter counted down mechanically. Harry thrust with his poles and shot out of the gate. Boyd went into the slot.

I checked my zippers and my helmet, panted once as my fingers fumbled with my goggles. I exhaled hugely to get the carbon dioxide of shallow breathing out of my lungs. Three neat parallel lines of tracks, evenly spaced apart, led down the mountain now. The starter was counting. *"Go!"* Boyd made a slow start, and I frowned after him. One minute before I went.

In the slot I fanned my goggles in and out, checked myself one last time, set my poles. "Ten seconds." At the count of five I began to flex my knees.

"Go."

I sprinted like a speed skater, tucked, set my skis running down the center groove in the course. Visibility was better than I had thought, my legs felt fine, my skis ran fast. As I picked up speed, I felt filled with joy, confidence, exultation. I went down toward Ruthie's rapt with speed and surety, and I wasn't afraid of anything.

It was an almost perfect run.

It was snowing very lightly at the finish. There was a big crowd. In the outrun, panting, I wiped my nose on my sleeve, my sleeve on my pants, pushed up my goggles. My father was leaning over the rope in front of me, and I raised a hand to him and grinned.

"Good run, Jackie?" he called.

I nodded. Brown was with Anne, and I waved at them and moved over to join Harry and Boyd. Boyd held up a badly bent pole. "Souvenir of Ruthie's Run anybody?" he said.

The loudspeaker crackled. "Time for Jack Roche, Norden, California—two:forty-four and three-tenths. That is fastest so far." My heart leaped. It would take 2:45 to win, Jean-Gaby had estimated—and that was before it had started to snow. I saw Harry angrily shake his head.

The loudspeaker said, "On the hill now is Chris Leary, from Colorado Springs. Chris was a member of last year's FIS team and won the Harriman Cup in Sun Valley last week."

"You really made a run, Jack," Harry said. "Go get married, will you?"

"What time did you have?"

"Two:forty-five and six."

"Well, I broke three minutes," Boyd said disgustedly.

We waited. The loudspeaker said, "Joe Hammond has started down. Joe was a member of the FIS team and was second Friday in the giant slalom."

Looking up the course, Harry said, "I guess Charley canned-up."

"On the hill is Dan Arganbright. Dan comes from Seattle, Washington—"

"Here comes Benny," Tom said.

McInerny came down the last schuss. He was covered with snow; he'd had a fall. When he slid over to us Boyd held up the bent pole again. "Where'd you clobber, Benny?"

"Didn't you see me?" McInerny was panting. "Just up on Norway there." He pointed up the slope with his pole. "Who's fast?" he asked.

"Jack," Harry said.

"See Charley?" Tom asked.

"Crashed and burned."

"That's only two stood out of the first five," Harry said.

The loudspeaker said, "Time for Ben McInerny, Stowe —three:eight and five-tenths. On the hill now is Jackie Samuelson. Jackie's a local boy, member of last year's FIS—"

Leary came into sight on the schuss down Norway. It seemed very soon after McInerny. He shot off a bump, off balance, a ski tilting, a pole flipping up. But he recovered and came down to the finish tucked and pumping, the black of his cap and parka grayed with snowflakes. In the runout he leaned head down between his poles.

When he straightened up a photographer in a red hat coaxed him into posing.

The loudspeaker came to life again. "Time for Chris Leary, Colorado Springs—two:forty-five and three-tenths."

He slid over to join the rest of us with the familiar swagger. "Who's fast?" he asked.

No one answered right away, and then the loudspeaker announced it. "Jack Roche of Norden has the fast time so far with two:forty-four and three-tenths."

Leary's eyes looked suddenly very close together, very hot, unbelieving, then frightened. He licked his lips. The loudspeaker announced the next racer. Leary poked one pole tip into the snow, then the other. He cleared his throat. "Good run, Jack," he said.

"Thanks, Chris," I said.

Joe Hammond crossed the finish line and fell when he stopped. Leary stood there poking holes in the snow, and everything seemed very quiet, slow, and strange. This should have been my greatest moment, yet I didn't seem to feel anything. Leary didn't say any more, and after a while I took off my skis and went to join my father. We watched the racers come down off the mountain one by one. After the first seeding group was down there was no chance of an upset, and, as usual, Leary and I were fast. But this time it was I, it was Jack Roche of Norden, who was first and Chris Leary second.

"Well, congratulations, Jackie!" my father said. "Wonderful, Jackie, wonderful!" He hugged and patted me on the back and wrenched my hand all at once. He let me go and said, "I knew you could do it, sonny!" His cheeks were flaming. In his new quilted parka he looked strangely smaller and of less consequence, out of place here in Aspen. "Positive thinking," he said with an embarrassed bluster, to remind me that he had helped. "Isn't that Georgie over there?" he asked.

I took him over to join Brown and Anne and Helen; I couldn't see Jean-Gaby anywhere. He hugged Brown and talked to her in a loud voice, and everyone congratulated me. Racers came over to shake hands, and other people

came up, some that I knew slightly and others I'd never
seen before. There was Bob Graves from the selection
committee, in his balaklava, and some other USSA brass,
and Aspen people, including three men who were part of
the syndicate that had bought me in the Calcutta. And
here was Bruce Carrington.

"Nice going, Jack," he said. "Got your name cut on
the big one. Hello, Mr. Roche."

"Hello there, Brucie. How'd you like this boy here?"
When Bruce had gone he said to me, "How'd Brucie
make out?"

"Not very well. He's out of shape." I looked up the
mountain. The sky was clearing now, and a little wind
had come up to flutter the flags. The last racers were on
course. Finally the afterrunner came down.

Then Jean-Gaby appeared. He embraced me; grinning
and gripping my hand painfully, he said, "It is very well
done, Jack! I am a good physician, eh?"

"You're a terrific physician," I said. "Thanks, Jean-
Gaby." I introduced him to my father.

"I saw you win the down-mountain at Squaw a while
back. Against some pretty tough competition too," my
father said, and Jean-Gaby looked pleased.

Helen announced that she and Brown had to go;
they had many things to do and couldn't wait to watch
the women's downhill. She came over to me and said, so
softly I had to bend down to hear her, "You skied wonderfully, Jack. Jean-Gaby is very impressed." She gave
me a smile like a trophy. Brown was flushed and looked
unhappy. Before they left, the photographer with the red
cap got her to pose giving me a kiss for winning the
Roch Cup.

Then I posed with Jean-Gaby congratulating me, and
with Leary and Harry Butler. With me in the middle, we
stood with our arms around each others' shoulders, being
good sports and good friends, grinning at the camera.
Leary didn't say a word, and Harry whispered, only half-
humorously, "I'm so effing sick of running third behind
you effing bastards."

My legs ached, and my back, and the only thing I

wanted now was to go back to Helen's to shower and change my clothes, and to be by myself—as though by myself I could get a grip on having won, fondle and savor it awhile before it leaked away. But it was time for the women's downhill.

As I stood with my father against the rope that closed off the outrun, I was thinking of the race at Altà, which I would miss because we ought to go to Reno after the wedding and fix things up with Brown's parents, and of the Nationals at Squaw, which was the last selection race, and after that the spring starts. I remembered Leary saying that he wondered sometimes if this was all one season.

We watched Lorraine and Alice and Evelyn finish, and then Anne was on course and I was tense again, as though it were myself I was waiting for. "My God, she's a pretty skier!" my father said as she appeared, round-headed in her big blue plastic helmet. She came beautifully around the turn above the last schuss and settled into a tuck with her legs working like pistons over the bumps that had nearly thrown Lorraine, pumping on the last flat. She almost clipped the side of the finish gate as she rocketed through and swept deep into the outrun. She hung panting on her poles for a while before she started back toward the timer's circle. When she passed us she turned her milk-white, exhausted, excited face toward me and smiled, and smiled at my father. Her eyes were startlingly dark in her pale face.

She won her first downhill of the year by eight-tenths. She'd won everything—the GS, the slalom, the downhill, and the combined—and I was jealous. I was jealous, and at the same time I was sick at heart that I could be jealous of Anne, and that I needed to be jealous at all.

12

I walked with my father along the packed path toward town, skis on my shoulder, poles in my hand. Once he laughed his loud, explosive laugh and banged me on

he back, but I didn't ask what he thought was funny. He
aid, "Say, I brought you a little wedding present. Drove it
ut here in fact."

"Wheels?" I asked.

"Sitting right over there." He pointed to a gray VW
ith blue Nevada plates. It had a big custom-made rack
n the tail that would hold a lot of skis. "Jimmy made
hat rack up for me. Isn't it a dandy?"

"That's a terrific rack."

"Got a new clutch in her. The clutch went out in Salt
ake, was why I didn't make it for the slalom yesterday.
he goes right along. Likes to switch ends when it's icy
hough."

"Thanks, Dad," I said, and he slapped me on the back
gain. I leaned my skis and poles on the rack and se-
ured them with the straps.

"I've got a ride back fixed up with Johnny Shepley," he
aid. "No strain there. Say, did you see those fellows taking
ictures of Anne? She's really a beautiful girl, a real
over girl."

"I'm getting married in an hour," I said. "I'd better
o get shaved and dressed."

"Have we got time for me to buy you a drink in one
f these fancy bars? Son of mine doesn't get married
very day."

"You can have a drink at Helen's. I'd better get
ressed. I'm still wound up pretty tight, Dad."

"Sure you are."

I moved around the VW and said, "Shall I go ahead
nd drive?" My father said, "Sure. It's your heap,
ackie." We got in. His suitcase was in the back seat.
he ashtray was full of cigarette butts, and butts had
pilled onto the floor. I leaned on the wheel and looked
t the mileage on the odometer and thought about Anne
anting a Facel Vega. I'd never even seen a Facel Vega.

"Say, I was trying to remember if I ever knew you to
ake out Georgie Brown," my father said.

"I took her out last summer."

"Oh, yeah." In an embarrassed, blustery voice, he
ent on, "Well, it sure is funny. You're out and around

203

all over the country, all over Europe too, and you come home and marry the girl next door, practically. But guess that's the way people do."

"I guess so," I said.

"But you are really in love with Georgie, huh?"

"Sure," I said. I started the engine and gunned it; it whirred noisily behind us. "This is a great car, Dad. Thanks a lot."

"Jackie," he said, "you're not feeling stuck, are you kid?"

"No, I'm fine." I gunned the engine again. "I'm still going like that, is all."

"I noticed you're a little scratchy. Well, you're supposed to be nervous though. I remember I was really nervous when your mother and me got married."

"It's not that," I said. "It's just that I've just won the Roch Cup and I'm wondering what the hell good it is." I felt him looking at me as I slipped the VW into gear and we moved out into the street.

"You're just wound up tight still, Jackie."

"I don't remember Chris Leary ever looking very damn happy when he'd won something," I said. "Maybe you're just not. And I know he feels like hell now. So if you feel lousy when you win and terrible when you don't, what good is it? Just because you have to see how far you can get?"

"Circuit's got to riding you a little, huh?"

I nodded, but it wasn't the circuit that was riding me. It wasn't even the regret that I hadn't won the GS along with the slalom and downhill. What was riding me was that I hadn't really won anything at all: I had only made Leary lose.

My father sat beside me with his arms folded in a thick bunch on his chest and his red face worried and unhappy. Finally he said, "You know, Jackie, I was talking to Bill Patten about you and Georgie getting married. You know the two of you'd make a pretty fine drawing card for his ski school there. Bill wants to see you when—"

"There's Helen's house," I said.

"Isn't that something?" my father said.

Inside, Leary was half sitting, half lying, in a red over-tuffed chair, his legs stretched out and his unlaced boots esting on a footstool, a beer bottle held upright on his tomach. He got to his feet to shake hands with my fa-her. We stood there uncomfortably. "Well, I'd better o up and get dressed," I said. "Chris is going to be best nan," I told my father.

"Well, you were best man this weekend," Leary said.

My father laughed his jarring laugh. "Yeah, it's hard o tell the best man from the groom today, I guess."

It was the worst joke my father had ever made. Leary nd I stared at each other; he looked as though he were oing to cry. My father said quickly, "Well, there's still he Nationals coming up, isn't there? You boys'd better vatch out for this little Buddy Jahncke from Sugar Bowl. Ie's only sixteen but he's just as apt to sneak past you in lalom as not. Too little for downhill, though," he said, hen stopped abruptly. Leary sat down again.

Just then Jean-Gaby came in and offered my father drink, and I hurried upstairs. I shaved and took a hower, got into my last clean longjohns and a black urtlenecked shirt. My black stretchpants had come ack from the cleaners in a plastic bag. I put them on nd, as Leary's footsteps came along the hall and his loor clicked closed, sat down on the bed to put on my fter-ski boots.

I lay back on the bed. All at once I felt like a spinning oin running out of momentum and circling eccentrically. was marrying Georgiana Brown in three-quarters of n hour. The slow minutes were passing and would ass. "Oh, Anne!" I whispered. I could make tears come o my eyes by whispering her name. "Oh, Anne, Anne!" elf-torturing, self-pitying, I thought of Facel Vegas, achts and private planes, places in Bermuda and Klosters, palaces in Acapulco, hotels on the strip in Las Vegas; people who didn't know what a chain saw was, r a backhoe.

I tried to think about being married to Brown. All that vould come was a picture of the four of us in a motel oom; but two were missing. I thought of the Roch Cup

I had won. My name would be engraved on the cup with the other names, illustrious names, names of champions. I was groom and best man today, best man and groom. I had beaten Leary. I had broken the barrier. And I had beaten Bruce Carrington too. I thought of all those years when, as a junior, I had gnawed at myself because I couldn't beat Bruce. I had beaten him this weekend as well as Leary, as well as everyone. I had at last become the one everybody trailed, and there wasn't any pleasure in it.

Jean-Gaby knocked on my door and called to me to hurry, then knocked on Leary's door.

When I went downstairs my father had changed into a gray suit, suitcase-wrinkled and badly fitting. With an amber highball in his hand he looked like a joke man-of-distinction ad.

Jean-Gaby said, "Ah, Jack, you will come back here after the banquet, will you? There is something we must talk about. It is of your future. You will come, please?"

"Sure," I said. "Sure, we'll be here." I thought of Brown with pity. After the wedding we wouldn't rush off for a happy honeymoon with people throwing shoes and rice; no, we would go to the banquet at the Red Onion because I had won the Roch Cup. And after that we wouldn't drive away either; no, we would go back to Helen's house because we had been summoned by Jean-Gaby. I supposed it was some job for me, part time and well paid, so I could support a wife and baby and still race on the Olympic team; so that I would be taken care of, and so would Leary, and, incidentally, Brown. And I supposed my father would be a little jealous because I had earned the job myself, by being the Roch Cup winner, by being a certainty for the Olympic team.

Going to the Hotel Jerome, Leary and I were in the VW, my father and Jean-Gaby in the green jeep. In the lobby Helen was instructing Bruce, Dan, Bill, and Ben McInerny, who were my ushers. Anne, all in blue, passed, carrying flowers; she didn't see me. Brown wasn't in sight. Two ski-bums in waiters' uniforms came along, wheeling a cart with a great punchbowl on it. One of

em called to me, "Hey, Roche! Here comes the big
up!" There was laughter. A photographer with a camera
ung around his neck went to talk to Helen. She started
way with him, saw me, and darted over. "Oh, Jack,
ear, have you got the ring? You haven't forgotten the
ng?"

"I've got it."

She laid a hand on her breast and closed her eyes.
Bless us. Give it to Chris."

I took the ring out of its tissue paper and handed it to
eary, who zipped it into his pocket. He and I joined
e ushers while Helen disappeared with the photogra-
her. Jean-Gaby and my father came up, and I let Leary
ake the introductions.

"Did you see the cake, Jack?" McInerny asked. "What
monster!"

Dan started to ask, "Where're you and Georgie—" but
elen reappeared, waving urgently at the ushers and
ean-Gaby. My father left with them, saying, "Well, good
ck, Jackie."

For a moment Leary and I were alone together. "Oh,
hrist, Jack," he said in a miserable voice. "There's no
ay to stop it now I guess."

"I guess not," I said.

People in ski clothes were coming into the lobby,
acers and ski-bums and tourists. I heard a Texas voice,
ut it wasn't Dixie Rigg. A flash bulb went off. Jean-
aby hurried up and took hold of my arm. "Please, you
re to come by here." He led Leary and me into a small
om off the banquet room, where the wedding was to
e. Through the open door we could see rows of folding
hairs and a dais. There were more flowers than there
ad been at my mother's funeral. On the dais was a little
ald man in a dark suit with the neat collar of a white
urtlenecked shirt showing. But it wasn't a turtlenecked
irt, it was a clerical collar. It was the first thing that
ad seemed funny today.

The ushers were bringing people in and seating them
the folding chairs. Someone began to play a little
rgan at the back of the room. The minister smiled and

beckoned to us, and Leary and I went out to stand before him.

I realized that the organ was playing "Here Comes the Bride." I turned and saw Brown. She was moving down the aisle with Jean-Gaby, and they came so slowly that her limp was not noticeable. She wore a veil attached to a blue earband, a white sweater, and off-white Bogners. Behind her were Anne and the other bridesmaids, carrying bouquets.

There was an awkward moment while Jean-Gaby helped Brown up onto the dais. Anne came up too, while Lorraine, Alice, Evelyn, and Joanne stopped in a line below them, and the ushers formed a similar line on my side. Reading from his prayer book, the minister said in a fruity voice, "Who giveth this woman . . ." Jean-Gaby said he did, then went back to sit with Helen. Brown stood with her face turned down as the minister went on. Anne's nostrils looked pinched and white.

Brown put out her left hand, Leary passed me the ring, and I said, "With this ring I thee wed." It seemed to be over almost before it had started. Brown took my arm and I helped her from the dais. We started down the aisle between the rows of people sitting in the folding chairs. Behind us Anne took Leary's arm, and behind them the bridesmaids and ushers paired off in procession.

Then we had to do it over again, in dumb show, for the photographers.

People were enlisted to hold up ski poles for us to walk under. There were pictures of me kissing Brown, of Brown throwing a bouquet to the bridesmaids, of the bridesmaids and ushers signing Brown's cast. Once everything had to stop when Brown got the giggles. The rest of the time her face was a small, dark, unsmiling mask.

The photographers were still at it when we cut the cake, and I was disgusted to see the way faces froze into phony smiles whenever a camera appeared. I got stuck talking to people I didn't want to talk to, like Lorraine, who kept saying how *wonderful* and how *perfect* it was about Brown and me. I talked for a while with one of the men in the syndicate that had bought me in the Calcutta about how much better skiing was in Europe than America, which is the dullest of all ski conversations, and I listened to Dan Arganbright explain how the downhill course had psyched him out. But finally Anne and I came together.

She smiled brightly at me. "How is it behind the glass curtain?"

"What?"

"Oh, I read somewhere that a couple went behind a glass curtain when they got married." She seemed nervous.

"I haven't noticed any difference yet," I said. "How does it feel to be a three-way winner?"

"I'm feeling a little shattered at the moment."

I tried to smile, thinking she was still talking about Brown and me. But she said, "I've been accused of hogging the photographers—among other things." She looked around to see who was near.

"Who? Helen?"

She shook her head. "The wicked witch of the north. And warned," she said.

"You mean Mrs. May? Warned about what?"

"I shouldn't even be talking to you now, Lilith that I am." She moved away to take a glass of punch from a tray one of the waiters held, then she disappeared.

Alice came up to whisper how glad she was that Brown had decided to marry me instead of Chris Leary.

When it was time for the banquet Brown and I rode silently over to the Red Onion, where there were prime-rib dinners and speeches and the Roch Cup. I saw my father staring at me, his face pink and anxious, as I rose to hold up the big, permanent cup for a moment, to applause. I thanked the president of the ski club, then sat down with my collection of trophies and pins, to clap for Harry Butler and Bill Birks. I worried over what Anne had said at the reception, and because she would not look at me when she stood up to get her cup and the three little medals shaped like aspen leaves for the three events she had won.

The dinner dragged on through coffee and ice cream.

Sitting with Mrs. May, Helen, and some of the brides-maids, Brown pushed listlessly at her ice cream with her spoon. But finally it was over, and for the few minutes' drive across Aspen she and I were alone together again in the VW.

She said in her small voice, "Where are we going tonight, Jack? Are we going to drive somewhere?"

"I'm pretty tired. Aren't you tired?"

"Let's not stay at Helen's house tonight."

"We can go to a motel."

"Let's do that," Brown said. She sat slumped in her seat. "I'm sorry it was so awful," she said. "It was so awful. Those photographers, and Helen, and Mrs. May —I keep thinking I'll be able to laugh about it all someday, but I'll bet I won't."

"It was pretty awful."

"Everything was so phony."

"Well, it's over."

"Well, you won the Roch. I was awfully proud. I really was, Jack."

"Did you hear Charley Catten broke his leg?" I said, and she nodded as I pulled over to the curb in front of Helen's house. The jeep and the Cadillac were already in the drive.

In a small voice she asked, "Do we have to stay here very long?"

"I don't think so. Jean-Gaby said he had something important to talk to me about."

"Oh," Brown said. I went around to help her out of the car. "I think your father's awfully nice," she said. We went slowly up the walk. The stars were out. They looked small and cold. It was a cold place.

"Maybe we ought to start west tonight," I said. "We could get to Glenwood Springs." All at once it seemed so far to Reno, where we had to go first: across part of Colorado, across Utah, across all but the last twenty miles of Nevada.

"You're too tired," Brown said. "You shouldn't try to drive if you're tired. Let's stay in a motel and start early in the morning."

In the foyer, as I helped Brown off with her parka, there was a pop like a flash bulb. Jean-Gaby had opened a bottle of champagne. He handed glasses to us as we came in.

"Isn't it too bad Dixie couldn't be here," Helen said.

Jean-Gaby made a toast in French that I was too tired to understand.

We all drank, and my father made a toast. Then we sat down, Brown and I together on the high-backed loveseat, where she leaned against my shoulder. Leary sat on the back of his neck in the red chair, Anne on the pile of cushions.

"Thank you so much, Helen," Brown said. She sounded affected and insincere. "It was just wonderful!"

"Thank you, Helen," I said, and I thought I must sound phony too.

But Helen seemed pleased and said we were very welcome. "Darling, you must hurry and tell Jack and Chris your plan," she added.

Jean-Gaby stood up, holding his champagne glass. He looked lean as jerked beef, and his dark face with its disfiguring mole was very serious. "Ah, Jack, we have already spoken of this to Chris. Now it is time to speak of it to you also. I must tell you I am very pleased with what you have done this weekend. The physician has had a very good patient."

Helen was smiling at me, Leary was studying his hands, Anne was frowning. She and my father looked puzzled. Brown leaned against me heavily as Jean-Gaby went on, "You will remember we have spoken of the difficulties of ski racers in America?"

I nodded.

"It is very clear that unless there is a disaster you and Chris will be chosen for the Olympic team. There is no question. Others will also be chosen, but they do not matter. You two have this certain chance—"

He held up a hand. "I go ahead of myself," he said. "This summer I have been asked to come to Portillo, in Chile. It is publicity. But perhaps I am to do a little teaching there—certain special guests; perhaps they want me to come to cause their ski school to go better, perhaps to help them develop a new ski area; perhaps many things." He shrugged as though none of that were important. "I have written these two letters," he said. "I have first written my friend Yves Valéry. You know of him, of course. He will be in charge of training the French Olympic team. Next year it will be very important for the French to win from the Austrians. For tourism, you understand—for selling French skis, for other things. Now: I have written my friend Yves Valéry perhaps it can be arranged that the French team will train this summer in Portillo, for very little cost to them, perhaps for nothing. It will be of mangificent assistance to them. Next I have written my friends at Portillo that perhaps it is possible to have the French team come to Portillo to train this summer, it will be magnificent for publicity." He raised his champagne glass again, almost in another toast. He smiled. "And two Americans will also come and train there. Helen will pay all their expenses. She has said she is very pleased to do this."

Helen whispered, "Very, very pleased. And of course it is something for Jean-Gaby to do, he has been so at loose ends."

Jean-Gaby flushed. He said, "I will coach you. You will understand this. We will work very hard. There will be excellent competition there. There will be the French team, I am sure of it. Perhaps there will be others—Swiss, perhaps even some Austrians. We will work very, very hard."

There was a silence. Anne was hugging her knees and squinting at Jean-Gaby as though she were seeing something she didn't want to see. I saw it too. What do you do when you're through being a champion? Leary had asked. It seemed that you plotted and scrambled to make a place for yourself and pretended you were not plotting and scrambling, that you were not desperate. If Jean-Gaby could make Olympic winners out of Leary and me, he would make a place for himself in this country. I was ashamed to look so cynically at such a gift.

"It sounds wonderful," I said.

"You two can be skiers of the world class," Jean-Gaby said. "Almost you are now. But not quite. And to me it is very sad that you can go so little farther. To go farther you must spend much time racing with people you can beat only if you are very, very lucky. You must train very hard against people like this. Then perhaps one of you can become a real champion. Not merely a champion in this country, which is still so very small in international skiing. This country has not yet won one medal, not even the bronze, in the men's skiing of the Olympic Winter Games. I would be very, very proud if I could help this to happen."

It was as though he were making a speech to many more than were present in Helen's living room. He bowed a little before sitting down next to Helen, who patted his knee and murmured something to him. Leary was rubbing his hands over his face.

"See my draft board," he said.

"You are not to worry about that!" Helen said.

Then everyone seemed to be looking at me. But Jean-Gaby stared at me most intensely, and with a sudden sweet bursting I realized that he was counting on me, not Leary. He thought I could be the champion.

I took a deep breath. "It sounds great."

"Say, that certainly sounds like a wonderful thing," my father said. "I hope you appreciate that, Jackie—Chrissie." Helen started to speak, but he leaned forward in his chair and said, "But just a minute now, Jackie. What about your little wife there?"

"I'm sure Georgiana won't mind if Jack takes a summer's absence for such a chance as this," Helen said smoothly. "Will you, dear?"

"She's asleep," Anne said.

Her face, and my father's and Jean-Gaby's, Leary's and Helen's, floated in my eyes, strange and demanding.

Helen said, "Oh, you mean the baby, Mr. Roche." She laughed. "Really, that's no problem either. Everything can be taken care of. There are no problems!" she cried in her soft voice.

"Wait! Just a minute, Jackie!" my father said. "You

have got your little wife now, and a kid on the way."

"Oh, Christ!" Leary said.

My father leaned toward me. It was as though he were trying to touch me with his eyes, to communicate without having to say it aloud. But he had to say it. "Jackie— it's a wonderful chance and you ought to be damn grateful to Mr. and Mrs. Michonneau. I mean, it's a wonderful thing. But you have got a wife, and a kid coming."

I managed to nod.

"Jackie, don't get me wrong. It's just that you have responsibilities now. You have to be a man now. You know what I mean. You have a family to— Jackie, I was trying to tell you before—I talked to Bill Patten again. He is real excited about you and Georgie for his ski school. It's the perfect thing. You and Georgie are pretty big names, you know. Everybody around the summit and the lake, and Squaw and Reno, is really— Jackie, if it works out you win big in the Nationals I'll bet you could write your own ticket with Bill Patten. Even if you don't. I mean, he is really interested. And that was before you even won the Roch!"

Leary said calmly, "You see now, Jack? You see how they try to cut you down?"

My father's face turned redder, turned angry. "You may like being a ski-bum," he said to Leary. "I know my boy's not counting on being a ski-bum all his life."

"That's so damned unfair, Mr. Roche!" Anne cried.

Jean-Gaby got to his feet again. At first he only stuttered. Then he said, "In this country you do not comprehend. Your son might be the greatest at this thing in the world—in the world, do you understand? A champion of the world. Is that not something of importance? Let me tell you, that is the immortal thing! Probably he will not be that, perhaps certainly he will not be, but there is a chance. Would you have your son throw away this chance for only a *position*? For only the making of *money*? Is it that there are to be no champions in this America but the champions of making money? I tell you it is a terrible thing!"

My father said, "Do you know anybody that used to

be a champion? Drunken bums. Listen—once I saw Maxie Baer—"

"*I* am a champion!" Jean-Gaby said in a terrible voice. He hit the flat of his hand against his chest. "Do not speak to me of it! I would not be any other thing! I am immortal!" He turned very red and in a thick voice said to the rest of us, "Pardon. You must pardon me for saying this."

"You think I like what I'm saying?" my father said stubbornly, miserably. Leary grimaced at me with a bony show of teeth. "Jackie," my father said. "Listen—"

"I've been listening," I said. I felt as though my head were going to split open. I felt filled with poison. "You don't know how phony everything is here. But you're being phony too."

"What?" he said. "Jackie—"

"But now I'm sick of being a phony," I said and glanced at Chris, who got sick of being a bastard sometimes. "You talk about my responsibilities," I said to my father. "I'll tell you what my responsibilities are. They are to me, to myself. I've been pretending I'm not that way so long I can't stand myself any more. I want to be what Jean-Gaby was talking about. I want to win. I've spent most of my life trying to win. Trying to beat people. I spent four years as a junior trying to beat Bruce Carrington so I could be best instead of second best. And I've done time trying to beat Chris Leary. I wasn't trying to be just second best." Brown stirred against me. Anne was staring at me with dark, wide eyes, and in a way it was to her I was talking. I felt cold and hateful and a little drunk.

"I want to be the best in the world," I said. "And so does any racer worth a lift pass. I guess it's just a thing you get born with or stuck with some way—like freckles, or cancer. And I'm sick of pretending I don't feel that way and just happen to be up in the first seed out of luck or something. I'm there because I want to be the best there is, and I think about it all the time."

I took a deep breath and said to my father, "You don't want me to be in the Olympics, do you?"

"What?" he whispered. "What the hell do you mean, son?"

"You pretend you can't stand to say those things to me," I said. "How I have to settle down because I've got a wife and a baby on the way. You got your medal in the Lake Placid Games, but not for jumping. You got one for doing a good job of work like everybody else. So you don't want me to go to the Olympics and compete, and maybe win a real medal coming down a mountain faster than anybody else in the world. You don't want me to be a real champion. You just want me to be a little bit of a one so you can go around telling your friends Jackie's doing great, isn't he doing fine? So I'm still Charley Roche's boy. But anything more than that and you get lost, don't you? Pushed out, I mean. I mean— I know it and I'm sorry, but why don't you face it too?" I began to run down, and all at once I was shocked at what I had said.

Anne got up and ran out of the room. I almost groaned. But she was the one who had to hear it.

My father rose. He stood facing me with his head hanging in that way I knew so well, looking at me through his eyebrows. His face sagged in hard red lines, and his fists bulged in the pockets of the cheap suit. I remembered the time he'd broken a man's jaw in a bar fight; the deputy who had come with a warrant had been afraid of him. I thought he was going to have to hit me to save himself, as I was trying to hate Anne for what she must think of me now. But he only shook his head once and walked heavy-footed out into the foyer. The front door slammed.

Jean-Gaby had his face averted. Leary's grin looked as though it hurt him. I heard Brown yawn; her weight was removed from my shoulder. I got up and said, "Well, I guess we'll be going along. We'll stay at a motel tonight and pick up my stuff tomorrow, if that's all right, Helen. Thanks for everything."

"You're very welcome to stay here tonight." She said it as though nothing had happened.

"I think we'll go to a motel, thanks." I helped Brown up.

Leary came over to shake hands. "See you at Squaw," he said casually. "See you in Squaw, Brownie," he said, not so casually. I shook hands with Jean-Gaby.

"It is a very difficult thing," he said. "It is very hard, Jack."

Helen came over to kiss Brown, and I looked toward the stairs up which Anne had disappeared. I wished I could have explained it further to her, but maybe there was nothing more to explain.

In the VW, Brown said quietly, "I'm sorry you had a fight with your father. Was it my fault?"

At least I could be thankful she had heard so little of it. "No, it was my fault," I said. "I just—" I didn't go on, and she didn't say anything more.

We found a motel with a blue VACANCY sign out, and, in a room that cost more money than I had wanted to pay, Brown sat on one of the twin beds with her hands in her parka pockets while I stood looking out the window at the blue steam rising from the heated swimming pool.

"Do you want to go for a swim?" she asked.

"I guess not tonight."

"Jack, you don't have a razorblade, do you?"

"I've got an electric shaver."

"I'm sewed into these damn pants."

We managed to pick and rip open the seam with a nail file, so she could get her cast out. She was shivering. I didn't know how we were going to handle the sex part. She said in a rush, "Jack, I'm so *tired*."

"So am I."

I turned off the light and we undressed in the dark, although I could see her in silhouette in the faint illumination that came through the window from the lighted pool. When I came out of the bathroom she was in bed. "Good night, Jack," she whispered.

"Good night, Georgie," I said and got into the other bed. I thought if I could have apologized to my father I would have told him I was sorry I had piled on when everybody else was jumping him, and that I knew the things I had said were only partly true. I would have liked to tell him I wasn't really mad at him, I was only mad at myself.

In the morning, with clear gray light streaming into the room, I went for a swim in the pool while Brown watched me through the window. Then we went to Helen's, where no one was up but the German woman, who was sitting in the kitchen with a cup of coffee. I collected my things and strapped my skis and poles on the VW's rack. We drove to Glenwood Springs before we stopped for breakfast. Then we headed west, Brown and I.

THE NATIONALS | IV

1

It was raining when we came into Reno. The tires made sounds like zippers, and there were soft streaks of color on the wet asphalt fron the neon signs. Squaw Valley was almost three thousand feet higher; it would be snowing there and on the summit, but spring was not far off. The VW's wipers squeegeed the water back and forth, back and forth.

"I'd better phone before we go home," Georgie said. She had been taut as a guitar string all day, talking too much and too fast about the Roch and the Nationals and Jean-Gaby's proposition, as though all that mattered to her was my racing; or as though she was trying desperately to keep off the subject of her father.

I stopped at a gas station where there was a phone booth. When I'd paid for the gas I counted the bills in my wallet, Georgie's and my pooled funds; a twenty, four fives, two singles—forty-two dollars left. I didn't know where any more was going to come from. But we would be taken care of at Squaw through the Nationals, and surely Mr. Gayley would be there—and then I had the almost frightened realization that I probably would be taken care of from now on: the spring races, then Portillo, then the Olympic team. I would be in Portillo in September, when the baby was due: Georgie never mentioned that when we talked about my training with Jean-Gaby. She would have to stay with her parents while I was in Chile.

I drove the VW over beside the phone booth to wait for her. I could see her through the rain-streaked windshield, smiling, nodding, shaking her head, and I turned to watch the evening cars passing on 40, some with their lights on. Rain drummed on the roof. Rain depresses skiers.

Georgie opened the door, dropped into the seat, and swung her cast inside. "How was it?" I asked.

"I talked to Mother. She said everything was—fine." She slid down in her seat and laid her head back as I started the engine. "She said everything was just fine," she said.

I counted down in a slow voice like a starter, while she laughed. "Go!" I said, and we moved out of the gas station into the line of cars. Georgie didn't speak again as we drove through the rain to her father's house. I turned into the driveway and stopped.

Mrs. Brown ran down the steps, holding her skirt. She threw her arms around me as I got out. I patted her awkwardly, rain dripping down my face. I heard the dog barking. Mrs. Brown cried, "Oh, dear Jack! We're so happy!" She darted around the car to Georgie.

The porchlight was on, turning the raindrops to quicksilver where they fell, and Mr. Brown appeared on the porch with a glass in one hand, the other raised in a gesture of welcome. Georgie's sister, in a red sweater, came out behind him.

"You shut up, Monte!" Georgie cried at the dog. "It's just Jack and me!"

"Come in out of the rain, you two!" Mr. Brown called.

Mrs. Brown and Georgie and I went up the steps together, the dog scrambling up and down past us. On the porch, Georgie and Carrie hugged each other, and Mr. Brown tried to wrench my hand off, saying in a loud, ragged voice, "Well, you won big, fellow! Well, you finally pulled it off!"

As I got my hand back from him, emotions I hadn't even known were stored up in me began to coil and move. It seemed strange that the first thing my father-in-law said to me, which was to congratulate me, should make me realize I hated him.

Inside, we all sat down, Carrie hugging her legs against herself in the chair by the TV set. Mrs. Brown immediately got up again. "Have you children eaten?" I said we hadn't, and Mr. Brown said, "Tell you what, let's all go down to Eugene's and have a steak. How about that?"

"Gee, we're awfully tired, Daddy," Georgie said with elaborate gestures. "Gee, I know Jack must be bushed." Mr. Brown looked disappointed. He went out to the kitchen to get us a drink, Mrs. Brown to make something to eat.

Carrie said, "Hey! You guys just got married! Yay for you!"

"How's the weather been, Carrie?" Georgie said in a low voice.

Carrie swept a hand back and forth in front of her face in a gesture I didn't understand. "Good!" she said. "He thinks it's really *great* Jack won the Roch. And *every*thing!" Quickly she said to me, *"Every*body does. *Really;* congratulations and everything, Jack. Terrific!"

"Thanks," I said.

Mr. Brown came back, bringing beer in Pilsener glasses for Georgie and me, and sat down holding his own replenished highball. I realized how much Georgie looked like him. He smiled at her, with the heavy lines around his mouth deepening. He smiled at me.

"You got a fine run in the papers here, Jack. Some fair pictures. I wish I'd been back there to see it. Quite a write-up on the wedding too."

"Life took a lot of pictures, Daddy," Georgie said. "And the sports magazines and ski magazines. *Life* didn't know whether they were going to use them or not though."

Hugging herself as though she were shivering, Carrie said, "Yay! Big deal!"

"So you found out you could whip Chris Leary after all," Mr. Brown said. "He didn't get in trouble, did he?"

"He ran off the course in the slalom."

"But you won the downhill clean?"

I nodded and sipped my beer. I felt resentful and confused because this was not as bad as I had thought it would be, or even bad at all. Mr. Brown was neither hurt nor angry at Georgie, but pleased, and proud of me.

"You couldn't see much of the downhill because it was

snowing," Georgie said. "But Jack was really cranking down the slalom. It was one of the best runs I've ever seen."

"Well, honey, if you hadn't hurt yourself you'd have been in there with him, wouldn't you?" But there was no edge to the words, and Georgie grinned and shook her head.

"Oh, I don't think so. It was Anne's weekend. Anne was so great."

He grunted. He said to me, "Well, the last big one's coming up, Jack. Do you think you can do it again?"

"Maybe," I said. "Chris is pretty hard to beat, but I'm skiing well now."

"He'll be sweating this one out. He'll be trying too hard. You see if I'm not right."

Mrs. Brown bustled in to say we would have something to eat in a minute. She sat down. "How was your trip out, Georgie?"

"Well, we had to take it awfully slow. I kept getting cramps in my leg and Jack would have to stop and let me walk around. I didn't think we'd ever get here."

"Those damned beetles," Mr. Brown said. "They may be easy on gas, but they are damned uncomfortable on a long trip. How's the ankle, honey?"

"Oh, it's fine."

"Wasn't it good to find out you'd be skiing again by Christmas?"

I glanced quickly at Georgie; she hadn't told me. She leaned down to scratch Monte's ears.

"Are there other married couples on the circuit?" Mrs. Brown asked. "We've been wondering about that."

"Some married guys," I said. "Joe Hammond's married."

"Well, it took you three days to drive out," Mr. Brown said. "That's about what it takes, from here to Aspen, unless you want to kill yourself driving." He looked at Georgie, and she flushed.

"Oh, I hoped you'd fly, Daddy!"

"Well, we considered flying," Mrs. Brown said quickly. "But—"

"You know your mother is terrified of flying," Mr. Brown said.

"Oh, Daddy, I'm sorry," Georgie said. "But there just wasn't time! Anyway, it was all Helen's fault."

"That's Jean-Gaby Michonneau's wife," I said.

"How do you mean it was her fault, honey?" he asked. But he didn't say it suspiciously, and I saw that he wasn't trying to give Georgie a bad time, he was only sorry he had missed the wedding.

Georgie must have realized it too, for she seemed more at ease as she said, "Oh, it all happened too fast! I mean, Jack and I were talking about it a little, then all at once everybody was talking about it. Helen was all excited, and there was this man from *Life*—" She went on to tell about Helen's plan for a ski wedding and the photographers' session after it as though we had been rushed into the wedding by all the people who were having a good time playing with it. And finally she said triumphantly, "Well, and you know what you used to say to me, Daddy."

"What was that, honey?"

"Oh, you remember! That if you wanted to win you had to grab every advantage you could get, something like that. Well, I wanted to grab Jack. So I did!"

"I thought I'd grabbed you," I said.

Everyone laughed. Mr. Brown cleared his throat. "Well, you made a hell of a good grab, honey."

"Hey, *yay!*" Carrie said. "You mean the wedding's going to be in *Life,* Gorgo?"

"Oh, wait now!" Mrs. Brown said. "Don't talk about anything interesting while I'm gone!" She hurried out to the kitchen.

Speaking loudly so her mother could hear, Georgie said, "Well, we're not sure it's going to be in. They have to decide back in New York. But they must've taken a million pictures. They took shots of everybody signing my cast." She thrust her scribbled-on cast out where her father could see it.

"We'll have to write Mrs. Michonneau and thank her," Mr. Brown said.

"Oh, I wish we could've gone!" Carrie said. "Oh, *darn* it!"

"How's your beer, Jack?" Mr. Brown said. "Another one?"

"No, thanks."

He started to get up, stopped. His throat worked as he swallowed; he pursed his flat lips. Then he said, "Honey, at first we were a little bit hurt about it. We wish we could've been there. But it's all right, honey. Everything's all right now." He looked at me out of the corners of his eyes and grinned wryly. "Okay, Jack?"

"Well, we wish you could've come," I said.

Mrs. Brown brought us plates on which were ground-beef patties and carrots and stringbeans, and she fussed over us, running back to the kitchen for milk and salt and pepper and paper napkins.

Georgie was silent now, round-eyed and serene, as she ate her dinner. We finished quickly, and Mrs. Brown took away our plates and brought coffee. Mr. Brown went to make himself another drink.

When he came back he said, "Well, that was quite a day for you, Jack. You won the downhill and copped the Roch and got married. I call that a full day."

"It was a big day."

Georgie said, "Oh, that wasn't all though. Can I tell about Jean-Gaby, Jack?"

I couldn't very well say no, now that she had brought it up. "Sure," I said.

"Well, after the banquet we went to Helen's, because Jean-Gaby had something he wanted to talk to Jack and Christy about—" She stopped and smiled at me; I was to continue. I told about Jean-Gaby's and Helen's proposition, and I thought, as I spoke of it, that I didn't really want to believe in the possibility yet—not until after the Nationals.

When I'd finished, George Brown said in a careful voice, "You don't sound like you think it's so much of a thing."

"I think it's a hell of a big thing."

He brushed a hand through his thick hair. The lines in

his face cut deeply. In the careful, almost gentle voice he said, "You sound like you're backing off a little from it, Jack."

They were all looking at me. I wondered how he could have known I was a little afraid. Someone had said once that in a race there was one winner and all the rest excuses. If all the possible excuses were taken away, and you failed, then there was nothing to hide behind. I was afraid of that.

"Don't make a mistake," George Brown said. "I made a mistake." For a moment I thought he wasn't going on, but then he said, "I was a very hot boy in the high-school football league here. Stanford offered me a scholarship. Cal and Washington too, but Stanford was the hot club in those years. Well, I wanted to take that scholarship, but my folks wanted me to go to school here. I'd be living here, and the people I'd be doing business with would be going to the university here. But I could've gone to Stanford if I'd wanted to push it. But I didn't. I was a little bit scared of finding out I wasn't as hot a halfback as I thought I was. But maybe I could've made All-American and—"

"Carrie," Mrs. Brown said quietly. She rose and began to take up the cups and saucers; Carrie helped her. They both went out to the kitchen, and George Brown watched them go.

Then he looked at me with hot eyes. "That's a joke around here," he said. "Wanting to be an All-American. Case of arrested development. Well, maybe that's the way development gets arrested. Don't you make any mistake like backing off from a thing like this, Jack. You grab this chance. Because if you don't you'll spend the rest of your life kicking yourself and everybody else because you didn't grab it." He paused, took a deep breath, and said, "You're not to worry about Georgie. She can stay with us. She'll be back on the circuit herself next winter, even if she won't make the Olympics. Georgie'll be just fine. And there'll be no problem about money either." He swung toward Georgie. "Jack's to have this chance, isn't he?"

"Oh, yes!" Georgie said. "Of course! He has to!"

I said, "I've been trying not to think about it until after the Nationals." It was as though you had a letter to mail, I thought, and because you were going to the PO everybody else gave you their letters too; until you could hardly stagger under the load. I didn't want to carry George Brown's mail.

"I've been talking about it too much," Georgie said. "I'm sorry, Jack. Mr. Roche was talking about this Silver Ridge resort, Daddy. Mr. Roche told Jack the man who's going to run it might be interested in Jack setting up a ski school. Co-director or something like that."

Her father stared at me as though he saw it all. "Sure I know Bill Patten's interested in you," he said. "He says it's time we had our ski schools run by our own people instead of a bunch of Austrians. He'll be a lot more interested in you if you win the Nationals. But everybody in the country will be interested if you win something in the Winter Games. Don't you worry about Bill Patten, he'll keep." He grinned at Georgie, "And don't think I'm not looking forward to having two champions in the family."

Mrs. Brown called from the kitchen, "I'm making some more coffee!"

"I guess we'd better go to bed," I said. "I'm pretty tired."

The twin beds in Georgie's room were both made up. We got into one so we could talk. Her trophies gleamed dully out of the darkness on their shelf, and a little light came through the window across the foot of the bed and the green bookcase beside the door that held her Book of Knowledge. We could hear the rain and the fainter long sound of the Truckee River running behind the house.

Georgie laughed shakily. "It was so easy. It was like being all braced for somebody to run into you and they don't and you almost fall over the other way."

"I didn't know the doctor'd said you could ski again by Christmas."

"He said *maybe*. If I take a lot of therapy and whirl-pool baths and things. But I'm not going to race any more. I'm going to school for my teaching credential in the fall. I can go to summer session while you're in Portillo."

I put my hand on her stomach. "When's it going to show?"

"I think if you have good muscles it doesn't show for a long time."

There would be trouble then, I thought. Or maybe not. Maybe no one really wanted to make trouble. But I felt low. Now the pressure was going to be on me instead of Georgie, and though I could take it better than she could, I was not looking forward to this relationship with George Brown. For the first time I wondered what I was doing here, where I didn't want to be, caught in a situation that had nothing to do with me.

"You're awfully quiet," Georgie said. "Jack, are you ashamed of me?"

"I think you're just fine."

"Are you depressed about Daddy? I was just so—surprised tonight. But I won't ever let him give you a bad time."

I said, "It's not that. I guess I'm just depressed."

After a pause she said in a blurred voice, "Jack, can't I do anything for *you?*"

At first I didn't know what she meant. Then I laid my hand on her stomach again and moved it beneath her pajama top. Her cast scraped my shin as she turned toward me. "It's such a funny way to be married," she whispered. "Jack, do you want to?"

"Can't you tell?"

She laughed shakily again. "Well, I thought you *might*. We'll have to be awfully quiet though," she whispered.

2

It was nine o'clock in the morning before we came downstairs, and Mr. Brown had gone to work and Carrie to school. Mrs. Brown was sitting in the breakfast nook in the kitchen, wearing a tan cashmere cardigan. She got up and kissed us both. Outside it had stopped raining, but the sky was still threatening. The dog appeared, to paw and smell at Georgie, and, when she sat down at the table, crept under it to lie at her feet. Mrs. Brown brought us coffee.

"Your father telephoned this morning," she said to me. "He said I wasn't to waken you."

Brown studiously stirred sugar and cream into her cup while her mother tore a leaf from the telephone pad.

"He said you are welcome to stay in the Culver cabin at Squaw. You can get the key at the realty office. He said you'd remember that Mrs. Culver is Mr. Gayley's sister. You're welcome to the cabin through the Nationals. He'll see you one of these days, he said." She handed me the notepaper, which had written on it: "Culver," "Gayley," "realty," and "thru nats." She had a sweet, quick smile that tucked the corners of her lips in deeply.

"That's awfully nice of them," Georgie said. She looked at me out of the corners of her eyes.

"Good deal," I said.

"I'm sure you'd rather honeymoon in a cabin at Squaw than here with us," Mrs. Brown said and smiled at me.

After she'd brought us plates of bacon, eggs, and toast, she sat down with us. "Georgiana, you can take the station wagon if you want—you can handle the automatic shift without using your bad leg. Daddy said he'd bring home a demonstrator for me."

"Oh, thanks," Georgie said. "I don't need a car though. I'll just sit on the deck at the lodge and wait for Jack. I thought I'd knit him a sweater. I like to think about myself on the deck knitting and waiting for Jack to come off the mountain."

Pushing her sleeves up on her fair-haired arms, Mrs. Brown said, "You are not to think Daddy is unhappy about this, Georgiana. He was a little shocked at first. Because we'd had no warning. But he's very pleased. He's very proud of Jack."

"Oh, that's good," Georgie said.

Mrs. Brown turned to look out the window. "Are you going to—to have babies right away, dear?"

Brown gave me a scared look with her penny-colored eyes. "Yes, Mother, I think we are."

"I was wondering if we should make an appointment with Dr. Weir for preventative things."

"Too late," Georgie said.

"When, dear?" her mother asked.

"I'm not really sure yet."

Her mother nodded primly. Then she smiled the quick smile and patted Georgie's hand. "It will be all right," she said. She got up to put the coffee pot on again. "You are not to worry, dear."

"I won't," Georgie said, and her hand caught mine and squeezed it.

"I think it will please Daddy very much once he gets used to the idea that it's going to be so soon. He was saying last night what marvelous little skiers your children would be. I hope it will be a boy. That would please him so much."

There was a silence. I said, "Well, you can sit on the deck at the lodge and *pretend* you're knitting something for me." Both Georgie and Mrs. Brown laughed, Mrs. Brown standing at the stove with her back to us, and Georgie raising her coffee cup as though to hide her face with it.

When we started for Squaw Valley the clouds were breaking up and slashes of brilliant blue sky showed through. Mrs. Brown had remembered at the last moment to hunt up the sports section of Monday's paper. Georgie was very pleased with the headline, which was: ROCHE ROMPS TO ROCH WIN. There was a blurred photograph of me coming through a slalom gate, and a photograph of Anne and me, under the caption: ASPEN WINNERS. Georgie read some of the text aloud while I drove.

" 'Summit star Jack Roche fulfilled his early promise today when he tore down a tough downhill course on Aspen's Ajax mountain to add the downhill crown to yesterday's slalom win and defeat arch-rival Chris Leary in the combined standings. On the distaff side, ski-lovely

Anne Patterson—' What do you suppose they would have called me if I'd won it?" Georgie said wistfully.

"Well, ski-cripple, as you stand," I offered, to make her laugh; but she didn't laugh. She finished the article, which included a paragraph about the wedding, and then was silent for a time.

"Brown Bungles for Big Bust," she said finally.

"How about 'belly'?" I said and hoped she would find that funny. She laughed until she cried.

There was snow almost down to the California line, and when we turned off the freeway onto 89 we passed a state pushplow hurrying and clanking along the edge of the pavement. Many cars now were carrying skis. The snowbanks along the sides of the road were four feet high when we turned into Squaw Valley, and ahead of us Squaw Peak gleamed soft and pure in the sun, with the top tower of Squaw No. 2 like a nipple on her breast. Granite Chief was laced with terraces of new snow, and houses wore thick white mats like thatched roofs. A rotary was chuffing up one of the subdivision roads, blowing a jet of snow. From the realty office we could see skiers carving up the powder on Red Dog and KT-22.

When we had the key to the Culver cabin, and directions, I had to put on chains and follow the rotary's slow progress to the house, which was an A-frame with a shake roof, looking down on the lodge. I shoveled a path so Georgie could get in, turned on the water and the furnace, and made a fire while she wrote out a grocery list. When I came back from the store she was sitting in front of the fire, looking unhappy, so we went in the bedroom and made love on the crackling plastic mattress cover. Afterward she cried and wouldn't tell me what she was crying about.

Later I went down the the lodge and managed to sell my Kneissl Riesen Slaloms to a ski-bum for sixty dollars. On the way home, feeling rich, I stopped at the store again and bought two cellophane-wrapped steaks, some Danish beer, and a couple of paperback mysteries for Georgie. She was lying in front of the fire with her cast in the air, reading a dog-eared comicbook she'd found.

"Did you see anybody?" she asked without looking up.
"Everybody's at Alta."

She threw the comicbook in the fire and watched the
pages char and burn. It was a pleasant, wood-smelling
house, and the slanting walls made it very cozy. "I sold
my Kneissls," I said. "Sixty bucks without the bindings."

"That's wonderful. Next time we go to Reno, let's bring
back my skis and sell them."

"Good idea."

I spent the rest of the afternoon shoveling snow from
the porch and bringing in logs and kindling, and drinking
beer with Georgie before the fire. For dinner we cooked
the steaks on a hibachi in the fireplace and drank the last
two beers. We found some stale marshmallows and toast-
ed them over the embers, and we made love again by the
red flickering glow, on the Navajo rug in front of the fireplace. Afterward we went to bed.

Outside the bedroom window there was a full moon.
The snow-marbled face of Granite Chief looked close
enough to hit with a snowball. The furnace made a
comforting, reverberating roar whenever it came on. I
was almost asleep when Georgie whispered, "Jack?"

"Yeah?"

"Are you awake?"

"Yes."

"Do you wish you'd gone to the race at Alta?"

"No."

"We're having a kind of nice long honeymoon, aren't
we?"

"Sure we are."

"Jack?"

"Yeah?"

"Maybe we oughtn't to do it so much. Isn't it bad for
you or something? I mean, bad for your legs?"

"The Austrians had it worked out that it's all right
before the downhill. Only once though. But never before
the slalom." I snorted, but she didn't seem to think it was
funny.

"Well, maybe we oughtn't to any more when you start
training again."

"Do you want to now?"

"No, I didn't mean that. No, I was just thinking about the Nationals. Is there going to be a new downhill course?"

"It stays a little higher and comes down that face above Tower Twenty. They changed it farther down too. It's not so much wax and tuck as the old course."

"But it's not really bad like Exhibition?"

"It's not so bad. There're some tricky places though."

"Do you think you'll win, Jack? I used to get mad when people would keep asking me that—but do you think you will?"

I supposed that she was thinking about Leary. "Yes, I think I will."

"Jack?"

"Yeah?"

"Did you ever do it with Anne?"

"No."

"Who've you done it with?"

"Girls."

"Any girls I know?"

"No. Why?"

"Because you're awfully good to me and I know you must've had lots of experience. I'll bet you did it with Eileen Porter."

"I'll never tell."

"Well, I know you did it with Anne."

"No," I said. "No, really."

"I wish you had. I'd feel better if you had."

"Why?"

"Oh, I guess I wouldn't feel so cheap and—crummy. If you and Anne had too. Didn't you want to?"

"Sometimes."

"Wouldn't she let you?"

"I didn't ask her."

"Jack—"

"Yeah?"

"I didn't want to. Really. I was so scared. But do you know? I was more scared *not* to than I was *to*. I'm so scared of people being mad at me."

"Well, you don't need to be scared any more. Don't you know that?"

"Don't I? Jack, do you know that it's being cowards that makes people so bad? Do you know that? I've felt sorry for bad people ever since I realized that."

She fell silent, and I lay awake staring out at Granite Chief. I wanted to know about Leary, and I thought it would please her that I would want to know. I said, "How was it with Chris, Georgie?"

"How— Oh! Oh, it was just messy. I was all frozen up and it was just terrible. Not like tonight." Then she said in the affected small voice, "But, Jack—it wasn't just once though. I lied about that."

I laid my hand on her belly, but this time she didn't turn toward me. "Look how beautiful it is out there," I said.

She sat up to look out the window. "Oh, it's so beautiful! Look, the shadows are just like daytime."

When I was almost asleep again she said, "Jack?"

"Yes?"

"Jack, are you having a good time?"

"I'm having a fine time."

"That's good. Because I'm having a wonderful time. Jack, I'm so happy."

"I'm happy too."

"Oh, that's so *good*. Good night, Jack. I won't wake you up any more."

"Good night, Georgie," I said.

3

On Friday, Charley Catten showed up at the Lodge, with a long cast and crutches. He sat with Georgie on the deck while I was up on the mountain, and that night he came for dinner. He was discouraged and thought he'd better give up racing. He had been hot as a junior and his first year on the senior circuit, but every time it looked as though he was getting somewhere, he said, he would bust up. This was his third spiral, and he couldn't ski for a year.

Saturday I called my father, and that night he took us out to The Pfeifer House for dinner. It was a stiff and uncomfortable evening. We all tried so hard to stay off the subject of Jean-Gaby and Portillo, the Olympics and Silver Ridge, and to say nothing that wasn't pleasant, that nobody said anything worth saying. My father didn't seem to be holding a grudge, but I didn't know if I was ready to be forgiven yet.

Sunday the slopes were so jammed with weekend skiers that Fred Wales and I set up slalom poles on the bottom of the Poma Hill and practiced running gates. Some of the local racers came to join us, and it was strange being made to feel like The Great Man by the juniors, and even by some of the racers I'd known in high school. It was hard not to be pompous. Georgie's mother had brought her some yarn and needles and a knitting book from Reno, and she sat on the deck in her Cowichan sweater, knitting and watching us bang down through the gates, and watching me trying to help the juniors. Someone had phoned the results from Alta. Leary had won the slalom but had Markered-out in the downhill for a DNF. Harry Butler had won the men's downhill and Lorraine the women's. There was no news as to how Anne had done.

Late in the afternoon when I came up on the deck to sit with Georgie for a while, Mrs. May appeared. In the Tyrolean hat, a shapeless tweed suit, knit stockings, and her heavy-soled shoes, she looked as though she had just hiked out from Utah. She kissed Georgie and shook hands with me.

"Well, here's the happy married couple," she said.

"Didn't you go to Alta, Mrs. May?"

"Had to fly to Colorado Springs for a little USSA do," she said, seating herself in one of the steel-mesh chairs. "So I came straight on here."

"Can I get you some tea, Mrs. May?" I asked.

"No, thank you."

"Georgie?"

"Please," Georgie said, smiling up from her knitting.

ent into the snack bar, and, when I came back, burning
my fingers on the paper cups of tea, they were both
watching me, Georgie looking flushed and rattled, Mrs.
May with a queer, smug, proprietory expression on her
unburned face. She sat with her legs apart, like a man;
she was peeling an orange.

"A scene from the ages," she said. "The male in his
ion skin or breastplate or whatever the uniform of the
period, and the female impregnated and contentedly
knitting." She had spoken loudly, and people at nearby
tables looked at us. Georgie held her knitting closer to
her face in embarrassment. But Mrs. May didn't seem to
have meant it unkindly. She smiled and popped a section
of orange into her mouth. "The indignities nature prac-
tices upon women," she said. "How is your ankle, Georgi-
na?"

"Oh, it's fine, Mrs. May."

"If you had to break something, you couldn't have
made a better choice. And so clever of you to get everything over with at once." She grinned conspiratorially,
showing teeth stained with orange. "You'll be racing again
next season," she said.

"No," Georgie said.

I watched someone weaving and twisting down through
the slalom poles.

"Oh, yes!" Mrs. May said. She pushed the pile of
orange peel aside, leaned toward Georgie, and said in a
low voice, "I talked with the selection chappies in Colorado Springs. There's a good chance you will still be
chosen for the Olympic team."

"Oh, no," Georgie said.

"Oh, yes, indeed! As you well know, the quality falls to
nothing at all after Lorry, Alice, and Evelyn. To zero. Jo
has *not* done well this year."

She hadn't mentioned Anne. I stared at her as she put
another piece of orange in her mouth. Her eyes, with their
discolored whites, met mine for a moment.

"But that wouldn't be fair!" Georgie said. "I mean, I
did so badly at Stowe. I was only in two tryouts anyway.
And I don't even know if I can ski—" She took a great

237

breath and whispered, "And I'm married! And I'm going to have a baby!"

"I'm very well acquainted with the Olympic regulations," Mrs. May said with mock severity, "and I can assure you there is no ruling against either wives or mothers. None. And I'm sure your husband would be proud to have you competing alongside him. Wouldn't you?" she said to me.

Before I could speak Georgie said, "But what about Anne? Anne's the very best. Isn't Anne—"

"Anne Patterson seems to have chosen not to be a member of the Olympic team," Mrs. May said. "Nor do I believe she is coming out for the Nationals."

I said, "But she— Where is she?"

She gave me a warning look. "In New York, I should imagine. She was going back to her mother, or so she said. I wouldn't presume to believe anything she said— I think she would be terribly hurt if I did. Apparently her mother and Roger Bernand are divorcing each other."

"I know that's true," I said.

"But why?" Georgie said. "I don't understand it. What's she going to do?"

"Professional modeling, I imagine," Mrs. May said. "I believe that is her chosen field." She finished her orange, took a handkerchief from her jacket pocket, and briskly wiped her hands. "I suspect she was given the first of a series of very salutory shocks at the wedding," she said. "I think she regarded Mr. Jack Roche as her own, personal, well-trained puppydog and was exceedingly embarrassed by his defection. Her fellow competitors have been snickering audibly." She sniffed and rose. "Well, I must be off."

I slowly got to my feet for her; crazy old bitch!

"Will you come and have dinner with us one of these nights, Mrs. May?" Georgie asked very formally.

"Wouldn't think of it," Mrs. May said. She put a hand up to my shoulder, the other down to Georgie's, and held them there for a moment. "Couldn't bear it," she said. "But you are two nice children, and you have my blessing." She removed her hands. "I will be focusing all of my considerable will power on the selection committee, Georgiana," she said and strode away across the deck in her heavy shoes.

"Oh, Jesus!" Georgie said almost tearfully.

I sat down and sipped my lukewarm tea. I poured sugar into it, for energy. The crazy old bitch.

"I'm worried about Anne," Georgie said. "Didn't she go to Alta even?"

"I thought she was going," I said. I remembered how strangely Anne had talked at the reception.

"Maybe we ought to try to phone her."

"I guess we ought to," I said. Besides being angry at Mrs. May, I was very uneasy, and I grew more and more uneasy as we sat in silence and Georgie tried to knit.

"Let's call her right now," she said suddenly, so we went home to try. But Roger Bernand's voice, in New York, told the operator that Anne wasn't there and was probably with her mother. He had no idea where her mother could be reached.

Monday afternoon I saw Leary, his black toque pulled down over his ears, adjusting his straps on his poles at the bottom of Squaw No. 2. We rode up together. He'd just arrived from Alta.

"How's married life?" he asked.

"Fine," I said.

He nodded, staring straight ahead. He sat on his poles and folded his arms on his chest with his hands in his armpits, although it wasn't cold.

"How was it at Alta?" I asked. It would have been worse not to ask. "Bad course?"

I could almost see him working out the proper expression, first blank, then sullen; but he managed to grin. "Terrible as far as I was concerned. No, it was a pretty good course. Did you hear Harry won it? He finally got his hot run off."

"I heard you canned-up."

"I lost a ski and hurt my ankle—it's still pretty sore. Jean-Gaby's really peeohed at me. You're supposed to finish if you have to crawl, it turns out. I made a hell of a

slalom run though——" He stopped, made a face, then sat
with his shoulders hunched, so that he looked like a big
skinny bird with a black topknot.

"Anne wasn't there, huh?" I said.

He shook his head.

"What the hell happened to her? Mrs. May said she'd
quit the circuit."

"I heard some of the girls saying she and May had a
big beef after you left Aspen. I heard she's quit the circuit too. Christ," he said, "everything's falling apart."

"She's really crazy," I said. "What the hell's the matter with the crazy old bitch?"

"She sure never did like Anne. She never liked me
either, when I was—— She really hates men; I guess she's
a really terrible old lez. Brownie's okay, huh?" he asked
suddenly.

"She's fine. She's knitting me a sweater."

"How was it with her father?"

"Not bad. He doesn't know about the baby yet though."

"Anyway he won't be a bastard like his dad," he said
in a stuffed-up voice. He laughed harshly. "Well, it was
good seeing *you* being a bastard for once. How is it with
your father?"

"It's going to be all right," I said.

He grunted. Then he sighed. "I don't know why the hell
I didn't stand at Alta, Christ sake," he said. "I don't even
know what happened. I just fell down. Really stupid."

"You got careless when you looked back and saw I
wasn't following you."

He scowled as though he didn't understand. Then he
snorted. "Yeah, maybe that was it," he said. "Maybe I
just missed you. Well, Harry thinks he's old king downhill
now."

But we weren't easy together; he was very nervous with
me, and I was sorry. As the chair climbed toward the top
tower he opened the bar. The footrest was one of those
that folded back and caught the tails of your skis if you
weren't careful. We went down the ramp, and, without
stopping, Leary headed over the long traverse, turned

and shot down over the moguls. He didn't want to ski with me.

That afternoon when I came down, the sun was behind the headwall, and Georgie had moved inside the Lodge. She was sitting at a table by the window in the cafeteria, with her foot in its cast up on a chair seat, talking to a man with thick white hair and a cigarette in a silver holder. He was nodding and smiling in a jerky manner to something she was saying, and when I came up he rose to shake hands. He wore a parka with shoulder patches from European resorts sewn all over it.

"Bill Patten, Jack," he said, gripping my hand in his two hands. "I've been talking to this cute little wife of yours. You shouldn't leave her sitting around here—somebody like me's apt to pick her up and take her home, cast and all."

"You're developing that Silver Ridge resort," I said. "How's it going?"

"Couldn't be better. We'll be starting on the road first thing the snow's off the ground, and the lift as soon as we get a road in. We'll have the first lift and the day lodge up by the end of August." We sat down, on either side of Georgie, and he kept talking in his rapid, non-stop, promoter's voice. "You'll be interested in this lift we're putting in, Jack—Georgie. One of those new Swiss ones, very high capacity—nine hundred skiers an hour."

"Silver Ridge is a nice name," Georgie said.

"Isn't that a good name?"

"It looks like a pretty good mountain," I said.

"We've got experts tell me we're going to have the finest skiing in the Sierra. Pepi Henke—you know Pepi?—he says it will be some of the finest skiing in the country. And we're so close to the lake, you see." He sounded as though he'd been wound up too tightly. "We'll be able to keep that lift filled with sightseers in the summer, magnificent view of Lake Tahoe. And we've got wonderful beginners' slopes—ski-school slopes. That's where the money is, of course. But there's some fine expert terrain too. Maybe not as much tough stuff for the experts as they've got here at Squaw, but——"

"Maybe that's to the good," I said. "The more expert a skier is, the more expert he is at scrounging a lift ticket."

He laughed a breathless, silent laugh, showing pale gums. "Right!" he said. A stream of skiers was coming past our table, heading into the bar.

"Daddy's talked about it a lot," Georgie said. "He's very excited about it."

Patten closed an eye at her. "Between you and me, I think your Dad's going to be a director," he said. "We think he's going to be bringing a lot of Reno money in, one of these days." He said to me, as though afraid of hurting my feelings by leaving my father out, "And Charley Roche is going to be doing a lot of work for us this summer. We're going to be really humming over there starting about May one."

"You'll be open next fall then,". I said.

"We sure will." He grinned and blew cigarette smoke. "Well, that's enough about us." He leaned forward as though to whisper a secret. "Who's going to win it this weekend, Jack?"

"Just about anybody in the first seed can win it," I said. I decided I didn't like him.

He gave me an askance look, as though I was being phonily modest. "Everybody knows it's between you and Chris Leary," he said. "Maybe you're so close to it you haven't heard all the talk. There's a lot of talk, a lot of interest. They'll have this valley packed to see it if the weather's decent."

Georgie said, "There is a lot of interest, Jack. I don't know how many people've asked me who's going to win."

"And what do you say?" Patten asked with his white-gum grin.

"Just what Jack said. You know, it's not like other kinds of races where you're racing against somebody. You're all by yourself. You're just doing the fastest you can against time. And so many things can go wrong. Just a little mistake with your wax, or you hit a bump a little bit wrong, or you catch an edge——"

"I've been told this downhill course is Jack's meat. Long and fast and easy."

"It's not easy," I said.

"Well, I meant comparatively," he said, flustered. He smiled and said, "Well, there's certainly a lot of interest. A lot of interest." He leaned toward Georgie, as though with a new secret. "How'd you like to run a ski school?" he murmured. He turned toward me and widened his eyes. "How'd you two like to run a ski school?"

There was a bad silence. "Well, I hadn't thought about it," I said.

"Think about it."

I said, "How'd you like to run a ski school, Georgie?"

She stared back at me, and I saw a melting in her copper-colored eyes, as if her heart were showing, that I didn't want to see, I shouldn't have asked her that, so lightly, and in front of Patten. She licked her lips. Then her eyes looked past me and she said in her small voice, "Oh, hello, Chris."

I glanced up to see Leary among the skiers filing by our table. "Oh, hi," he said. "How are you doing, Brownie?"

Patten and I rose, and I introduced him to Leary. "I've just been asking Jack here who's going to win this weekend," Patten said.

Leary looked suddenly stiff, suspicious that we'd been talking about him. "What'd he say?" he asked without looking at me.

"Oh, he backed and filled. What do you say?"

"Nobody knows who's going to win," Leary said. "That's why they have these races, to find out who's going to win."

He said it snottily, but it was what Patten deserved. Leary didn't know who Patten was and wouldn't have cared if he had known, since it would never occur to him he might need a job from Patten someday.

Patten flushed. "You won't mind if the local people are strong for the local boy, will you?"

Leary shook his head. He turned his back on us and went on along with the traffic moving toward the bar.

"Did I say something wrong?" Patten asked as we sat down again. He began to make a big business out of looking at his watch and being surprised at how late it was.

"Well, you two be thinking about this ski-school proposition," he said. "Maybe we can get together for a good talk after the Nationals are over. I'd like to hear any ideas you have, I really would."

I started to say I wouldn't be interested next year, but I didn't say it. When Patten had gone, Georgie and I went downstairs to the Beer Garden, which was dark, loud, and where the racers who had arrived from Alta would be. Of the girls, only Jo Grimes was there; she had driven out with Harry Butler. We had a beer with her, but she knew nothing about Anne except the rumor that she and Mrs. May had had a fight and the fact that she hadn't come to Alta. Harry joined us, swaggering when congratulated, and very pleased with himself. Leary didn't show up.

Tuesday night Mr. and Mrs. Brown came just as we were finishing dinner. We didn't have anything to offer them to drink except coffee. "Oh, coffee's just fine!" Mrs. Brown said. "We just thought we'd drive over and see how you children are getting along."

"You kids finish your dinner now," George Brown said.

"We're finished, really," Georgie said.

Her mother helped her carry our dishes into the kitchen, and I put a log on the fire while Mr. Brown looked out the window.

"That's quite a view," he said. He came back to sit by the fire. "How's the downhill course look, Jack?"

"It's not in shape yet."

"I'll bet you could just about run that course blindfold, couldn't you?"

"Oh, they'll build some new bumps into it."

"Everybody's expecting you to win," he said. There was an edge to his voice. He grinned, flat-lipped and intense, without humor, but the severity was gone almost as soon as I'd noticed it. Everybody's expecting great things of you, Jack."

I wished everyone would stop telling me I was a sure thing to win the Nationals. Every time it was mentioned a chip was knocked off my confidence, and at the same time I had a dogged feeling of rebellion. I didn't want to be told that everybody was expecting great things of me.

Mrs. Brown called from the kitchen, "Oh, George, I forgot to bring in that package for Georgie. It's in the glove compartment."

He snapped his fingers. "Our excuse for coming over here," he said. He went out to the car and returned with a small package wrapped in brown paper, which he took to the kitchen to Georgie.

"Oh, Jack, look!" Georgie came out of the kitchen holding Anne's bracelet. It jingled with her movements like the soft clink of trophies in a box in the back of the station wagon. "It was addressed to me, isn't that funny?" she said in a strained voice.

"What is it, dear?" Mrs. Brown asked.

"It's Anne's charm bracelet."

"Loaded with lucky pieces, isn't it?" George Brown said.

"Isn't that Ullr an ugly fellow," Mrs. Brown said. "He's supposed to be Norse, isn't he?"

"Yes," I said. "Norse."

Georgie was looking at me anxiously.

"But isn't Anne here?" Mr. Brown asked.

"We don't know where she is," Georgie said. She told them the rumor that Anne had quit the circuit, and blessedly Mr. and Mrs. Brown left it at that.

We sat by the windows and had coffee. Below us were the colored lights of the Lodge and the amber lights of the Inn and headlights flowing along the road. Above the ghostly-snowy line of the peaks were great stars like Christmas tree ornaments.

The Browns stayed for two cups of coffee, then left, saying they mustn't keep me up. As soon as they had driven away Georgie took a folded slip of paper from her sweater pocket and held it out to me. It was a sheet of notepaper, one side of it covered with Anne's small, graceful handwriting:

Dearest Brownie,

   This ought to be yours. I'm not going to be racing any more. If you haven't heard story, please don't ask why the bell tolled. If you have, it's all right, and I swear I won't ever *bother*. (I have to be cryptic in case it's still mysterious, and hope it is.)

   Saw proofs of *Life* thing. Sorry I hogged. Now interesting propositions and things. (Who is this Anne P?) But I'm being very cool. Mother and I may take trip to Acapulco to think over the course. Isn't it funny how when things you thought you always wanted are dumped in your lap, they're not really what you wanted? Att: Jack.

   Ullr has additional medicine on for Jack to win all the races ever, because that's what he wants.

Love, and love,
Anne

"I don't understand," Georgie said.

I shook my head, seeing Anne's face staring at me in Helen's living room that last night in Aspen. "I don't know what she means either."

"She did have a fight with Mrs. May—everybody says so. But it sounds like more than just that." She stood looking at me, with the fire's warmth and shadows flickering in her face. I crumpled the letter in my hand; I held it crushed inside my fist.

"Maybe I'd better ask Mrs. May," Georgie said.

"She doesn't want you to ask, she says."

"I'm going to though," Georgie said. When she had turned away from me I flipped the crumpled ball of paper into the fire.

"I guess I'd better get to bed," I said.

In the downhill course for the Nationals there was a straight shot to a sharp turn, then the schuss down Siberia, where you would be running up to sixty or seventy miles an hour. Although some of this speed would be lost on the flats, you would still be going fast when you came to the difficult part—down a narrow gully, between trees, and over two ridges, the first built up, that we called double-trouble. The reverse slope of the second ridge was the face above Tower 20 on the Squaw No. 1 lift, and the face was steep and moguled. If you were going fast enough and lifted at exactly the right moment, you could sail over the two ridges, come down just on the downslope of the Tower 20 face, and ride it out. But there were lots of ifs. If your speed was wrong or your lift bad, then you hit the second ridge too soon. If your line was wrong, you came down in the moguls; or, worst of all, the upswing of the second ridge could loft you clear out over the face and onto the flat below it. Landing on a flat like that, instead of a steep downslope, would be like running into a concrete wall.

Wednesday afternoon I spent some time at the top of the Tower 20 face, watching the racers lift over double-trouble. Leary lifted well and let down perfectly far over on the right side, where he had to turn almost immediately to make the next control gate. Both Harry and McInerny took falls, McInerny an eggbeater. I reminded myself that the course would be in much better condition by Sunday and ran down toward Tower 20, to watch from the bottom of the face for a while. Someone called my name; a thin man in a black parka came through the moguls toward me. It was Jean-Gaby.

"Ah, Jack," he said. He seemed very glad to see me. "What do you think of this very fine course? It is a true downhill course, is it not? Very, very fast."

"It gets pretty tough right here," I said, indicating the face above us. "Did Helen come out with you?"

"Ah, no; she had business. She will come Sunday, for the downhill." Gripping my hand, he said, "I have heard from Yves Valéry. He thinks it is very possible the French team will come to Portillo."

"That's great," I said.

"So we must decide. You will come?"

"Sure," I said.

He clasped my hand hard, then released it. *"Bon!* I am

so pleased." He brushed at the porcupine quills of his hair. With a suddenly hard mouth he said, "I went last weekend to Alta. Chris did very badly."

"I thought he did pretty well in the slalom."

He shrugged. "He did very, very badly in the downhill. I do not like it. I am very disappointed. He is DNF."

I said, "Well, if he Markered-out—"

"I will tell you why I am disappointed. He wins the slalom. He skis like a crazy man. It is not skill, it is only luck he stands up. Do you know why he skis like a crazy man? Because he is so rattled you have beaten him at Aspen. I am not interested in someone who is so easy rattled. In the downhill he is a crazy man again, and he falls, he loses his ski. He has no chance to win, so he does not finish."

"Well, it wasn't a tryout race. He probably—"

He shook a finger at me. "Listen! Do you know why one must always finish? It is not merely because a DNF is disqualified in the combined. It is because everyone has a coward inside, and this coward must never know it is allowed not to finish. Always, always, always to finish. It is the first thing I have been taught. It is the first thing I will teach."

He looked angry, so I didn't say anything. He said again, "I am disappointed. You see, there is this thing. One must begin racing always against people who are better. So one must lose and lose. Finally one wins perhaps. You have done this. Finally you have won the Roch." He paused and gazed at me as though what he meant must be evident without his having to continue. "Chris has won and won and won. Then he has lost. So he is rattled and he skis like a wild crazy man. Stupidly."

"I'm sorry to hear that," I said.

"It is very easy to win when one is winning," Jean-Gaby said. "Very. But when one is losing—that is the test. He must arrange himself very quickly."

I gazed into the hard, dark eyes behind his glasses, at his jerked-beef, mole-marred, hard-mouthed face, and I thought this must be the face of the thing-inside that gnawed and pushed and was never satisfied. I felt a wave of anger and disgust, and loyalty to Leary, and I saw what it was going to be like to train under Jean-Gaby Michonneau.

"Come," he said less harshly. "We will examine very carefully this place here. It is very interesting." He swung on down the swale to get on the lift at Tower 20.

I didn't know why I looked up. In a chair almost directly above me was Leary; his face, made almost savage by the black bar of his eyebrows, was filled with jealousy. He looked as though he hated me.

As soon as our eyes met, his face turned blank. He waved a hand in greeting as his chair climbed on upward. I waved back and, shaken, skied down to join Jean-Gaby.

Thursday, after the required non-stop downhill training run, there was a competitors' meeting. The Chief-of-Course was worried about weather reports of two storms coming in, and rain probable below seven thousand feet. There was danger of the course softening up and then freezing with ruts in it, and he wanted to reschedule the downhill for Saturday, the slalom for Sunday. There was a lot of grumbling because it meant one less downhill training day, but if the course softened we wouldn't be able to train on it Saturday anyway, so we voted for the rescheduling. Thursday afternoon we were to help ski-pack and sideslip Friday's giant slalom course on KT-22.

When we came down off KT I went into the Lodge through the downstairs lobby to go to the men's room. Someone called my name; it was a man I'd never seen before, although he shook my hand as though we were old friends. He had on black-rimmed glasses, ski clothes, and a brand-new pair of Molitor boots. His face was chubby and tanned, he spoke with an eastern accent, and he carried a rolled-up magazine under his arm. The card he handed me gave his name as Milton Hite, of Twentieth Century-Fox.

He tapped the rolled-up magazine with a hairy forefinger. "You don't photograph too badly. We'd like to schedule a screen test."

I didn't know what he was talking about. Then I said, "Is that the new *Life?*"

He showed me the cover. It was Anne. Her face was in action, smiling but tense, her hair alive with speed, a blue pole and flag showing behind her, and snow and blurred trees. It was a wonderful photograph. Hite and I moved over toward the lobby fireplace, out of the traffic, and he showed me the other photographs in the magazine. There were two pages of the Roch Cup races and two more of the wedding. Anne was in most of the pictures. The worst was the one of Georgie and me under the crossed ski poles. It didn't seem to me I had photographed well, and Georgie's face looked like a muffin with raisins for eyes.

"Maybe you can tell me where I can get in touch with Anne Patterson. I was skiing at Mammoth when I saw this spread, and I shot on up here. But now I understand she isn't here for this race."

"She won't be here," I said. He was interested in Anne, not me. *Interesting propositions and things, but I'm being cool,* she had written. I told him to try Roger Bernand in New York and asked if I could keep the magazine. I looked closely again at the face on the cover. I could just make out the chipped tooth, but I wouldn't have noticed it if I hadn't known it was there. I knew the sweater and those gloves gripping her poles and, behind her, Aspen's Ajax Mountain and the bare-limbed tan trees against the snow, but I didn't know Anne any more.

"I think somebody heard that she and her mother were going to Acapulco," I said vaguely.

Hite thanked me and we shook hands again. "Get in touch with us when you come south, Roche," he said.

I watched him start up the stairs in his big, shiny black boots. Then I went on along the hall to the men's room, where I flushed the card he had given me down the toilet.

That night my father was to come to dinner. It was

much easier this time. He had convinced himself that Georgie was the cutest, finest wife anybody could have, a good cook too, and that I was very lucky. For her part, she seemed fond of him. He made many jokes about the baby and about becoming a grandfather. After dinner, while Georgie did the dishes, he sat in front of the fire. It was the first time he and I had been alone since Aspen.

"Had a call from Bud Gayley," he said. "They'll be up tomorrow night. He's really proud of you, Jackie."

"Well, I'm glad."

He lit a cigarette, blew a gust of smoke and studied me through it. "How's everything look?"

"I like the downhill course. Jean-Gaby went over it with me this afternoon."

"He's a good man. How's the GS look?"

"Everybody likes it but Tom Boyd. It's a good course."

"Well, I'm going into Reno tonight and get a little bet down on you. Did you know they were making book on the Nationals over there?"

I hadn't known it. I called the news to Georgie, above the sound of water running in the sink. "Oh, you can get a bet on anything in Reno," she called back.

"Thought I'd go over and see what the odds are anyhow," my father said. "You're the favorite this time, I know that much. Jimmy heard it over there."

But the more I thought about it, the less I liked it. And I didn't want to be the favorite. "Don't do that," I said. "Don't bet on me."

"Why not?"

"I just don't want you to."

"What I was going to do, I was going to put up five hundred on you, and you and Georgie can have the winnings. It might help when the baby comes along."

I shook my head irritably. Everything seemed in a very delicate balance. I wished he hadn't mentioned the betting in Reno.

He shrugged, and we sat in silence for a time, listening to the fire crackling. "You feeling the pressure pretty hard, Jackie?" he asked quietly.

"Not as bad as Aspen, I guess."

"You were really feeling it there, weren't you? Sure, I should've known that."

"I'm sorry I blew like that."

"Forget it," he said. His face reddened. "You said some pretty hard things, Jackie."

"I'm sorry."

"I don't know what hurt worse," he said, "the hits or the misses."

Georgie appeared, stopped, and retreated into the kitchen again.

I looked into the fire. "When you were jumping, did you know any guys who were real competitors? That's what we say about somebody who's really in it for blood, all the way: he's a real competitor. Did you know anybody like that?"

"Sure. I—sure."

"I guess I'd been trying to sit on it—that I was like that. And I had to own up to it, to myself. All the guys like that I know are really crappy guys inside. Always trying to crash the lift line—that's the way somebody put it. I hadn't really known I was like that till the Roch Cup, and getting married, and a lot of things. And you know how when you get really ashamed of yourself, you —I don't know. Anyway, I guess I'm a real competitor, Dad."

"Sure you are, son."

He was missing the point and I didn't know how to explain it any better. I didn't want to get into another quarrel with him. I took a deep breath. "I mean—I guess when you're like that you're competing with everybody in everything all the time. I can look back and see how it's always been that way. With your parents. And your brother, if you've got a brother," I said quickly. "With people you love at the same time. And you get so goddam sick of yourself."

"I've known you were that way," my father said uncomfortably. "I mean, I've always known you were going a hell of a lot further than I ever did. Wanted you to. I haven't ever really tried to cut you down like Chrissie said that night, have I?"

"Hell, no," I said. "You've been terrific."

His face was heavy and rueful. "Well, but there's some things yet you don't know. You'll understand about it better when you've got a kid. See, it's not so much I'm for your winning or not winning or making the Olympics or not. It's that I'm for *you*. I'd hate like hell to see you in a bind where you're chewing yourself up, or where it seems like the circuit's riding you so hard you—" He shook his head. "You know why I'm for you? Because you're a part of me, like a leg or something. Sure, there's some oddball things mixed up in it, but— Well, you'll start to understand about it one of these days when you've got a boy of your own."

"Sure," I said.

"No hard feelings here," my father said. "I've already forgot about it. It's all over." He leaned forward to flip his cigarette into the fireplace. "Well, you're not feeling the pressure so bad this time, huh?"

"It's different anyway."

"Jackie, don't you worry about yourself. You'll be all right. You've always had a good head on you. I'm not going to worry about you."

"Thanks," I said as Georgie came limping out of the kitchen to sit down with us.

When my father had gone I brought the *Life* magazine in from the VW, and Georgie and I looked at the pictures of the Roch, the wedding, and of Anne. I hadn't produced it earlier because I had been afraid my father would make too much, in front of Georgie, over what a beautiful girl Anne was.

4

Friday morning when Georgie and I got up it was snowing, and Granite Chief was freshly frosted. I stood in the living room with a cup of coffee and watched the snow turn to water as it struck the windows. It slid down the glass in wiggling lines. Just before it was time to leave the cabin the snow turned to rain, and Georgie decided to stay home. She could see more of the race through the binoculars that hung by the windows than she could from the Lodge. She seemed despondent when she kissed me good-by and wished me luck. "Somebody make this god-dam rain stop," she said.

It stopped, and the clouds began breaking up, as I rode the KT-22 lift. I'd been so depressed by the rain that the pressure of the GS didn't catch up with me until starting time. Then the phone hook-up failed, and we had to wait on top an hour in the wind that was blowing the clouds past, fast-moving and close above us, while finish-to-start contact was made by radio. I ran third, and I didn't feel really right until I got off the first face. Then I went down in a hurry, in 1:58.7. Leary ran right behind me in 1:59 flat.

Because it was Friday and rainy, there was not much of a crowd at the finish, but my father and Mr. Brown were there, my father in his new blue parka, Mr. Brown wearing a gabardine topcoat and a modified rancher's hat. I stood with them while the rest of the first seed came down, achingly taut as the race was held up with communications delays and clouds began filling the sky again. No one else broke two minutes.

I managed to grin as they congratulated me, and Jean-Gaby came to shake hands, and others gathered around us. I was shaky because it had been so close, disgusted with myself at what I felt when Jean-Gaby said Leary had made a good run too, and caught by the irrational rebellion and resentment again, as though Jean-Gaby and George Brown, and even my father somehow, were trying to make me want Leary to fall apart. And I was sorry for Leary as I watched him disappear, alone, over toward the Lodge.

Mr. Brown was sucking up to Jean-Gaby and ignoring my father, and I excused myself, saying I had to get my downhill skis and go up to see what the snow was like in

254

Siberia. I rode up Squaw No. 1, hunched in my chair in the rain that had started again, and looking down at the snowpack dimpling with it. Above Tower 12 the rain turned back to snow, but very wet, and what had fallen on top was hard to move—dangerous, leg-breaking garbage. The few racers who were already up looked apprehensive. Harry Butler and Joe Hammond and I stood in front of the quonset at the top of Siberia and watched the Chief-of-Course slowly slipping the course. The blue gates looked desolate in the snow, and their flags drooped damply.

Leary came off the lift and past the quonset, ignoring us. He traversed over to the course and started down the schuss without a pause.

"He's out of his goddam mind," Harry said savagely. "He'll break his goddam ass."

Leary ran down Siberia in a tuck, blurred and grayed in the falling snow, diminishing, gone.

"Let's go see what the Chief-of-Course says," Joe said.

Looking worried, the Chief-of-Course said if this kept up he would close the course to training and keep sideslippers on it. The temperature was supposed to drop tonight, and he'd open the course for training before the race if the snow set up hard.

We skied on down. Toward the bottom the snow had softened badly. When we went up the ramp at Tower 10 to get back on the lift, the attendant rapped on the window of his little shack to stop us. He called out the door, "Say a phone call just came in for Jack Roche. One of you him?"

"Here," I said.

"Your wife wants you to come home."

I kick-turned, went down the ramp, and schussed the golf course with rain blurring the lenses of my goggles. As I came off the last face I saw Bill Birks, skis on his shoulder, trudging toward the lift. He stopped and raised a hand as though he wanted to say something to me, but I needed my momentum to get across the flat to the Lodge, so I didn't stop. There were only a few people on the Lodge deck, and in the rain everything had a chill, dreary, unreal quality. I was shivering as I got out of my long-thongs.

"Jack!" someone called from the deck. Bruce Carrington's face, encased in his parka hood like the face of a peasant woman in a shawl, peered down at me. "Say, that's tough about Patterson," he said.

I tried to grin back at him for his irony, but his face was strangely stiff. Charley Catten appeared beside him. Hanging on his crutches, he said, "Did you hear about Anne?"

"What?" I said.

"She got killed. It was on the radio just now."

I cleared my throat. "How?" I said.

"In a plane. She and her mother and that guy that was in Sun Valley, Rigg. Down in Mexico. They hit a mountain, it said on the radio. They all got killed."

They both stared down from six feet above me, Bruce with the stiff, almost severe expression, Charley grimacing as though he were afraid I was going to be mad at him.

I leaned my skis and poles against the deck, turned, and walked away. I broke into a heavy-booted trot going out the turnaround to where I'd left the VW. I drove up the hill, pulling at the neck of my shirt. Rain and occasional snow splattered on the windshield.

Georgie wasn't in the living room. The embers of a fire smoked in the fireplace. "Georgie?"

There was no answer. I went into the bedroom. She was lying face down on the bed in her blue robe. Something scraped tinnily under my foot. When I stopped to pick up the bracelet, blood rushed to my head so my brain ached and pounded. Georgie's face turned slightly toward me, revealing one eye, and she raised her cast and dropped it with a thud. The plastic mattress cover crackled as I sat down beside her on the bed. The rain on the roof was loud and close.

"Anne's dead," Georgie said.

I nodded.

The *Life* magazine was on the table beside the bed, with the alarm clock on top of it, partly covering Anne's face. I dropped the bracelet on the magazine and lay on the bed beside Georgie, shivering in my wet clothes. I felt as though a shackle had broken loose inside me and I was no longer connected to anything. I was crying for Anne, but I felt only a kind of empty horror that I felt nothing. The speeding and vivid-colored photograph on the cover of the magazine was not the face of anyone I knew; I didn't know the girl who had been killed on a mountainside in Mexico in a plane with her mother and Dixie Rigg. She was no longer real, none of it was real, and I was crying but I didn't know what for.

Georgie whispered close in my ear, "You loved her so much."

With my face pressed into the pillow I shook my head. It wasn't true. I saw clearly and in pain and revulsion that it had never been true. No one loved anyone but himself, and not even himself so much as a lovely, golden, impossible daydream of himself. I had not loved Anne Patterson, who had needed it so much and was so honest she never claimed to be able to return it; I had loved a glamorized picture of myself walking, talking, dancing with, making love to, a soft-focused, soft-haired, soft-colored image on slick paper, who did not exist.

I heard someone sob. Georgiana Brown Roche, who was no competitor, who was simple enough to feel pain for my false pain, was sobbing for me. Or maybe she had simply loved Anne.

I tried to reach back with my mind to find Anne, who had loved me loving her and had trusted that I did, who had loved the attention, the eyes admiring her aesthetically, like a painting, who had loved beautiful clothes, beautiful cars, beautiful trips to bright jewels of places like Acapulco. *Isn't it funny how when things you thought you always wanted are dumped in your lap, they're not really what you wanted? Att: Jack*, she had written. Attention: Jack, who had sent her to Acapulco with Dixie Rigg when she had seen my true face, as two days ago I had seen Jean-Gaby's. But what had she meant: *I swear I won't ever bother?*

"Oh, Jack," Georgie said, sobbing. "You're so closed in.

I have to tell you things, but you never have to tell anybody anything. Don't you need to?"

I turned toward her. She was leaning over me, her eyes swollen, her cheeks shining with tears. She said, "If there was only some way I could comfort you! I'd be good for something then."

I put my hands to her cheeks and pulled her face down against me so she would not see me crying. I held her hard against me.

She said, "Did you ever tell Anne anything you felt?"

"I guess not."

"Oh, Jack, what can I do?"

"Nothing. It's just it's—it's just such a—shock." That wasn't enough of a word.

"If I could just do something! You've done so much, and I can't do anything back." Her voice broke apart. "Jack, I haven't ever done anything but cheat you and lie and gyp you and—take you away from her! I was so proud! Jack—Jack—Jack, I *killed* her!"

"Nobody killed her, Georgie."

"*I* did!" she cried. "Jack, I did! You don't *know!*"

"Hush."

She pulled away from me to sit up again. Wildly she shook her head and caught her hair in both fists as though to pull it out. And I thought: she is doing something she has seen in a movie, she is faking feeling something, as we are all fake and pretense. But something in her voice impressed me. "Jack, it was because I was so afraid!"

She loosened her hands from her hair and said more calmly, "I thought I was, I *really* thought I was. And I was so scared. Then it was like when I broke my ankle. I was still scared but it was such a relief too. Because with my ankle I knew I wouldn't have to race any more this year. And with the baby I thought I wouldn't ever have to race again, ever. It's because I was so scared, Jack!"

"What?" I said, not understanding yet.

"I'm not pregnant. I mean—I wasn't."

I stared at her.

"It's so! Jack, it's so!"

"Don't be silly," I whispered.

"Why won't you *believe* me?"

I didn't believe or disbelieve; I couldn't think. But I shook my head.

"Jack, I got the curse that night we had dinner at Helen's house and talked about the wedding. It was so awful. I cried and cried because it was such a gyp. And I was afraid to tell you. I was afraid of Helen, and everybody'd got started—" She slapped her hands punishingly to her face; she shook her head wildly again. "I lie and lie! Oh, make me stop lying! It wasn't that. It was just that it'd been so wonderful not being afraid. Because I wasn't ever going to have to race any more. You'd marry me, and I'd have the baby, and—oh, I don't know what I thought!" She stopped; slowly her hands slid down her face until her eyes were uncovered, full of tears and fear.

I said, "I didn't know you were so afraid, Georgie."

"I don't know how to tell you! Every time it was worse. Daddy and Mrs. May were so sure I was going to be great. But I knew I wasn't. And every start I'd think that this time they were going to find it out too. I didn't know what they'd do, they'd be so mad." I watched her round, sunburned throat work. "And I was so afraid of getting hurt. I kept thinking about Janice Haney in a wheelchair for the rest of her life. I knew I was going to get hurt.

"It was so terrible at Stowe," she rushed on. "And then at Arapahoe it·was worse. I've heard there are people that have accidents because they really want to. It must've been like that. Because at Arapahoe I couldn't remember how to do anything. I'd think: bend the knees; and, get your shoulder through that gate. But it wouldn't work, and I'd edge so much my skis would chatter and chatter. After the slalom I went up the hill again—remember, you were standing there? And it was like going·up to an executioner and when I got up there he'd chop off my head. I mean, I knew what was going to happen, but I—" She leaned down again awkwardly until her face touched my shoulder.

"Oh, Jack, you don't want to hear all this. When Anne's—"

"Yes, I do," I said, stroking a hand over her hair. I couldn't hear the rain on the roof any more.

"Jack, don't you see I killed her? Because she needed you. But I thought I needed you more. I guess everybody thinks what they need they need more than anybody else. Jack, are other people the way I am? If I could just think—"

"We're all the same," I said. All the downhill racers.

I turned over on my back and gazed out the window at what I could see of Granite Chief. It wasn't raining now, but a cloud was drifting through the valley, trailing gray veils.

"She was going off with some Dixie Rigg sometime," I said. "She said she was going to marry lots of times, like Helen Michonneau. She was going to get divorces and big settlements. She was going to be one of the ten best-dressed women in America. And she wanted a Facel Vega. That's a sports car." But that night in my bed in Aspen she had said that she was going to win the Nationals, and that she was going on to win in the Olympics, and then— "Did it say on the radio if she and Dixie Rigg were married?" I asked.

"They didn't say. It was just—short."

I said slowly, "I just don't know why she'd go off with Dixie Rigg when everything was opening up for her. Because of that stuff in *Life*, I mean." And all at once I thought of Anne's mother, who had been killed too. Maybe Anne had not been on her way to marry Dixie Rigg because of me; maybe she had only been getting her mother away from Figgy. I nearly groaned, because I knew I was never going to know. I said, "But you aren't to blame for anything, Georgie."

"Yes, I am."

"No."

"I knew I wasn't pregnant but I was going to get pregnant right away and then try to pretend— I don't know how I could've done that to you. Oh, Jack, I was so jealous of her. I knew nobody was ever going to look at *me* that way, the way you used to look at her sometimes when you thought nobody was watching."

"No," I said.

"Yes, you did," she said harshly. "Other people noticed it too."

I got my arm around her and pressed her against me again, but this time she strained away.

"Jack, don't treat me like a baby. Jack—I hurt so much inside."

"She went away with Dixie because of me," I said. "She thought I was one way and she found out I was another. After the wedding, at Helen's house. When you were asleep."

"I wasn't asleep. I saw her go upstairs."

"Well, then if you saw her, you know."

"If she thought you were any other way about that, then she was stupid. We're all hateful that way. You don't really think that was why she went away, do you?"

"Yes," I said. "Partly."

"Well, it wasn't," she said in the harsh voice. "Do you want to know why she went away?"

"Why?"

"I talked to Mrs. May yesterday. To ask her what happened about Anne. But I already knew. Inside I knew."

I raised up on one elbow to look at her face. Her eyes were tightly closed, her hands caught tightly in the lapels of her robe. "There's some new FIS ruling about professionalism," she said. "It's like using your Name and Fame—you know. Only now it's even using your picture. For advertising and things, even if you don't get paid for it. And she'd seen you look at Anne like that too," she said, her eyes still closed. "She did it for me."

"Did what? Who?"

She didn't seem to hear me. It was as if she were watching and listening to something behind her closed-up face. "She said Anne had lost her eligibility posing for ads in that catalogue of Roger Bernand's," she went on finally. "And some other things she posed for last summer too. I don't know why she hated Anne so. Anyway, she and Anne had a big fight after we left Aspen. I guess Anne told her to go to hell, she'd been posing for her stepfather for three years, even before she had any Name and Fame or anything. Anne was going to fight it out with the eligibility committee. But then Mrs. May phoned up Mr. Bigdammit, you know—the International Olympic Committee guy. And I guess there was some question about the FIS ruling, but there wasn't any about the IOC. Anne couldn't compete in the Olympics." She opened her eyes and, looking into mine, said, "That's what Mrs. May told me."

"What do you mean, Mrs. May did it for you? So you could be on the Olympic team instead?"

She continued to stare into my eyes, as though looking at her reflection there. I remembered her eyes melting when I'd asked her how she'd like to run a ski school; these were hard, and hot, and unforgiving. She nodded almost imperceptibly.

Then she shook her head. "No! She said Anne was going to take you away from me. She said Anne couldn't stand it that you'd married me. She said she could see it so clearly—she'd known someone like Anne before, and someone like you, and she said Anne would just hang around with us and before I knew it you'd have left me. She said she did it to get Anne away where she couldn't ever *bother* us. She—" She squeezed her eyes so tightly closed that the tears spurted from them. "She said it was her wedding present."

I said hoarsely, "She's crazy. The goddam rotten crazy old bitch!"

"No, she's not! She was right, you would've. It's just—" She cried out, "It's just, I didn't see any point in telling her, Jack! I mean, in Aspen. I mean, what was *really*— what was the point of telling her? I didn't know what she was going to do. And what was the point of telling her yesterday? She'd already done it to Anne."

"Everybody'd already done everything," I said.

"Jack, don't hate me!"

I moved to sit on the edge of the bed with my head in my hands. She hugged me from behind, sobbing. I tried to say, "It wasn't anything you did," but it came out wrong. I disengaged myself from her arms and stood up. Crouched on the bed like an animal, she stared up at me.

"Don't hate me."

As though all she had to do was ask, it turned to a kind of sweet liquid that dripped through me, changing to pity, changing to something beyond pity. "I don't hate you," I said and bent and kissed her wet mouth. She dropped back on the bed.

She whispered, "Once I almost thought— The other day when you asked me—"

She stopped as I knelt beside her again and pulled at the belt of her robe. I parted the robe, and she whispered in a shocked voice, "Oh, *no!*" She turned her face aside, holding one clenched fist to her mouth. I looked at the sallow, taut-muscled flesh beneath the tan line at her throat and the dark thimbles of her nipples. "No, it's —no," she whispered, but she made no move to cover herself or to stop me. The plaster at the top of her cast was crumbling a little. "No," she whispered as though to herself only.

When I went into her I said, "I love you." I said it over again each time.

She had her eyes tightly closed. "No," she said, shaking her head.

"I love you, Georgie."

"Don't say that. It's not true."

"I love you," I said.

"You don't have to say that."

"I love *you*."

"You can't."

"I love you."

"No." She shook her head again.

"I love you."

"Just so you don't hate me."

"How'd you like to run a ski school? You and me."

"Oh."

"I love you."

"Oh, Jack," she whispered.

"I love you," I said, over and over, and this time I didn't have to think about Anne, who was dead. She came for a long time after I was through, and I had to help her finish. Afterward we lay together without talking.

"Say it now," she said finally, her face against my throat.

I said it, looking out the window past her rumpled hair; but now I was thinking about Mrs. May.

After a long time she said, "You'd better get some dry clothes on. You don't want to catch cold or anything."

"It's stopped raining. I'd better get back on the mountain."

"Downhill tomorrow," she said.

"Right."

"Did you win the GS?"

"Yes."

When I got up she quickly covered herself and turned away from me. "Jack?"

"Yes."

"You're so good. But I know you didn't mean it."

"I mean it." I stood looking down at her. "I meant it. Do you want me to show you again?"

She turned her face into the pillow. "Only once before the downhill," she said in a muffled voice, and I couldn't tell if she was laughing or crying.

Slogging through the soft snow toward the bottom of Squaw No. 1, carrying my downhill skis, I saw two figures standing together by the Poma lift. One of them wore a round white racing helmet—I couldn't tell whether it was Lorraine or Alice. The other had on a Tyrolean hat, I could see the jut of the red hatchet face beneath the green brim, and my breath hurt suddenly in my chest.

I halted and leaned on my skis. It seemed important that she should feel me watching her, feel that I knew, feel—I didn't even know what I wanted her to feel. Presently the red face glanced toward me, away, toward me again. I had thought a little while ago, lying spent with Georgie, that I must kill Mrs. May, not in revenge so much as merely to stamp out something evil and vicious. Almost matter-of-factly, I had thought of ways, seen her standing beside the downhill course as I came down, and with a simulated loss of control, a slight deflection of line, I would crash into her, killing her with a pole, my skis, my body, and the fact that I would break myself up as well was right and just too. But I couldn't hold the hate, the need. It was a remembered thing rather than immediate, and it was as though, trying to call it back, I were poisoning myself, not her. For how had she killed Anne any more than I had, or Georgie, or Anne's mother and Figgy, or Dixie Rigg, or Helen, or even Anne herself? I shouldered my skis and started on again, tears stinging cold in my eyes.

Riding alone up Squaw No. 1 over the men's course, I thought of the days that now seemed from another age but were only a few weeks past, when everything had been exciting and gay and full of a sweet tension, when all I had to do was try to beat Leary, when there had been joy in the racing itself; when if someone had asked if any of us could be hurt, or killed, I would have said, yes, of course, but I would not have believed it. Now I saw no joy ahead in racing, and it was as though a door had opened, and kept opening wider, revealing things that were terrible to see and understand, that were not merely downhill racing, but life, with death at the end of it.

The clouds were gone now, though there was still a little wind, and racers were training on the course. When I skied down from Tower 26 to the Squaw No. 2 terminal, I saw Leary in a chair above me. He was waiting for me on top, and I thought he must have heard about Anne.

He said, "What've you and Jean-Gaby been talking about so much?" His eyes were hostile behind the amber lenses of his goggles.

"Just the course," I said.

"What's he been saying about me?"

"Nothing," I lied. I started to say, "Chris—"

"The hell he hasn't! That son-of-a-bitch! Well, I know all about him. Marries Helen to get himself into this country, then all he does is bitch he doesn't have anything to do so she'll buy him a couple of boys like you and me.

So he can bring us along, pretend he's made something out of us. Only it'll be us that'll make something out of him." He was talking so fast drops of spit showed in the corners of his lips; he wiped his mouth on the back of his glove. "Don't you see what it's going to be like in Portillo? The son-of-a-bitch, he'll just keep chewing on us. He'll keep playing us off against each other the way he's trying to do now. He's not trying to do anything for us, he's just trying to do something for himself."

"Like everybody else," I said. I remembered asking him once if he would turn himself into a machine just to be a champion. And he had said maybe that was the way it had to be. My eyes began to water again; I didn't know why we were talking about Jean-Gaby. "Listen, Chris," I said, "didn't you hear about Anne?"

Two racers came off the lift and ran over toward the schuss. Leary put a hand up to pull his goggles out from his face, then fit them back again.

"What about her?"

"She's dead."

"What?" he said, as though he hadn't heard me.

"She and Dixie were flying down to Acapulco and the plane crashed. And her mother—her mother was with them."

"*Jesus,*" he whispered. He grimaced furiously. "Oh, for Christ's sake!"

"It's pretty awful," I said senselessly. It was like talking to someone I hardly knew about another person with whom we were only remotely acquainted.

Leary stared at me for a long time, his face contorted into the grimace. Then he whispered, "What am I supposed to do, feel sorry for you? Well, I don't feel sorry for you. Why the hell should anybody feel sorry for *you,* Mr. America?"

I didn't understand. All at once I couldn't get my breath. "What?" I said.

He rubbed his glove over his mouth again. "Boy, did you psych *me* out," he said. "You get married to Brownie, and you're a big hero and I'm a crummy bastard, so you walk off with the Roch. What a job you did on me! On everybody! Making everybody think you were doing it for Brownie. And for me.

"So I get screwed out of the Roch," he said hoarsely. "And screwed clear through to Alta, while you're out here training for ten days and the rest of us get screwed out of a training day. And I'm probably getting screwed out of the set-up with Jean-Gaby and Helen I fixed up in the first place. *I* did." He was talking so fast he was almost panting. "And Anne gets screwed!" he flung at me. "Boy, does she get screwed! She goes off with that Texas prick and gets dead. You must've really been laughing that night I almost took a crack at him for you. My friend," he said. "Hell, no, I'm not sorry for you. I'm sorry for Anne and I'm sorry for Brownie and I'm goddam sorry for me. But you are really in great shape."

I said, "I beat your ass in the Roch, and I beat your ass this morning, and I'm going to beat your ass tomorrow. And you can't stand it, can you? You goddam jealous shit!"

He shook his head as though to clear it. "I finally saw through you," he said. "And Anne did that night, didn't she? Didn't she?"

"Shut up!" I said.

"What a phony deal you made out of being so big for the four of us. What—"

"Shut up!"

"What you did to us, you rotten—"

I lifted a ski and slammed it down across the front of his skis. Awkwardly I swung and hit him in the face.

He hit back at me with both hands, his poles, hanging from his wrists, flying wildly. I managed to get more leverage when I swung again. This time I hit him in the mouth, and he sat down, his skis still pinned beneath mine. I backed off his skis as Tom Boyd and Benny McInerny came down the ramp from the lift get-off. They hesitated before starting toward us. Leary sat on the snow with his goggles askew and his mouth pursed tightly. He spat blood on the snow. He got to his feet just as Tom Boyd came over.

"What's the matter here?" Tom asked. "Little pre-downhill tension?"

Leary kicked around and skated away from us. He stopped about a hundred yards away, leaning out over his poles and gazing down Siberia. There was a sharp, bony ache in my knuckles, where I had hit him. Tom Boyd had the sense not to say anything more, and after a moment Leary started down the bowl in a schuss. Tom and McInerny traversed over toward the downhill course in single file, McInerny turning to glance back at me. I started down the bowl too, but my legs were shaky and I didn't take it very fast.

5

The night before a big race your body is like an engine finely tuned for one purpose and one occasion, and you are the mechanic concerned completely with it. Your mind is part of the engine, disciplined and concentrated in the same way. Before a crucial downhill you are intolerant of any interruption or intrusion on your concentration. You don't want to talk to anyone unless it is at your own choosing and on your own terms. It is irritating even to be wished luck because of the demand for attention and the need of acknowledgment. You are sunk in a deep preoccupation with yourself as that engine waits for its trial.

Everyone connected with racers and the circuit knew this, and Georgie and I were left alone Friday night. And Georgie knew it and left me completely alone to work and fuss over my skis, leaf unseeing through old magazines, lie early and sleepless in bed. That afternoon and evening I would lose that essential deep preoccupation but always, quickly, I could get it back.

Then it was Saturday morning. The thermometer had fallen to ten degrees during the night. The downhill would be glare-ice, and now there was no room in my mind for anything but rethinking the running of the course in terms of ice.

When Georgie and I went down to the Lodge there were many cars coming into the valley, and in the parking lots skiers were taking skis off roof racks. I shouldered the rucksack containing my racing gear, and Georgie and I went into the downstairs lobby to look at the mimeographed lists of racers on the race board. Mr. Gayley appeared, to wring my hand and congratulate me for winning the GS. He was wearing an inflated-looking quilted parka, and his nose and cheeks were red with cold.

"This is a great day, Jack," he said emotionally. "Wouldn't miss this for anything in the world. I suppose the course will be like glass. Dodo couldn't come up with me, she had some exams—she was sick about it." He said to Georgie, "I don't suppose you remember me. I'm Dodo Gayley's father—she was a couple of years ahead of you as a junior."

"Of course I do," Georgie said. "How are you, Mr. Gayley?"

"Shame you hurt yourself," he said, pumping her hand. But he wasn't interested in her. "Well, it's the National Championships and you're already a leg in," he said to me, with a smiling cock of his jaw. "I hope you've managed to get Jack *up* for the downhill, Georgiana." He forced a laugh, then abruptly sobered. "What a terrible thing about Anne Patterson," he said.

I turned away from him to confront Jean-Gaby. We shook hands, and he said quietly, "I think this will be a big day for you, Jack." Out of the corners of my eyes I saw Mr. Gayley tucking a packet of folded bills into the sidepocket of my rucksack. I introduced him to Jean-Gaby. Georgie stood very close by me. I knew I couldn't take seeing her father or my father, or anybody else who was going to wring my hand or knead my shoulder while they told me it was going to be a great day for me or wished me luck, or who felt they had to tell me what a terrible thing it was about Anne.

I said to Georgie, "I'm going up on top now."

"Ah, there is no hurry, Jack," Jean-Gaby said. "There will be a postponement. One hour at least."

"I'd better go up," I said. I had to shake hands with Mr. Gayley and Jean-Gaby again. They wished me luck.

"I want to walk outside with you," Georgie said, and she clutched my arm as we started out. But now Mr. Patten appeared, very loud and cheerful and acting as though we were old friends. Before we could get away from Mr. Patten, Leary came by in his skin-tight striped racing pants. There was a small Band-aid stuck to the corner of his mouth. He didn't even glance at us.

Outside there was warmth in the sun, but the snow was still set-up hard. It would be hard for a long time yet on top.

"Did you and Chris have a fight?" Georgie asked in a low voice as I set the rucksack on the snow beside my skis and poles and squatted to look through it for my racing number.

I nodded. I took out the wad of money Mr. Gayley had put in the sidepocket; there were five twenty-dollar bills. Straightening, I handed them to Georgie.

She pushed the money down inside her glove, looking at me with hurt, red-brown eyes.

"I'll tell you about it tonight," I said. "I didn't want to talk about it last night."

"Okay," she said. There was a little jingle under the sleeve of her parka as she put out a hand to touch my skis. She was wearing the bracelet.

Then she looked into my face and I felt a kind of stubborn demand like a current of electricity. I kissed her firm-lipped, pink-lipsticked mouth. When I stepped back the hot, hurt look had gone out of her eyes and the current had been turned off. "Good luck, Jack," she said and stood a moment longer, watching me get my skis, poles, and rucksack organized. She turned and limped back inside the lodge while I started with my burden for the lift, walking gingerly on the ice.

I rode up Squaw No. 1 with a ski patrolman who wanted to talk and was offended because I didn't. Below the chair the icy trails reflected the sun fiercely. Skiers coming down were having trouble edging, and their skis scraped and clattered. There was a little wind. A few racers had preceded me to the top of Siberia, where the wind whipped in gusts up over the ridge. Twenty-five hundred feet below, Squaw Valley lay clean and shining in the sun, with its clusters of bright-colored buildings and Squaw Creek twisting down its center.

There was a fire in the wood-burner in the quonset hut, and I joined the racers who were already there, warming themselves and sharpening edges. After I'd filed my own I went out behind the quonset to steam a yellow hole in the ice. Returning, I saw Leary limbering his legs with deep-knee bends after the cold ride up the two lifts. He looked through me, purse-mouthed, as though I did not exist. I yawned, and my mind turned slowly and shallowly on nonessentials. I had heard an estimate once of the equivalent of how many deep-knee bends you made in a downhill race, but I couldn't recall whether it was five hundred or a thousand. It seemed important, and I kept trying to remember as I walked up the shoulder of the mountain toward the start where a few racers had congregated. Harry Butler came down to say that the Chief-of-Course had authorized an hour of training on the ice.

There was time for two or three runs, but I made only one and returned to the quonset to file my edges still sharper. The race was postponed another hour, and the time passed painfully. I ate a chocolate bar. At last a slow procession moved up toward the start, where there was now a crowd of officials, ski patrolmen, spectators, and racers. No one talked much.

On top I stood with Bruce and George Wurz, looking down the still-gleaming course. Leary came by, the bit of adhesive at the corner of his mouth no whiter than his face. My slow-turning mind pushed him out; if I thought about him I thought about Anne, and about my father saying, "I don't know what hurt worst, the hits or the misses," and then so many people and demands and promises and needs came crowding in, and all the other things I could not have with me now. The starter began counting, testing the phone, and I noticed Bruce flexing his knees unconsciously to the counting. Tom Boyd, in his red, white, and blue parka came to stand with us. I watched Leary tighten his bootlaces and put on his skis.

The loudspeaker hissed as the starter called for the forerunners. It was time to put on my skis and do some climbing and turning to limber up.

I stood above the starting gate to watch the first forerunner start down. Tucked into a ball in the Siberia schuss, he looked like a bomb falling away at a steep slant through air.

There was a long, bad wait before the second forerunner started. He wind-checked down the long schuss. The starter called for number one, Tom Boyd. Two was Joe Hammond, three the Canadian, Markle, then Leary, then me. Leary slipped down toward the start, buckling on his black and white helmet. Tom Boyd stood poised in the slot for the count-down. On the first turn he chattered out almost to clip the outside of the gate. Then he was gone in a long, fantastically swift, descending arc.

"Number two next, three on deck. Number four get ready."

Joe Hammond went. In one minute, Markle; in two minutes, Leary; in three minutes, Roche.

"—number five, get ready."

I moved up behind Leary, pulling my goggles out to keep them from fogging.

Markle went. One minute for Leary, two for me. Suddenly my stomach came up to gag me, and I bent over, puking weakly. When I could straighten up again I didn't think my legs were going to hold me. I wiped my mouth, panting. Leary turned to stare. I spat to get the taste of bile and chocolate out of my mouth.

An official in a fur hat took hold of my arm. "Are you all right, Roche?"

"All right," I said. "Okay." I slid up behind Leary as the starter counted. He was kneading Leary's back. I spat once more.

"Are you sure, Roche?" the official demanded.

"Sure."

"Go!" the starter said, and Leary shoved off.

I didn't watch him go, coming on into the slot, checking everything in my mind, cool all at once, my stomach clenched like a fist but no longer queasy. I breathed hugely as the starter's distant voice counted; his fingers worked at the knotted muscles of my back. I began to bend my knees in rhythm, tightening my grip on my poles, leaning out.

"Go!"

Not too fast down to the first turn so as to hold the high line: I bared my teeth to the cold wind in a grin as I cut close inside the gate. Then I tucked, and the bottom of Siberia began to rush at me. Dimly there came, through the focus of my senses, the mounting racket of ski clatter and cloth snapping, the wind numbing my face and making my teeth ache. Leaks in my goggles made my eyes water. When I reached the bottom of the bowl I knew I had made that schuss very fast, and my mind began to click ahead to the lift over double-trouble.

Now there were places where the ice had softened that pulled at my skis, but it was very hard and fast still in the gully under the shadow of the trees. Too fast, I thought, and checked a little, checked again. There was the ridge rising. I lifted and sailed over it. Too short! I pulled my skis up farther, missed the top of the second ridge, dropped them to make contact on the down slope, pitched forward as they hit slow snow but caught my balance. Now down the Tower 20 face with the hard jarring of my skis on the moguls, and ahead the blue, double-poled gates leading the course on down the flats below Tower 20.

There was someone on the course ahead.

I became aware of him through my cocoon of speed: a racer, a number on his back, a black and white helmet. I had a flashing impression that he was skiing like a crippled bird running. I tucked again at the bottom of the face just as he fell, awkwardly, off to the right, where he didn't interfere with my line. He was up again and trying to pole when I shot past him. His face, turned toward me, was bright red. It was Leary, his face was covered with blood, and he was falling again.

Instantly I straightened to wind-check. I cut crashingly uphill to a halt. Stopped, I was horrified that I had stopped.

Leary was up again, poling, holding his downhill ski slightly raised. A ski patrolman was running and sliding along the side of the course. Leary fell again, trying almost in the falling frantically to push himself up with his poles. I skied down into the course toward him. There was blood on the snow where he had fallen. Trying to ride his uphill ski he came on again; he had lost his goggles. "Chris!" I yelled at him. Now more people were hurrying down beside the course from Tower 20.

I ran alongside him and caught him in my arms. He was making a moaning, panting sound. His bleeding face looked as though it had been grated and his right cheekbone was shockingly sunken. "Let me go!" he panted. He fought me weakly.

"Stop it, Chris!" I said, and he sagged in my arms.

"I came down all—" He panted. "I came down and busted— Jack, something's busted in my leg!"

"Let's get off the course."

He wiped a glove over his face, smearing blood. "Jack, what the hell did you stop for?"

Someone yelled a warning as McInerny sped past, deep in a tuck, the white diamond of his nose and chin showing between his gloves and his goggles. Leary slumped against me as though the sound of McInerny's passing had knocked him over. The ski patrolman was shouting at us to get out of the course. He and I managed to drag Leary off, skis trailing.

"Bring the goddam doctor!" I yelled at the others hurrying and sliding toward us. Leary seemed unconscious now. The ski patrolman was gently unwinding his longthongs.

"Jesus he hit," he said. "He came off there like he was trying for the ski-jump record and came down on his face."

"He said something was broken in his leg."

"Achilles tendon. You could see his foot flopping." We got Leary's skis off as the others came up. The patrolman began to wipe the blood from his face with a handkerchief.

"He's got a fracture here."

Another ski patrolman brought down a toboggan. They covered Leary with blankets until the doctor, sandy-haired and snub-nosed, came to examine him. I jammed my Vectors into the snow beside Leary's Kaestles.

"What the hell did you stop for?" someone asked me.

"He had to stop. The other guy was all over the course."

I shook my head; it wasn't true.

"You better get back up and make them give you another run, Roche."

I watched Harry Butler flash over the flats. He didn't even see us. When I turned back the doctor had his hands on Leary's leg and Leary's eyes were open. "I kind of pulled something loose," he whispered to the doctor apologetically. His eyes turned toward me, the pupils framed with white. "Hey, Jack, I really busted myself up."

After the doctor had fussed over him for a long time the ski patrolman loaded him onto the toboggan, mummied in blankets. There wasn't anything for me to do, as there had been no reason for me to stop. One of the ski patrolmen started down the hill with the toboggan. The doctor clamped his skis back on. "Hadn't you better be seeing about another run?" he said, frowning at me. He began to herringbone back up the hill.

Leary's skis stood with the red thongs dangling from the turntables. There was no release from the bindings in a forward fall. I put on my skis. It seemed important that I take Leary's skis and poles off the mountain. A racer racketed by on the course.

"I thought he'd killed himself," a gatekeeper in a red parka said, offering me a cigarette. When I shook my head, he lit one himself and blew smoke. "But he just got up and started on down. I'll bet he fell ten times between where he hit and here."

"I'll take these down for him," I said. He helped me

275

gather Leary's skis and poles, and my own poles, put them on my shoulder. Skiing slowly, I started down the way the toboggan had gone—by Mogul Hill and the south side of the creek. From time to time I would see a racer running down the last schuss to the finish, over on the north side. At a distance racers looked so much alike in their goggles and helmets, racing parkas and pants, that it was impossible to tell them apart without seeing their numbers.

The ski patrol had carted the wire basket from the toboggan over toward the bottom of KT, where the ambulance could back up to it. A few people had gathered around, and others were watching from the deck of the lodge. I left Leary's skis and mine leaning against a tree, took off my number and helmet and hung them on the tips of my skis. An offcial with an armband on was hurrying up. I wondered why he was down here and not up at the finish, until it occurred to me they must be worried because the two stars of their race had DNFed.

"What happened, Roche?"

I didn't answer him, feeling a kind of cumulative irritation with all the race officials I'd ever seen. I moved over to the basket to talk to Leary, but his eyes were closed; he was snoring; I supposed the doctor had given him something. Blood still oozed in places on his scraped face, was drying darkly in others. Jean-Gaby was running toward me, awkward in his ski boots. He slipped and almost fell on the ice.

"Jack, what has he done? How is he hurt?"

"He broke his Achilles tendon," I said.

The race official sucked his breath through his teeth with a sharp sound.

Jean-Gaby's fingers gripped my arm like steel tongs. "But what is wrong with *you?*"

I didn't answer. More people were coming over from the bottom of Squaw.

Jean-Gaby's eyes glared at me out of his dark face. "But you are Did Not Finish!" he said. "One does not do this! In a downhill race one does not stop if one's own mother lies and bleeds to death at the feet. Chris was in your way?"

I shook my head.

"But why did you do this? It must be that someone interfered. Why did you stop?"

His hand shook my arm, his harsh, almost hysterical voice continued, and it was as though his hand twisting the flesh of my arm twisted everything inside, and all that had been so tough and determined and wanting was beginning to dissolve in the hurt of his fingers digging in and the scraping ache at the backs of my eyes.

"You must listen!" he cried. "You are DNF, you are disqualified in this race. You must demand that they give you another run—"

"Let go," I said, and instantly his hand fell away. A number of people were crowding around us now. There were Bruce Carrington and Bill Birks, and Charley Catten on his crutches. And there was Georgie. She was with her father. They hurried toward us, and she cried, "Jack, we heard you clobbered!"

I shook my head at her. "Chris," I said, but not loudly enough for her to have heard. I saw my father, with Mr. Gayley and Mr. Patten. The ambulance was backing slowly up to where Leary lay in the steel basket. When it stopped the driver came around to open the door. I knew him; he had been a ski instructor at Sugar Bowl once. I said, "I'm going to ride along, Bob."

Voices rose, Jean-Gaby saying, "You do not comprehend—" And someone else, "But won't they let him run again?" And Jean-Gaby, "You must hurry! Jack, there is no more time!" And my father, "Jackie, you're not hurt are you? You look—" And George Brown, his grim mouth bracketed with deep lines, "What's the matter with you?"

I heard the voices in an echoing hollowness, but I felt their force, and I knew I would have to be very strong now in asserting my membership in the race of humans, not machines. Yet I knew that I was cheating them. I felt so miserably guilty for having cheated everyone, and I tried to think how to apologize to them, how to phrase what must be said. To Jean-Gaby: I'm sorry I let you down; now there will be neither Leary nor me for you to work with, make champions of, but maybe you ought to try Harry, Harry Butler, maybe he is the real thing. If there was a real thing. And I would say to Mr. Gayley: I'll pay you back. I didn't ever ask for much, you know, mostly you just sent me money without my asking or you'd tuck it in my pocket the way you did today. It's true I accepted it, but I'll pay all of it back. And say to George Brown: I'm sorry I let you down too. I guess I am afraid, but not quite the way you meant. And listen: when Georgie and I have kids you must not try to make them do this for you, be this, that no one has a right to impose upon another person. And say to my father: what could I say to my father? Maybe I didn't have to say anything to him. But I would say to Georgie: we'll take that job at Silver Ridge with Mr. Patten, that's what you want more than anything, isn't it? That's what we'll do now, because I've quit too.

The word, when it came to me, shocked me, as I'd been shocked when I discovered that I had stopped on the course. And just then George Brown, standing very close to me, said it, in a hoarse, ragged whisper: "I never knew anybody to quit like that in the middle of a race before."

"Leave him alone," Georgie said, taking hold of my arm, but not as Jean-Gaby had grasped it, and her father said, "Well, what the hell's the matter with him? He looks like he's drunk."

"You don't *know*. Leave him alone!" Georgie said, and I felt a surge of pride in her that she would talk like that to her father.

"Did he crack up too?" someone else asked.

"Let me go tell them you'll be along, Jackie," Mr. Gayley said.

My father said nothing. A hand thrust a piece of cloth at me, my racing number. I shook my head again.

Jean-Gaby said in the almost hysterical voice, "But what can one do? What can one do with these *quitters*, these—"

"*Shut up!*" Georgie cried.

Mr. Brown started to speak, but my father, standing

red-faced beside him, said, "You people leave him alone now," and George Brown glanced at him and was silent.

They were loading Leary into the ambulance. "Come on if you're coming, Jack," the driver said.

Then Georgie and I were in the back of the ambulance on a bench beside Leary, who was swathed in blankets and snoring. Faces gazed at us through the glass that shut the voices out. The ambulance trundled slowly out toward the road. On the road it began to pick up speed, and the siren came on; not loud, it was a bitter parody of the wind singing in the skis on the top of the station wagon.

Some kind of fever seemed to be clearing from my head. I watched Georgie lean over to look at Leary's face. She grimaced with pity. "They gave him something to knock him out," I said, and she nodded. She put her arms around me and leaned against me.

"You're the only one of us left."

"I'm not left either."

She was silent for a time. When she spoke it was very carefully. "It doesn't really make any difference about the Olympic team. I mean the DNF. Nobody else has nearly as good a record as you have. You—"

"No, I want to quit," I said.

"But you can't," she said. "I know you feel like it now, but you can't. Can you?" In the stubborn voice she had sometimes she said, "Jack, you're too good to quit."

"I thought you and I would take that job at Silver Ridge," I said, and I was pleading with her.

She shook her head. "No. Don't do that for me."

"Why not?"

She continued to shake her head, and I said, "Do you know what's happened to me, Georgie? I don't give a damn. I don't have to beat everyone any more. It's like being out of jail."

She didn't seem to remember that she had said that once. She was in profile to me now, her eyes squinted almost closed, as though against bright sun, her lips tightly pursed. "But don't you still have to know?" she said.

"Know what?"

"If you can go all the way?"

I looked at my face, reflected, distorted, in the shining chrome of the stretcher rail. From the top of the green oxygen bottle the owl-eyes of the two dials there watched me. Once Leary snored more loudly. I said, "I know I don't want to end up a goddam machine."

"But you won't," she said. "You couldn't. But, Jack, you can't not be what you *are*." She looked at me with flinching, darkening eyes. Her face was filled with pity. "I can help; maybe I can help. But don't you have to finish it?"

I almost groaned, because she was right, and stopping for Leary and the DNF were beginning to seem meaningless. Maybe you could quit, deliberately, irrevocably, without regret, if it was your father's need that had driven you, or your desire to prove your quality or courage, or a means to some other end. But none of those had driven me.

I had wanted to beat everyone in the world at this one thing. Today that wanting had been cast out of me like a devil exorcised. Yet I still wanted to be the best, and maybe it burned as a purer fire with the old, corrosive envy gone. There still remained the question that could not be begged: how good was I? And with a sudden pride I thought that bending all my ability to running downhill the fastest was no more self-seeking or meretricious a goal than many another star-reach of human endeavor.

"You're the only one of us left," Georgie said again. "But maybe you were the only one that could've gone all the way anyway."

She was thrust hard against me as the ambulance swung out of Squaw Valley onto Highway 89, heading for the hospital in Truckee, the pitch of the siren rising as we gained speed. I held her tightly, straining forward a little and gazing past the driver, trying to see the road ahead, through the curves and trees.